Buddy!
Love!
My protect
craft, man
Thank you for
such a blessed
part of this
journey.

# Dream Wakers

Book One of
*The Veiled Prophecy Series*

Rebecca Wright

| | |

*Rebecca Wright*

*Dedicated to all those who bravely imagine without rules, rebel against the status quo, and believe in following their heart.*

# Author's Note

In life we are faced with the patterns of our past, of society's beliefs, and the outline for what is successful. I wanted to take a moment to thank those who have supported my unique, and sometimes rebellious way of creating. Without my high school Creative Writing teacher, Mr. Harrison, I would have never taken the time to consider my passion for writing. I will never forget the day he pulled me out of class and forced me to admit that I was, in fact, a writer. I want to thank my parents for giving me the opportunity to discover myself with the freedom of my own choices, and mistakes, so that I might come to this very moment and know that I followed my heart. You have always kept my happiness in your best interest and to me that is heroic. Gail Becker perhaps deserves an infinite hug from me for her presence in my life. She pulled me out of the darkness and flung my eyelids back with a sharp tug. I haven't looked back since and the expansion of my spirit and awareness is owed to her. Lindsay, my sister from Saturn, you are my blood and my heart and have loyally stood beside me through this journey regardless of where it has taken us. My little Ellie Pearlman, I will never forget the enthusiasm you showed for the entire process of this book. You may be the only person who was more excited than I for its creation. Jeff Happ, thank you for your contribution and efforts. I am endlessly thankful for your help and conversation. Lastly and not least, I want to thank Dylan Robison, Miriam Kilby (and her kids), Rebecca Ravitz, the regulars of It's A Grind in Castaic, and all of my friends who have read, edited, and listened to this rambling process. I am forever grateful to all of you.

*Chapter One*

Henry closed his eyes and repainted the night sky as he had seen it so many times. Each constellation tilted and adjusted as time went on, lending encouragement for the future he always seemed to be waiting for. His fingers reached out to the glittering guides above. It had been a long time since he was able to reach past the gateway star to the gods of his ancestors. Bright colors swirled around him like old friends. Lives and stories passed before him as they did every night. Details and turning points of her life recounted themselves so that his old memory couldn't forget. A day would come when he would no longer hide the truth. He would no longer have to be the guardian of her secrets.

"Papa, Papa!"

Henry smiled as his dream faded.

"Papa! Wake up! I want to play the game."

He opened his eyes to find the little girl standing impatiently next to him.

"Okay, Emmy."

He chuckled and smoothed down his granddaughter's wild hair. She wouldn't have understood the truth behind the strings of color that beckoned her when she slept. She was six years old and too young to understand the gift. She only needed to practice her ability to synchronize the energy, not comprehend it. There would be plenty of time to tell her about the prophecy. No child needed to be burdened with a future like hers. He would wait for the signs just as he had always done.

.......

Emmy pushed the gas pedal hard against the floor. White lines ran together and she pulled over, summer bushes scratching the paint of her truck. Six years of her life had been wasted.

"Why?" she muttered between tears. "Why me?"

Her fingers slipped from the wheel and she let her body bounce against the bench seat. She stared at the dashboard in front of her, waiting to dissolve into a different life, a different time, where she could be anyone but who she had become. A wave of nausea rolled over her and she swayed against the feeling. Anger always made her dizzy. Red dots flickered and danced behind her eyelids and she lay with her face calling to the breeze. Emmy begged the earth to swallow her, but only the silence of dawn rang in her ears.

She thought of the lilies on her kitchen table and how they'd wilt. Her horses would no longer have spiced apples to eat in winter, and her grandfather wouldn't know she left town. She hadn't spoken to him since she'd been married. Emmy ripped her wedding ring off her finger and threw it out the window. She couldn't have gone to Henry now, she didn't deserve to. He had warned her about Ethan. She shifted her legs, wincing as tender flesh slid against her jeans. Emmy breathed carefully, not wanting to stir her temper, and counted three lightening bugs inside the cab of her truck before she turned the ignition. She didn't have time to wish for what could have been done differently.

"I have to leave," she whispered.

The smell of dirt warmed in her nose and she pushed the hair off her neck along with the rest of her mistakes. She needed to find a place to rest; hours would pass before she could be sure Ethan wasn't going to come after her.

Emmy cursed under her breath. Life had not proven to be the fairytale her grandfather had painted. Her eyes grew heavy and memories of her childhood rolled in her thoughts. Every time she thought of Henry, small veins of light popped and danced in her mind, searching for a path to connect to. The familiar tugs of Henry's game asked for her attention. She hadn't played since she'd met Ethan and tried to fight the impulse to give into it now. Emmy didn't want her grandfather knowing she'd left. She didn't want to feel the shame of what had happened. He didn't need to know. The air in the truck grew cold, and her vision faltered. Her entire body constricted, her knuckles white against the wheel. A piercing sound screamed far off in the distance and pinched at her temples. Emmy groaned, trying to break free from the magnetism that sucked her consciousness away. The strings of color danced frantically when she refused to give them control. Her shoulders ached and the sound became louder, blaring against her forehead, making the back of her eyelids flash red. They weren't searching for Henry, they were searching for the woman. This couldn't happen now. She gritted her teeth against the pressure.

"Not now," she yelled.

Emmy's eyes flew open and she swerved away from an oncoming vehicle. Her truck charged into the dirt on the side of the road. The woman had been haunting her dreams for years because of Henry's game. She waited to regain control of her numb body as cars whizzed past. The game had always taken its toll.

"Finally," she breathed, seeing a town on the horizon.

When she could move her arms, she pulled back onto the road. The first time she had tried playing Henry's game, the darkness had scared her. Henry had told her that her big mind was too smart for her little body and she had gotten lost between memories. They didn't play often after that, and Emmy grew too preoccupied training her horses to care. Once she married Ethan, she had no choice but to ignore it all together. She sighed and pushed the thoughts out of her mind. It didn't matter anymore.

Small town buildings filled her windows. The roads were uneven, and the storefronts were weathered. She read signs until she found a motel and parked. When she slid out, her legs buckled, making her fall back against the bed of the truck. Inhaling through her teeth, she pulled her suitcase and backpack out of the truck and headed to check herself into a room.

The man behind the desk smiled at her.

"Morning, ma'am."

"Morning," she repeated, self conscious of the bruise on the side of her face.

"I'd like to stay until tomorrow evening."

He nodded and handed her a key.

"You're number seven. My name's Charlie if you should need something."

Emmy smiled, frozen at the front desk, feeling out of place.

"You need help with that suitcase?"

"Oh no, sir," Emmy said, shrugging off the kind gesture. "I just need to rest, I've been driving all night."

"Honey, call me Charlie."

Emmy only nodded. She picked up her things and headed toward her room. Flower pots hung from red trimmed window sills, and the porch seemed to smile. She opened the door, and the smell of fresh linen crowded her senses. Exhaustion crept in her weary body. Emmy set her bags on the floor, too tired to unpack whatever she had thrown in there. She tenderly pulled off her jeans, and placed them over the foot board. Her toned legs flexed sorely before resting against the sheets. She unhooked her bra, pulling it out from beneath her thin T-shirt, and slid a hand over the bruises along her sides. Her delicate frame sank into bed and she tugged the sheets to her chin. She'd have a plan before she left tomorrow evening.

She tossed in her sleep, muttering and sweating. All the suppression she had forced down her own throat reared its ugly head. Years of buried trauma detoxed from her body as she dreamt.

*Unfamiliar faces jolted her as they yelled and screamed in coded languages she couldn't understand. Heavy mist rolled from their eyes. Shadows melted into the darkness. The sound of Ethan's laughter rung in her ears before he pinned her underneath his fists. The weight was crushing her. His black eyes twinkled. She scrambled to free herself, wishing to disappear. Her body started to fade and her golden brown hair was turning black. She could feel her flesh tearing from her body. The veins of light were weaving themselves into her bones. Suddenly she fell.*

Emmy sat up in bed.

Something was wrong. She scanned her surroundings, convincing herself it was only the dream. A large body moved across the window frame. Her heart stopped; the silhouette was indisputable. Ethan had come for her. Death crawled up the back of her neck. Heavy feet crushed the gravel outside. Sweat started to collect at her temples. Emmy screamed at herself to get up and do something, to remember the courage she had only a day ago. *But that was before he...no.* She pushed it out of her memory. *No.* Bruises throbbed in pace with her heartbeat.

The creak of her car door drifted through the walls and she clamped her moistening eyes together. Most of her money was in between a book shoved in her glovebox.

He was entitled to everything. He invaded all that was hers. He did what he wanted without permission. She had sat back for years and allowed him to dictate what cruelty she'd have to endure next. She was still succumbing to his manipulation. Emmy leapt to her feet and grabbed the letter opener on the desk. It couldn't happen anymore. Her eyes darted after his footsteps, waiting as he moved closer and closer to her locked door. She watched the knob twist soundlessly against the lock, its brass gleaming in the late morning. She blinked once. Ethan would not be touching her again.

The door splintered and broke from the frame. He stood in the doorway; a statue of muscle and satanic intention. The dust of debris rose and fell around his still body. Every feature on his face was sharp and clear. He was too calm. Emmy didn't hear the manic terror rupture from her throat, didn't hear the pieces of furniture tumble as she jumped towards him and dug her weapon into his shoulder. A roar broke from Ethan's slackening jaw and his open palm pushed Emmy to the floor. He leaned against the wall, laughing at her, unaffected by the open wound that stained his perfectly pressed shirt.

"When will you ever learn that you can't stop me?" Ethan laughed wretchedly. "Now get up!"

He licked his lips, trying to maintain his precision. Emmy rose achingly slow from the ground, groping to find a way up. She grabbed the knob of the bed frame for support and it wobbled underneath the pressure of her weight. She ripped it off its threads and whirled around.

"Don't even try it, Emmy."

Ethan pointed his gun at her without a hint of remorse. There wasn't a tick of uncertainty as he held it cocked between her eyes. The iron knob slipped from her hand and Emmy stared down the smooth shaft. Her heart beat steadily, almost as if she had prepared for this moment, as if she knew it would all come to this. She looked down at her palms and swallowed hard. Her throat felt like cured meat, and the light around her fingertips was white. She could feel all her blood pulling towards her heart as she prepared for death. Emmy looked up at him. Ethan was sweating, and she watched him try to maintain his focus. Emmy had to break his concentration. She had to live.

"You know Ethan," she said delicately, "if you killed me, what would you do afterwards? You'd have no one to torture."

The pistol wavered. His eyes were black as they watched her mouth move. Her body grew hot. She needed to control the temper bubbling on her tongue. She had to persuade him to put the gun away.

"You'd be alone. You'd have to live with the filth you've laid in your bones. You can't stand who you are, so you distract yourself with me. If I'm gone, Ethan, you'll have nothing else. Don't make a choice you'll regret."

"No, Emmy," he spoke carefully, "if I decided not to kill you, *you'd* regret it. If I had it my way, I'd make you beg me to kill you. You just might today."

"Maybe I will, and maybe I won't," she threatened against her better judgement. Her limbs were going numb.

His voice cracked when he laughed.

"You have ruined everything. If you think I value your life, I don't. It's because of you I am this way. Your disgraceful upbringing has forced me to build laws and perimeters so that you would understand how to function in the real world. Because of you my business has faltered. Because of you I am alone. You have no idea who you are, do you? I almost deserve to kill you."

His fists clenched.

"After you writhe for the last time at my feet, I will have to dispose of your body where your useless grandfather will never think to find you. I'll put you under your beloved flower garden and as your body turns to bits of dirt, I will watch each petal wither and die, poisoned by your unholy soul."

He thought of the clean click her neck would make if he snapped it. *No*, he thought to himself, *I'll wait until the bullet has done the dirty work. She shouldn't struggle in my pleasure. She will lay quiet and enjoy it as my wife.* He smiled.

"I will burn your barn. Your horses will heave and convulse, and look wildly around for their mother only to find that you've left them to suffer."

His voice rose with the excitement. Emmy's throat closed and the hair on her arms stood on end. It was as if the whole room was made of ice. She couldn't ignore how cold she felt. Panic rattled her teeth.

"After your eight babies are dead, lying in a heap to rot just like you, I will have one last task to finish before I need to worry about living with myself," he mocked.

"I will go to the house you grew up in and find your beloved grandfather. I will choke him with my own hands and laugh into his pallid, bluing face. His body will fall to the floor, and as he sucks his last breath before death, he will whisper your name, pleading for you to save him. But you won't, because you have failed him once and always, Emmy. You will be responsible for the death of all of your beloved things."

Henry passed in front of her eyes, and Emmy screamed, hands clasped over her ears. Ethan laughed again, penetrating her attempts to muffle the repugnant fantasy he was creating. He settled the pistol's muzzle square on her forehead. Emmy only felt the constricting of her back.

The small breeze lifted the scent of her hair to his nostrils and he closed his eyes in lust. She smelled of earthy idealism. His body was tense with joy as he watched her crumble before him.

"It won't be long, Wife, before you are mine."

Emmy's body gave into death, and she fainted.

Ethan laughed in satisfaction and stepped forward to collect his prize.

"Hey!"

Ethan looked over his shoulder before the baseball bat made contact. His head slammed against the floor without his large body to break his fall.

"Get up!" Charlie yelled as he stood over Ethan's limp body.

"He won't be down long and you've got to get away from him."

Emmy opened her eyes, disoriented. She saw Ethan huddled on the floor and slowly looked up at Charlie. He lifted her from her waist. She stood unevenly for a moment as she regained full consciousness, staring at the broken bat.

Charlie shook her shoulder, trying to restore her.

"Didn't you hear me? Get what you can and get out of sight. I'm not sure what more I can do to stop the giant, so go!"

She stared at the man from the front desk as he shoved her things towards her.

"Go sit in your truck with the door locked, take a minute to breathe."

Life crept slowly back into her veins. Emmy hugged all her belongings against her.

"I need to pay you," she mumbled.

Charlie's eyes widened and a smile softened the severity of his face.

"Honey, you've got more serious things to worry about. A night's stay will not put me out. Now get on in the truck. I called the police already."

Emmy only turned, unable to process beyond the movement of her sluggish body. Closing up her last bag, she took one exaggerated step over Ethan. She glanced at Charlie over her shoulder, slid her sunglasses over her eyes and walked out of the door. She opened the door to her truck and slid in. The cab smelled like the threat of death through her dried nostrils. Her bruises felt like rot beneath her clothes and murder danced between her shoulders. The noose tightened as she waited.    Policemen wouldn't solve his insanity, they'd get paid off like everyone else. A tear fell on her shirt before she noticed she was crying. She wondered when she'd become so weak and tired. There had to be a point where her capacity for strength had ceased, when it had become easier to lose herself and coexist with him. Emmy turned the keys in the ignition and pulled onto the road. Dotted lines blurred ahead once more. Ethan would be eager to fulfill the promises he etched into her brain. Everything was dead. No one would come for her, or know where to begin searching. She didn't even know where she was heading. Her fist came crashing down on the dashboard.

"How did I let it come to this?"

She pressed down on the gas. She pressed it to the floor, trying to break through to the road spinning underneath. There was no pinpointing where she stopped being strong and unafraid. She had transformed without even seeing it. She looked back upon all the years spent compromising herself to subdue him. All the things she chose to give up to please him. The steering wheel rattled beneath her fingers. She was still running away. Everything else would suffer in her absence. The horses' lifeless bodies passed over her.

Startled by the gory image, she pulled over. Her hands cradled her face. She didn't cry anymore for the death of her horses, but for the truth that swept undeniably over her. She couldn't go back. Not even to save her animals. Ethan would be sure of her arrival, certain the horror would manipulate her back. It had worked before, but he had finally broken her. In the pit of her soul she knew there was no more history repeating. Not even for Henry.

The skin cradling her eyes was tight and swollen.

"Oh, Papa!" she sobbed, choking on the words. "I'm sorry!"

*Chapter Two*

     *The woman pointed down the hill, tears of vibrant color running down her cheeks and into the ground. Lillian could hear the horses' hooves stamping nervously against the barn walls below them as the flames licked up the sides of the building. White paint curled away to ash. Shrill cries pierced her ears. Lillian's own screams caught in her throat and her legs stood as still as the tree she hunched under. The river of light twisted around her legs like roots. She tried lunging forward without success. She panicked. The damp dirt chilled her bones. Flames swallowed the roof. The silhouette of a man moved up the hill; he hunted them every night. Lillian's hair whipped wildly around her face as she choked for help, hearing the screams of the noble beasts burning a few yards away.*

     Lillian's eyes flew open, her black hair plastered across her forehead with sweat. Blankets and pillows were tangled with the exhaustion. The nightmares had been ruining her sleep since she'd left the city. She tugged on her earlobes with a trembling hand and looked carefully into the corners of her dark cottage where shadows lurked against her walls. She reached to her nightstand, groping for the porcelain lamp, exhaling as the light filled the room.

Her wrought iron bed frame creaked. Lillian swept shaky legs over her bed, touching her toes gingerly to the wooden floor and pressed her fingertips into her closed eyelids, trying to massage the nightmare from her memory. She wondered if she'd ever be able to escape all that had happened in the city. A flurry of beating feathers rattled the cage behind her.

"Hush, hush," she cooed as she turned, "it's okay my little Hoot."

She opened her eyes more clearly, and stood now that she was certain her knees wouldn't buckle beneath her. Lillian touched the iron birdcage next to her bed where the small Tawny Owl recuperated inside. He settled the creamy feathers ruffled at his breast and gawked at her in distress. For the first time, his nocturnal habits were comforting. Lillian smiled at him softly and made her way to the kitchen in search of some tea.

She lit the pilot on her stovetop with a flick of the wrist and relaxed against the cool white tiles of her kitchen bar. The waning moon winked at the tops of her shoulders through the window and the forestry beyond beckoned to her in the silence of night. A cup of tea to calm the last of her nerves was going to be perfect. Her quaint cottage seemed to relax in the chilly English air. She thought of the safety her stone wall brought just beyond the front gardens and the strength of the warm brown stones that had held up since the 1860s. They had probably survived events far worse than anything from her past.

Lillian turned to open a cupboard. She sucked in the countless smells from the containers in front of her. Each shelf was packed with antique bottles of herbs and teas. Lavender for comfort, peppermint to calm the remains of the dream in her stomach, and chamomile to soothe the tightness in her throat. Her long ivory fingers caressed each handwritten label as she pulled them off the shelves. She could hear the old man's laughter in her ears and a fond sadness blanketed her. Each bottle had been a gift from sweet Aillig. It was only a few weeks ago that she was sitting in the apothecary shop with him, solving the curiosities of the day. She plucked out a tea bag and blew into it.

"I suppose I should treat myself for all this troubled sleep," she mused aloud, grabbing a pinch of dehydrated orange peel from one of the baskets on her countertop. The familiar routine of making her own tea always soothed her.

She placed the satchel in her mug and leaned against the sink, painting pictures in her mind's eye. Her dreams had been a source of great inspiration when she had lived with Aillig. The crackle of flames whispered in her ears as she recalled his burnt apothecary, understanding the connection to the barn. She yearned for the friend she had lost in the fire and the peace he had brought her.

Lillian had done her best to carry on since his death. She'd even managed to open the doors to her own apothecary shop. Keeping busy was the only thing that dampened the fears she'd worked so hard to forget. Memories of her suffocated upbringing tainted her subconscious and turned her dreams to nightmares. She'd always suffered from an overactive imagination, and now that it seemed to be returning, it was too easy to recall how the nuns had handled her stories about strange faces and the ghosts she used to see moving in her old room. They had quarantined her from a normal life and told her the devilish hallucinations had to be controlled. Lillian shivered despite herself. No one was here to correct her wild ideas, but the remnants of their rehabilitation were hard to forget. It had been a priority to beat it out of her, and without Aillig as a protector, Lillian couldn't help but worry that they would try to drag her back to the city.

"They haven't come for you, and they aren't going to come for you now just because it's happening again," she whispered into the silence.

It had been a long time since her life at St. John's got the better of her and she didn't like the returning feeling. With her upheaval to the North, she had been too busy mourning Aillig and restarting where he had left off to let it affect her. It had been a lifted burden. She sighed and tried not to obsess. The sooner she let the memories fade, the sooner the dreams would go with them.

Hoot called from behind the half wall separating her room from the kitchen. Lillian smiled and spooned some honey into her mug before she made her way back to bed. She was worrying for nothing. Her legs slid under her heavy blankets and she sipped her tea. The thought of her little friend being awake while she slept did offer some comfort. Lillian set her empty mug on her nightstand and leaned against her headboard, hesitant to turn out the light. He was the first animal Lillian had ever tended to and it looked as though his foot was healing well. His unblinking eyes stared at her forehead. She didn't want to return to the gruesome images that had woken her.

"Hoot, at least I have you to protect me should the dreams grow too terrible. You'll screech and wake me?"

He ruffled every feather on his body. Lillian smiled. Her long, black hair fell in stark contrast against white bedsheets. She pushed it to one side self soothingly and turned out the light. Blackness formed into bodies as Lillian lay in bed. She closed her eyes. Though the man in her dream was unrecognizable, the woman seemed vaguely familiar. She had dreamt of her before. Ribbons of light danced in her mind, forming into the familiar blue eyes. The dream was going to start over. Her arms shook involuntarily. Long forgotten memories rattled around the edges of her thoughts without permission. Lillian clenched her teeth, forcing her eyes open.

She looked out her bedroom window and counted the stars as the minutes ticked on, trying not to think of the alarm clock that would ring in a few short hours. Her eyes grew heavy. The dark walls shifted. The shadows were waiting for her to look at them. She tossed in the covers and dug her hands under her pillows, refusing to tug on her earlobes. Her imagination would be the death of her one day. She was a grown woman. She was too smart to be scared by something so silly. Morning would come and she would remain unharmed. The nuns weren't here to yank her out of bed every time she dreamt. She muttered to herself as she drifted off, her fingers twitching restlessly under her pillow.

"Just no more dead horses."

*Chapter Three*

Emmy woke, rubbing the smell of lavender from her nose, wondering if she'd been dreaming of strange women again. Days and nights ran together in fits of incoherent dreams. She sighed, pushing the mop of sun bleached chestnut hair out of her face. Pale yellow walls mirrored the blankness in Emmy's face as she stretched, her oversized T-shirt rising dangerously up her toned thigh. Her hands fell against her legs, and she thought of nothing. She'd been on the road for weeks, driving nowhere but far away from home. Her pale skin had tanned from long hours in the sun and in the heat of summer she had cut her jeans into shorts to keep herself cool. Today she needed coffee. Her feet wiggled into her sneakers without socks, and she grabbed cash from between the pages of her book.

"At least he didn't find the money," she thought to herself.

*No, Emmy, no thinking.* She pushed away from her memories, and went to check out the detached lobby. Small dust clouds kicked up around her ankles, and clung to her exposed skin as she walked through the parking lot. A woman with mousy hair sat behind the main desk, engrossed in an article on her computer. Emmy stared at her, annoyed that the woman had nothing better to do than avoid her job. She should be grateful to be employed, and to have a place to live without the fear of being hunted. The heating pad hissed and complained as black coffee bubbled and fell over the edge of the pot. Emmy grimaced at its prospect and stood still in the center of the empty lobby. The woman looked at her, inconvenience disfiguring her face.

"Can I help you?"

Emmy stared back for a moment before turning on her heel and heading out.

"Well, I guess I could see what this place is all about," she said to herself, shrugging. "I don't even know what state I'm in."

Emmy almost laughed at the numerous small towns she had driven through. The bitter education that her hometown was bigger than most in the Midwest had disappointed her more deeply than she wanted to admit.

The morning light delicately warned her of the afternoon heat as she walked. Emmy hoped the town was as remote as it felt. A handful of trucks rumbled by, kicking up the dirt now clinging to the ends of her hair. She glanced sheepishly to the side as they passed, nervous it'd be a face she recognized. She had become very capable of knowing how to slip in and out of places without talking to anyone. As long as she could stay anonymous, there was little chance she could be found. Emmy made certain to keep her eyes carefully on her toes. She was too familiar with the interested glances burning into her back as she moved by a few locals. It was no different here as it was anywhere; a group of bodies with nothing better to do than put her in a fishbowl and watch.

She didn't want to be translucent to judgmental eyes and second guessed her decision to penetrate through the outskirts she'd been living in. It made it impossible to ignore what she'd been running from. Her throat closed tightly and Emmy swallowed hard, trying to keep her composure. Her blue eyes scanned more wildly for a place to hide. A couple of women came out of the post office. *They know what's happened. They recognize you. They'll tell Ethan.* Her vision tunneled and the deep laughter of one man rang in between her ears.

Her heart pounded, and her feet stumbled frantically beneath her. Emmy's screams were caught in between her clenched jaws. The faint scent of espresso trickled in through her flaring nostrils and she pushed the nearest door to her, nearly falling into an empty diner. Everything went silent and time swirled once around her neck before falling still. She froze, not daring to move should Ethan come from behind the counter.

"Can I help you?"

A middle aged woman stared at her. Emmy eyes were blank and glossy. Memories and reality desperately tried to separate themselves as she stood lost in between. She tried to push Ethan's image away. Seconds felt like hours. She blinked once and lowered her gaze to her feet.

"Coffee?" she spat quietly, touching her fingers to her lips. She wondered exactly when she had last spoken to someone.

"Yes, there would be coffee here."

Emmy lifted her right foot, turning it on her heel, noticing where the glue had lifted off the canvas of her shoe. *God, Emmy! Order a coffee and just get out! What the hell are you doing?*

"Do you speak English?" the woman insisted. "I swear I don't get paid enough to deal with this."

The woman turned to start a fresh pot of coffee. Emmy slowly raised her eyes to watch, wishing the scalding water would seep out and flow over the counter to drown her. Her fingers flicked at her side and she looked to the barstools, begging her feet to take her to sit down. The place was as clean as a doctor's office. Emmy felt guilty that she didn't stomp out her shoes before entering. The sun warmed her back through the window behind her. Somewhere outside, trucks moved down the main drag, humming faintly in Emmy's ears.

The woman whipped around, snapping her towel as she placed her fists on her hips.

"Really honey, you gotta say somethin' or get out. I just can't have you sitting there, staring."

The door swung open. Emmy barely managed to stumble out of the way. The first few men left her unnoticed, but not all were oblivious as they walked to the counter. Emmy had gradually backed herself against the wall, trying to melt into it. Ethan had friends everywhere.

"Don't mind her, fellas. I think she's a mute or something."

They raked their eyes over her body. Her knees weakened. She refused to make eye contact and stared at the floor. Losing interest in her silence, the group turned back to order what they'd come for.

"Mornin' Sherry Jean."

The woman beamed. She must have had ten years on the young men standing in front of her, but Emmy was certain she pretended otherwise. The sounds of their conversation fell away from her ears as they found seats at two tables in the dining area.

"No, I don't know her," she whined to the group of men. "She's just been frozen there. I tried to tell her to get out if she won't sit, but then all you handsome devils came in."

They smiled respectfully but said nothing.

"The girl is making me nervous acting like that," she went on. "I'm going to kick her out after I take your order."

Sherry Jean looked back at her.

*Just leave, Emmy. Go back to the lobby. You've had bad coffee before. Drink it and hit the road, this isn't a place for you to be wandering. They might know who you are.*

"Excuse me, ma'am. Are you feeling okay?"

Emmy looked up. A pair of misty green eyes gently scanned her cheekbones.

Emmy stared, screaming at herself to speak like a normal human being. She opened her mouth, then closed it, swallowing hard. Her hands pressed against the wall for security.

"Maybe you should come away from there and sit down."

His palms wrapped around her shoulders for support and Emmy winced.

"Jesus," he whispered, stepping back.

She stood frozen in place, eyes closed so tightly that bright bursts of color fell across the backs of her eyelids. The abstract patterns mesmerized her, drawing her far from where she stood. She wanted to disappear, not call on Henry's game.

"I won't hurt you," he cooed, "I won't touch you again, just sit down before you make yourself faint."

Emmy couldn't budge if she wanted to. She waited for her body to regain movement. She opened her eyes. Strangers surrounded her.

"Look," he whispered, "I don't want to scare you, but if you don't sit down those guys are going to keep staring at you. You, um," he hesitated, and raked his hands over his short, brown hair. "You don't have a bra on."

Without thinking Emmy crossed her arms over her breasts, the heat of embarrassment reddening the skin under her scattered freckles. *They probably think I'm a whore. I have to get out of here. Or they'll be just like Ethan. Stop thinking about it.*

"Will you sit down? If you sit down where they can't stare, I promise to leave you alone."

Emmy looked over his shoulder into stale air and walked stiffly to a booth where she would be concealed. The man did as he promised and rejoined his friends. Emmy's shoulders slumped and she put her face in her hands. Whatever small part of her that believed she'd be able to escape her nightmares had been killed in the last half hour. Her first attempt to venture out since Ethan's attempt to kill her was a complete disaster. Tears grew near her jaw. She felt helpless. She was never going to get out of the booth.

A ceramic mug smacked the table. Emmy lifted her face from her palms to see the waitress hovering over her.

"Cup of coffee. Compliments of my regular. He says if you were wanting something else, to say, and he will cover it."

When Emmy said nothing, Sherry Jean stormed off. Emmy glanced down at the small bubbles popping on the surface of her coffee. Her fingers wrapped instinctively around the mug. She controlled her breathing and tried to rebuild her walls of security. *Something familiar, finally. This is a start, Emmy. Time to collect yourself.* She brought the rim of the mug to her lips.

She glanced slowly to the man to see if he was watching. His back was turned, his worn shirt tight across his back. The numbness she'd built within returned, and she sipped, thinking of nothing. Emmy emptied her mug and glanced to Sherry Jean for a refill. When she made no move to offer more, Emmy slid her cup to the edge of the table and dug in her pocket, pulling out a few crumpled bills. She rose with arms crossed protectively over her chest and walked towards the door.

"Tell him thank you, but I have my own money."

The hot air outside welcomed Emmy's nerves to thaw. She leaned against the western decor of the wall for a moment before rising to head back to the motel. She would pull out the map in the desk drawer and figure out where to go from there. She paced herself. Weariness shadowed her as the adrenaline of the morning subsided. *Maybe a short nap would do me some good before trying to figure out what the hell I'm going to do.*

"Do you know where you're going?" a voice called behind her.

Emmy whirled around to find the man from the diner standing behind her. She noticed how green his eyes were against his honey toned skin and thought she must be too tired to be afraid anymore.

"I'm not going to hurt you. I'm afraid you won't make it back to where you came from, you look ill. May I walk you there? Or near there? That way I know you won't get hurt."

He rounded his shoulders and lowered eyes, keeping his distance. She reminded him of the horses they drove in from the mountain range; wild-eyed and on the defense in an environment they didn't understand. Though the city had proven to be mostly good, its inhabitants still possessed the danger of their ancestors. It would be naive of him to think that his coworkers wouldn't be curious about her. Chivalry bested his usual apathy, and he was compelled to ensure her safety.

Emmy stood, evaluating the man a few inches away. She looked down at his arms, watching them lay still against his sides. She didn't want to talk to anyone. Her broken experience in the diner had exhausted her. She glanced half heartedly at the stranger and felt her hands twitch. When he made no move to lift his arms or lunge toward her, she nodded once and started to walk.

"Okay," he smiled.

"What state am I in?"

He raked his fingers through his short hair.

"You mean, you don't know where you are?"

"No."

Emmy decided it'd probably be best to reveal little, just in case. Not that she would've been capable of saying much more.

"You're in Wyoming."

A truck pulled up next to them.

"Cutter! We don't have time for this shit!"

Emmy's arms flew over her breasts.

Cutter stared at his friend before turning to Emmy.

"Are you close to where you are staying? If not, I can tell them to go on without me."

"I'm close enough," Emmy stammered.

Cutter looked at her with sympathy and moved into the street. The door slammed behind him and Emmy turned back towards the motel.

"I didn't get your name," Cutter yelled out the window.

Emmy opened her mouth, but the words only came as a whisper. The truck disappeared from view and Emmy stood a moment longer before resuming her walk, feeling overwhelmingly defeated in the middle of the afternoon.

When she unlocked the door, she threw her keys onto the desk and flipped on the air conditioner. She kicked her shoes off, and stepped out of her shorts, letting her body fall onto the mattress. The cold air raised the skin on her legs. She nestled her face into the pillow and closed her eyes. Sleep came quickly and soundly for the first time since she left home.

*Emmy watched the woman floating uneasily about a darkened room. Wrought iron bars skewed her vision as she searched for the cause of her distress. Emmy's heart fluttered irregularly, and the blood rushed from her chest. In the corner, lingering near the window, stood the silhouette of a man. She went to call out to the dark haired woman to warn her, but all that escaped from her belly was an owl's coo. She flapped her ruffled wings and watched the shadow dissipate. The gentle woman looked at her and smiled, a mug of tea in her hand as she spoke.*

*"You'll screech and wake me?"*

*Emmy stared hard as she watched her sleep. Veins of color dripped and wound together from the tips of her dark hair. Emmy couldn't remember why Henry's game included her.*

The flirtations of evening mingled in the air of her room as she woke. Everything around her seemed illuminated and a flash of peace possessed her. Holding on to the sensation of the dream, Emmy rolled onto her back, stretching her arms out to her sides. She could still hear the sound of feathers tickling her ears. She wondered if the shadow had been Ethan. The thought soured her mood and she rose from bed, drawn to look at the moon. She didn't want to dwell any farther on what imaginative fairytale had met her in slumber. She sat in the door jam of her bungalow, soaking in the fresh air. Her lean legs bent in front of her and the summer breeze tangled playfully between her fingertips. She rested her head against the open door and thought about the distance she had put between herself and Ethan. She had to admit that knowing she'd put a few states behind her was a small relief.

It also meant he intended to keep a promise. There was no way to find out if he had returned to Kentucky. Emmy wanted to call her grandfather, but she was afraid it would only put him in danger. She longed to be in the comfort of Henry's home. It was never in her plan to become an abused wife, or a negligent granddaughter. She had always wanted a big family, not the life of a spinster like Henry's friend, Ms. Beckett, as sweet as she was.

"Ms. Beckett!" Emmy shot up with enthusiasm.

If her Papa was still unharmed, his long time friend would be able to help. Ethan had never taken the time to learn about her life outside the estate and wouldn't even pay a passing glance to their elderly neighbor. Emmy walked to the desk and pulled out a pen and paper.

*Ms. Beckett,*
*It's Emmy. I can't contact Henry in case Ethan is waiting for that.*

She hesitated, biting on the cap of the pen.

*I'm in Wyoming for now. Please tell Henry I'm okay.*

She folded the paper, and shoved it in the pocket of her shorts before she could change her mind. Emmy sat on the edge of her bed, heavy from the dark pit that Ethan left in her stomach. Delicate fingers grazed over her thighs. The bruises had long faded, but her skin still prickled to the touch. She'd go to the post office tomorrow and send it. She doubled the pillows under her head and curled into a ball, clenching and unclenching her jaw. She swore she would never misjudge a man again.

As she dozed off, she expertly pushed the bad memories aside before it could penetrate her dreams.

"If it doesn't exist," she said to herself in slumber, "it can't hurt me."

.......

Ethan sat up from the hard floor, cradling one side of his head. The drink whispered for him.

"I want my lawyer," he growled inside the jail cell.

"You'll get your chance," an officer mumbled.

Ethan's rage grew as he recalculated her escape. His error in thinking she'd never run was going to cost him. Ethan's superiors had been caught off guard when he called to inform them of Emmy's disappearance. He was forced to wait while they figured out what they needed to do about his failed assassination. It was never simple with witnesses.

Ethan had wasted too much trapped in this little box. He needed to get back and get his revenge. He punched the wall of the cell, cursing her and their forced marriage. He had obeyed his father's wishes but had never forgiven him. The best years of his life had been wasted trying to contain the darkness of her prophecy. His arms grew hotter as the anger fumed under his skin. She would ruin his life forever unless he took matters into his own hands. Ethan squeezed his face against the bars.

"Get my lawyer, now!"

The guard's eyes widened in surprise and he stood silently to fetch the phone. Once free from the cell, Ethan yanked it from him and dialed.

"No, you idiot, I'm in jail," he went on, teeth chattering with fury. "We have a lot to accomplish. I don't care what they're doing! I've waited long enough. Why are you asking so many questions? No, forget about her, I broke her. She's probably at home waiting for us. Be useful for once and get me out of here!"

He slammed the phone on the desk, smiling at the warden.

"I hope you have a good defense for arresting me."

The officer swallowed, strangely affected by the giant man in front of him.

"I don't care what anyone saw, I will be released and you will regret it."

*Chapter Four*

*Lillian strained to see the words scribbled on the paper in front of her. Unfamiliar addresses and names illuminated and changed. Her heart raced in her throat. Her eyes ached as she tried to still the moving letters long enough to read. She had to decipher what was written in front of her. The air grew cold. It wasn't going to be long before her caregivers would be back. Thick, woodsy notes lingered in the thin air and Lillian ran to the door, tugging against the lock. She had to escape before they came. They couldn't know about the letter. Tears streamed down her face. She was trapped. The woman appeared beside her and stared out the window of her old room. Lillian banged her small fists against the door, waking to her own cries.*

........

Lillian reached absently for her receipt book and pen. Her apothecary shop had been unusually busy and she was feeling ill prepared for the attention new customers required. She'd spent the night hiding from her night terrors.

"Thank you Ms. Beckett."

Lillian shook her head and closed her eyes.

"I'm sorry Mrs. *Duckett.* I'm afraid I'm a little tired this morning."

She crossed out the receipt she had started in the wrong name.

"Please, let me know if the willow cucumber bark tea helps. I also threw in a small vial of White Oak Oil I mixed for your massage therapist to try at your next appointment. It should help with the passage of pain. It's a new blend, do tell me how it works."

Lillian smiled, watching the gray haired woman scuffle out of the door.

"Don't forget to take your walks in the afternoon before it gets too cold," she called after her.

The shop was finally silent and she sat at her desk. Pressure hung dully behind her forehead and her eyes begged to close. She looked around the cramped quarters and ran her fingers through her hair. She should be overjoyed with the immediate business she'd received. The small town had been in dire need of easily accessible treatment and it looked like she had come at the perfect time. If only Aillig had been here to see her. Tears built behind her giant green eyes and she felt exhausted. The obscure letter she had dreamt of was interfering with her work, her dreams were only growing worse, and she couldn't help but feel anxious.

Her memories resurfaced in analytical lists, and forced her to link the darkness of her dreams to something meaningful. Aillig had taught her about subconscious messages and the psychology of what she had been repressing. If she could decipher the symbolism in her dreams, she'd be able to let it go. Lillian let the faces of her clients pass through her mind in a neat line. Maybe one of the local church ladies had triggered her haunted dreams. Lillian shook her head. All of her clients up north were lovely and welcoming, none of them would remind her of

St. John's. Her muscles tingled with tension and all she really wanted to do was get into a hot bath and unwind.

"Perhaps an herb pillow will ease my mind before bed," she sighed.

She stood and grabbed dried herbs from various jars in her store, placing them in a satchel to take home before locking up. Picking apart her subconscious had not been a part of the plan when she had decided to move. Forgetting it, however, had been. As she walked, Lillian couldn't help but feel overwhelmed. Her list was long at work between building inventory and the flood of customers. Her sleeping habits were starting to affect what was most important to her and she couldn't find a way to stop it. Herbalism was a way to healing others and yet she had trouble healing herself. Lillian had to bury the trauma of her past if she wanted to continue working as an herbalist. She quickened her pace as the evening grew late. She had always felt the world around her was most alive in the silent hours of night. She blamed the shadows she was prone to imagining. Darkness, like a magnet, drew the darkness from her. Lillian's arms prickled with goosebumps. The fear that she'd be ripped out of bed and reprimanded for her night terrors didn't need to control her. These dreams needed to be settled for good. She unlocked the door to her cottage and wasted no time in drawing a bath.

Water sang and tumbled down the drain as she waited for it to warm. She gathered her handmade soaps off the counter in her small bathroom. She invited the list of oddities to recreate themselves in her mind, hoping to find clarity amongst her chaotic introspection. Aillig would have known exactly how to fix it. He had done so before. She wondered if the woman she dreamed of was her mother. The man who'd lit the barn on fire the night before had dark hair like her own, perhaps she looked like her father. Too gruesome to accept, she chided herself for taking a fabrication of her imagination so literally. Lillian's face fell and she looked in the mirror.

"The nightmares must be symbolic of the abandonment I felt as a child," she muttered shaking her head. "And my desire to be free of my confinements."

She watched the steam dance on the surface of the water. It was obvious that growing up in the church had left her with harbored illness towards being given away. The nuns, strict and unforgiving, never ceased to remind her of the damnation she faced as a forgotten child. She slipped into the tub and let her body rest heavily at the bottom with her weakened sense of control. Without Aillig to comfort her when life stilled, she could not ignore the facade she had created. Lillian was still terrified. He had been the only reason she had ever felt safe. Now he was gone and all that had tortured her six years ago remained. She shivered once remembering Sister Roy. She could still hear the woman's voice in her ears.

"Stop your crying you little prat," she would scold.

"I want to hear none of your demonic tales about ghosts. Blessings your parents had the sense to leave you here, where we could correct your nasty habits. Only evil things can talk to the dead."

Lillian had learned quickly that whatever met her in the hours of the night were her secrets to keep. Her back tightened impulsively, and Lillian closed her eyes. Sister Roy had stripped the joy from Lillian.

"No point in bothering about it now," she assured herself as she focused more closely on the calming scents of her bath. She had spent eighteen years in that hell and couldn't stand to think of it a moment longer. Lillian toyed with a rose petal as it curled against the steam and she felt her frazzled eyes turn heavy. She lifted herself from her soak and dried her body before bed. Recognizing the insignificance of her dreams would likely return them to the pleasant inspirations she'd known with Aillig. Lillian snuggled under her sheets and stared out her window, counting the stars as she drifted off. The shadows jumped on the walls and crept cautiously around the perimeter of her room. Lillian shut her eyes tight. She could feel it move to the edge of her mattress.

"If it's not real, it can't hurt me."

She tugged on her ears and counted backwards, forcing herself to fall asleep. Lillian's hands trembled and she whispered under her breath. She was haunted whether she slept or not.

............

The man tried explaining to her that he wasn't there to scare her, becoming too aware of his formidable height. He moved farther away from Lillian's bedside, aching with the desire to soothe her. He could see the companionship of their childhood had long dulled from her memory. They used to escape the adults that plagued their upbringing together. Now it seemed as though she had all but forgotten him. Stripped undoubtedly by the hands of the woman who raised her.      She was aware of him, but being demoralized to a ghost tightened his chest. He slowly let his shadow fade from her room. He blamed himself for becoming a stranger to her in the time he had been away. He couldn't help but think of his own life to the point where he sat now, rotting in a cell. He had tried valiantly to live up to the nobility of his name and his father, but had failed. Now he was only a killer and a fiend, left to linger in the stench of his shadows before death, centuries apart from the love that had carried him through war. The darkness that had skewed their innocence now damaged the time parallel connecting them. He couldn't blame her for being afraid of something she didn't understand.

"But young man, you did not fail at all."

"Who is that?" he called to the darkness.

An old man shuffled his way forward to sit next to him, his sacred robes dirtied with imprisonment.

"You sacrificed your life for the wellness of your people, and have protected the one who carries a responsibility heavier than your own."

"How do you know me," he demanded.

He felt unrecognizable from the brilliance of his days in battle, but the old man spoke of an intimate knowledge. He had been alone the day he sent his sister across the sea with the premonition of Lillian's prophecy.

"Please," he whispered gently, "tell me what you know."

The old man only smiled and rested his head against the wall, closing his eyes.

"There is time for that yet."

..............

Lillian woke at sunrise to take a walk before work. She had spent most of the night peeking from underneath her covers, praying the shadow moving in her room was only her imagination. The musty smell of the church dampened her exhausted mind and she wished her haunted memories would have stayed in the city where she left them.

"It's just ridiculous," she mused to herself, scolding the fear she should have long outgrown.

The dense footing below cushioned her step and the cold air pressed against her forehead. Her footpath to the forest behind her cottage was already worn. Walking had always been her favorite way to work through her problems. Lillian toyed with the edges of the paper she'd scribbled on as she moved through the tangle of trees, studying the list of herbs she'd imagined just before waking.

"Really, Lillian," she spoke to the air, "you must find a way to stop it. You cannot work without proper rest. Stop obsessing over it, and the dreams will fade."

Birds chirped sleepily from their cozy nests. She walked through the mist, watching tiny droplets weave between the whispering trees. Despite the dull ache in her bones, the world was at her fingertips and she slipped into the sing song pattern of procuring healing lessons from the Earth. The trees that grew above her had weathered many storms, and the dew soaked grasses had been flooded by rain on a regular basis. They had not only survived what overwhelmed them, but flourished in the aftermath. They had learned to adapt and thrive from what should have killed them. Lillian would survive and grow from her set backs as well.

When she returned home, her cheeks were flushed with rosy invigoration. She made a quick cup of tea and headed out for work. It was almost a mile to her shop, and she had grown fond of walking there. It was the only time she allowed herself to remember Aillig; to cry if she wanted. He wouldn't have liked her to get lost in the sadness of his death. He had never thought much of death himself. Aillig had always been so different than anyone she'd ever known. For the first time since she'd moved, she smiled in his memory.

The sun was bleak in the morning light and Lillian softened to the metallic overtone it gave the world around her. The steam from her tea escaped her travel mug and made her lip dewy as she sipped. She admired the small gardens she passed, acknowledging the eccentric colors of each flower bed. Not a soul stirred in the waking of a new day. The seclusion of a small town was a gift not taken for granted and she owed it all to Aillig. He had left her everything in his will. It hadn't been much, but enough to start again.

Lillian unlocked the door to her apothecary. Customers wouldn't come for another hour, so she headed towards the back to work. Clear glass bottles fell away to darker tinctures and essential oils as she wound further, and she beamed over the varieties that stocked oak shelves. She twisted the knob to her procuring room, and something slipped by the corner of her peripheral vision. A tickle spread from her chest and made her arms weak. She rushed through the other side of the door, closing it quickly behind her. Lillian pressed against the old wood, listening in the darkness for the shuffle of feet. After a moment, she sighed, shaking her head as she pulled the cord to her light.

"Really, Lillian," she scolded herself, "you are not a child anymore. No one is here to get you and there are no such things as ghosts."

She inhaled deeply and closed her eyes before blowing out her nerves.

"Now," she muttered, "what was it that I was mixing in my dream?"

Lillian pulled out her notes and lost herself to another new creation. The weight of her silky black hair swung in its plait as she plucked bottles from her shelves. The herbs called to her as she uncorked them, and Lillian's green eyes brightened in the depth of her mix. She could feel the herbs rise to her nose and expand towards her chest, loosening the tension in her strong walking legs. The walls of the room fell away. She could see the forest behind her house and could feel a fresh rain against the damp bark of the trees. The sun peeked gently through the density overhead and Hoot's low call was gentle in her ears. Her pupils dilated and for a second the silhouette of a man stood in front of her.

Lillian gasped and the mixing room returned to sight. She could feel her heart slamming against her chest as she blinked to gain composure, systematically reading the labels of the herbs she'd mixed. She had always created imagery of her mixing, but in all her life she had never seen a person in any of them. A last time, she looked at the bottles in front of her.

"Kava, rose hip, blue mallow. None of these should cause hallucinations," she stressed to herself.

The bell rung on the other side of her door and she glanced at the clock. Time had lapsed too quickly. She opened her procuring room and moved toward the front of her shop. Though startled by the vision, her mind and body worked clearly. The new mix had successfully relieved the anxiety of shadows and old memories. Lillian shrugged to herself and prepared for another work day.

........

His eyes flew open, hoping to see her standing with him in the woods. His heart slammed dangerously against his broad chest, breaking in disappointment as the walls of the prison returned.

"What did you do?" he commanded, handing a small vile back to the old man.

"You are so dejected from the famine of war that it seems you have forgotten the heart of your own culture. You cannot recall the sacred teachings of your druids? You do not remember the very earth oils your beloved creates?"

Brightly silvered eyes shone in single minded silence. He didn't like his attention to detail challenged. Not when it came to her.

Nodding, the druid continued as he tucked the liquid away.

"The Hooded Spirits must not have had the time to explain before returning to the Isle. Sacred Oak thins the veils between time and aids your ability to reach her without relying on the realm of dreaming. Her herbs do something similar, but she doesn't know it. The synchronicity of your experiences brought you together.

The connection you share with her is strong and it will need to be now that the prophecy has wakened."

"How do you know about her," the man demanded, feeling violated.

"I have lived many lives my young nobleman. I know many stories. You and she are one of them."

*Chapter Five*

*Emmy watched her gather plants. She could see a foot path in front of them, and birds flustered in the branches above their head. She had to adjust her eyes to the darkness of the forest. Flickers of light popped and danced in the air around her, brightening the places between the shrubbery. The shadow moved between the trees and walked out in the middle of the path in front of them. He stood stoic and vacant as he approached. She strained to make out his face, but even her lights could not illuminate him. Emmy tried calling to the strangers, desperate to know their identity, but no one seemed to hear. She was getting frustrated. She wanted to talk to them. Her body started to separate itself from her and Emmy gritted her teeth. She had felt this unbearable pull before. The woman rose from her clippings and screamed at the sight of the dark shadow, jolting Emmy out of sleep.*

She stretched and rose from bed, readying in haste. One slender leg slipped through her shorts after the other. She strapped an arm over her chest. She would not be repeating yesterday's disaster. It was time to start over.

Her dream had been inspiring. She had felt free walking behind the woman. She reminded Emmy of the Indians Henry used to tell her about. She looked softly to the book she'd stashed in her glovebox. He'd read it to her since she was little. Looking at it now made her homesick, and she resisted the urge to open it. She couldn't continue reminding herself of the past if she expected to move forward. Cutting the fat out of her plan was something she had learned from watching Ethan operate his giant thoroughbred farm. *Stop thinking about the past.*

"So what first," she asked herself, deliberately changing her focus. "The post office. Then coffee."

Emmy needed to do something productive. Shirt wrinkled and hair wild, she set her errands in a list, and walked less tragically toward town. The dry air whisked playfully around her waist, harkening to the bare skin underneath her shirt. Ethan wasn't here to control her choices anymore. Whatever she wanted the people here to see, she had to make it known now. She would not be the crazy outsider in a town she was determined to make her home. She was tired of wandering.

Emmy set her jaw in a hard line as she approached the post office. Her slender fingers curled around the handle of the door. It was time to make her first impression. Her heart skipped. She glanced sideways to notice a drop box on the outside of the building and slipped her addressed letter through the opening before she could think. Her eyes shot to her feet, and she hoped the people behind the desk hadn't seen her as she hurried away. Panic built a defensive wall against being recognized and Emmy rushed into the diner, stopping as she faced Shirley Jean's sharp, punishing eyes.

"Seriously?" Sherry moaned.

*You're doing what you said you wouldn't do.* With effort, she recollected her composure, taking a deep breath.

"My name is Emmy. I'm gonna be here awhile."

She stuck her hand over the counter, praying the harsh, fried hair on Sherry's head was no representation of her personality. Sherry stared indifferently at the unkempt, but undoubtedly beautiful young woman in front of her.

"I'm Sherry Jean," she whined with practiced judgment.

Emmy's explosive temper flared, sensing the cruel nature she'd escaped. Crystal blue eyes pierced through the dull pupils in front of her, unwilling to submit to people like Ethan again. Seconds passed like minutes, and the diner's humming machines fell from Emmy's ears. Her heart pounded once when Sherry Jean's eyes dropped to the counter. Emmy wasn't going to be intimidated by anyone from now on.

Emmy broke in with purpose, letting the dismissal of her handshake slide. She turned her back to the woman and towards the diner.

"So can I just help myself to a seat, or do you wanna show me one?"

Sherry Jean held back a snort as she slid a menu off the bar.

"Pick whatever seat you like."

Emmy set her eyes on a booth in the far right corner. She sat and opened the menu, glazing over its contents with decisive interest.

"I'll have a cup of coffee, a water, and the eggs and bacon. May I have hash browns and white bread for toast, please?"

She intended to stay there until closing, hoping to figure out what she had decided to get into. There was no mistaking that work would be hard to find, so she needed to start making connections immediately. Her grandfather had always teased that her good looks would get her everything in life. She recalled being seventeen with the world at her fingertips and pulled that version from far inside her soul. She had kind of believed Henry then, and she would now too. If that's what she needed to survive, she'd use it.

Emmy stared out the window and watched the vehicles passing by, trying to guess which were moving through and which belonged to locals. She curled a lock of her mane around her pointer finger, and bit her lip in contemplation. She was determined to make something of herself and quit the nomadic life. Sherry Jean slid her breakfast in front of her, interrupting the barrier of Emmy's quiet thought.

"Do you sell newspapers here?" Emmy asked, continuing her process out loud, "I'm not sure I even know what day it is," she laughed.

Sherry Jean pointed to the newsstand near the door, wondering what hole the girl had crawled out of. This was by far the strangest person she had ever met.

"How much?" Emmy said, rising.

"Seventy-five cents."

Emmy dug three quarters out of her pocket, and dropped them on the table. Returning with paper in hand, she glanced at Sherry Jean absentmindedly, engrossed in making a list of things to accomplish.

"Hey, do you have a pen I could use for a while?"

"Sure," Sherry said slowly, still calculating the disaster sitting in front of her. She couldn't decide if she should lure her into action as entertainment on a slow morning, or run for cover and prepare to kick out the time bomb. Yesterday she had shown up dazed and shaking. Now, she sat functioning as though it had never happened.

Sherry shrugged as she turned and walked back to do busy work. She thought that unstable people had it easy if they could forget their odd behavior as they pleased. She thought of a few things she'd like to forget about herself as she wiped down the spotless table tops. Her relationship with her boss was one of them. She blamed girls like Emmy for her miserable life. This pretty thing sat completely unaware of herself. She had captured the interest of the elusive Cutter Maben without even trying. Sherry touched the hair at the nape of her neck and glanced with disdain at

Emmy. For once she wished that beautiful people understood what it was like to struggle.

Emmy scribbled furiously in the margins of the newspaper, making notes of what needed to be done. First among them was to look around for some new clothes. If she wanted to be noticed, she'd have to get an unwrinkled shirt or two. In having to find a general store, she'd also have the chance to map out the rest of this place. She felt certain it'd require a trip to another neighboring town, where more variety existed. Making acquaintances rolled smoothly into the rest of her checklist, and she set the pen down to take another bite of her toast.

"Now," she muttered to herself, "what day is it anyway?"

She looked to the header of the front page and smiled. "Saturday, July 25."

A weekend crowd was bound to gather. She silently hoped that this was the diner they all gravitated to. She gazed out the window, wishing to see some movement around the little shops. A few people littered the quaintly western walkways. She took a sip of her coffee and shifted her attention back to the newspaper, scanning for all the information she could absorb.

Though rural, the community was richly influenced by a variety of artistic mediums, and boasted a large selection of galleries. She wondered how such modernism reached this dustbowl. As she continued browsing, Emmy noted that a national juried art show was being held the entire month of July. Scribbling next to it as a marker, she made a mental note to visit the showing tomorrow.

Skimming over each section, the rest of the city seemed typical besides the promise of an extensive museum of local history. There was a small sheriff's station and a church. Local high school heroes were spotlighted, along with the usual quirky gift shops. A local rodeo was held almost every weekend. Her skin burned and ached at the thought of attending. Going tonight would place her close to what she left behind. Again, she gently pushed the past from present plans, and practiced forgetting the painful loss of her horses. She turned the page and noticed a thrift store. She circled the ad feeling as though she had made a good start. It seemed she had picked a good place after all. Emmy sat back and enjoyed the last of her coffee.

"You want more?" Sherry Jean squawked over her.

"Eh, yes," Emmy said distracted, "thank you."

The door opened. Both women looked up to see a handful of customers waiting at the counter. Sherry Jean flattened her apron with one hand and scurried over with exercised gentility. Emmy sunk back against the seat as she watched and analyzed. The assortment of western attired people trickled into tables and barstools. A husband and wife toted their child, a middle aged man sat gruffly at the bar to sip his black coffee. A handful of friends crammed into a booth to shovel in some breakfast, hopeful to get rid of their hangovers.

Emmy smiled at them. She had never experienced that part of life. She had passed up parties for marriage and business. That really worked out well for her. She flicked a page of the paper, consumed with self loathing, and a blown up photograph from last weekend's rodeo caught her eye. As usual, the cowboy was sitting on the back of a gnarled and mean looking bull. She defiantly chose to go to the upcoming rodeo. If her past didn't exist, then the whole thing shouldn't bother her, and she'd plan to have a few drinks while she was there. Emmy was going to have the experience a free woman ought to have. She was determined to change the pattern in her life and make up for lost time.

More people arrived as a convenient distraction to the fire building quickly inside. A tall man walked passed, and Emmy dove at the opportunity.

"Hey," she said, nodding her head once.

The man stopped, towering over her table.

"Morning."

Emmy was surprised to hear his subtle east coast accent and made quick conversation.

"That's a different accent. Where are you from?"

"New York."

"Wow, are you just passing through? Sure are a long way from home."

"No."

"Oh, so you live here now? I'm staying here awhile, maybe I could pick your brain for information."

Emmy blinked slowly and leaned over the tabletop with inquisition. The man stood indifferent to her flirtation. Emmy tossed her hair to one side, and craned her neck to expose its delicate skin. His hazel eyes glanced at it briefly before matching her stare.

"There's not much to it," he stated simply and moved to his booth.

Emmy managed a smile until he was out of sight, then slumped against the window in disappointment. She hadn't caught his attention, and was certain she must be out of practice. She brushed off the loss and continued scouting for someone to talk with. Sherry Jean silently gloated from behind the bar. She must have seen the whole thing unfold.

A few hours passed as Emmy watched hopelessly ignored at her table. Even though the town offered diversity, her original generalization held true. The locals were so used to passersby that they offered a short glance of acknowledgement and continued to gossip in circles about other locals. She scrunched her nose as Sherry Jean went scurrying from table to table, clearly overwhelmed by the full house. This whole endeavor seemed so much easier when she scribbled it out on the newspaper.

"You aren't going to learn about this town by sitting here all day."

Emmy jumped as the tall New Yorker walked by her table.

"Go to the rodeo tonight, you'll learn all you want," he said, walking out the door.

Emmy took it as a small triumph. If she could catch him there, maybe he'd be less stiff and consider her acquaintance.

.....

Henry patted his friend's hand as she collected her nerves. Ms. Beckett huffed, and tried to catch her breath.

"The dear girl has no idea what she's done, we should have told her, Henry."

"Tell me what happened," Henry cooed.

"I heard them fighting. Then silence. The air felt different. So I hurried home and stayed on my porch to make sure he wasn't going to drag her body off somewhere in the middle of the night. When I saw her leave the next morning, I knew it was only a matter of time before he went after her, Henry. I waited until I was sure no one would see me come to you. She finally left. You know how the prophecy starts."

Henry nodded.

"A broken pattern. We have a year and a day. It's time to gather our things. You will need to know more about her prophecy too, my dear friend. She has remarkable dreams about it, but I never had to the chance to tell her the truth. After she married Ethan..."

Henry's anger grew. He should have prepared her for the chaos that was bound to follow her. She wouldn't know how to control the past lives as they surfaced. She wouldn't know what the mood swings meant. She didn't even understand the synchronicity game he'd started with her and the strings of light. He closed his eyes for a moment. There was nothing he could do now. Henry could only hope that she would remember his fairytales. They were her story.

*Chapter Six*

Lillian watched the aging man saunter through her aisles. He had made brief eye contact when he entered, but nothing more. He read every label of every bottle, his eyes dancing with humor. Her temples grew tight and insecurity warmed her face. She could pick out every small inadequacy as he passed it. She rubbed her hands and took a break from writing notes, observing him behind her busy desk.

Though heavyset for his short stature, he moved with little effort between her tight quarters. His white hair was kept neatly under a tweed cap and his face was tinged with rosacea. She guessed he suffered from pressure headaches by the deep crease between his brow, and perhaps mild pain in his fingers by the way he held his hands so tensely.

"May I help you, sir?" Lillian spoke with gentle humility, oddly nervous before him.

He smiled and came to a deliberate halt before her.

"Quite an inventory, my dear, for your humble location."

"Thank you," she replied.

"May I ask what brought ye to decide on a storefront so far away?"

Lillian wondered what he meant. She never felt comfortable with personal questions and thought about her answer carefully. It wasn't her job to talk about herself and she liked it that way.

"I enjoy the scenery and quiet surroundings."

He paused before speaking again.

"Pardon me," his mild brogue slipped past, "but perhaps I should ask ye differently. What's brought ye so far from the success of the city?"

She smiled politely, uneasy about his mention of city life. Something about the man was starting to upset her. No one here ever talked about the city. They didn't need to, they didn't live there. Her palms started to grow clammy.

"I'm sorry if I don't understand sir, but my answer would still be the same," she lied.

He looked at her thoughtfully.

"Perhaps then, I should ask ye who instead of what?"

Lillian felt the pit of her stomach drop. Her legs began to shake behind the desk. Aillig wasn't there. He was dead in the city she fled from. She was alone without anyone to protect her.

"I'm sorry," she stumbled, "I don't believe we've met. My name is Lillian."

She extended her delicate hand.

"Oh, I quite know who ye are, Miss Blake."

His wide palm engulfed hers, shaking it with a rough strength.

"My name is Dougal."

Lillian's nerves rose to her throat. She didn't recognize him at all.

"I'll not be forgetting my question."

Her stomach grew hot in the silence that stretched between them. Memories flashed behind her deep green eyes. The sensation of the city crowded her, broke the seal on the barrier of safety she'd built. She could hear the distant roar of flames booming in her ears and she could feel the threat of tears weakening her composure. His suspicion felt threatening. This stranger no longer piqued her interest.

"You were such a nervous creature that day."

Lillian glared at him.

"But I don't know you."

"No, ye don't lass," he sighed, "but ye knew my brother, Aillig. I saw ye at his shop the day it burned, but couldn't decide how to approach ye. Then ye were gone and I wasna sure if it was right to try and find ye."

The color drained from her face. The squat, strong man in front of her looked nothing like her dear Aillig. *But the eyes, those all knowing eyes.* She should have seen it. Lillian felt dizzy. She wasn't prepared to talk about him with someone else. She didn't want to share the mystery surrounding his death. It was as if her dreams had been trying to warn her this was going to come.

"Ye couldn't have recognized it, lass," he laughed, knowing well the only trait he shared with his brother. "It's hard to see something you're working hard to forget."

She wanted to coil away from him.

"Twas a terrible thing to have seen. I canna blame ye for wanting to erase it."

Dougal watched as the girl struggled with composure. Even in shock she had an air of gentility. He could see why Aillig was so fond of her. She had the same curiosity that was constantly working to save the world. Aillig must have trained her meticulously to forget what the church had done.

"What do you want from me?" Lillian asked.

She was lost in a barely faded memory. Aillig was the only person to show her kindness; the closest thing she had to a parent. He was her only attachment to Norwich and her reason to leave when he died.

He smiled painfully for the girl.

"Och, I want nothing from ye."

"Then why'd you come here?"

"I suppose I just wanted to check on Aillig's special apprentice. Maybe recount a few memories."

After his brother's death, he had received a mysterious letter in Aillig's writing and Dougal had been sent out to speculate on her well being. He had been asked to make sure she hadn't learned too much from his cunning family member. It was hard to imagine the frail girl he had seen at the sight of the burned apothecary would amount to anything worthy of a holy prophecy. Until now. The town had already started gravitating toward her, and he grew as suspicious as his superiors. Her type always had a way of beguiling people into believing in them.

"I didn't know anything then, and I don't know anything now. His apothecary burned. That's all I can tell you," she snapped.

Lillian wished he would leave and take the memories with him. A man speaking fondly of the city never had good intentions for her. That she had learned early in life. Aillig's death crept all around her.

Dougal silenced his efforts. A worn hand touched his vest pocket, and he decided to press the girl another day. If the announcement of his identity upset her, the presentation of Aillig's letter would leave her lifeless and he wanted to savor it.

"I'm sorry to have come and hurt ye," Dougal whispered as he headed towards the door.

Lillian's face fell.

"I'm sorry to have bitten at you like that, really. I just don't know what..." she choked, "I can't seem to believe," she wrung her hands, "Oh, Aillig," she gasped, standing to find privacy to weep.

She turned in every direction, all of them unfamiliar through blurry eyes. She could feel a recognizable panic crawling in her chest. Talking about his death out loud somehow made it more real than it had been. All the mystery that surrounded that day came bubbling up from the abyss of her consciousness. She had never wanted to think about it again. There wasn't a reason. She'd never know the truth. No one cared enough to search for it.

"I'm sorry," she blubbered, ushering him through the door. "I'm closed. I don't know what you'd ever want from me."

She locked the door and turned to make the long walk home, leaving Dougal dumbfounded on the side of the road. The walls were closing in around her. She could smell the burnt hell in her memory. Lillian didn't look back but watched her toes in the dimming light, counting down the steps to her front gate. The city had finally come for her and she had handled it poorly. Lillian blamed it on her nightmares. She could feel the ghost at her back.

"If I was sleeping well, none of this would have bothered me so terribly," she tried convincing herself as she wiped tears from her lashes.

......

He hung back in the shadows behind her, feeling the limits of their connection. She had every right to be scared. He had seen what these people were capable of in his own time. The fat man's tactics were a trademark. They found her after all.

"Divide and conquer," he hissed, "nothing has changed. They rip her away from her own, from us, and control her with fear."

"Calm now," the druid whispered. "Your soul in rage is too strong for this old body to guide into her time projection. If you cannot wait to see her on your own, you have to remain sedate."

The man took a deep breath. A sweet, floral scent lingered nervously in the air. He'd know it anywhere. The long angles of her thin face called to a life from more romantic times and her wide, observant eyes shone in the gentle green of memories she didn't understand. He blessed his mother for teaching him the stories in faces. His night haired beauty had chosen all the signs for awakening the prophecy.

Lillian needed to stop running from her past. She needed to remember it. She needed to remember him. Lillian had no idea what danger was in front of her and there was little he could do to help. His chest ached as he watched, hoping that he could find a way to her.

"I love her," he whispered, apologizing to the old man.

He stood, pacing his small confines, letting her fade from view. The dampness clung to his dirtied clothes and suffocated him.

"You will again," the druid said, catching his breath, "I suppose we may need to train you to walk through the veils on your own. I simply do not have the strength to contain you."

He pushed his fair hair away from his face and sat back down.

"I could kill them all for what they've done to her."

"And you will."

He looked at his tired cellmate, waiting for him to elaborate.

"In time, young man. We must show her what's been lost, first. I must teach you some of our secrets too, while I can."

Muffled voices of enemies streamed in the distance and the young man recalled the years he'd spent in her life. They had grown up together and his heart ached to feel close to her again. She had to know ghosts were a creation to keep her from the truth. If she could remember their childhood, perhaps she could break her pattern of fear and he could guide her towards the prophecy. Their forgotten civilization could thrive again. He closed his eyes and tried to make a plan.

Lillian was tired and it made her defense against his presence weak. Even though it was immoral to take advantage of a distressed woman, chance was not in abundance. He'd try to reach out to her tonight.

*Chapter Seven*

Emmy looked around the strange room and tried to remember how she'd gotten there. The shelves that towered above were crammed with millions of things and she felt lost. A gruff voice drifted to her ears and she looked up. A fat, burly man stood in front of her. She could recognize malicious intent without trying. Her hands trembled, and her heart slammed in her chest. Bottles tipped and Emmy whipped around. The same silhouette from the forest hid in the shadows of the shelves. Her stomach grew hot, and when she looked down, wisps of black hair fell against her clothing. The woman was so close she seemed to be a part of her. That was impossible. A sharp pinch constricted her ribs and she pulled away from the dream.

......

She could see the lights glaring from her motel room as she set out. Handfuls of people gathered and walked down the edge of the street as trucks cruised carefully by. The stars were winking above her; wiser about the predicament she was putting herself in. Henry always told her they knew first. He'd learned astrology from the

Native Americans when he was a young boy in Kentucky. She smiled, remembering him recount old Indian tales. Emmy often wondered if he'd mixed in a bit of his own Irish history with it. He would have loved to see the rodeo. He had raised her in a western saddle.

"Now he's gone," Emmy sighed, distancing herself.

She thought of the dream as a distraction. It wasn't the first time she'd seen that frightening man or the woman with dark hair. Emmy couldn't be sure if she'd known them or only dreamt of them. Henry would have known what it meant. He always asked her about her dreams when she was little and offered explanations, even if they usually tended to stretch the imagination. He liked to make her laugh.

The low buzz of the event announcer relieved her from her failed attempt to forget and called focus to her surroundings. People passed by in dirtied jeans and leather boots. Accents of travelers and locals mixed together into marbled gibberish. She followed the crowds through parking lots filled with stock trailers. Emmy rubbed her neck. She had to go watch for a few minutes, at least.

"ID please," the man at the booth asked.

She handed him her driver's license with little enthusiasm.

"Okay, have fun," he said cheerfully, wrapping a neon yellow piece of paper around her wrist.

At least she could have a few beers. Emmy shrugged to herself and kept walking. The stands rose gently above the main arena and the dirt had been carefully dragged between each event. People sat waiting with excitement, and Emmy decided to see what was causing so much anticipation. She passed a portable bar, and determined to numb some of the heartache, she detoured to order a drink.

"What'll you have?"

The New Yorker from the diner. Instantly, she turned on the charm, happy to refocus her energy into something productive.

"Just a beer," she smiled. "You working the booth all night?"

"Only for another hour."

Taking it as an invitation, she leaned casually over the serving table.

"Well, maybe when you're done, you could come on up in those stands and find me."

He stared at her, sliding a plastic cup across the small space. Emmy's confidence waned. She could have sworn men were all the same. They loved attention from girls. She furrowed her brow and looked at his left hand, expecting to find a wedding band. When there was none, she glanced upward, half hoping that he was into men to save a little of her pride. He glanced over her shoulder, and she followed to see a string of people forming behind her. She stood with a stiff back and started towards the stands.

"I'm meeting friends later," he called after her, pity almost penetrating his hard exterior.

Emmy didn't turn, but held up her hand and waved in acknowledgement as she continued moving towards the bleachers. The fizz from the beer was soothing as it settled in her stomach. The condensed crowd gave her an edge and the loud noises seemed to jar her more than she had expected. She settled in between the crowd, hoping to adjust.

In the arena below, cowboys tried their hand at staying on top of wild broncs in the bareback competition. Emmy held her shoulders tightly, trying not to get nudged. The children screamed and whined about the popcorn they didn't get. Their mother pacified them the best she could while their father sipped numbly on his own beer. The crowd yelled and clapped as each hero exploded out of the shoot on another wild eyed beast. Emmy hadn't realized how quiet and introverted her life had been in the past few weeks. It was becoming increasingly obvious how little she had interacted with people, even before she had left home.

The ominous task of readjusting herself to the exuberance of human nature started cracking her fragile walls. She could feel the chill crawling up her knees and the cold pressure of panic on her back. She looked down for a moment to regain her composure and saw her hand shaking. Emmy managed to bring the cup to her mouth, letting the cool elixir soothe the quiver in her lower lip. She sipped eagerly, wishing the effects would kick in.

The gate slammed open to let another gnarling horse leap from its pen. The crowd thundered and shook her bones. The whine from the P.A. pressed against her forehead and Emmy felt dizzy. She stood unevenly, desiring no longer to be one of the crowd. The groups surrounding her looked up with mild interest before cheering again for whatever cowboy came jumping out of the gates. Emmy's tingling legs wobbled out of the row and she gripped her free hand tightly against the rail as she made the descent out of the stands.

When she hit the bottom, a breeze twisted up her legs, the intensity of the crowd waned, and she exhaled. She walked to find a less populated area of the event grounds and another drink. Intoxicated couples walked by her, eyes happily glazing over one another. A twang of longing passed by with them. Competitors watched as she walked through them. The desire for adrenaline grew in her. Children ran past her in a flurry, giggling as the energy of the night surged through them. Magic and innocence tickled the backs of her thighs when they disappeared from view. Emmy's head started to swirl with the things she had promised to ignore. She cursed herself for thinking that alcohol would help her, and she instinctively looked to the stars to check if they were amused.

The distance from the crowd quieted her. She walked languidly between holding arenas, admiring the greatness of the bucking bulls and contemplating the glare in the eyes of the broncs. Emmy stopped when she reached a pen holding a tightly wound group of young horses. None had the flare of a competitor. Nor did they have the wise stature of a seasoned rodeo animal. They stood together in nervous comfort, shyly absorbing their surroundings.

She could feel a tug towards their overwhelmed expressions. It was something she picked up on easily, she lived in that space herself. She hesitated to move closer. Their little nostrils expanded and deflated as they tried to make sense of the commotion around them. She couldn't bear seeing them as upset as she. Emmy peeked inside the pen, transfixing herself to their movement, giving into the tugs she'd abandoned years ago. She closed her eyes and watched the pulses of light dance and search for a connection. The horses edged cautiously forward. The ends of her hair trembled and she slowly reached her free hand out to the sorrel colt in front of her. His nostrils flared. Emmy opened her eyes and smiled. A paint mare crawled inward to get her share, and Emmy leaned lower to blow gently into her nose. The mare's eyes steadied as she blew, and she nudged in even closer. Emmy murmured in a low voice, whispering confessions of her abandonment to her captive audience. She reached out to stroke each of their foreheads before they parted and went back to the herd.

"That was incredible."

Emmy turned in slow surprise. The man from the diner stood a few feet away, watching her with gentle eyes. She cleared the evidence of sorrow from her face in hopes he hadn't seen. She wondered idly how long he'd been watching. Emmy prayed he wasn't referring to what she'd learned to hide from Ethan. She smiled despite herself. The beer had definitely curbed her nerves.

"Cutter, right?" she asked with a thicker, mixed accent.

"Yeah, that's right," he smiled. "I'm sorry I didn't catch your name."

"Emmy," she replied, sticking out her hand.

The air popped around her ears when his fingers wrapped around hers and the world tilted her off balance. Sparks of memories she had never seen flew between her eyes. Her body was going numb and she pulled her hand too carefully away from his. She felt inexplicably certain they'd done this before. Emmy glanced at her empty cup, trying to remember the last time she drank. Alcohol made her strange.

"How'd you coax them over here?" he asked, regaining her attention.

"What do you mean?"

Emmy turned her dizzy body to lean against the rails, trying to recover.

"They're completely wild. The only human contact they've had was whoever chased them in here this morning."

Cutter turned too, but kept his eyes intently on her. She wore sneakers like they were boots and moved too fluently through the horses of waiting ropers to be unfamiliar with rodeo. Her legs stretched freely away from the fence; toned and golden from summer. Cutter forced his eyes beyond the dangerous curve of her jean pockets and over her back as she leaned forward to get a better view of the herd. Her hair fell in a mess of reddish, golden brown flames around her. He blushed at the curve of her chest and the admittance of yesterday's memory. He almost wanted to apologize for remembering so selfishly.

"Why are they here?"

Emmy frowned as she watched the angels standing a little distance away.

"It's a part of a competition to see who can get a saddle on them and get their ride first. It has a huge pay out."

Emmy watched and analyzed the small movements of the animals in front of her.

"They're so young and uncertain. It's such a shock."

He smiled, eager to reassure her.

"I'd hate it too, but the guys usually never catch one. It's mostly comedy."

Emmy smiled and Cutter's heart almost stopped. Since he had seen her shivering in the diner yesterday, he couldn't stop thinking about her. He had laid awake all night wondering where she had come from and what had scared her so badly. Emmy dangled her fingers over the rail and the paint mare stepped hesitantly towards her.

"Ah, *báibín*," Emmy cooed, kissing into the air as she wiggled her fingers.

The young horse moved no closer, eyeing Cutter. Emmy rested still.

"She's nervous of men. I hope she kicks them in the balls."

Cutter blinked. Emmy was broken in the face of a stranger one moment and spitting fire towards another the next. She was exciting.

"How'd you coax them over?" he asked again.

"Not sure," she shrugged. "I was just watching, wishing they'd come over. No animal needs to be so afraid. I just started telling them so and they came."

The truth about what Henry had taught her always got her in trouble. He didn't need to hear the details. She knew they were strange, and she didn't want to explain anyway.

"What was it you just said to that filly to get her attention? How did you see she was female?" Cutter continued, completely intrigued.

"It means baby in Irish."

Emmy went to elaborate, but Henry's memory caught in her throat.

"And I don't know how I knew she was a filly. I felt it, there was something in her eyes."

Emmy looked at Cutter once he turned to consider the horses. He had broad shoulders and an athletic build. It was obvious whatever muscle he had was because he used them. It wasn't like the manufactured muscle of the Kentucky gym rats she'd known at home. He wasn't as threatening as anything, or anyone, there either. His jeans were well worn, as were his boots. He had to be a local. Somewhere deep inside, her heart sighed in isolation. Her chest turned pink under her shirt. A dull magnetism drew her towards him. Emmy swore they'd met before, but she would have remembered a man like that.

The gate at the opposite side of the pen slammed open and Emmy jumped. Cutter's arm wrapped around her waist instinctively. She looked up at him and her entire body stiffened. He let go and dropped his hand against his side.

"Sorry," he spoke softly, "I heard you gasp. I guess I wasn't really paying attention to myself. I won't hurt you."

Her shoulders relaxed and she took half a step away. She couldn't allow the beer to dissolver her guard. Emmy didn't like that he seemed so familiar.

"It's okay," she shrugged, carefully wiping the concern from her face.

Hooves pounded in a flurry, dragging both their attention away from the tension already dissolving between them. The herd climbed over each other as a few ranch hands pushed them down a chute towards the main arena.

"Want to go see some of my friends get kicked in the balls?"

She knew what he was really asking. Every man liked attention from a girl. Tonight was her chance to change the pattern of her behavior. She desperately needed to make a friend and being suspicious of everyone would do her no good.

"Sure," she smiled a little forcibly.

He lead her away from the pen and to the bar for some drinks. The tall New Yorker stopped before leaving his shift.

"What ya want, buddy?"

Cutter looked to Emmy.

"Can I buy you another drink?"

She shrugged and nodded as she threw her empty cup into the trash. It was probably a bad idea, but it made her feel less afraid. She also wanted to rub it in the bartender's face. Cutter winked at him in thanks before they left. Emmy smiled despite herself.

"Thank you, Cutter."

"My pleasure."

He was surprised to see such a shift in her demeanor, though the hesitancy lingered as she walked. She wouldn't walk too closely to him. He knew he was still a stranger, and her walls were thick. She was refreshing and he wasn't going to take this opportunity for granted.

"Do you ride horses, Emmy?"

"Not anymore," she sighed.

Emmy was feeling looser as she sipped the beer he had gotten her. They watched their new acquaintances elude the cowboys from the far side of the main arena. The paint mare fired a hoof into someone's thigh. Emmy laughed. She silently thanked the golden liquid for dulling whatever was still wrong with her. It'd been such a long time since she had enjoyed the company of someone else. She let herself indulge in his interest and smiled as he went on about the rodeo, grazing vaguely over this person and that, filling the time with stories about the city around them.

"The locals aren't bad once you get to know them. They just don't waste their time on travelers. Unless it can make them a penny or two."

"I noticed."

He laughed quietly and let his leg brush lightly against hers. Goosebumps prickled her skin. He looked down and frowned.

"Are you cold?"

She only managed to shake her head once before the burn of embarrassment set into her cheeks. She couldn't control what her body remembered. She slid her fingers through her hair, feeling like she should be focused on the horses and not a man. That's the mistake that forced her to leave home. That's what made her skin tingle every time it was touched. Emmy felt nauseous.

"Hey, you wanna get out of here?"

He must have seen her shift away from him. Men loved attention from girls. Emmy panicked. She eyed him warily.

"I meant that it will be a thick crowd when this thing is over. I didn't want you to feel crammed. I wasn't saying..." the beer wasn't helping him either. He sounded like a creep.

"I'm sorry. I just noticed that too many people make you nervous. I saw you in the stands." He stopped. "That sounded likes something a stalker would say. I'm not doing a good job of explaining myself." Cutter laughed. It'd been too long since he'd been interested in charming a woman and he was out of practice.

She was drunk and didn't want to walk back to the motel alone. She considered him carefully before nodding.

"Yeah, I don't like crowds."

Cutter only smiled and held out his hand. She grabbed it in bravery. Her ears popped and Emmy felt a rush of old memories she didn't have. She glanced at the hard line of his jaw as he turned to lead her out. Emmy knew she'd remember a man who looked like that. She couldn't understand what Henry's game was trying to connect to. It had been acting up every since she left. She looked down and concentrated on walking as the world around her grew fuzzy. She couldn't give into the tug, she couldn't let her body fail. Cutter was a stranger. She couldn't lose control now. Emmy's entire body tensed as she tried to fight against it.

"It's okay," he said squeezing her hand. "You're safe."

She forced a smile. It was simple for him to say, he didn't know what she'd lived through or what she was fighting against. Her legs started to numb. She linked her arm in his for balance and felt fuzzier. *What are you doing? Terrible idea. He is still a stranger. If this goes wrong you're going to be sorry, just like before.* She'd needed to make a gentle exit soon. They walked through town in silence, both caught in their own thoughts.

He softened watching her struggle to keep every emotion under control. He didn't need to press her for explanations, if he played it right. There would be plenty of time to learn the meaning behind her stormy eyes. It was hard not to be straight forward about his attraction. He had never been an indirect man and most people couldn't appreciate it. It had never bothered him until now. Her arms fit too well in his. Her company felt too good. When they reached the hotel parking lot, he spoke up quietly.

"Do you want me to walk you to your door?"

Emmy knew she shouldn't let him, but resisting against the light now blurring her vision had exhausted her. Her nerves were ragged and her surroundings dimmed. Emmy's arms had gone completely numb a while ago. She longed to feel human; to feel a human. She was sick of being alone. She needed Cutter and couldn't tell him.

"Okay," she almost slurred, damning herself.

She couldn't understand what she was doing, but didn't want him to leave. Emmy tried with difficulty to understand why he felt so familiar. She was certain they'd never met before. She was mostly sure. Her memories felt blurry and unimportant. They reached her door and stood a moment.

"It was nice to meet you, Emmy. I hope to see you again soon." Cutter was light hearted and optimistic.

"You too," she almost giggled. She couldn't believe herself. She couldn't control the tingling in her body. There was something crawling inside. She blamed it on the beer. It must have done this to her. Not Henry's game. Cutter went to leave, and her hand shot out to squeeze his arm. Emmy looked down at it with as much surprise as he. Her eyes were wild and bright when she looked up to him, searching for answers. Her entire body longed to recognize him.

"Are you okay?" he asked slowly.

"I don't feel like myself," she whispered.

Her soft lips pressed against his in impulsive daring. The plump curve of her lower lip had touched his before. Her breasts had pressed lightly against his broad chest a thousand times before tonight. A strange sigh danced in her throat.

He wrapped an arm delicately around her waist. He was afraid to touch her. Afraid to spook her. Afraid to break the thread of memory he was following to find her. She teetered and pressed harder against him. His mind exploded into silence. When she pulled away, his eyes opened slowly through heavy lids. Blue eyes gleamed like moons, full of mischief and surprise in front of him.

"Okay, good night," she said, opening her door and stepping in.

"Night," Cutter stammered just as the lock clicked into place.

Time rolled slowly back into motion as he readjusted to his surroundings. He hadn't seen that coming. Laughter rumbled in his chest and he turned to walk back to his truck. He would need the time to recover from the shock of her kiss. When his friend had described her from the diner earlier that day, he couldn't believe that they were talking about the same girl. Cutter owed John some money and a thank you for suggesting she go to the rodeo.

*Chapter Eight*

Lillian was drained. The walk home was long and all she wanted to do was crawl under the covers and never get up. Warm homes glowed from a distance through double paned windows. Aillig's brother had surprised her and she couldn't help but feel small in light of so many unexpected events. Aillig had died mysteriously. All of Norwich seemed suspicious of her. She fled to a town she'd never lived in to escape the chance of being taken back to the church. She'd rebuilt the business. Her night terrors had returned. Now Aillig's brother came to interrogate her about Aillig's death. Lillian could feel the bags under her eyes. Even the fear of being followed did not affect her. The pain of Aillig's death hummed in her veins as she unlocked her door, half hoping that the ghost who followed her would hurry up and haunt her to death.

........

The shadow man hung back from her, feeling the draining effects on her spirit. Her walls of defense didn't restrict his presence and the usual pinch of fear in the air was gone. Not being able to soothe her like he did in childhood was taking its toll. He was a warrior, and yet he was unable to help.

He longed to tell her about the thin veil that separated them, that he was alive and just out of reach. She needed him and he could do nothing but watch. He had lead men into war and rebelled against an infamous army, but he couldn't reach out and comfort the woman he loved. The shackles on his wrists seemed to extend into his soul, chaining him into a reality far away from her. He tried not to torture himself for being absent during the years he'd spent fighting her opponents. He had tried to defeat their growing empire before it could ever reach her. But he had lost the war, and Lillian. All that he had set out to do to save her from them had failed. He turned to his old friend.

"Why can I not move through the underworld and reclaim a life she understands? One that will allow me to fight for her?"

The old man smiled. "Lillian has to learn to fight for herself. She needs to break from her old beliefs if she wants to truly be free of what controls her. That is the pattern that the prophecy speaks of. All her lives she has allowed someone else to dictate her life." He shook his head, considering. "The underworld is difficult to navigate. It would be unwise of you to try before you are ready. Tonight will be practice when you veil walk through her subconscious with my guide. If she is willing to accept your presence, your influence on her dreams will help you."

"And if she is not?"

The druid realized what little comfort he offered and smiled.

"Then it will likely turn into another nightmare. Just like the underworld, you cannot always control what happens. The subconscious is our personal underworld."

.........

Lillian listened to the silence. She had come to the northern country to be left alone. Too many people in the city asked about Aillig's death and Lillian found it impossible to process the loss. She thought of Dougal.

Lillian didn't even know that Aillig had a brother, he'd never mentioned him. She wondered what had driven Aillig to erase Dougal from his life. He wasn't known to exclude anyone. She tossed onto her side in between cool sheets. Dougal was abrupt and cryptic and encouraged no kindness in her. Perhaps it had been the same in Aillig. Lillian fought against the urge to fall asleep. She was tired of dreaming about terrible things and she worried that the thoughts she wouldn't approach about Aillig's death would haunt her tonight.

"Dreams of my past haunt me when I sleep. Now the sorrows will haunt me awake."

She thought of her mentor's contagious laughter and insatiable hunger for knowledge. He made life exciting. He had a way of making her feel like she was constantly on the edge of a new discovery and pushed her to learn more about the art of healing. It was almost as if fate had brought them together. Her eyes grew heavy. Aillig had been such a bright light in her life. He was generous and kind hearted, even if a little strange. But he was never careless. He'd never have allowed his beloved shop to burn.

Lillian stopped herself. Tears welled in her eyes. To assume worse would only invite another nightmare. Hoot flapped his wings and somewhere between sleep and wake she felt the ghost stand near the entrance of her bedroom. Too late. The pressure of the shadow weighed on her back. Lillian squeezed her eyes together. Sister Roy wasn't here to hurt her anymore. She was exhausted. Lillian was tired of fighting against it. Darkness curled around her conscious mind.

She picked through her memories as they came, desperately trying to face them before the distortion of dreaming made it any worse. Through a squinted eye she saw the shadow shift closer to her. She tensed under her blankets. Lillian's breath deepened, and the edge of her bed bent. She lay facing the window and decided she was too old to be afraid anymore. Her body was motionless. She opened one eye. The outline of a man formed against the moonlight. Her body tingled and a hand rested gently on her ankle. Lillian turned toward the shadow man and surrendered to slumber, hopeless to escape her night terrors.

*Her cramped room swayed in sticky, humid air. Tucked tightly under her covers, she clamped her eyes shut, praying she hadn't bothered Sister Roy with her fitful sleeping. A whisper slid by her ears and she could feel the shadow on her bed.*

*"It's going to be okay, come on."*

*She smiled at the comfort of her invisible companion. The boy placed his hand on hers and she rose to sneak out. Lillian followed the vague silhouette down the hall and slipped outside to bathe in the light of a full moon. They sat together, laughing under the tree nearby. She could see his fine blonde hair and bright eyes. He watched her with patience. She giggled and crawled around the tree trunk to play tag.*

*Sister Roy appeared over her, sending a chill of terror down her spine. Her friend laid over her but his shadow did little to defer the woman's anger. Sister Roy clenched her arm, dragging her past Lady Julian's statue, and back to her chamber.*

*"I'm sorry," she cried, "I only wanted to play with him."*

*Lillian looked up to the deadened, soft eyes of the concrete patron, praying for the protection that would never come. Lillian swore she'd never speak of her shadowy friend again.*

Lillian shot up in bed, her camisole stuck to the dampness of her skin.

"How have I forgotten him?"

Pieces of memories that had been stripped away slowly began to wake. She could feel the nostalgia of innocence quivering in the air around her.

.......

Dougal glanced at the clock and shifted his stiff body. He hated sleeping in stranger's beds. Sitting up, he turned on a light and grabbed the letter sitting on top of his night stand. It was no coincidence that Aillig had intercepted the girl. He was notorious for meddling in affairs that had nothing to do with him. It must have been his delight to harbor her, especially once he realized who she was. Now, his gentle brother was no longer able to counteract their work of suppressing her prophecy. Dougal smiled in anticipation of showing Lillian the page riddled in Aillig's eclectic cursive. Just mentioning him had sent her near hysteria. He folded the paper neatly back into the envelope. Maybe it would reveal a little of the woman his superiors were so afraid of.

He had come expecting Lillian Blake to be more like the legendary tales they had revealed to him upon promotion. Instead of a woman well versed in unholy practices that promised to end the modern era, he had arrived to see the same frail girl he had remembered. He had envisioned a woman that needed to be scared by a strong arm. Dougal had to admit that he was disappointed. He had come assuming his new assignment would be more exciting. He had driven all the way out to the middle of nowhere for a task that she seemed to do on her own. Dougal only had to make certain his brother hadn't taught her more than she needed to know. It was never easy untangling his brother's agenda.

If she had learned anything about the prophecy, she would have gone somewhere farther than Northern England. He rubbed his gnarled hands over his eyes and turned out the light.

*Chapter Nine*

*....her hand slipped out of his and she fell into the darkness, watching the strings of light snap and break above her.....*

Emmy woke tangled in her sheets. The pressure on her forehead was dull and pin needled behind her brow. The booze blurred the lingering dreams that churned between her aching temples. Pressing all her fingers into her eyes, she tried to focus on what happened the night before.

Emmy was mortified. She knew better than to let a simple attraction get out of hand. She couldn't be known as a loose girl. She wasn't.

"Twenty-four hours and you already kissed him," she groaned to herself.

The air conditioning hummed overhead and light seeped shamelessly through the thin blinds. Emmy rolled over, trying to remember just how many beers she had last night. She cursed under her breath. She'd never slept this late. Slowly, she attempted to rise out of bed, leery of acquiring any more demons pushing behind her eyes. The bed sheet untangled itself and slid to the floor. Emmy stretched on her toes and ran her fingers through her tangled hair. She scrunched her nose, wondering when she had last brushed it and sauntered to the bathroom to fill a glass of water.

In the time she had been alone, Emmy found great peace in living out of clothes. It was a luxury she had never known, always afraid that the sight of her body would remind Ethan of what she was not giving him. She closed her eyes, touching the tops of her thighs for a moment before pushing the memory from her mind. She stared at herself in the mirror as she drank.

The past few weeks must have taken a toll on her. So had the weird episodes. That was why she was acting out. Deciding to dwell no longer on something that upset her, she shrugged and went to get dressed.

"Now," she muttered, "what do I need to do?"

She paced around the room looking for her clothes. She found them crumpled by the door. Her shirt was dusty and smelled like horses and salt. Her jeans were disfigured from too many days on her body.

"Well, I guess investing in some clothes would be good to do today."

She reluctantly put on her wrinkled outfit and headed toward town for her usual breakfast. Emmy never cared for being fashionable, but she had always been clean. When she arrived, the unkept mess she had put on made her self conscious. The diner was packed at one o'clock with families well dressed and fresh out of church. Tugging at her jeans, she crammed herself in a corner booth when a group vacated, trying her best not to be noticed.

Sherry Jean whizzed over to her, scowling as she poured a cup of coffee.

"I can't believe you came in here looking like that," she scorned, jumping on the chance to scrutinize her. "If you aren't going to show up at church, the least you could do is look presentable on the Lord's day. You said you were staying a while, didn't you?"

Emmy shrunk into the corner.

"Eggs and bacon please," she whimpered.

Sherry Jean went buzzing off.

"More coffee, Mr. Fassenbach?"

"No."

He watched Emmy. Ethan had undoubtedly screwed her up, there was no question about it. The poor girl barely knew which way was up. He frowned, thinking about the potential she could have had, the money he could have made, but the superiors had their reasons. He shoved a piece of toast in his mouth, wanting to be sure it was her before making any calls to her husband.

......

Cutter woke lazily in his bunk, feeling rested and alive. Sunday was the only day he could submerge back into life before Wyoming. He slept in too late and grabbed the cold leftovers in the mess hall where the cook had made habit to leave some. He leaned against the large sink, gnawing on a hunk of bread, still reeling from Emmy's impetuous kiss.

She was hard to peg. She constantly tried to hide whatever made her nervous. She shied away from human contact, and traveled alone. Then she'd turn around and talk to him like an old friend. And kiss him like a familiar lover. His shoulders relaxed thinking again of her body pressed against his. She had stared at him with fire and he knew he had gotten a glimpse of who she was. He had to see her again, whatever it took.

A door opened at another end of the large house and he heard the low tones of his friends. Travis came through the swinging doors into the kitchen.

"You just get up, dude?"

He opened the industrial fridge in search of leftovers. Cutter shrugged as he slid the plate of bacon to him.

"Where did you go last night anyway? You were supposed to compete!"

"Oh," Cutter mumbled, remembering. "I lost track of time and got drunk."

He lied, but for some reason he couldn't bring himself to share the truth. He didn't want to share it with anyone.

"You totally banged that chick!" Travis accused in marked excitement.

"What?" Cutter yelled in shock.

He was certain none of the other ranch hands had seen him sneak off to Emmy.

"Dude, that chick's been on you since she saw you!"

"How do you know?" Cutter started, growing protective.

"Dude, tell me," Travis went on, "is she really blonde? Do the drapes match the carpet?"

Cutter stood upright, boiling beneath his skin.

"Blonde?" he asked, dumbfounded.

"Yeah, idiot. How drunk were you last night? The blonde from the Windy River cabin."

"Oh," Cutter said, slowly realizing the mistake Travis made. "No, man. I don't want that."

Travis' golden eyes lit up. He ran a tanned hand through his hair, making it stand up.

"You're kidding me," he breathed. "Care if I go after it? Man, you're dumb."

Cutter only shrugged again, silently relieved that he hadn't been seen.

"I don't know what chick did you wrong in the past dude, but it must have been bad."

Cutter said nothing, a skill he had practiced well when it came to the subject of women. When Travis got no elaboration, he turned to leave, unaffected.

"Well, the rest of us are going into town for a while if you want to ride with us."

"I got some stuff to do around here. I'll meet up with you later."

Once the rumble of the trucks had faded, Cutter went back to the bunkhouse to grab his backpack and headed out. Walking gave him privacy and peace of mind. It reminded him there was a world bigger than himself. He'd have the freedom to think of Emmy there. When he saw her next, he would be sure to ask how long she was staying. Considering her slightly nomadic appearance, he wouldn't be surprised if it wasn't long.

The mountain range seemed desolate in late July and the wild bush surrounding the main lodge had almost lost its color. The sun was sharp against his clothing and his skin dampened. He worked his way through the still, ancient guide of trees. The ground still held a little moisture from the cool night and cushioned the sound of his boots. A cool breeze sang to him as he moved into open ground and up the gradual incline of rolling hills and craggy rocks. Coarse mountain grass called him towards his destination.

The wind pushed eagerly against Cutter's shoulders. Most tourists made a laundry list of things to do in town, maybe Emmy would wander to the town's art show like she had the rodeo. Maybe he could try seeing her there. He smiled when reached the hidden lake just beyond the hill top. Cutter had found the sparkling pool on one of his more turmoiled walks. Disturbed by his own demons, he had set out looking to remember why the world was still beautiful. The land had lead him here. He could almost hear centuries of secrets whisper between their peaks.

Sitting at the stoney edge, he closed his eyes, listening to the small lap on the water's surface. The lake beckoned him in shades of dark blue. He tried imagining the life of the cool water, but the only thing that came to his mind was the blue light in Emmy's eyes.

.......

Emmy shuffled through racks of clothes, picking at the thin wire hangers as she went. Still ruffled by the judgmental glares at the diner, she couldn't seem to find anything suitable at the thrift store. A few basic T-shirts hung on her arm and she looked nervously over her shoulder every few minutes. Deciding to move on from her past was proving to be a lot more difficult than she had expected. Ethan's raving hatred of her still singed her confidence. Simply choosing to be okay didn't allow her to forget its effects.

The store clerk approached her.

"Can I help you find anything in particular?"

"Oh, no," Emmy stammered, "just browsing, I guess."

"If you're looking for something nice for our gallery showing tonight, we have a great selection of formal wear."

Emmy smiled, uncomfortably. The girl carried on without notice.

"I know there's a lot of basic stuff," she admitted, "but every now and then the folks who relocate here bring in something really cool. I can show you if you want."

The girl's eagerness to befriend her was encouraging after this morning's debacle. It'd be the perfect distraction from the old emotions the diner had conjured.

"Thank you," Emmy tried. "I do need something for tonight. What is the expected dress code?"

The girl flushed with excitement. In a flurry she had Emmy by the hand, tugging her to a far corner of the store.

"Well, you can't tell, but I keep the coolest stuff kinda hidden over here."

Emmy prickled at the unexpected touch. For a moment she was instinctively tense from the girl's tight grip.

"Normally it really wouldn't matter what you wear, but this weekend is the national show. There are people from all over coming tonight and well, you don't want to look like a bumpkin in front of the important city crowd. That's so embarrassing!"

Emmy nodded blankly, reminiscing over the stiff suits she had to entertain every time Ethan had business meetings. At first, she had enjoyed experiencing people from all over the world. They found her charming and conversational, often preferring her company over his. Fueled by jealousy, Ethan would send her to the kitchen for drinks until he was drunk and angry. Eventually, the routine became so regular Emmy found no delight in the dinners and withdrew from the heated business discussions shortly after eating.

The chattering blonde looked over her shoulder at Emmy.

"So the dress got left here by a pretty blonde from Los Angeles. Passing through on a road trip to New York she said. Said she couldn't bear to own it any longer. What a dummy, right?"

The girl hugged it to her body as she looked in the mirror. Her eyes grew tender and dreamy as she swayed from one side to the other, fantasizing about the life it had before collecting dust in Wyoming.

"Why don't you buy it?" Emmy asked outright.

"Are you kidding? I wish I could fit in this! We eat too many hearty meals around here. But I think it'll fit you," the girl coaxed.

"Oh, I don't know," Emmy stopped, thinking. "I'm sorry, but what was your name?"

"Kelly!"

"I'm Emmy. I can't remember the last time I wore a dress, not sure I really want to."

Kelly stared, conflicted. The silence hung in the air. Emmy shifted her weight.

"But it'd be so perfect!" Kelly exploded. "You're the first person I've showed it to since it's been here! It's been a year. A year! Please, Emmy, I can't bear seeing anyone else wear it. At least just try it on, please? For me?"

Emmy stared, slightly in shock. It was the first time anyone had treated her like a friend since she had left home, apart from last night. She blushed.

"Oh, God, I'm such an idiot! I'm so rude, I'm sorry. I never should've been so blunt."

Emmy burst into gentle laughter realizing the girl had misinterpreted her embarrassment.

"It's all right," she drawled after a moment. "I'm flattered. I just haven't really talked to anyone in this town since I got here. Seems they like to keep outsiders at a distance."

Kelly's eyes almost popped out of her head in elation. She shoved the dress into Emmy's arms, and yanked the shirts away from her.

"I'll put these at the counter while you change. I can show you all five minutes of this town! I know almost everyone here, and who I don't know my father does. I like you, Emmy! We are a lot alike in that we're different from everyone."

Emmy smiled politely. They were nothing alike at all, but Kelly was contagious and Emmy longed to feel liked again. She appreciated the girl's buoyancy. She slipped into the dressing room, making Kelly squeak with pleasure.

"Oh my God," Kelly stared in approval when she emerged.

Emmy walked to the mirror barefoot, tugging at the hem.

"I don't know, it's so fancy, and so short."

"Not any shorter than the jeans you came in with! Thank God too, or you'd have horrible tan lines."

Emmy stared at her reflection.

"I just don't know. I haven't, I mean, it's just..."she trailed off.

"My God, girl, you're hot, just own it! Plus, it's gonna be so rad to walk in to the art show with you looking like that!"

Emmy glanced at Kelly.

Kelly shrugged confidently.

"Well you can't go alone. Plus, I can introduce you to people."

Settling in was appealing.

"Okay, but I better not be overdressed. I'll walk out, trust me."

Kelly considered the woman standing in front of her. She didn't seem like the dramatic southern belles that occasionally passed through, though she looked like one. She didn't wear makeup and that was ballsy, so Kelly took her seriously. *Finally something interesting in this town,* she thought.

"Let's get you a pair of heels. I have the good ones stashed too."

Emmy followed her, still unsure this dress was appropriate after the mishap this morning.

"I'm not going to walk in looking like a whore, right? I already embarrassed myself this morning. Wore my clothes to the diner after church was out. Not exactly the impression I wanted to make if I plan to stay."

"No way," Kelly went on as she scrummaged through the pile of heels. "I can't wait until you see the mess that these girls show up wearing. What size are you anyway?"

"Eight."

"I subscribe to all the magazines. I know what's fashionable, trust me."

Kelly stood with a pair of heels, swearing they were perfect.

"Can't go wrong with basic black."

Emmy shrugged, having given up on an argument with her new fashionista friend.

"I'm getting out of this thing."

She paid for the jeans and T-shirt she wore out, plus a handful of shirts and the ensemble for the event later that night.

"Thanks Kelly, I'm really glad we met."

Kelly smiled, handing her change back.

"Me too. So you want to just meet outside the store at six-thirty and we can walk over? I found this totally gorgeous blue dress in the pile last week. Makes my tits look amazing."

Emmy nodded.

"See you then."

She walked out to explore a little more of the town, wondering if Cutter would be there tonight and if he'd even want to talk to her after her behavior. Except Kelly, everyone she'd met seemed mild mannered and steeped in a conservative way of life. Even the New Yorker was stand offish toward her. He must have been quick to see the inconsistent behavior she was letting herself tumble through. Emmy set and unset her jaw. She couldn't let her schizophrenic habit continue, tonight seemed like her way into the community.

It made her remember a year she and Ethan coexisted peacefully. The idea of being young business entrepreneurs was dreamy the first month of their marriage. All their fantasies had materialized, and Emmy had to admit the ease of a rich family wasn't horrible. The international world she found herself mingling in seemed magical and surreal. Determined not to disappoint her well practiced, ambitious husband, she decided to become the most professional host she could, and spent most of her time learning about their clientele so she'd know how to converse with them. Henry had tried to warn her not to fall too deeply into the superficial race she was running in. Still young, and hurt by his disapproval, she shut him out.

Regret filled her now. It was a painful mistake to have made. Emmy straightened her back.

........

Henry squinted to see the smoke rise from Ethan's property. His heart constricted as he felt their flesh and spirit fading. If Emmy didn't return in a few days, he knew Ethan would turn on him next. He gathered books and memories from hiding places, preparing for the future he hoped his granddaughter would someday realize. Her prophecy was well maintained through the generations and he blessed his Irish blood. They had a talent for preserving history in fairytales and he hoped his had done the same. She'd need to remember them soon. Ethan was a serious man and he'd go looking for her once he realized she wasn't here. Emmy needed to be long gone by then, whether he survived or not. He regretted not storming into that big house and beating Ethan to death, but it would've only ended grimly for Emmy. The hierarchy of the system Ethan was in would only come for her if Ethan couldn't. Letting that corrupt man cage her was the only option he had to keep her alive.

He remembered her as a little girl with misty eyes. She had been born a ball of fire, nipping at his heels in the pasture since she could walk. Particles of the past coiled and burned inside of her, as a rebirthing of great importance would. Henry had quickly recognized her uncanny communication with horses and the vision of colors she liked to ramble on about as a child. He had been born her grandfather to teach her in this life, for it was the most important of all her lives. He couldn't help feeling like he had left her ill prepared for the awakening of a prophecy.

Henry closed boxes and refocused on what he needed to leave for Ms. Beckett, deciding there was no time to dwell on what could have been done better. Emmy Mulcahy was born into a greatness she'd soon be discovering and he needed to have everything ready.

.........

Ethan slumped against his leather recliner, drunk and feeling satisfied with himself. He had walked away to the house, already inebriated with alcohol and his psychosis, listening leisurely to the cracking of the old wood behind him. His empty glass slipped forward. He savored the tedious task of starting fire to her barn. Ethan wanted to make good on his threats as a lesson. The screams pierced through the walls now as he poured more gin and sat back. Her weak heart would shatter to submission at the sight.

Ethan was certain she was hiding at her grandfather's. It was the only place she'd be kept in secret. The nature of the social web he worked in was too loyal to keep her away from him. It was just a matter of time before she would be begging for the torture to stop. Ethan's madness was teased lustfully with the fantasy he unfolded in his mind. Once someone caught sight of the flames, he would feign innocence and blame Emmy for being a jealous lunatic. It'd be simple to obtain a warrant to find her and bring her back if she didn't instantly return. They had to play by the rules after Ethan's last explosion.

He was too important. He couldn't spend anymore time locked up if they were going to keep her under their control. Ethan smiled. After this outbreak, he'd be allowed to do whatever he wanted to her. She was never going to see the light of day again. His black hair fell out of place as he started to doze off. All he had to do was wait for someone to see the fire. She'd be back.

"I will have her as I want," he muttered. "Dead."

*Chapter Ten*

Lillian had grown fond of her dream counterpart. The grass was high above their five year old heads as they ran with laughter bubbling from their throat. The heat of the day struck her more intensely than she was used to. Lillian could hear heavy footsteps just out of sight and worked her short legs toward the sound. Large, leathered hands appeared and lifted her to the soft muzzle of horses. Her hands were small and innocent as she reached for them but instead of touching their soft coats, she grabbed a handful of herbs instead. Yarrow, dandelion, sage, chicory, frankincense. A mix for self-transformation. She looked up and grew. The woman grew with her. In their adult height she could see far in the distance. He stood there. His dark, clipped hair shone in the afternoon. The man who'd burned down the barn had been watching them.

The other woman was still with fear and Lillian could feel the string of light break from her wrists as she separated herself from her and walked towards him. She was determined to find answers. There was a dull pressure on her forehead.

"Find me."

It lingered in her ears. The accent was thick and strange. The sky turned black around her and she lost sight. Lillian kept walking. Lines of dancing silver light twisted *and softened, curling around her until she could feel the damp air of England. The walls of the church formed to her sides and Lillian's dark hair fell near her waist. The ghost waited at the end of the hall, smiling. She followed him to the garden, studying his remarkable appearance. He showed her plants, and walked next to her as they explored their old playground. He turned, grabbing her hand.*

*"Remember me," he whispered.*

*Her feet rooted themselves into the ground, forcing her to stay in the moment. Green light danced in the grass they stood in and she could feel the breath of the tree give life to her lungs.*

...........

The morning was cooler than normal as she walked to work. She could feel a serenity that wasn't entirely hers. She'd spent the night lucidly experiencing the shadow man. Lillian could remember more memories of him than she had ever recalled before. She wondered idly how many stories she had told Sister Roy before she learned to stay quiet. She shrugged and focused on what was tangibly in front of her. Her client list had grown rapidly since opening and there were plenty of packages to assemble. There wasn't time to indulge in imaginary friends.

Lillian stopped and squinted her eyes. Her heart dropped to her stomach and she sighed. Dougal was waiting outside the shop. The last thing she wanted to do was ruin the mood she'd woken up in, but she couldn't avoid him. She had to unlock the door to her shop. Lillian straightened her back and continued forward. Dougal had come for a reason and it was her duty as a healer to help pained souls regardless of her own opinions. Even if it might mean that she would be reliving Aillig's death.

"I wanted to apologize to ye," Dougal said as she approached. "It was not right of me to surprise ye like that yesterday."

"I don't think there could be a delicate announcement for it," she replied through a stiff smile.

She unlocked the door and invited Dougal in.

"I've an hour before official opening. Perhaps we can sit and talk for a while."

"I'd like that, lass."

Crammed in between shelves in the back corner of the shop was an antique table for consultation. She motioned him to sit, allowing his bulk to settle before speaking.

"It's been over a month since Aillig's death," she started in. "What made you come now and not sooner?"

He couldn't tell her he'd been quarantined in Rome, earning a promotion for his work to suppress her, so he danced around the truth.

"Lass ye are much harder to find than ye think. Ye live in the northern most part of the country in a town that the Queen hardly bothered to put on the map. You've no relatives to call, you've no friends that see ye on a regular basis, and your customers speak of ye in whispers, fearful that a lightening bolt might come down and strike them for the magic ye work."

Lillian felt invaded and reminded herself to be careful. She didn't even know what her customers said about her and was shocked to hear of their superstitious view. Her green eyes changed as she analyzed. It wasn't a surprising opinion from rural folk, but she wouldn't think they'd cling to the impression after knowing her. The success of her craft was like any other that a person spent years studying. Irritation crept at the back of her neck and she had to remind herself to be calm. *Compose yourself,* she thought, *it will do you no good to get defensive.*

She smiled indifferently as she would at one of her clients. Dougal had lived with Aillig his whole adolescent life and knew that behind the carefully manufactured frame of mind was a storm of thought, always dancing one step ahead.

"What's happened to ye, wee lass, that ye worked so hard not to be found?"

He was careful to keep the suspicion from his voice. There was no doubt she had secrets to keep. These types always did. Aillig's got him killed.

"With all due respect, Mr. MacIntyre, I like to keep my personal affairs to myself," she smiled warmly.

Lillian seized the opportunity to turn the attention off of her and encourage their common sympathies. Between her supervised childhood at the church and clients prone to gossip, she had become very good at controlling the direction of a conversation.

"You know, Mr. MacIntyre, I do have a question for you if that's permissible?"

He nodded once. She was going to be harder to crack than he anticipated. He was going to need to take a softer route if she wasn't going to share when he asked for personal information.

"I spent quite a few years apprenticing your brother. Aillig and I had become very close, and yet I never met you. What makes you interested in his life, and death, now?"

She could see the tight lines around his mouth, as if he were frowning to himself. *Guilt.* It was the hardest admission to pull out of a person.

Dougal said nothing and stared far past her at the faded paint on the wall. He remembered Aillig's best trick was silence. If he couldn't say anything without giving himself away, then he would wait. She would relieve something definitive about herself in her assumption. He couldn't count the times his brother had extracted secrets from him out of silence.

She did not hide or fake the sadness in her voice when she spoke. Maybe she could heal both of their regrets.

"I am still mourning the man too," she said, patting his gnarled hand. "It doesn't matter how long you've been away. Brothers always love each other. I'm sure Aillig never stopped loving you. There's no need to feel guilty."

Dougal smiled at her self-projected confession. Apparently Aillig hadn't taught her as much as they feared. She couldn't read him with the dark magic like his brother at all. Part of him felt relieved.

"How about we share our stories together? Maybe we can put rest to his death," Lillian whispered gently, trying to be brave for both of them.

Dougal made eye contact then, working to keep the mist in his eyes. He hit his mark. The girl was a healer, she couldn't help but want to save the wounded. This was the role he would need to play.

"It's hard to conceal my feelings in front of ye, lass. Aillig was the same, could see right through ye. Aye, I suppose we should go at it together."

"That would be lovely," Lillian smiled.

If he could gain her trust now, it was likely he'd find out any secrets she kept locked away. He could see another promotion forming in front of his eyes.

"Aillig was my older brother by four years, though you'd not know by his size. We were opposites from the start. He took after our mother's side and to the healing early, always helping Mother in the garden. I was a typical boy however, rough housing through most of my life," he chuckled. "Wasn't until college that we grew apart. I followed Father's wishes to go to a Catholic school, but Aillig refused. Father's temper boiled over it. If it'd been me, I'd have my ears boxed. But Aillig was so gentle, it wouldna be right. Our different opinions drove us apart. The last time I saw Aillig I was yelling, trying to understand why he couldn't just please Father. He wouldn't say a word, just kept staring into my eyes like he was reading my mind.

I couldna bear it and stormed out. I was hard headed and refused to see him in the years that followed, though he'd send medicine for my bones as I aged. I still don't ken how he'd find me to send it. When word was sent about his death to his last remaining relative, all the guilt I ignored came washing over me."

His face was twisted with self loathing and Lillian couldn't help but feel sorry for him. She tilted her head before rising to pull tea bags from the shelf. Dougal barely noticed her moving around as he cloaked himself in past regrets for effect. She'd either lead him to secrets about Aillig's kind and her prophecy, or she'd start talking about her beloved mentor and fall to pieces. There wasn't a bad outcome to this meeting. He'd be a hero no matter what happened.

Lillian sat back down, and he lifted glassy eyes to the tea now steaming under his nose and smiled. He was playing his favorite game.

"If I believed in it, I'd swear you could be Aillig reincarnated."

Lillian said nothing, but sipped on her piping concoction and watched him. She didn't fully trust Dougal yet. He had abandoned Aillig one way or the other. Aillig's life could have been saved if family could have intervened. Lillian breathed deeply and realized that judging the old man for his mistakes would not get her any closer to letting Aillig go. This could be her only chance and she desperately wanted it to stop haunting her. She wanted the tea's calming effects to take hold before continuing. Speaking about herself was never easy. Hot water singed her throat as she swallowed.

"I could never believe he had fallen asleep with his burners on," she admitted.

She shrugged, testing to see if a weight had lifted. Lillian had never breathed the words aloud.

"The night of my eighteenth birthday, I left my caregivers. I had planned terribly, spending a few nights in a scummy hostile. I snuck to the farmer's market early one morning for herbs to heal infection, and in my rush back into hiding I ran head on into your brother, almost knocking him over. That was the only accident I ever saw him make. When I lived with him, he had never displayed thoughtless behavior. In fact, I always marveled at his ability to foresee what was coming and prepare for it."

She paused in recollection, wringing her hands behind her mug. Speaking to someone else about it brought her past into the present. Lillian had conditioned herself to consider his death to the likeness of a bad dream. She had opened a gate she'd sworn to leave closed and started to feel trapped by Sister Roy's violence. Dougal didn't need to know exactly what Aillig had saved her from.

"It was as if he was always there right when I needed him, as if he knew what would happen before I did."

Dougal could feel his chest rattle with anger. It certainly wouldn't have taken Aillig long to discover what woman he had tripped upon. What a prize he had found in her, the foretold savior of their heathen beliefs. Dougal spent years digging to discover Aillig's association with the *Genius Cucullatus*. How his own blood could believe in tales about reincarnation and mystic healing from the mouths of hooded spirits was beyond him.

If Aillig had grown as close to her as she said, he may bring back more information about these people to his superiors than they expected. He would be famous for giving them the tools they needed to extinguish the trouble they caused. He smiled gently so as not to pique her nerves to his excitement. His curiosity was sparked and he wasn't going to scare the skittish girl just yet.

"What happened, lass? What makes you question his death?"

"My apprenticeship was over and he wanted to initiate me into a master's course. Just as I was about to delve into the deeper learning, he changed. Then, one morning I showed up to his burned apothecary and the police. I fled in shock of his death and swore never to cross into that part of England again."

"What do ye mean changed? What do ye mean deeper learning?"

Dougal pressed more than he wanted. He cursed himself.

"I'm not sure."

Lillian recoiled, wanting to protect herself. Revealing too much would only get her hurt, and she regretted saying anything now. She ran a hand through her long hair, toying with the ends. No one was here to hurt her. She needed to focus on acceptance and staying open. She was a healer.

"It wasn't obvious, but I knew. I could see a subtle difference in him. He was worried. He spent more time in his mixing room concocting the strangest things. I meant to ask him what was the matter but he wouldn't have even heard me."

"Aye," Dougal nodded, surprised that she had continued.

"When he was young, he'd spend hours sitting alone on the stone wall bordering our garden, talking into the air. No one bothered him. It was like we knew then he was solving the problems of the world."

Lillian frowned. She had wondered if his knowledge had somehow gotten him into trouble. Something told her so now more than ever. Aillig was a man who knew the secrets of life, indeed.

"What do ye ken, girl?"

Dougal watched from across the table, jealous that she had access to secrets no one could pry from his older brother. It was dangerous in the wrong hands.

She snapped her head to look at him from wide, forest eyes. Her rosy lips parted as she tried formulating words for the intuition she'd never been asked to explain. The bell rang from the front door and Lillian's trance vaporized. She stood, looking at the clock.

"I'm sorry, please excuse me. The customers are arriving. There's no rush for you to leave."

Dougal sat, curling his gnarled fingers as he watched her go. She frustrated him just like Aillig, maybe more. He wanted to strangle the girl for what she might know about the mystery of Aillig's culture and her dreamy reluctance to share it. He was growing tired of searching for answers with no clues. He touched the letter still tucked in his vest. He had meant to show her this morning, but had lost track of his intention. He wanted to know more about their hooded community than believe in a sorceress disguised as a fawn. He stood slowly, trying to ignore the pain in his joints. They all needed to be wiped out.

Lillian looked up from the register as he made his way to out.

"Mr. MacIntyre, I've this for you."

She pushed a cluster of bottles his way. He recognized them instantly. She smiled and nodded her head.

"Take it. He'd have done the same. Will I see you tomorrow?"

He grunted as he grabbed the bottles and left.

"Who was that?" her client asked.

"Oh, no one. We have a mutual friend," she smiled. "We were just talking of him."

The woman nodded knowingly.

"A suitor for you then?"

"Oh no, Mrs. Bixby, our friend died."

Lillian smiled sweetly in dismissal, and watched the middle aged woman walk out. She made a mental note to increase her rose scented collections and to be careful her ever curious customers didn't pry too easily. It was overwhelming enough going through the past with Aillig's brother. Lillian knew too well the consequence of opening up her mind to rural England now.

Dougal's nonchalant comment about their whispers made her wonder. She felt herself growing more paranoid and uncomfortable as the day went on. She eyed customers casually, straining to hear what they might say as they talked to each other. It made her feel separated and different for the first time since she'd moved. Lillian looked at her shelves for comfort and tried to push all the nonsense from her mind. It would take time to build strong relationships just as it had always been.

She sat behind her desk and started balancing the day's books. Mrs. Bixby's delicate face passed through her stream of thought. She was fond of the nervous woman. She felt guilty for being so curt with her. Mrs. Bixby had a genuine interest in Lillian's happiness and she'd only been excited over the idea of a man in Lillian's life. It was a thought Lillian hadn't taken time for, and it seemed strange that it tugged at her attention now. She couldn't recall ever being interested in romance. She had always been too busy pushing her nose in herbalism books. Lillian balanced the cash drawer and closed shop.

The constant emptiness that had sat dully inside for so long beckoned to her as she walked. The long grass teetered against her knees, reaching for the uneven road to her left. Between Aillig's absence and Ms. Bixby's inquiry, Lillian's independence had been redrawn. It hadn't bothered her until now. She tried to convince herself it had nothing to do with trust, but Lillian knew she was lying to herself. She'd been abandoned by everyone she could have loved. There was no escaping the stereotypes of being an orphan.

"So instead I've created fake people to befriend instead," she laughed into the evening mist. Lillian thought that if she'd taken more time to experience normal relationships with other people, particularly men, then maybe she'd stop imagining them in the confines of her cottage walls.

"I don't want to be a crazy, old maid," she muttered to herself, "but it looks like I've become one already."

Unlocking her door, she walked straight to the kitchen, preoccupied with the idea of love. Looking over her sink window, the woods seemed farther and more foreboding, the grass moved more desolately. She watched each reed bend in the gentle breeze, almost expecting to see someone appear from the tightly bound trees. Moments passed and when nothing changed, she turned to make tea.

"It was a hallucination, Lillian," she sighed. Her imagination would be the death of her one day.

Hoot rustled awake behind her while she pulled aimlessly at her loose leaf jars to make tea. She knew why never dated. She was incapable of nurturing the idea of a man's love when her own parents couldn't give her that experience. Sweet orange peel curled delicately around the rich and sensuous aroma of currant berry as the warm elixir slid down her throat. Her skin warmed and grew heavy. She was feeling sorry for herself. Lillian veiled her darkened green eyes behind thick black lashes, gazing at her blankets in wanton. The pressure to pursue the reason for her failed love life faded with the last evening light. Lillian licked her lips, savoring the last trace of honey that coated them. She set her empty mug in the sink and resolved to rise early for a walk in the woods. She could analyze all she wanted then.

Long legs moved languidly between half partitions as she found herself undressing, already near dreaming. She pulled her shirt over her shoulders, letting her angelic fingertips linger under the petite curve of her breasts. Her mouth parted and she sighed before slipping between her sheets, brazenly wondering what it'd feel like to have the rough skin of a man run over her. She had been so lost in Ms. Bixby's inquiry of romance that she had made a sensuality tea.

She felt the shadow move from the kitchen as if on cue. Lillian lay on her back with her eyes shut in nervous curiosity. Her skin tingled in his presence and her heart was in her throat. The luxurious intoxication of her mind called for his attention. Hoot cooed once when she felt the ghost sit on the owl's side of the bed. She was heavy and fluent in the sheets, unable to push off the slumber edging closer to. Her arm extended to her pen and paper, scribbling the words that so often tickled in her ears before sleep. He drifted sweet nothings against the gentle curve of her neck. Darkness cloaked her and her body relaxed against the pillow.

........

The shadow man smiled despite himself; she was ethereal. Her silky hair fell like water around her and his ribs constricted, longing to feel it. He whispered to her, wishing it offered her comfort in her loneliness. He wanted her to understand who he was. Who she was. With the help of the druid, they entered her subconscious projection to encourage memories about his presence in her life, hoping she'd remember. The dominance of her fear could filter into what should be a pleasant experience any moment and change the imagery. It was a risk not being able to control the movement of the dreams.

"I don't like this. It's too painful watching her struggle, knowing we're part of it. I never wanted her to feel lonely. Especially now, with those vultures crawling around her. I wanted her to remember our memories and feel comforted. I want her to feel safe when she senses my presence. Not ridicule it as a filler for the love she never knew."

He refrained from admitting that he didn't want to push her into the thought of being courted by another man. Though he couldn't himself, he selfishly wanted no other to try, even at the expense of her solitude.

"These things are never easy, young hero. But if Bixby desires to get closer, Lillian might find out who she is, and who you are, much faster."

"Why is that?"

"Bixby is a Veil Walker like myself. It is a foundation in the science of the old knowledge. This is what defines our group of Hooded Spirits. Our job is to move through the parallel of time to inspire the completion of her prophecy. Bixby can weave into someone's subconscious activity and open the barriers of time reality. As I have helped you reach your woman, Susan Bixby can help her reach us. But only by Lillian's consent or it will be no more successful than our attempts in her dreams. Pray, my friend, that they grow closer."

The man's pale, silvery eyes lit as he absorbed the old man's words, hope swelling his heart. All he wanted was his little, black haired dove to open her eyes and see. He could hear the guards shouting outside the dripping walls of their confines. They'd be moving soon. He rubbed a large hand over a weary brow, feeling the constant ebb of worry.

The old man touched his shoulder. "Have faith in her. She is stronger than even she is aware."

*Chapter Eleven*

Emmy could see Kelly from a distance. She had to admit that the dress was perfect for her new friend. It plunged dangerously to her empire waistline, leaving the fabric to flow freely over curvaceous hips. Kelly wasn't kidding about her fashion sense, which relaxed Emmy a bit on her own attire.

"Hey," Emmy called.

"Hey, girl!"

As they walked to the conference center, Kelly filled her in on some of the people she'd want to meet and who she would introduce her to.

"I'm making it sound important," she admitted, "but it's just a bunch of boring country folk."

"I grew up in a small town, I understand. They don't know how small theirs really is."

"Yes!" Kelly giggled. "I knew you'd get me!"

Her childish energy was endearing. Emmy enjoyed being around an exuberance that she had lost a long time ago. Somewhere deep inside yearned for it now. She thought of the dark haired woman and the dream she had of them running together at Henry's farm. She had woken up wishing they'd really been friends. Kelly would have to do. Their heels clicked on the side paths and Emmy was lost in her thoughts.

"Girl, don't be nervous," Kelly misinterpreted. "You have to know how serious that dress looks on you."

"Oh, it's not that. I've been having really weird dreams since I've been on the road. Sometimes they get me thinking too hard."

"I totally get it," Kelly offered, though she didn't at all. Truthfully, she couldn't remember a single dream she'd ever had. Kelly appreciated the deeper levels of Emmy, and the idea of befriending her seemed even more impressive.

"Get ready," Kelly scoffed as they approached the building, "we can play local or not. So easy to guess by the level of tacky."

They walked through the large doors to the softly lit display. Wooden partitions zigzagged through the open auditorium, and people wound through them, carefully considering the hanging art. Sculptures sat atop faux stone pedestals, and farther beyond she could barely see the tall New Yorker working the cocktail bar aside the long table of refreshments.

The handful of those standing near the door stopped to stare at the pair as they walked through. Kelly was glowing from the attention, comfortable with the crowd. Some looked with lust and others with mild surprise. Emmy froze in her tracks, suddenly aware of every curve her dress was hugging.

"Oh, don't be a baby," Kelly whined, tugging at her arm. "Let's go get a drink."

Without argument, Emmy stumbled after her, dislodged only physically from self doubt. They hurried by the artwork, and Emmy's eyes dragged over what they could focus on.

"Lemon drop," Kelly ordered coyly.

"Kelly, you aren't old enough."

"John, my father owns the bar you work in. He doesn't care unless I go whining about not getting my way."

John glared at her as he poured. "Don't get me in trouble. I will not get you drunk while I'm clocked in."

She smiled in the way a spoiled child might.

"What about you," he stopped, stumbling his eyes over Emmy in disbelief. "Is that you?"

"I'm gonna need a shot of whiskey, quick."

Kelly glared at her in surprise. Emmy slid the honey brown liquid down her throat and cleared it, handing it back to him.

"Emmy, if you want to impress these people, you might want something more fem!"

"Put it in Coke then, and make it Irish this time. That other stuff chokes me."

John grinned so quickly that Emmy almost didn't catch it.

Henry wouldn't allow anything else in the house. She remembered the first time he let her try it at sixteen. One tiny sip had fallen hotly down her throat and into her chest before she coughed. Tonight, she needed the comfort of home as she moved uncomfortably through the growing crowd.

Low voices filled the building, lulling in with the background instrumental music. Every side glance they passed felt like a pinch. Every introduction grated on her nerves and her cheeks hurt from smiling. Names escaped her, faces were fuzzy and similar. Emmy heard herself talking smoothly, but she was somewhere far away in the safety of her own mind. She was on autopilot and her memory committed nothing from the information bubbling out of the strangers before her.

A few years ago, this whole production would have impressed her. Glancing around, it was easy to see the locals and the visitors, Kelly was right. Not by the judge of clothing, but by the air in which they carried themselves.

For those who obviously had no comprehension of rural life, Emmy found it bizarre that they'd be drawn to this town to buy art they had little connection to. She laughed sarcastically, wondering what schemer took up residence in Wyoming to lure a bunch of rich people into making him money.

"Daddy!" Kelly called to a stout man across the room.

"Emmy, come meet my dad. He runs this place. Maybe he can help get you started."

After another sip of her drink, Emmy hauled herself back to the moment. Kelly's father grinned widely, watching his daughter practically prance to him. The man seemed generous, in stature and demeanor, and by the way Kelly clicked around, she was certain it only grew when it came to her. By the time they reached him, the man was nearly shedding a tear.

"You look beautiful, sweetie," he said, gently washing over Kelly's ensemble. "Who's your friend?"

"Oh, this is Emmy. We are a lot alike. She's thinking she may want to stay awhile. Could you find her work, Daddy? I don't want her to leave. I'll be forced to hang out with all the same boring girls."

"Kelly," he scorned, "mind your mouth, honey, especially tonight."

"Sorry."

"Well, where do you think I could put her? Summer season's closing."

Emmy's heart sank and her eyes threw themselves to the floor in childish despair. Her mind raced for the next plan, already expecting to have to pack her bags and ship out. She had to remind herself again that life was no fairytale.

"Well, what about at my store, Daddy? I'm manager and you said I was in charge," Kelly whined.

"Honey, you barely need to be there for how busy you are. This isn't Los Angeles or New York as much as you'd like it to be."

Despite the affection he had for his daughter, George Fassenbach was still a business man. The deep wrinkles setting into his forehead made no admission for whimsy, regardless of who he was dealing with. He eyed Emmy with distant severity.

"And what's your friend think of staying here? Is it her idea or yours, Kelly?"

This certainly didn't seem like the woman he'd seen in the diner earlier that morning. She was well put together in multiple ways, he thought, and raked his profit evaluation over her body. There was no mistaking her up front sex appeal, every man in the house watched her. The string of frantic calls to look out for her arrival were justified now. There was no questioning why Ethan wanted her back. Dollar bills wagged in his ears and George was interested to see what he could squeeze out of her stay before dumping her back home. If she lived up to the grand reputation his superiors built, he would be tempted to make a little financial gain before calling Ethan. No one would have to know about it.

"I will literally die if she can't stay! You can't think of any place to hire her?"

Kelly's knack for drama was impressive. Emmy forced herself to look the man in the eye if nothing else than as a plea to stop the embarrassment of Kelly's act. George met her with the glassy stare that business people have when they are dissecting possibilities. Emmy had seen it one hundred times when large clients of Ethan's came to stay in their home. After a while, all those hard looks seemed robotic and mathematical, as if they had all read the same book on how to be successful.

George, however, held no robotic qualities behind his eyes. There was something inside far more wild, and

Emmy felt a fire of warning stir in her heart. She wasn't surprised to see the bustle he brought to the small town anymore. Only a real business man could get something like a national art show to host their event in the middle of nowhere. She forced herself to keep eye contact.

George's face broke into a smile and he raised his eyebrows. Whatever doubt he had about her disappeared; it was the girl. They had said she used to be a rambunctious little brat, and that fire burned towards him now. Her magnetism would make a high profit in a place where people come to stare at each other.

"I suppose she could try a few days at the diner. It is busy year round and Sherry Jean can use a little help."

"Oh, you're the best!" Kelly squeaked, completely unaware of the exchange that unfolded in front of her.

"Thank you," Emmy replied with relief.

She stuck out her hand and he clasped it firmly with a wink.

"Anyone who Kelly claims to be so much like her is worth the investment to me."

The sarcasm slipped delicately past his daughter and into the ears of his new employee. An odd pinch settled between Emmy's shoulders. No doting father would sell out their child's misgivings to a stranger.

"Come to the diner Tuesday morning for your first shift, five o'clock in the morning."

The girls departed, and Kelly was buoyant with excitement. Emmy tried not to let the exchange bother her.

"I knew Daddy would help," she hummed.

"Thank you, Kelly," Emmy replied, "Sherry Jean hates me though."

Kelly dismissed it with a wave of her hand, "Sherry Jean hates anyone without a cock. She'll have to get over it. Let's get another drink."

"Mine's still pretty full. Think I'm gonna go look at the display."

"Suit yourself, more John for me," she grinned.

Emmy wandered off through the partitions of art, absorbing. She didn't want to ruin the opportunity with her silly prejudices. Instead, she forced them away and lost herself in the souls of strangers. Her talents never were artistic, but she loved it deeply. It made her feel small and unimportant in the mystery of creation. Western paintings sprung with texture and vibrancy on the walls, capturing the lively, rural lifestyle. Other pieces gracefully shared the quiet and subtle beauty of nature. Nerves escaped her as she submerged herself into every stroke of every painting. Each piece pulled her farther and farther into it, calling her to the world held between their frames, where nothing and everything existed. A photograph beckoned her from the corner of her eye.

Dangerously jagged mountains stood like knights, guarding the heavily textured clouds behind and above them. The layers of rock were magnified in black and white, and spruce fir trees scratched at the bottom of the range, spreading wildly like children towards the most unusual rolling hills. The shadows that fell upon them made it look painted. Danger and serenity stirred in her, begged her, dared her to walk the hills, climb the range and dive into the clouds. Ancient stories whispered in her ears and she stood frozen in front of the photograph. She could feel her body numbing, transfixing her to the image. She swore she could see movement in the mountains. Her wild imagination seemed to be waking, and all of Henry's old stories came flooding between her ears. She strained to listen to the words, but they only grew more muffled. The Seven Fires story had always been her favorite.

The long journey of its young Moon Horse had been Henry's creation between old Indian tales and those of his ancestors in Ireland. Emmy looked deeper into the valley between the mountain range and couldn't remember how the tale ended. Lights flickered and the wind rushed from the photograph towards the tips of her hair.

"But I'm inside," she muttered to the picture hanging in front of her.

Something moved from the corner of her eye, jarring her back to the present. Voices came rushing to fill the trance of the photograph. Bodies moved by her, and she looked around to see if anyone had noticed. The crowd mingled as if nothing had changed. She blinked a few times and blamed it on the whiskey. She looked down at her diluted drink. She couldn't move her arms yet. Unnerved by the experience, she shifted her eyes to find what had distracted her.

She peeked through partitions, breathlessly recognizing Cutter's back. There was no mistaking his lean body and broad shoulders. Her lips tingled, she blushed. Her legs flexed and she found herself gliding slowly towards him. Her body swelled with a nervous desire. She rounded a display board, putting him in better view. His crisp white shirt stretched relentlessly between his shoulder blades, leaving only enough room for movement at his trim waist. His black slacks were cut low, perfectly hugging every muscle below his thin, black belt. She couldn't remember ever seeing a man who wore such fitted formal attire. She was instinctually drawing closer, quickly learning every hard line and texture about him.

Cutter felt her before he saw her. Every muscle in his body tensed and he couldn't move. As she neared, the circle of people around him turned their eyes to the approaching ball of electricity. He looked over his shoulder. Her black heels rose dangerously high from the floor as she came towards him, her legs a mile longer and even more shapely. His fingers twitched at his side. The dress was dangerous. The scalloped hem of black lace melted against her toned thighs, hugging her hips, holding steady to her small waist. The neckline scooped demurely under her neck, leaving her shapely chest hidden for the imagination. Chestnut hair fell down her back and over her bare shoulders, quivering like a crackling fire as she moved. Not an ounce of makeup covered her subtle freckles and the offset from the glamour of the dress made Cutter swallow hard in pleasure.

"Hey," he called to her softly.

He stepped from the circle to receive her before she reached their dissecting glares. He touched her shoulder and turned her in a direction that would be more secluded. He felt selfish.

"You look beautiful," he whispered.

She let one shiver pass through her twitching insides before she spoke.

"Thank you."

Every intention to apologize for the night before left, and her voice went mute. She didn't want to apologize. She didn't want to bring it up and ruin the memory of touching him. Emmy had no control of herself and couldn't care enough to recompose. She was a different person around him.

"So what brings you here tonight?" Cutter asked, hurrying past the awkward silence.

"Contacts," she choked.

She clenched her fists with frustration. Her body and her mouth seemed disconnected. She felt a little dizzy and couldn't hold on to her surroundings. Cutter patiently waited for elaboration and when none came he spoke again.

"Are you entered in the show? Is that what brought you to Wyoming?"

He was hopeful to know more about her, wanted nothing more than to know everything. He would wait all night if she needed.

"No," she swallowed, working out the kinks, "only attending. I came to know more people. For work."

Cutter smiled, Emmy's knees buckled. His mouth was wide and genuine and she felt herself remembering the kiss. She took a long sip of her drink.

"What kind of work has you come all the way out here for an art show?"

The condensation collecting on her glass ran indulgently across her fingertips. Cutter wanted to reach out and touch them in a familiarity he had no right to. He desired to hold her against him so badly his body stood stiff from restraint.

"I meant to find local work. Relocation. Sorry," she flushed. "I don't know what's wrong with me."

"It's okay, it's probably the crowd. You're safe with me."

His fingertips grazed her forearm. Electricity surged through them both and the room turned white. He stepped back for composure, his arm dropping reluctantly to his side. Days ran before him in a flurry of the future. He could see their life together in flashes before it faded. Strange instances burst too brightly to hold onto. Cutter felt he had seen it before, as if he suddenly remembered her from one hundred dreams he'd never thought of until now. He blinked.

"So you're planning to stay a while? Why here?"

"Needed to start over. I don't know why here," she admitted, laughing.

Cutter's heart fell to his stomach. Her laugh was light and tragic. She was going to stay.

"Do you live here?" she asked quietly.

"Yeah, I work on a guest ranch about thirty miles out of town."

"Oh, right," she blushed. "Your friends in the rodeo. I should've put that together."

"It's okay," he assured her, trying to clear his mind of the strange images.

"That's a far drive to come to an art show, isn't it?"

He gave up trying to remember why he felt as though he knew her and nervously considered his next response. He didn't enjoy talking about himself.

"I have work submitted," he confessed before he could change his mind. Her eyes grew, and she looked like a fawn; leggy and wondrous in front of him.

"What pieces are yours?"

Taking a chance in pride of her excitement, he bent his arm. It didn't matter that he didn't take his art seriously. He took her seriously. She gracefully wrapped her arm through his. Nothing existed around them but the vibration radiating from their bodies. Everyone stared as they walked by, helpless to ignore the twinkling energy they created.

George watched from a distant group of colleagues. He knew little about Cutter and wasn't happy that he seemed to be helping the girl out of the control they had worked so hard to get. Ethan's reputation had catapulted because of it, and George was nervous to consider what would happen if she was returned stronger than when she left. She was practically floating. Every eye watched her in curiosity. He couldn't let his new sideshow slip from his fingers without testing what all his forefathers had whispered about. If it was true, the girl was a land mine of money in a town full of men and horses. George knew it would be risky putting her near the things she should stray from. His bitter relocation to the rural country still stung after all these years and he figured this little financial endeavor would more than settle the favors they owed for it. He just had to return her as scared as she was when she'd left Ethan. It would be easy to do.

"Mr. Taylor," he inquired, turning to a man in the group, "have you ever seen Mr. Maben's work?"

George smiled generously when Emmy caught him staring as they walked by. He nodded his head and her mouth twitched at the corners before moving behind one of the partitions. She'd never know what hit her.

"Like a lamb to slaughter," he mumbled under his breath before redirecting his attention.

"This is yours?" she breathed in disbelief.

Cutter shrugged, slightly self conscious.

"This is it."

The photograph she had gotten lost between vibrated in front of her. She merged into it again, now absorbing the man and the art, feeling slightly imbalanced from the collision of two worlds. Her mind raced with questions she couldn't ask. He'd think she was insane if she told him what had happened when she'd first seen it. She could feel the whispers and rushing wind edging from the back of her mind and she turned to him, searching for any recognition of the feeling in his demeanor. He stood, staring back at the storm in her eyes. He tried helplessly again to recall whatever memory he had of her from before. The harder he tried, the smaller the feeling became. Time passed as they stood drowning in the mysteries between them.

"Cutter, this is amazing, I had no idea. I mean, I guess I really wouldn't know."

Reality stole her ease with him and she went to take a sip of her drink. Ice clanked against her upper lip. She felt anxious from the confusion and couldn't help moving closer, wanting him to dissipate the feeling he created.

"Right before I saw you, I was completely lost in this photograph. I mean, it looks like a painting. It's perfect, it's, it's you..." Emmy clamped her lips shut in shock.

"I meant I can tell you put your soul into it," she tried to save herself.

Cutter looked at Emmy, unprepared for the barrage of compliments. The back of his neck was hot. He rubbed it instinctively. She was impulsive; she was a roller coaster. She was beautiful.

"Thanks. Can I get you a refill?" He wanted to change subjects.

She smiled. "No. I can get us one."

Emmy felt alive again as they walked to the bar. There was a casual acceptance about him. He allowed her to trip through her words until she could stabilize herself. The pressure to control whatever affected her didn't exist. She smiled and bravely wrapped her arm into his, not caring that the white dots of light blurred her vision. If it wanted to connect to Cutter, she was okay with it tonight.

Kelly was leaning over the bar, daring John to look. John smiled tensely, avoiding the display being offered up with some trouble. Quick to find a moment's relief, his face brightened at an opportunity.

"Cutter!" he called. "What are you drinking buddy?"

Kelly shifted, turning expertly toward another potential target. Her eyes widened in surprise before mischief settled in the crook of her grin. Emmy was tucked into Cutter's side. The boys shook hands over the bar. Emmy smiled a little shamefully.

"Rum's a good idea," Cutter laughed.

John nodded and turned to fix Cutter's drink.

"Hey Cutter." Kelly let each word roll too sweetly off her tongue.

Cutter grinned uneasily, flexing his bicep a little tighter against Emmy's arm. Emmy looked up and saw Cutter clean slate his face.

"How are you, Kelly?"

"Oh just fine. Emmy, when you said you wanted to look at the art, I assumed you meant the stuff hanging on the wall," Kelly smiled widely.

"I did," Emmy stammered, blushing.

She pulled her arm from Cutter's. She started to explain but realized she had no explanation. She didn't have a reason for even walking up to Cutter to begin with.

"Emmy had insisted to repay me for the drinks I bought her last night," Cutter stepped in.

Kelly's eyes widened before she broke into laughter, subduing some of her small town scrutiny.

"Girl, you have it backwards. Wherever you came from must be something else. The man always pays."

John handed Cutter his drink with Emmy's next to it. Kelly glanced at him in mock hurt.

"None for me, John Boy?"

John stared at her and with an exasperated sigh and turned to make another lemon drop. Ceasing the physical separation between the two, Kelly grabbed Emmy's hand and pulled.

"Please do excuse us, Cutter."

Cutter tensed every muscle in his body to keep from protecting her. Emmy hated being grabbed like that.

"Really, Emmy?" Kelly almost shrieked. "Cutter? Cutter Maben? How long have you been here? I mean you couldn't have been here too long or I'd have seen you before yesterday. You're gorgeous, don't get me wrong girl, but Cutter is stone cold. How'd you even get his attention?"

Emmy stared in confusion.

"Every girl in town is going to hate you!" Kelly laughed in devious pleasure.

"I, I don't know what you're talking about. I mean, I met him a few days ago. I didn't know, I don't think..." she trailed off hopelessly.

"Oh my God, you totally wouldn't know." Kelly was beside herself with laughter. "Well, good for you. I gave up on him a few months after he showed up here. Barely spoke two words, kind of like you do. Still can be a total mute most of the time. Good luck, girl. I didn't know you had that in you."

Emmy glanced at the boys talking at the bar. A few men came to shake Cutter's hand. She watched as their praise reddened the back of his neck. When they waved their hands toward his exhibition, he moved to go, but turned first to where she stood with Kelly. She met his eyes with a smile and he moved to her quickly.

"I've got to go talk to them for a while. Don't leave without finding me."

She nodded, watching him hesitate a moment before he left. Kelly's description seemed wildly opposite of the man she had known in the past few days. As much as she tried to warn herself to be careful, she couldn't stop from giving in to the temptation of his companionship. She wasn't acting like herself. *Who am I?* She pushed her self judgement away with too much enthusiasm. *Whoever I want to be now,* she thought a little humorously.

"I've been admiring your artistic display tonight, Mr. Maben," the man went on, "and I'd really like to speak with you about a job I'm offering."

Cutter smiled at the straight backed man as they walked towards his display. He was not a local swept up by the allure of city money. He had seen plenty outside of this little town and knew what opportunity a man like this could bring him. He also knew what kind of trouble they brought to Wyoming. He looked over his shoulder as they analyzed his photograph. Cutter knew what Emmy could attract without meaning to. Danger was in the air and he knew every eye watched her. These events always turned into a meat market.

"So where was this taken?" the man carried on.

Cutter tried to refocus on the business at hand. He looked to Emmy and caught her attention. He smiled warmly to let her know that he was keeping an eye out for her through the crowd. He was tuned to every move Emmy made.

"I took that one here," he finally responded.

Emmy watched him a moment longer. She ordered more Jameson and Coke. The atmosphere was light next to Kelly and John. They talked easily about nothing, and watched all the people as the hours passed. Emmy felt as though she was getting a first glimpse into her new life and it felt good. Nobody knew her story and didn't have to if she chose. She could feel what made her strange slowly unravel from its hiding place.

"How'd it go, buddy?"

Cutter made his way to the bar as the crowd died off.

"Good. He took my number, gave me a card. The usual. I've got work early so I'm going to head out. Can I walk you home, Emmy?"

Cutter wasn't tired at all, but he hadn't spent as much time with her as John and Kelly. He shouldn't have been jealous, but he was.

Emmy looked at Kelly for approval.

"Go on, girl. Get some, um, rest! I've got to stay and help shut down anyway."

John rolled his eyes.

"Okay. Thanks again for everything, Kelly."

Cutter bent his arm and she tucked herself close. as they made their way out. The whiskey made her warm and she relaxed when they touched. The cool summer air played wistfully around her hem. Stars winked in bliss above and the town seemed to be sleeping. This time of night had always been her favorite.

"So how did you meet Kelly?" Cutter asked.

"Oh. At the clothing store. She picked out this outfit for me. To be honest, I'm dying to get out of it."

"Yeah, sounds like Kelly. She's a good friend to have," he half muttered, trying not to literally imagine her out of her dress.

"She sure has it for John."

"This month."

They both laughed, bending closer together. When her swimming head bobbed against his arm, he tensed to support her. Emmy kept it rested there for a sweet moment before catching a quick glance up at him. His eyes were gleaming. She wanted to know him as well as she felt she did.

"How long have you been taking pictures?"

"Spent two years traveling all over with a camera. Wound up here a year ago."

Emmy was fascinated.

"What made you stay here?" she asked.

"I'm not really sure. Something told me to stay."

"That's what happened to me," she giggled.

Cutter's grin split his beautifully structured cheeks. The lightness in her laughter made his heart break. He longed to collect her up in his arms and assure her she'd never have to be frightened again.

"What brought you here?" he asked.

Emmy froze. Her two worlds intersected, and swept the color from her face. Never missing a beat, Cutter recovered her.

"It's okay, you don't have to tell me."

It took all his self control to keep the concern from his voice. He wished he hadn't asked.

"It's just a long story," she explained lamely.

The words rattled in her throat. The alcohol would only make it worse if she dared to tell it. He'd never want to talk to her if he knew anyway.

He wrapped a wide palm around the side of her face and lifted her chin.

"If you never told me, I wouldn't care."

Her worry seemed shallow and she looked at the ground.

"So, what happens to your artwork now?" Emmy asked, eager to change the subject.

"I'll go pick them up on my break tomorrow."

"I really loved your work, Cutter. It was beautiful."

"Thanks," he choked.

They walked in the silence of night. Emmy wished she could point out some of the constellations she'd learned as a child, but all she could remember was the story about some Wolf Star. She ached for her horses and Henry. They were dead. Her esophagus tightened. She tried to believe she was done with the past, but it was impossible to simply cut the ties in Kentucky. In her entire life she never would have guessed this is where she'd end up, so far away from her Papa in a town full of strangers. Emmy wished Cutter would have never asked why she was here.The whiskey made her emotional now, uncomfortable in her own skin. She remembered a few days ago, when she was shaking and afraid, having ventured into human contact for the first time since Ethan had considered killing her. Cutter had looked her in the eye so gently, without prejudice.

"I'm not crazy," she blurted.

Cutter looked down at her, brushing a piece of hair from her face.

"I know, Emmy."

"But you saw me just days ago, and now..."

"Some days are harder than others. I'm glad I don't scare you."

"The opposite, actually," she thought out loud. She was never touching another drop of whiskey.

Cutter laughed. He hadn't thought much about the track they were spinning on. It had been so long since he had been excited by the presence of a woman that he didn't care to question it. He had learned quickly in life to tune out what didn't work. Painful memories were dull and faded to him. Dwelling on what couldn't be changed did nothing. He created spaces for only the best things. The road. The Wyoming terrain. The ranch. Emmy.

They had reached her front door and she was shifting her weight uneasily. The alcohol was tweaking her emotions, making her irrational, and she didn't know if she should go right inside or brazenly kiss him again, being more aware of her intention. Her heart reached out for him to save her from her demons. Her legs were tingling. She should go inside before it consumed her again. She wondered what it was about him that triggered it. Light danced in the sky behind him and Emmy blinked it away. Losing physical control for the sake of curiosity seemed to dangerous.

"Thanks for walking me home," she stalled.

"Thank you for the company."

His eyes were shining.

"My feet are killing me," she said, rambling as she kicked off her shoes. *What the hell are you doing?*

She shrunk six inches. He wrapped his arms around her waist, lifting her mouth to his. Her body tensed and she made herself relax, wanting to give in to the moment. She wrapped her arms around his warm neck, twining her fingers at the base of his head. His mouth pressed firmer against her than last night. She could feel her body tearing towards the darkness behind closed eyes. Her toes tingled, barely touching the ground. Emmy gave in against her better judgement. She wrapped her arms tighter around him. She was searching for a connection, gently pleading to find answers for her behavior. Henry's game glowed to life and searched to bind to Cutter. Her legs started to numb. She could feel herself separating from her body and a hum rattled her ears. The intensity grew and Emmy thought her heart would explode. She opened her eyes and gasped, unable to withstand the pain. His arms loosened around her waist. They fell apart slowly, and Emmy sighed. She cold never hang on long enough to finish the game. Her limbs felt fluid and she leaned against her door for support. Cutter grabbed her hand, toying with it gently in his.

"Can I see you tomorrow afternoon when I come to get my pictures?"

Still shaky from the kiss, Emmy only nodded. She couldn't plant herself in reality. Her mind was refusing to ground itself.

"I'll pick you up at noon? We can go get the photos and some lunch?"

"Okay," she whispered.

"Good night, Emmy."

"Good night, Cutter."

She opened her door, leaning her head in the door jam, hair cascading to one side and smiled. She flicked her fingers to wave and locked up. Emmy could feel him linger a moment before turning to go. She considered switching the latch. Her arms were still too weak. *No, Emmy, too soon.* She stumbled to bed not caring if she ever recovered from the spell.

........

Ms. Beckett sat back in her rocking chair. The piece of paper fell like a sigh of relief to her lap. Emmy had made it out of Ethan's grip. The moon hung happily above her and she patted the Labrador at her feet.

"She made it, Bess."

She'd phone Henry in the morning to tell him.

*Chapter Twelve*

They sat together on a stone wall, wind rushing around them. His hair was kept neatly behind his neck, beckoning to times long before her own. There was a softness in his eyes and butterflies dusted her stomach. Lillian studied the movement of his mouth, unable to hear his voice. He pointed to the open hills and more shadows appeared in front of her. An ancient battle quickly unfolded. Warriors sped in horse drawn chariots. Tattooed bodies ran with spears. A rabbit darted between their feet. Fearful it would be caught amongst the violence, she started to panic. She tried to get up to save it but green light had wound around her knees, keeping her tied to the wall. Sensing her distress, he grasped her hand and the people disappeared from view.

Lillian could feel a presence to her other side and looked to see the woman. She also tried speaking, but no words came to Lillian's ears. She strained to hear, tried speaking herself but sound did not flow from her lips. She watched the girl rise, orange strings of electricity popping behind her. Lillian followed. Her shadow man held out his hand before dissipating. Lillian tripped into darkness. She tried to scream for help, but moonflowers and herbs fell from her mouth instead. Smoke made her eyes tear, and the *crackling of fire pierced her ears. She could feel her body reaching for a notepad, and the dream faded.*

The sun had not risen when she woke. The sky outside was lavender and Lillian looked as tired as she felt. She pulled a large cream sweater over her slender frame and slid outside. The apples of her cheeks reddened on the footpath to her woods. Green eyes looked through swollen lids and Lillian sincerely tried to wake up. The dim light peeked through the density of her trail as she walked briskly to keep warm, trying to sort out dreams she could no longer ignore. Aillig had always told her dreams were important messages from the subconscious. Before recent, she had agreed faithfully; she derived most of her herbal concoctions that way. *Yet you shove off the strange ones, as if they are to be treated separately from your herbs. Dreams are dreams,* she argued with herself.

She had to admit their presence had evolved from fearsome hauntings. Now, they almost offered her a sense of comfort. She pulled her hands to her lips to warm her chilled fingers. Repressing the shadow man's existence had saved her from abuse in childhood. Opening up to the realism of his companionship wouldn't hurt her now and Lillian's hungry curiosity started analyzing.

"I suppose ghosts are real enough if I've seen it my entire life," she whispered between the trees.

Mist curled around her legs as she wondered if the woman was also some form of haunted soul. Sometime in the night she had dreamt about her and the man that followed her.

"Maybe she died in a terrible way," Lillian guessed to herself.

Lillian tried to match their faces to someone she knew without success. It was too peculiar to feel so familiar with people she'd never seen before. She shook her head.

"Who knows, Lillian, maybe they're just symbolic of all the commotion going on. Maybe their image is only a physical representation of your thoughts, which are currently fear and love."

She smiled at the slumbering greenery around her. *The shadow is a handsome man*, she allowed herself.

"Unfortunate he's not real," she said playfully.

Reaching her garden, she clipped her rose bushes before going inside. She'd be needing to mix and replenish her stock soon. Lillian glanced at the clock as she picked up her dream notes, muttering under her breath.

"Time escapes me too quickly," she murmured, folding the paper and heading out.

She toyed with it in her pocket as she walked to the shop, a gentle crease pressed between her sculpted brows. She tried focusing on Aillig and the matter at hand, but for some reason she felt distracted to look at her notes now. It wasn't like her to push responsibility aside, but it was such a painful duty to recall Aillig's death. Dougal was also likely to show up again, and Lillian felt procrastinating the drama a little longer wouldn't hurt.

Pulling the paper out, she opened it like a candy wrapper, savoring each swish that brought her closer to discovery. Her eyes grated over the ink stains. There were no herbs, no ailment cures. The words seemed to be written in a foreign language. Her pace quickened as she stared, feeling a strange sense of urgency to decipher it. Though it looked like it may be Latin, it matched none of the words used for any herb she recollected. She had to find the book of Latin she'd stashed in her shop.

"Oh!" she squeaked, startled to see Dougal from the corner of her eye. Lillian shoved the paper out of sight and mind. Procrastination was over.

Dougal refrained from shaking the lost mindedness out of her.

"Good morning, Mr. MacIntyre," she stuttered, unlocking the door. "Please come in."

After Mrs. Bixby's comment, she was determined not to die alone. Lillian decided to concentrate on the possibility of a friendship. She may not have her family or a romantic prospect, but she may at least be able to make a new friend in spirit of sweet Aillig. She grinned as he followed her in. Maybe he wasn't as bad as she had made him out to be.

"Back to it, I suppose. Shall we make some tea first?"

He followed her through the store, watching as she pulled bottles from her back inventory, praying to God that he may not be fooled by the mystic woman. Spending so much time around her irritated him. He only needed to confirm that she knew nothing dangerous. Aillig's passing wouldn't sound correct to anyone who knew him. But, as long as she believed he had only been distracted, everything would go well and he could return home.

"So ye said he wasna himself, lass? If ye can explain that a little better, I might be of some help."

She placed a steaming mug in front of him. He smiled, recognizing its sweet and earthy aroma immediately.

"Did Aillig teach ye this tea?"

She nodded from behind the rim of her cup.

"Aye, I know it well. My mother taught it to him."

Lillian could feel her heart soften. "He would always brew this when we had late nights studying. The red date focuses the mind, and well, the vanilla I suppose is for comfort," she laughed softly.

Dougal shook his head. "I canna understand the obsession you folk have over mixing strange things."

Lillian only smiled. She took another sip and refocused to Dougal's question.

"A couple of weeks before his death, I noticed his attention started wandering during our talks. He was normally such an attentive man. We would be discussing the local growth and he'd suddenly look at me and ask something obscure like the name of a customer. If it wasn't that, it was the long hours in his mixing room, scribbling down the strangest recipes. I was always glancing over his shoulder as I apprenticed. He said they were important for me to remember though they made little sense at the time. He grew persistent about my memorizing things without writing them down. He said it was important to only make them when necessary."

"What kind of recipes?" he asked, feeling the hair on his neck prickle.

Lillian bit her lip.

"That's the trouble. None of them were directly for healing which I thought was odd. Some I remember were sleep aids. I was so distraught over his behavior that memorizing took the lesser priority."

She ran her hand through her hair, watching the dark strands twist over her knuckles as she drifted through her mind's eye. She could see Aillig with his scraggly white hair, pieces falling from behind his ear. She remembered his frame, hunched and frail, as he scribbled furiously on his notepad, steam from his infusers crawling around him.

"I could swear he had mixed some hallucinogens too. I had no experience or knowledge of that. I'm afraid I can't recall any of them."

Dougal sat quietly as he listened. The frantic behavior of his brother worried him more as she spoke. That was a trait the gentle man never possessed, he must have known something was about to happen. He always did.

"The night before he died he had come into my room. I suffered from terrible nightmares time to time and he'd wait for me to wake. I suppose I had a particularly bad spell that night, for when I sat up, I found him on the edge of the bed instead of the chair. His face was contorted with worry and his hands were clamped around my legs. He was whispering something under his breath, but said nothing to me. I settled back to sleep and when I woke, he wasn't home. Curious to ask about it, I dressed quickly to find him. The shop had burned by the time I got there. Nothing about those days seem right. Aillig wasn't made to be anything but peaceful. I would have never learned to master my anxiety without his example. The more I think of it, the less his death makes any sense at all."

Dougal looked paler and his gnarled hands gripped his knees tightly. He slowly reached to his vest pocket and pulled out the envelope, placing it on the table between them. He was hoping it wouldn't be necessary to show her. He damned his brother for knowing what he shouldn't. They'd need to see what Aillig left behind for her to find. Her catastrophic prophecy had to be prevented or the struggle of Lillian's abduction would have been for nothing.

"Three days after they came to tell me of his death, this letter arrived in my mailbox. It wasna signed, but when I opened it, I recognized his writing immediately. This is why I've come to find ye, but I didna want to bother showing ye unless ye felt the same as I did about his death. Look at it lass, see if ye canna make sense of what I couldna."

With a shaking hand, she carefully unfolded the deep creases. The familiar handwriting jumped off the thick paper, drawing the memory of his front desk in her mind. She could smell the lemon wood conditioner he soaked into its dark grain, could see the ink stains from the spills of his antique brass pen. Her name was scrolled thickly across the top, and underneath were barely legible addresses. Lillian's eyes swelled with tears and she had to look away. Aillig was so alive in between the scribbles.

"It's all becoming so real. All this at once is a little overwhelming. I've had so many unanswered questions, and all this time I thought I was the only one who wondered."

He rubbed the white stubble of his beard, trying not to press the girl to decipher Aillig's wild notes. He was always wasting his life waiting to figure Aillig out. Now he had to wait longer still if he wanted to wring secrets out of the flighty woman.

Lillian stood and caressed some of the bottles sitting close by on her shelves, trying to keep her tears from spilling. *So much for a jovial time making new friends*, she thought.

"I searched those addresses one hundred times but they do not exist. Can ye make sense of it?"

She nodded her head slowly, speaking near a whisper.

"You're right, they do not exist. They're parts of addresses that I'd know. He wrote them that way so no one else could figure it out. I suspected something had happened when he asked me to remember these. He was keeping secrets, I was afraid he was in trouble, and now I'm sure. I knew he would cause controversy in that town."

Fueled by her admission, Dougal's impatience grew. He cursed himself for opening a can of worms. She probably had packed it all away and now an otherwise closed case became precarious in front of his eyes. He should have never been sent out here to meddle.

"What are these addresses then, girl!" he yelled as he stood, knocking the chair over.

She looked at him and took a small step back. As much as she wanted to trust the burly man in front of her, his intensity was threatening. The information separated and organized quickly in her mind. She could feel herself prickling in the face of fear. Aillig's secrets were crawling up her throat. Lillian needed to think quickly.

"I'm sorry, Mr. MacIntyre. It's not so simple. Anyway what are we going to do? Go and search for a needle in a haystack? I cannot know why he chose these. He had been so unlike himself then. They are all back in that dreadful city anyway," she lied.

She could feel her nerves twitching and his growing anger constricted the air around them. She wanted him to leave. A strange weight pressed along her shoulder blades, and it took a moment for her to realize what had caused it. Her ghost was near by. Lillian glanced at the clock and took a deep breath.

"I do apologize, my first appointment will be here shortly. I can look at this more closely tonight once I'm home and try to remember the importance of these addresses. Perhaps tomorrow we can meet again?"

She dismissed him professionally. Lillian needed him to leave. Dougal shook his head as he strained to control himself.

"How am I to know ye won't run off with that and ye havena been a part of his death the whole time?"

Her eyes widened at his accusation.

"Certainly you do not believe that."

"Why else would he have your name here? Maybe those places hold proof of your guilt. Of course ye wouldn't want to tell me then," Dougal reached. He needed to coax the secrets from her tightly pressed lips. Accusing her of something so terrible would have to inspire a counteraction to prove her innocence.

"Aillig was the only family I'd ever known," Lillian huffed. "I loved him. I just need time to focus, and frankly you're frightening me."

Dougal's shoulders slumped. He watched her face go blank. He was losing her.

"Okay, lass," he sighed, "take it. But if ye don't show tomorrow, I will find ye."

She nodded, sure of what his threat implied.

"Tomorrow then," she whispered.

Dougal's temper had exposed itself. He turned and made his way out in haste. Her back tightened as it would have when she was child, facing the wrath of Sister Roy, and Lillian sat back down once the door closed behind him. She closed her eyes and focused on the density growing behind. Real or not, the ghost had given her enough comfort to remain calm when Dougal's aggression had slipped out of his control.

"Thank you," she whispered into the empty room.

Lillian allowed quiet sobs to bubble from her throat as she clutched Aillig's letter against her chest. She could adjust to reliving the memories she had of him, but the responsibility subtly hidden in between this letter felt too great. Again her life was being uprooted and Lillian was ill prepared for what was being asked of her.

People moved in and out of the apothecary in routine as the hours passed. Lillian filled orders and restocked her inventory as her mind wandered through Aillig's riddle. Dougal was partially right not to trust her, though he couldn't know why. Aillig made her swear complete secrecy to two more addresses within the letter. She knew he'd have something hidden for her, but couldn't guess what. Lillian couldn't imagine being asked to go back to the city either. She had managed to escape entrapment once, but twice would be unlikely. Yet Aillig was asking her to go.

She locked up and started home, working through the code in his letter. She stared at the lit windows, lost in the blur of finding answers that she wasn't sure she wanted after all. St. John's howled in her head and she could not ignore the degrading laughter of Sister Roy. Nervous bile rose in her throat. When she left Norwich, she had left it permanently. Lillian's panic elevated and Aillig's riddle twisted in her fore mind, overwhelming her with the responsibility to solve it. He had known what was coming for him and left it for her to avenge. Her hands shook. The smoke from the chimneys irritated her. It was as if she could feel the heat from Aillig's apothecary on her back again. She glanced over her shoulder to the distant silhouette of her shop to be certain she hadn't been pulled back in time. Letters in his handwriting reorganized themselves in the darkness and she was sprinting home before she knew it.

Her door flew open and her hair whipped across her wide eyes. She walked swiftly to her kitchen, before sinking to the ground, unable to make a soothing tea. She breathed deeply and pulled her legs to her chest, trying to focus on the information flooding her mind. Hoot stirred restlessly in his cage. She snapped a warning eye on him to settle. Whispers swirled in her head and she clamped her hands over her ears as she tried to focus. She hadn't needed to control her anxiety in years.

Memories pushed at her, and she felt herself slipping away. Her pale fingers trembled and turned pallid against the moistening skin underneath her leggings. Lillian squeezed her eyes shut, floating away from the walls of her cottage. Aillig's writing buzzed in the darkness around her and reassembled into symbols and shapes she couldn't decipher. The sound of the notes she had written in slumber were recited in a voice much deeper than her own. The voice that had been inaudible when she was sleeping. The shadow man's face flashed before her; smooth, angular, and cloaked in stubble. Her eyes flew open.

Numb legs stumbled to her nightstand. Grabbing her pen, she steadily scribbled down the vision before flopping onto her bed. Lillian fainted into slumber, having used the last of her energy to survive the psychotic episode. Darkness crept into the corners of her room as the sun hid behind the horizon. She had tricked herself into thinking she had mastered her anxiety attacks.

.......

His steely eyes moved back into focus and he looked to the old man. His face was taut with stress.

"I think she heard me this time," he said solemnly.

The druid nodded. "If only there could have been more time to teach her about what she thinks is psychosis. As her prophecy grows more possible, her subconscious will intensify in an attempt to prepare her. But without the ability to accept what has been taught to her in a past life, she will only recognize her experience in the Veil as something she can understand, which is psychosis and imaginative fabrication."

The man stood, deciding the will of his love could guide her. He called to their famed Sun King from the depths of his soul for strength, and focused on the war at hand. He was angry she had to suffer.

"No one ever took the time to explain the truth to her, not even her mentor. He was one of us. I will teach her what it is to travel through Veils, with your help. She needs me more now than ever. My little dove has been tortured enough by the secrets they keep from her. She only needs to read her notes now, she will remember."

The old man nodded, a bit of nostalgia glazing over the deep wrinkles around his eyes. He had lived many times and longer, and knew how to read in between the lines of youth. He could feel the younger man's emotions writhing beneath the surface.

"You won't be the only man she loves. Do not be jealous of the deceased, he was like a father to her."

He looked at the druid. After a moment, he sat down a little shamefully.

"I only wish I could be there for her like he was. Her suffering seemed eased because of him. Now she has no one at all."

"He was not meant to carry her always," the druid whispered.

"How do you know old man?"

The man grinned. "I am Aillig, the first of my name. Her Aillig is also me. I have relived many times to create movement towards the prophecy throughout her lives as a part of the Hooded Spirits. I had secured messages to her mentor before his death and the letter she has seen proves my success. I have been captured by my own will so that I may continue her movement through you. You will one day relive too, but to love her. Afterall, it is what will carry the prophecy to completion."

*Chapter Thirteen*

*Emmy thought the woman had followed her, but she turned to find herself alone. Wind rushed around the hillside where she stood next to Cutter. He was rigid, looking out to the wild grasses. His hair had grown long, and she smiled, wrapping her arms around his bare waist. His face was covered with the ancient blue markings of the old Irish Henry had taught her about, and on his chest a spiral lay over his heart. He gripped her tighter and called her by a name that was not her own. She traced the spiral with a shaky finger and the edges of the Wyoming terrain started to foil. Scared, she looked up to Cutter's sorrow stained eyes.*

*"Henry," he whispered, still looking behind her.*

*She blinked the tears back and when her sight cleared, Cutter no longer stood embracing her. The black haired woman was there, searching for recognition from the other end of a hallway.*

Emmy woke smiling at the photograph Cutter had given her. She could hear the faint whisper of wind as she uncurled her legs in the sheets. It'd been such a pleasant dream until Cutter disappeared. Rising, she reached her arms above her head, and let the sheets fall to her waist, sighing with the pleasure of stretching. Her room was full of light from the late morning.

They'd been nearly inseparable since the art show a few weeks ago. Cutter had a way of making her feel unbridled from the memory of Ethan. There was something about the velvet tone in his voice that called to her, as if she'd been hearing it her entire life. She pulled on her jeans. Ethan's reign floated far from her and the inconsistent schedule at the diner kept her mind busy and distracted from whatever still lingered. The lunch shift had already started picking up since she began working. She figured between Cutter and Kelly's promotion, most of the town had been rallied to go while she worked. It made her happy to feel supported again. She felt like she had gently eased into a life that frightened her only weeks ago. Her strength was returning and Emmy realized that most days she thought little of what had happened. For the first time she was in control of her own destiny. She pushed her hair out of her face. The only thing missing was Henry. He would have laughed at her choice to stay in Wyoming.

"I ended up in Henry's fairytales," she mumbled, shaking her head.

Her life was changing and for the first time she took notice with playful excitement. She looked out to the distant mountains, her blue eyes shining to their call. She felt herself breathe in more of the wildness as she walked to work. There was something about it that catered to her spirit. Cutter's company had made everything exciting too. He'd been eager to show her the Wyoming at her fingertips. She had even met some of his friends as they trickled through the diner with interest. They wanted to take a look at who had finally caught Cutter's attention. Which caused quite an escapade whenever Kelly was there.

Her adventures with the boys around town were epic. Now that Kelly was freshly twenty-one and full throttled for John, they spent a lot of nights at the bar.

John would loyally have their drinks poured when they walked in. Regulars recognized them with a grin and the jukebox was always playing a tune they could sing along to. The girls had become thick as thieves and she couldn't think back on a time she had a real girlfriend.

Emmy could feel herself molding into the person she had imagined as a child. Her laugh had become heartier, her confidence stronger. She had dedicated herself to living in the moment instead of working her way through the past. She couldn't change what had happened, but could control what came next. She had been given a rare opportunity to start fresh, and though it came with terrible sacrifices, she tried to count it as a gift. Emmy felt lucky to have found people who nurtured the damaged places in her heart.

She wiped down counters, thinking of how the past weeks had been filled with Cutter's goodnight kisses.

Every time they touched, he sucked her into a different world. Her lips tingled, and she looked around to see if anyone caught her blushing. She walked behind the shining counter, brushing cool fingers across her face, lingering on the memory. Every day felt like a rush. He was taking her on a small trip after her shift and she couldn't help but wonder what expectation Cutter might have of her tonight. Nerves bit at the excitement but she was hellbent not to ruin it. Every minute dragged by and when Emmy clocked out, it felt like days had transpired. She walked back to her room, anticipating what might happen. Emmy knew that an overnight trip was out of her comfort zone. She hadn't escaped her past completely, but she couldn't manage to refuse him. The shadow that Ethan had cast over her was still present, even if distant, trying to decapitate whatever ground she stood on. Just like the man, it wouldn't be ignored and forgotten. She clenched and unclenched her jaw, refusing the desire to touch the tops of her thighs. It had been long enough that her soothing habits started to annoy her. She didn't want to think about what Ethan had done to her, not tonight.

.......

"I don't care what ancient bloodline is in her blood or his," he boomed into the telephone line.

"If the old man goes down, I will get her back."

"That kind of murder is harder to fight in court, Ethan, too many people know and respect him," his lawyer gently argued. "If it was possible they would have done it years ago. No, it will create too much attention."

"I'll cover my tracks, you idiot. The old man goes tonight."

Ethan threw the phone to the floor, strangled with rage. It'd been more than a month since she disappeared. The only person that could keep her in secrecy from Ethan was her grandfather. His network was too loyal to keep her appearance from him. Rome had assigned her to him in good faith of his ability. He had not taken his calling lightly, and felt weighed down by it now. Ethan's shoulders slumped as he sat back in his recliner, dizzy from the brandy.

Hours passed as he grew drunker, the house dulling into the pit of night. He numbly recounted the duty his father passed to him through generations of preceding noble men. He had been descended from the high born blood of Romans, sworn to protect the throne the Vatican sat upon. For centuries the College of Cardinals had built a strategic method to keep their power safe from those who threatened it. One century after the next, they worked to erase such dangers. Now it was his duty to do the same. Her dark prophecy was hidden from common knowledge but Ethan had not been spared when he took on the job of controlling her. They had told him how she'd been born to awaken an uprising against their beliefs. He was told that she would be responsible for ending the world as they knew it. No detail went unshared to him about the dark reign that could return to the earth if she was not watched carefully. She was descended from the ancient druids, a people who believed in total madness. Without him to confine her, she was accessible to those who still lingered in today's society. The lunatics would manipulate her for their own ideals, just like her grandfather had done.

Ethan didn't need anyone to tell him he was in a deep hole for letting her slip through his fingers. He could hear threats bubbling under conversations with those above him. If he couldn't recover her, there would be no more backing him on business endeavors, no leisurely support to the life he had acquired. If he hadn't been forced to spend so much time containing her, he could have gained unsurmountable wealth on his own. His fist sailed into the wall and he rose to prowl through the house. He'd prove his devotion to his spiritual conquest. His father may not be alive to remind him of the sin he'd committed in losing her, but there wasn't any doubt they'd send someone else to do that. His body twitched with failure and the fear of their reprimands. He was too powerful to be submitted to the punishment of lesser ranks; he was a protector of their entire religion. If she would have only behaved, his righteous path would have been so much easier. She didn't deserve to take away any more of his life than she already had.

He'd go to the house at night. One whimper from her old man would reveal her hiding spot. His heart quickened and he went to his bottle of brandy for a nip to calm the excitement. He grinned, imagining the way he'd wring her neck and drag her to the estate. There was only one way this would end for her; he'd been waiting for it all these years. Finally he would have a good enough excuse and he would be free of his burden.

Unable to contain what lulled heavy behind his forehead, he threw his empty brandy glass against the wall. It shattered like stars to the floor and he burst outside, straight for her grandfather.

*Chapter Fourteen*

*Aillig smiled at her from his desk. Lillian rushed to him, throwing her arms around his delicate neck, tears rushing down her face. He pulled her away, turning into the face of her shadow man. He gently cupped her chin in one hand and wiped away the wetness on her cheeks with the other. She grinned feebly and watched as he pointed to Aillig's books. She leaned towards them and tried to memorize whatever he was trying to show her. She could hear the door of Aillig's apothecary swing open and when she turned to see who had arrived she saw the woman standing in the doorway. St. John's was grimly in the distance. She held her hand out to Lillian, light beaming softly from her fingertips.*

When Hoot stirred in his cage, she slowly came to wake. She stretched an arm out toward him and yawned, staring at the brass clock ticking gently beside her, taking too long to focus on the time. Lillian pulled her heavy body out from the covers and shook the lingering panic attack from her mind. It had been years since she'd had one so intense. She smiled to Hoot as she grabbed his early morning feeding from the refrigerator.

"Soon we should be feeding you something more lively, don't you think?"

She placed the paste in his feeder.

Lillian wished she could make sense of the episode she had experienced. She crawled across her bed and sat on the other side, feet planted firmly on the wood floor and picked up the paper she had scribbled on while she'd been submerged in her psychosis. The last time this had happened Aillig had worked through the meaning with her. Now she was alone. Lillian sighed and looked to see what her madness had construed, forgoing her walk in the woods.

She had listed the four addresses Aillig had sent Dougal in their proper form. Then she had written again whatever language had come to her the night before. The rest of the page was filled with impractical scratches and lines. The markings looked familiar, but she couldn't recall where she'd seen them before. Despite the fear laced into the mystery of Aillig's letter, Lillian thrived in the art of deciphering. The old man had used it to calm and distract her many times.

"Still using it even now," she whispered, grabbing a piece of paper to organize what she'd already uncovered.

First was Aillig's guest house near Brighton. Two weeks out of the year he would leave the shop in her management and disappear, always returning misty eyed and happy to see her. He had sworn her to secrecy about the location, laughing that he would never get a break from his clientele if they knew about it. He had been adamant about keeping her private life private. He learned the hard way and suggested she didn't.

"Oh, Aillig. You had no idea how right you were," she murmured to herself as she made her notes.

The second address she was sworn to keep secret was to a PO Box she had known nothing about. It was close to her cottage and she knew Aillig well enough to understand that was probably no coincidence.

"Perhaps I fled to this town without the random impulse after all. Perhaps somewhere deep in my subconscious I remembered it, and I came here."

The third was County Hall near the city and the last she read slowly. It was the address to St. John's. If she decided to return, it would undoubtedly be with Dougal. She would have to give him some sort of information from this paper as promised. Lillian sat back and examined her notes. She was unsure about what to do. Dougal would be waiting for her at the shop. She needed to form a plan if she had any hope to conceal the secret locations. She pressed her fingertips against her forehead. She was a horrible liar. Her panic rose in anticipation of his temper. She could feel the push of another attack. She forced her eyes to work on something tangible. Lillian sifted through more of her madness.

The writing below the addresses looked similar to Latin, or what she knew from her proper plant names. She rose and tip toed down the hallway to her mixing room, skimming through her shelves before pulling out her translation book. Its ancient cover felt like velvet in her hands and the dust and moisture tingled in her nostrils. The smell of old books always calmed her and she took it back to bed, hoping to find a translation.

She scrolled through the worn pages. The rhythm of research settled her. Lillian located the words with delicate efficiency. She closed the book and picked up the translation to read it.

*Only you, my dove, forever.*

The paper fell from her fingers, swaying lightly to the floor. She glanced breathlessly from her bed, replaying the trace of dreams filled with speechless faces. There was no mistaking it was not she who thought these words. Lillian felt invaded. She was suddenly aware of the sunless morning and the hauntings that slid in the darker corners of her room. There was no mistaking his presence now, nor hers with him. Her neck prickled with goosebumps.

She crawled backward from the edge of the bed and slipped silently underneath the covers. She could see her scribbled notepad still covered with Aillig's addresses and the scratchy patterns that filled the empty space around it. For the first time Lillian was afraid of her own strangeness. She pulled on her ears and forced her eyes closed, concentrating solely on falling back to sleep for a little while to ignore what was happening. She didn't want to deal with whatever madness was unfurling. Maybe the nuns had been right about her foolish conversations with the dead.

"If it's not real," she whispered, forcing herself to doze off, "it can't hurt me."

*Dougal stood over her as she cowered in a corner of her shop. His voice boomed incoherently, making bottles crash around her. Tears streamed from her cheeks and fell in rose petals to the floor. One gnarled hand wrapped around her throat and Lillian could feel herself choking. Her forehead ballooned from the pressure of his grip and he laughed. The shadow man came running from the distance, but it was too late. Lillian could feel her eyes bulge before she exploded into millions of moonflower blooms and darkness shrouded the apothecary.*

The ringing of the brass clock ripped her out of the dream. It vibrated painfully in her ears and she tried to sit up. Dizziness filled her and she had to lean against the headboard to regain composure. Her eyes were swollen. She pressed her fingers into the base of her neck and sighed. Dougal would be waiting for her at the shop and she was in no condition to deal with him.

She swung her legs heavily over the bed and rose slowly. Her toes touched the edge of the translation paper and she did not move her eyes to look. She could feel its intensity burning in her chest and she stepped around it with some difficulty. The lightness in her face was absent as she tugged from her tea jars. The density of a black ginger tea was sure to set her ajar with energy. Lillian grimaced as she sipped the smoky liquid, feeling sorry for herself. If she wasn't so fearful that Dougal would come looking for her, she'd stay under the covers and keep the shop closed. Bitterness clung in her ribs.

Lillian gazed out the kitchen window at the meek light of northern England. Another vicious dream only heightened her intolerance for the disruptive man. Her shoulders slumped in defeat and she set the half finished mug in her silver sink. Lillian had no choice but to prepare for the meeting with him. She recalled his terrible face from her nightmare and cringed.

"The moonflower," she whispered, recalling how she had exploded.

Briskly, she moved to her herb room down the hall, and made a quick pressed oil for Dougal before her good judgement returned. If she could manage to have him inhale enough, she could level his mood substantially. Packing it in the folds of her thick sweater, she made her way out the door. The note called her from the other side of the bed as she passed by. Lillian's intrigue about the shadow bested her. Before she could think too much about it, she walked over and shoved her haunted notes in her pockets.

She was thankful for the walk to the shop. She had to practice what she'd say to Aillig's brother. Her loyalty to Aillig made it impossible to tell Dougal the truth. Lillian couldn't help but wonder what kind of man Dougal really was. Aillig wouldn't have kept secrets from his own family without reason. Lillian squared her shoulders and walked with purpose, forcefully trying to ignore the nerves pounding between her ears. Dougal was waiting as she approached.

"Good morning," she said curtly.

They moved into the shop and made their way toward her consulting table. She made no offer to serve tea, only sat and stared through the aged man in front of her. He hadn't the charm she'd seen once, and perhaps she was seeing Dougal for the first time through Aillig's eyes. His wrinkles did not seem in sufferance but in stubbornness. His arthritis was not from the endurance of hardship but the infliction of his own blind anger.

"I looked at the addresses. There are two as I mentioned. They're back in the city I came from and I'm not willing to return there. Perhaps Aillig only wanted you to see me to decipher his writing."

Dougal rolled his eyes. She was clamming up. He had taken the chance to trust her, and it seemed she was taking advantage of it. Showing her the letter had been a mistake. He had to take control of the situation.

"I'm sure there's more you're not telling me, lass," he coaxed gruffly.

She shook her head, allowing the exhaustion from last night to show in her favor.

"No, I'm afraid not. I spent all night picking this information apart. There are two addresses. The rest was distraction. Take this note with you. Maybe it will help you find what you're looking for."

She wrote out the two addresses and handed it to him before rising to readjust bottles and slip the moonflower oil onto her hands. Lillian sat back down with slumped shoulders and watched the clock ticking behind him, wishing away the minutes until the distraction of her customers would relieve her from his undermining stare.

"Have ye given up on your beloved Aillig, lass?" he asked with dripping sympathy.

Her sudden lack of interest in his brother's death was marked. He wasn't sure how to play along to make sure it was genuine. He worked to keep the impatience from setting into his bones.

Lillian nodded her head despairingly. "I'm afraid so. I honestly cannot go back to that city, Mr. MacIntyre."

That was not a lie.

Dougal was growing more uncomfortable with her surrender and she knew it. She let her eyes brighten and she reached a cool hand across the table to squeeze his a little roughly, hoping to set his attention to his arthritis.

"If you should find anything I might be able to help with, I will do whatever I can to help solve the mystery."

Dougal rested his palms against his chin, rubbing his stubble, contemplating the situation. The idea of babysitting a heightened version of her in the city sounded like self torture. He already had his fill of her. He nodded his head once and stood. He knew where to find her if he needed. It'd be easier to search for Aillig's secrets without having to conceal his motivation in front of her anyway.

"I'm sorry, I can't be of more help."

She glared at him with wide eyes in apology.

"If anything comes up, I shall see ye again."

She walked him to the door.

"Do tell me if you find anything at all, Mr. MacIntyre. Anything to avenge sweet Aillig."

Dougal nodded and left her shop feeling utterly confused. He made the walk to his car in a haze of debate. He couldn't decide if it was disappointment or distrust that left him dissatisfied. The fear of returning to the city strangled her interest in the unlikely death of his brother. He couldn't blame her hearing what they'd done to her. However, the mysteries that had not been uncovered in the remnants of Aillig's shop would be easily guarded if the girl had been warned by his brother. It was impossible to tell what she did or did not know. Dougal's judgement of character had been blurred in all of her ups and downs.

"That cramped shop distracted me," he mumbled.

He assured himself that she couldn't know the real cause of his death, at least. The cover up was too strong. He sat heavily behind the wheel and started the car. The drive home was a long one and Dougal needed it to sort out his analysis of Lillian. St. John's wouldn't be happy to hear him stumbling through a possible threat to their world.

*Chapter Fifteen*

Henry sat looking into his fire. He had dozed off in his chair and dreamt of Emmy. It was the same dream he'd had every night in this life. She ran in his field, bound by the bright light that set her apart. What he hadn't expected to see was another little girl, bound by a similar light as his granddaughter. More of the prophecy was starting to reveal itself. Emmy was not alone in her journey. The Native stories had preserved an accurate version. He smiled, silently thanking the indigenous tribes who had sought him out all those years ago.

Ancient histories long made into fairytales and myth resided in the particles of Emmy's soul. Too long ago people use to believe in the higher learning that now burned inside of her. Numerology was not a trade of tinkers but a practice of science. Astrology was not a laughable guide to life, but a delicate documentation of the solar system's influence on living things. Time parallels were common knowledge and the truth about death was less frightening. Dedicated scholars translated messages from the ether to enhance the quality of life. It was a time when every living person was united. The names in the stories changed through demographic and language, but all of humanity had understood the importance of the old words.

Even the Romans had been a part, until their talent for dividing and conquering grew their obsession for power.

Many lives he had watched Emmy fall to their hunger for control. Henry couldn't see it another time. The repetition of her story had grown weaker in the mouths of those who preserved it as lives passed without change. Henry felt tired of holding on to so many memories of his past bodies. He had lived many lives in hope of helping her realize the prophecy. He fixed his stare on the flames in front him and tried to ease the ache of remembering all the centuries that had gone astray.

He criticized himself for always keeping her under wraps. He had always been so careful in his approach to teaching her, too afraid that speaking openly would harm her under their tight watch. Instead he had spent lives creating stories, hoping that she could piece together the information on her own. Emmy was alone in her adventure now and Henry couldn't help feeling angry that he hadn't done more, that he let his own fears dominate his decisions. She needed to be taught about the strength she once possessed, not how to hide it like he had. It made him feel like even he had succumbed to erasing knowledge to preserve personal interest. He was frustrated with his own repeating patterns.

The quietness that wrapped around the event of the barn burning made Henry suspicious about the plans Ethan and his superiors were making. The whole thing had stayed out of papers and people's mouths, almost as if it hadn't happened. It was what they did best, they had spent centuries perfecting their cover ups. He thought of his family in Ireland and the countless sacred sites that had been erased from history, lying unnoticed beneath the foundation of their buildings and cathedrals. They had simply burned them down and made his belief a fiction. Burying a tragedy like the murder of horses must have been simple. Henry knew whatever scare tactic they had tried ended in failure; she hadn't come back.

He could feel the tinge of death around him and knew the last thing Ethan had to hold over her was himself. His shotgun sat resting against his recliner, prepared for war. Henry knew it would come to this as it had many lives before. It was a pattern that repeated over and over until Emmy could wake the prophecy. He knew the pattern well, along with the hard truth that a controlled path didn't exist. There was no concrete promise in the story of her lives, only a probability. Her lives before had the same opportunity and ended unknown to her. Only Emmy could control the course of the prophecy.

Henry's giant hands itched as they rested on the navy arm chair in the darkness of night. She had shifted in this life, and so would he. He would choose to fight. Every life of his had been given up willingly in the idea of protecting her, and it never helped or harmed her. He couldn't waste another life on such balanced consequences. Henry realized he couldn't be responsible for her choices or her memory, but he could take charge of his own. A fire struck undeniably deep inside of him. That bastard wouldn't get him without a fight anymore.

Branches broke in the distance and he could feel his horses moving restlessly in their stalls outside. Henry picked up his gun, moving to his window. He watched as the shadow moved around his property, searching for the simplest point of entry. Ethan wouldn't be very careful about it, probably expecting no trouble. Henry's mouth twitched once at the corners. Boots moved up his porch steps and he shifted in front of the door, shotgun already loaded. His broad shoulders held steady. Henry couldn't subject himself for Emmy's sake any longer.

The walls shook from the impact of the door as it swung open. The air was cooler this time of year and Ethan stood with the moon shining behind him.

"Tell her to come out, old man," Ethan demanded too calmly.

Henry didn't move, didn't speak.

Ethan's impatience rung hard in his ears.

"I said tell her to come out. Or you'll regret it," he whispered through his teeth.

"She's not here, Ethan. She's outsmarted you again. Emmy finally decided she was done being controlled. Now you're going to regret what you've done to her."

Henry raised his gun to the giant man. All the years of anger, all the lives of standing by made his heart burst. He pulled the trigger and Ethan howled as the shot dug into the ball of his shoulder. Before Henry could get another shot off, Ethan leapt at him, throwing their bodies to the floor with a crash. He clenched the old man's throat in his palm and laughed.

"Go ahead, choke. Cough out for her, she'll come. I know she's here."

Henry held his breath and tried to relax. Physical abuse was not going to change anything. It would only make it worse.

"Speak!" Ethan yelled, crashing his fists against the floor.

"I told you she isn't here," Henry spoke hoarsely, "Let her go, Ethan. Whatever they've told you isn't true. Don't be the violence of your childhood."

Ethan smiled, then raised a fist above his head and let it crash into the side of Henry's face.

"You mean like that? You can't trick me, Grandpa. You won't be getting out of this so easily. Judgement Day has come for you."

Henry's head was numb. He could feel his body giving in, he was so tired. With huge effort, he dug his knee into Ethan's side and knocked the wind from his lungs. He pushed him off and rose unevenly.

"They've made a trained monkey out of you. Look how well you serve them. Look how well you exemplify the love of your God. Do you think he will accept the murder you've committed in his name on your Judgement Day? You know the answer, Ethan, it's why you drink. You're not serving Him, you're serving the Vatican and their lies. When will you learn it is not one and the same?"

Ethan worked to regain his breath, bent over on the floor. A fear stirred in him. The old man was using his dark magic to trick him. Ethan closed his ears to the words and rose with blinding rage. He dove towards Henry with abhorrent intention.

"Where is she?" he screamed, strangling the man in between his palms.

..........

The sun was warm on Cutter's face as he drove. A smile curled at the corners of his mouth in anticipation of seeing her. She brushed across his imagination in flashes; a piece of warm, chestnut hair streaming like gold across her face, the curve of her shoulder when she looked over it, and the deep blue that rimmed her eyes as the only mark of the darkness she carried. The woman was undeniably exciting to him.

His mind flipped through moments of the weeks they spent together and locked onto the night at the rodeo, watching her from a distance, when for a few minutes she had been completely and naturally herself. Cutter shook his head, trying to regain a memory of her that he'd not been a part of. He dreamt of them often in complicated snaps of events as if his mind had taken stills of things that hadn't happened. He liked to remember certain ones, like how she looked on a horse under starlight or sitting clad in black on a river's edge crying. She struck a cord that he had abandoned when he left home.

Cutter stretched his arms against the wheel of his truck, genially guiding himself away from the deep thought. Life was more simple when he didn't torture himself with things that couldn't be changed. But Emmy moved him, pulled him towards the place of soul bearing. His foot pressed against the pedal. He longed to feel her against his body. He needed to feel the slight curve of her lower lip as she pressed it between his own. Never in his life did his body call to a woman beyond his chivalry. Cutter exhaled and rolled down his window. He was quick to reign himself in, knowing too well what was at stake. Everything rode on this overnight stay and she couldn't have her trust broken in a moment of lust. He pulled into the motel and parked outside her room. Before he could knock twice, the door swung open and she jumped into him.

"Well, hello," he chuckled, pleased to have his arms around her.

"Hi," she whispered into his chest.

"You ready?" He ran a hand over her hair, pressing his lips delicately on top of her head.

"Oh, just a minute. I got side tracked. Come in."

Cutter hesitated before stepping across the threshold. He'd never been invited past the doorway and the sudden rush of intimacy was shocking. For the first time he felt too large in the room of a woman.

The walls were bare but for a few generic prints of western cliche framed in plastic. The late light of the day seeped lazily through the only window and turned everything yellow. His photograph stood crisply against the lamp on her nightstand. He swallowed hard. It was the first thing she woke up to. He sat on the end of the hard bed as he waited, noticing the clothes scattered on the floor in her rush to pack. There was a wrinkled map on the desk with a half hearted line drawn in pencil. Sudden sadness washed over him. Her journey had started in Kentucky and dragged through the barren parts of the country, to where she was living now. He couldn't bear to think of what had driven her away from home. He stood as she walked towards him from the cheap bathroom. He wrapped his arms around her waist, and lifted her up.

"You ready now?" he asked, struggling to keep the sorrow from his voice.

"Yeah," she chirped, unaware.

He grabbed her bag in one hand, and intertwined their fingers in the other. She locked the door and headed towards the parking lot.

"I just wanna make sure my truck is locked," she sang, jogging towards it.

He watched as she went, realizing he'd never seen it. The green paint on the old body was faded and flat. The door rang as she closed it in assurance. Cutter wondered how she had traveled so far in such a tired looking vehicle. He couldn't guess if that had been her only choice or not. His heart beat heavily with the hurt surrounding her and his green eyes were veiled in gray. It was like she'd been misplaced into a life without him all this time. He smiled softly as she opened the door to his Dodge with wide eyes.

"Wow, this is a nice truck, Cutter."

The air toyed through Emmy's hair from the open window as they drove. She admired the landscape as they passed out of town. Soil and earth mixed with the leather essence of Cutter and she thought this could be heaven.

"This is perfect, Cutter," she breathed sensually.

She smiled at the Wolf Star, the brightest star in the sky, which already shone above them. Emmy thought of all the stories Henry had told her in fondness. For the first time since she was a child, she could feel herself living inside his lore. In a moment of vulnerability, she lingered on the tribal fairytales she'd memorized since she was a girl.

"Henry would have loved this place," she murmured under her breath.

Cutter glanced at the picture beside him, straining to hear what she'd said. Her arm hung in the air as she let her fingers dance through the wind. She tilted her head as if she were hearing its secrets. He swore she was not real. Her serenity stopped time, pulling energy to and away from her as she breathed. She was otherworldly, the soul he had looked for all his life. He hadn't a right to the closeness he claimed over her. As much as he wanted to break the silence with questions about her past, about her mention of someone she knew, he dare not breathe a word, fearful of breaking her spell. Such peace was rare to her.

In the weeks they had spent together, Cutter's tendency to observe had been his guide to her intimacies. She spoke little of her life. He had to learn by watching. He couldn't move too quickly without her tensing. If a place became too loud, she'd grow anxious. But most intriguing was her reluctance to share her past. It was like she tried to gain control of a life she'd lost. She lashed out like an abused horse if you ventured too close to the source of pain. He had sworn to himself not to ask about it, but it was hard not to want to know all of her.

They pulled into the guest ranch just as the last of twilight wove above them. The night promised a beautiful tapestry and a silver moon shyly presented itself. The guest ranch sat nestled in the rolling hills in front of them, and the big house was lit warmly from inside.

"This is where you work."

"Yes, but I don't think we will be going in tonight. We are camping. Is that okay?"

"I think that's perfect," she smiled in spite of her growing nerves.

"I thought it would be a good chance to see the stars. I always catch you looking at them."

"Though my soul may set in darkness, it will rise in perfect light. I have loved the stars too fondly to be fearful of the night," Emmy recited.

"Did you make that up?"

"No, it's the poet Sarah Williams. Just a quote I remember."

Emmy choked back the memory of Henry. He had often read classic literature to her as a child. The melody of poetic minds would always send her to slumber. He had always said that poem was written about her.

Henry had hung dully in the background of her mind the past few days, and it gave her hope that Ethan hadn't followed through with all of his plans. She hadn't felt the tug of her horses in weeks and somehow she knew they were gone. She watched Cutter pull things out of the bed of his truck, his shoulders rising and falling as he lifted. Emmy still couldn't share stories about her grandfather. The distance it put between her and Cutter made her sad. She stepped forward to grab a bag.

"Let me help carry something," she said, letting her fingers graze his if only to feel connected again.

After slinging all the necessities over their backs, they set out under an inky night, the cabin glowing behind them as they went. They walked peacefully in the silent communion of their surroundings. Soft shadows and still air wrapped over Emmy's shoulders like Henry's embrace. Without the distraction of daylight or social scenes, Emmy found the cries of the recent past tugging at the ends of her tangled mane. She breathed in deeply, hoping the pine would burn away the constricting of her throat. Fallen needles crunched under their feet as they passed the tree line. The air seemed to sigh and expand over the vast, gentle rise of the hill before them. Cutter reached into the dark of the crescent moon to wrap his hand around Emmy's.

"We're almost there," he whispered.

She moved closer to him, the long summer grass hushing against her jeans. She had parted her lips, but the words nestled deeply in her chest. The unruly land had surrounded her in a loud silence she couldn't interrupt with sad stories. The breeze whispered answers to her burning past and she tried to decipher it. When they reached the top of the rise, a gust of wind rushed by. The ground flattened beneath them and the air became noticeably cooler.

"Just a few more feet and we can set up camp," Cutter breathed through his own thick intoxication of the land.

The stars above them cut through the sky like shattered glass. Emmy sat in the rocky earth, watching Cutter build their tent. She shook slightly not from the chill of the ground below her, but from the reality that was quickly approaching. Sharing a bed with him suddenly ballooned all of her unshared history, making her feel like a stranger in her own bones. The familiarity she had always felt between them slipped away. She flicked small stones beneath her feet, feeling like a liar.

"I didn't bring anything to make a fire with," Cutter said, as he finished the tent and sat beside her, "we can't build them here, the land is protected."

"I don't mind at all," she drawled.

The cloak of night came as a relief. Emmy couldn't keep up with the rise and fall of what she was feeling and the darkness helped conceal it. Ethan's destruction crawled around her legs and Emmy cracked her fingers. She breathed deeply, reminding herself she was miles away. He hadn't come for her.

Warmth emanated from Cutter's skin. Instinctively she moved closer, breathing him in. He wrapped his arm around her waist and they sat in the silence.

"Where are we?" Emmy asked, trying to distract herself.

"My favorite place in the world. But I will tell you more about it tomorrow, when you can see it."

Emmy shivered once. His arms wrapped tighter around her.

"Are you cold? I can get a blanket."

"No," she paused.

Emmy couldn't stand to hold the truth any longer. It was time to tell him. She wiggled harder against his chest. She could hear the chatter of wildlife around her like bones in the breeze.

"Cutter, I need to tell you something that's been on my mind."

His heart skipped once. His hand steadily stroked her hair and he pressed his lips to the top of her head. She was shaking.

"Okay."

Cutter could barely make out her profile in the darkness as she sat away from him. She pulled her knees to her chest.

"I was thinking on the way here how much we don't really know about each other. I know you said you didn't care if you ever knew about my past and I liked that. But I think...sharing a tent...got me a little nervous."

Cutter sat completely still. He hadn't thought this through. She seem to choke on the words as they rose to escape her body and there wasn't a thing he could do to stop it.

"I think I need to tell you about what has happened before I can get in the tent with you."

Cutter swallowed hard, frozen. The cold tone in her voice rang in his ears. His arms felt numb and he wanted to reassure her that he didn't care about her past.

"I was raised by my grandpa, Henry. His parents had immigrated here from Ireland. He was raised on their farm in Kentucky, the same one he raised me on. He was kind and I loved him. He was the reason I know the stars, the horses, the literature, that quote from earlier. Certain stories he would repeat so often I have them memorized."

He could see her shoulders shaking in the dark. He could hear the quiver in her voice. He waited silently for what she didn't want to say. Emmy was reentering the gates of hell.

"When I was eighteen, I found work on this huge Thoroughbred farm as a hand. The owners were real yuppies, but I loved horses and especially the power of such athletic champions. I was happy to exist in the shadows, mucking stalls, daydreaming of being small enough to jockey. Then there was Ethan. For some reason he took a liking to me. He spent so much time giving me attention, I guess I got caught in the whirlwind and let it sweep me up."

Cutter felt his stomach twist. His name stumbled like rocks from her lips. The pain in her voice made him desperate to stop it, but even Cutter knew there was no distracting her now. The story unraveled like a nightmare, and he anticipated the worst. He was losing his beautiful, wild horse. To him.

"His father had told him he could have the rights to the family business when he was a grown man, and typical of Ethan's ambition, he proposed to me when I was twenty. Just another business transaction towards his success," she drawled bitterly.

Cutter panicked. His eyes raced over her body, searching her fingers. He watched for the gleam from her ring finger. The night was too dark and he could feel it swallow him.

"I should've known better than to rush into it. But I guess I was too excited about those horses to see it was headed for disaster. I should've known that he'd never let me near what made him money."

Her words grew colder and her voice cracked between quiet sobs.

"I served my purpose in his mind. Ethan's desire to move ahead towards international fame left me isolated the first year we were married. All the social partying made him violent and when he started losing clients to it, he'd come home to unleash his rage on me. I learned quickly to be safe in the guest room if I wanted to avoid getting hurt."

"Then changing like night and day he spent his time coaxing me to attend his lavish business affairs. The lure of riches and international exposure seemed romantic to a girl who grew up with such simple surroundings. Not to mention feeling like less of a failure in a life I swore myself into. I just wanted the hardship to end. I caved to the bait. It was fun until I realized that a businessman is the same conniver in every country. When I no longer charmed Ethan's way into money, I was discarded to be a house wife. A maid."

"I spent years in the small barn of my own horses from Henry's or locked in the guest bedroom for safety. I wouldn't talk to Henry. I was afraid of my own failure, couldn't face him because of it."

She tried to catch her breath. Cutter could feel his heart racing along with her. It was far worse than he could have imagined. His eyes grew tight and his entire body tensed. He cried silently out to her, begged her to come to him. She cried in the darkness alone.

"Then one day, Ethan showed up in the middle of the day drunker than I'd ever seen him. I could hear him banging and yelling in the house from the barn. He liked to tell me how awful I was. He liked to tell me just how he planned to fix what was wrong with me. Something snapped. I raced in there yelling back, tried swinging a wrench into his side. I got him once, but the second I wasn't so lucky. He drug me back to the master room," she stopped, choking on her tears, feeling the bruises that no longer deformed her body.

"He pinned me underneath him and I could smell the alcohol in his sweat. He told me I should enjoy being underneath him. That I was his goddamn wife, and that I should act like one. I told him that I hated him. Told him I would never be his proper house wife. That he could burn in hell."

Her voice was raising with anxiety and Cutter was shocked into stillness.

"He knocked me out with a single blow. I woke up the next morning alone with bruises all over and torn clothes. Every part of me ached. I left before he came back. I was too screwed up to think that he'd come after me." She cried freely from her heaving chest.

"He found me at the first place I stopped. Broke open the door and put a gun to my forehead. I was so broken, I don't remember being scared. I remember almost wishing he'd just kill me. Instead he went on about how he'd kill my horses, and Henry too," she sobbed, growing more hysterical. Speaking it out loud made the fear so real that she looked hard into the darkness to make sure Ethan wasn't standing there.

"Then the man from the motel hit him with a bat and knocked him out. Somehow I drove away."

She was filled with a sadness older than her years. There was defeat and broken happiness all around her. Cutter wasn't sure how she had managed to pick up and carry on. He thought of his own journey to Wyoming and tried to catch his breath. He thought of what he would have needed when he felt as lost and hopeless as she sounded now. Her voice was ragged from sobbing and he could not take the torture any longer. Emmy would not be alone anymore.

"When I did stop, rest only came filled with nightmares. I was too afraid he'd come for me again."

Cutter inched soundlessly toward her.

"I can't quit thinking about how I abandoned my horses and Henry. I left them to die. I dream every night about people I've never seen. I can't always control it. It's like I switch between versions of myself without knowing all of them. I mean, look how I was the day I first met you.

It'd been the first time I tried interacting with anyone since Ethan...hurt me."

She was swallowed by cries so foreign that Cutter wasn't sure they were coming from her. He reached shaking out to her. His touch sent a moan from her lips and she scrambled to pull her entire body against his. He leaned backward to gather her between his broad chest, squeezing her tighter as she tried melting into him. He could feel his worn shirt moisten and his own throat tightened.

He hated himself for thinking an overnight was a good idea. The terror she had survived was rubbing too closely to the intimacy of sharing space with him. Her quirks became clear and he understood all of it. He felt like a selfish imbecile.

"It's okay," he choked, his voice rough and unfamiliar in his own ears. "You are safe with me. Emmy, I won't let anyone hurt you again. It's okay."

She relaxed a little, the confidence of his voice soothing her tremors. Her arms tingled without feeling and her legs ached. She tried to find her way back from her memories. She could feel his fingers kneading into the panic at the base of her neck. Leather and soil lingered around him and she could feel herself returning.

"I'm sorry, Cutter, I've probably ruined your surprise trip," she whispered raggedly, coming down from the high of her release.

"Not even close," he cooed, wanting to feel calm.

Silence fell between them as they both concentrated on relaxing. Emmy looked to her stars as she focused on stilling the racking in her chest. Her head felt heavy against Cutter and the confession of all her torture exhausted her.

"I'm sorry," she whispered.

Cutter looked over the top of her head, trying to think through his own pulsing anger. His limbs were on fire. He stroked her hair, hoping to regulate himself before it upset her. That bastard had taken pleasure in destroying her.

"I should've told you to start. I wanted it to be untrue. So I just didn't..."

Emmy's throat felt like glass daggers.

"I'm glad you told me. Everything makes more sense now. I understand you better. I know you better."

He wasn't glad at all. He wanted to take the long drive to Kentucky and hunt the man down. His thoughts were spinning. It hurt to hear anyone else had been near her heart. The whole story seemed out of place and wrong. Cutter stared into the night, wishing his own confusion would quit. Her body still trembled and he worried he couldn't stop it.

"I can't imagine what's happened at home, Cutter. Ethan is not someone who exaggerates. I'm afraid of the truth, and Henry...it's too much, what I've let happen."

Emmy's heart hit her ribcage with the admittance of her guilt. She should've gone back.

"Have you called the police? Do you know anyone back home that you could call?"

"No, I haven't and I don't. Only one person knows what state I'm in. I was a recluse for so long before I left I'm sure everyone thought I was already dead. Ethan's got so many rich friends anyway, he would just buy himself out of whatever trouble he got into. The whole town is run on his money, including the police. Well, except for Henry."

"Jesus," Cutter exhaled.

Emmy's heart sank. Whatever excitement she had for his surprise had been completely extinguished. She had ruined Cutter's night. She could feel him breathing deeply behind her, and she was too afraid to ask what he was thinking. After a confession like that, she was sure he'd retract whatever interest he had in her. No one wanted spoiled goods. She could face that reality tomorrow. She closed her heavy eyes and submitted to the exhaustion curling around her. Tonight she would savor the last night she'd have with him. She pressed her lips once against his chest before falling asleep in his arms, completely drained.

She muttered in small fits, apologizing to Henry and Cutter interchangeably under her breath. She cried softly and her jaw clenched when she was silent. Cutter only continued to hush and coo to her, helplessly trying to chase her unsettled deams away. He wondered how many nights were filled with restless sleep like this. He gently patted her shoulder.

"Emmy," he called softly.

Her eyes flew open with a start and her hands strained straight. Cutter wrapped his arms tightly around her until the recognition of her surroundings came. She turned to looked up at him through half opened eyes. Her mouth parted to speak, but he placed his fingertips against her lips and shook his head.

"Emmy, you're safe with me," he hushed. "I am not going to let anyone hurt you again."

She blinked as he lifted her face up towards him.

"I don't care what's happened to you. There is something that draws me to you, Emmy. Nothing can deter it. I don't know what it is, or what it means. I can't explain it. But I will keep you safe. You aren't alone anymore."

A small sob escaped from her throat and she wrapped her arms around his neck. A pinch in the back of her mind softened. All the time she'd spent trying to be strong was finally over.

"I'm so tired, Cutter. So tired of running from the fear, so tired of running from my memories. I'm tired of hating myself and doing everything wrong. I'm tired of living in the past. I'm sorry I'm so screwed up, I'm just so tired."

He kissed her forehead and his fingers spiraled against her back.

"You must be tired. It's okay now, just rest."

"Cutter?"

"Mmhm?"

"Can we go lie down? I think I'd like that," her voice sounded thick in her own ears.

He smiled against her hair. He gathered her in his arms to help her rise.

"Yes, we can do that."

They walked to the tent and Cutter unzipped it. She crawled in, a smile edging at the outskirts of her mouth. He had covered the floor in layers of blankets and pillows. It reminded her of something in a children's book. She let Cutter slip off her shoes to keep outside and waited for him to crawl in. They sat for a minute, awkwardly staring at the blankets. Cutter realized he hadn't slept next to a woman since he left home.

He pushed his own past with strength from his mind, too indulged in making sure Emmy felt comfortable. Cutter smiled, and pulled her to him, stroking her hair. They spoke not a word, afraid to break the fragile comfort zone they were exploring. When he felt the weight of her body lean into him, he slowly lowered himself to the ground with her securely wrapped in his arms. His head hit the pillow and she snuggled deeper in the crook of his shoulder.

"You're safe with me, Emmy."

She listened to the rich tone of his beating heart and her eyes grew heavy. He lay awake until he felt her sleeping. She stirred only to tangle her legs in his, innocently grappling for the warmth of his body and he smiled contently.

The night stirred as they slept. Whispers and hushed grunts jumped between the mountain peaks as men moved in silence. Shadowy figures shifted noiselessly in the distance of the tent with curiosity. The horses nickered in the pines and one of the men noticed.

"They recognize her," he whispered.

*Chapter Sixteen*

Lillian sighed and leaned against the wall once she was certain Dougal left. The moonflower oil had worked. She walked to the sink in her mixing room and scrubbed her hands. The thought of deceiving anyone bothered her and using herbalism to negatively alter anyone was even worse. Once the oil was thoroughly cleansed, she wiped her hands and walked through the shop, preparing to open. Dougal would be at least four days checking in on those addresses. She had at least that long to see what Aillig had hidden for her at the other two. Tomorrow, she'd travel to the PO Box.

Lillian turned an aisle and jumped. Mrs. Bixby waited at the front door. Too nearsighted without her glasses, she pressed her face against the window with squinted eyes. Lillian's pulse subsided and the elderly woman smiled as she unlocked the door.

"Well hello, Mrs. Bixby," Lillian greeted patiently, having snagged a glance at the time. "I'm not open for another half an hour."

"I'm sorry, dear," she cooed, shuffling her way in, "I'm afraid I'll be leaving town in an hour for a vacation and I had to pick up my week's subscriptions beforehand. I hope I'm not imposing too terribly."

"No, not at all. Why don't you have some tea while you wait."

Lillian fixed a chamomile orange infusion to settle the woman's hurriedness and made a mental note of what she needed to pull for the order.

"This is quite lovely, dear. Thank you, really. I'm going to miss it."

"I'll be here when you return, Mrs. Bixby," Lillian laughed from an aisle over.

"The trouble is, I'm not sure I will be back."

Mrs. Bixby ran a frail finger across the rim of her empty cup, trying to force the shaking from her hands. She knew the tea would calm her, but not quickly enough. Seeing Dougal at the shop the other day had left her startled.

Lillian rolled her eyes from behind the shelves before rounding the corner with a double order. Mrs. Bixby was marked by her nervous flare, as sweet as she was.

"Well, that's unfortunate. I hope this permanent vacation suits you?"

Mrs. Bixby looked fondly at the girl now perched on the chair across the table from her. Hopefully, Aillig had the presence of mind to set her up with a road of escape before he died. Even though he had been distraught before his death, Mrs. Bixby had to have faith in his intuition. It seemed the whispered prophecy between her sisters may carry some weight after all. She planned quickly to visit them down south to tell of what she'd seen and to ensure they were safe as well. If Dougal's superiors were planning to make a move, they could all be in danger. Strange things were shifting and Lillian seemed to be in the center of it. Her shop had been crawling with indecent people and Lillian seemed too frazzled to notice. She would know soon if Aillig hadn't lost his kenning. Her eyes grew damp and her voice teetered.

"I'm afraid there's been some trouble and I've to go to my sister's."

"Oh, there, there," Lillian fussed, suddenly alarmed. "Have some more tea. I'm sure it will be fine. Time with your sister sounds lovely, really. Doesn't it?"

Her wrinkles smoothed and a faint smile curled the edges of her mouth. "Yes, I suppose it does."

"Good," Lillian said patting her hand. She pushed her care package across the consulting table.

"The second bag is from me."

"You are too kind, my dear."

Lillian shrugged and raised her brows.

"Have fun, Mrs. Bixby."

Lillian was thankful for the extra chamomile tea she had laying around. She had thrown a tin in for the poor woman. She walked her to the door and watched until the horizon swallowed her in the mist of morning. She flipped her sign and watched her first appointment approach. Lillian had a feeling it would be a very long day.

The apothecary seemed busier than usual. Lillian bustled through shelves and scribbled receipts. It was uncanny how much product was being pushed out and she thought for a moment with some resignation that she'd be taking work home with her the next few days. The time she'd usually dedicate to mixing had been swallowed with Dougal's intrusion. With his pushing presence removed, she could finally focus more clearly on important matters.

Through the rush of bodies passing between the aisles of her shop, Lillian had noticed a handful of new customers. It was refreshing to see some younger faces and she was eager to open the realm of healing to them. They wouldn't find silly things like love spells but they may find aromatherapy oils to encourage self confidence. She almost giggled as she made notes to mix some new products over the next week. When the last customer had gone, she locked up feeling more exhausted than she had anticipated.

The long walk home provided decompression from the day, and her free mind wandered back to what she had chosen not to think about. She carried them with her for a reason. They called to her attention now as she caressed them in her pocket, toying with the softening edges. The words were sweet and romantic, just as she had pictured him in her dream. The writing was clear in her mind's eye as she dazed off alongside the road. The passing homes were blinking in her peripheral vision like Morse Code. The night was cooler than usual and her skin prickled under her oversized wool sweater. She'd never heard of ghosts infiltrating a person's mind. The idea didn't seem entirely impossible, but Lillian couldn't understand the purpose. She was not interesting or worth being reached out to. Nor was she smart enough to understand how it worked. It had become easy for her to decipher the madness for herbalism and healing, but now that the message had changed, it was strange to her again.

She gripped the paper more tightly and quickened her pace. It sounded too close to the church's stories of evil possession. Flashes of her childhood morbidly bombarded her mind as her only point of reference. Sister Roy's disapproval tightened her back. The darkness of evening allowed shadows to slip around her. Lillian felt as though she were doomed to live in fear. She quickened toward her porch light in the distance, locking onto the glow until it seemed to swallow her whole. She couldn't be controlled again, by human or ghost. The pressure hung behind her. She moved faster, too aware that she was alone in the night. Her heart beat in her throat and she prayed to make it to her cottage unharmed. The door slammed behind her and she slumped to the floor. Her chest rose and fell from exertion and her legs shook with adrenaline. She pressed her palms against the floor and stared down the hallway, confused. She was completely unsure of what was happening to her. She hadn't been this unravelled in years and she didn't like that she was dusting off her stability. Lillian tried to remember the last time the darkness outside scared her like that. She closed her eyes and slowed her breathing, trying to find a trigger in a multitude of possibilities.

Lillian gave into her childhood memories. The more she fought against their presence, the worse their affect seemed to become. Refusing their existence was becoming tiresome. Her mind turned to a particular night when she was fourteen and had snuck out to watch the Moonflowers bloom. She shot up from the ground, and walked down her hallway, pushing open the door to her mixing room, half expecting to see Father Crassus waiting to scold her for sneaking out.

The Father's nervous, contorted face flashed before her. His eyes had been distant that night and his heinous twitching had been redirected to her presence. His dry and cracking lips muttered madly in her ear as he grasped at her, picking at her robe with obsession. She had frozen into silence next to the moonflower, scrambling to release herself from his hold. He chased after her when she fled deeper into the garden, diving into the thick rose bushes and crawling mercilessly through the thorns to escape him. She sat shivering through the night, praying to God to save her as she listened to him wander in mindless chatter with himself. God had not saved her. Just as the sun began to break the horizon, she snuck herself back into bed before the Sisters made their morning rounds. Father Crassus had been found shortly after and quietly rushed to the hospital for poisoning. The whispers between the nuns had revealed his attempt to relieve his addiction to LSD by ingesting the seeds of the moonflower.

Lillian's eyes glazed as she searched for the flowers she had used earlier. She went to her press and found no trace of the oil lingering where the crushed flowers lay. Her equipment was clean, but the refining tools were not. She ran her finger through the debris from her refining tool, and in a moment of desperation, coated her gums with the last of the oil, hoping to dull her violated encounter with past atrocities. The room grew fuzzy and her heart slowed. She sat against the door frame, hoping that the potency could bring her away from the rotted image of Crassus' sickly hands and give her a break from her troubles. Lillian felt the blood coursing thick through her veins.

Aillig had told her ingesting the seeds could be lethal and that to provide them to anyone could be a responsibility over their life. Her attention faded from the past as the oil absorbed into her pores. She knew she hadn't used enough to worry, she had seen Aillig cut larger amounts with Valerian Root to aid her insomnia when the nightmares were too intense.

Her reality was manipulated and it wasn't long before she felt the shadow moving in her mixing room. Lillian sat against the wall, her nerves completely dull. She could feel her fingers curling around her ankles as the darkness shifted from one corner and moved towards her. Lillian's eyes grew heavy from the moonflower's effects. Her hair swayed gently in front of her breasts and a weight wrapped around her hands. Her breathing deepened and she barely heard the whisper before the world around her went dark.

"*Auxilium meministis.*"

Lillian rose to her knees and groped her way down the hall without vision. She could feel her fingers tremble. The shadow was following carefully behind her, she could feel it. Her body moved too slow and she felt like crying. Dreaming of him was one thing, but hearing voices with open eyes was too much. Lillian collapsed into bed, exhausted from working against her drugged reality. Worried whispers lingered in the air. Lillian clasped her hands over her ears and waited for the moonflower to wear off. Hours would pass before relief came.

*They stood, waiting for her to accept him. He looked so deeply into her eyes she could feel her head buzzing and the blue eyed woman reached our her hand. Light curled around the corners of Lillian's peripheral, weaving together, building a wall of translucent hexagons. He tried to reach out for her, call her over the wall before it got to high, but Lillian didn't move. The sound grew louder and vibrated in her chest. She covered her ears and screamed against the high frequency. She reached out to push the shimmering curtain away and it shocked her fingertips before turning black. She had lost him again and turned away.*

Her eyes opened and she licked her lips. Lillian reached for her pen and paper to write down what she had heard now that she could move her arms on command. She rose delicately and went to the refrigerator for water, letting it fall down her throat, fighting the last of her grogginess. She thought of her moonflower vines in the garden and frowned darkly, starting the kettle to make ginkgo black tea. She felt weak for using the oil to suppress her fears. She dressed and readied for work. Lillian wasn't sure what was getting into her. She would have never thought to take advantage of her healing knowledge like that. She straightened her bed before work, catching a glance at the paper stained with ink. Cautiously, she picked it up, and folded it into her pocket without reading. She would deal with it when her mind was sound again. She left the house later than she liked and set a brisk pace to her shop. There was too much to catch up on at the store to worry about what was happening to her. All the strange riddles and notes were only dragging her back to a stagnant past. Including her planned lunch errand to the PO Box.

"This is getting incredibly out of hand, I don't have any more time for it," she huffed stubbornly.

She couldn't understand why Aillig's ghost wouldn't just come to her and explain it. She could see ghosts after all. Lillian suddenly grew angry and she wanted to blame the madness on his memory. If she wasn't strange enough to summon help from the dead then she would be better off forgetting them. The mental list of what she needed to do just in her apothecary was long and she could feel the stress of what she couldn't understand weakening her. She unlocked the door to her shop, went straight to her desk, and shoved all the loose papers from her pockets into the drawer, pushing it closed.

"What does it matter," she muttered to herself. "The man's gone. No sense in living in the past. It certainly hasn't helped me with anything."

Lillian made the firm decision to give no more concern to the strange circumstances of her recent life. She couldn't be pushed to a limit that allowed her to misuse her craft. She wasn't going to solve the mystery of her hauntings. She wasn't going to think about Sister Roy. She wasn't going to visit the PO Box, she was done. She walked to her mixing room. Though the air felt heavy, she gave it no attention and forced the familiar follower from her thoughts as she closed the door.

"Whoever you are, I do not want to be bothered."

She could feel what was now a constant presence subside and withdraw from her proximity. Loneliness filled his absence. She ignored it. It was time to simplify. Her life up north would not require her to go beyond what she knew she was capable of. She would focus on the only important thing in her life. Mixing never abandoned her, never scared her, and never asked her to be more than what she was. It provided the comfort she sought so desperately now that her entire life had been turned upside down with mysterious murder and dead houseguests. She glanced at the list of things she needed to restock. The shop was closed for two days after this for inventory. Lillian welcomed the idea of some downtime from clients to catch up on all the chores she had been neglecting.

........

The man cursed as he was pushed out of his projection.

"I went too far. Now we can't even get to her. She's too scared by what she can't understand."

"She'll come back to us. Her past lives are aligned too strongly to allow her ignorance."

Aillig sat back against the crude wall of their confines. He contemplated the power of their adversary's lineage and tried to push the doubt from his mind before his young student could pick up on it.

"But the prophecy! She's supposed to awaken to her destiny, to me! How can she come back to us if she thinks I'm only a ghost?"

Aillig glanced at him solemnly.

"My young hero, a prophecy is never set in stone. Hers has been written many times, in many lives, and it hasn't yet been fulfilled."

He started feeling helpless as Aillig spoke and his death approached too quickly. He didn't have time.

"Then why bother," he sighed. "We have failed her."

"Do not think so low at the first complication, man. She has the power of nine in this life, the number of completion, the definition of our philosophy as druids. If ever a life of hers existed to succeed in bringing Enlightenment it would be this one. I will need to explain this philosophy to you soon. And the rest of what I know about her prophecy."

The young man's fair hair fell from its leather plait, dirtied from imprisonment. He wasn't hearing the druid anymore. The concept of reality he was brought up to understand had not been taught to her. The truth about a human's existence had been stripped from her learning and he was losing faith in his ability to show her. His legacy was soon to pass and all he wanted was to spend his last undecided amount of days in her company, even if they could not save her. He ran grubby fingers through his mustache.

"How are we going to reach her when it seems we are eons apart?"

"We are only separated by a delicate veil created from the concept of time. She has already started to accept your presence. Keep your faith, she is going to need it."

*Chapter Seventeen*

    *Cutter sat next to her along the creekside. Her eyes were ignited with daring. Emmy slowly lifted the hem on her long skirt and his eyes widened. She stood to wade in the water, turning to look at him over her shoulder, her legs bracing against the current. Cutter walked in to meet her. As the water rose, her hair shone in a million different colors and swirled all around her shoulders. Transfixed on the growing electricity between them, he extended his arm to cup her breast and thousands of lights burst into memories around them. Through the veil of colors, Emmy could see the woman standing on the other bank. She reached her arm out toward her, breaking the dancing honeycomb of lights, but the woman only turned her back and disappeared.*

    "Emmy," Cutter whispered gently. "It's time to wake up. I want to show you something."

    She stirred slowly to the deep tone of Cutter's voice. The night had passed in moments and Emmy found it difficult to pull herself from sleep. She could hear him, low and sensual, through tired ears and she snuggled into his chest.

    "Okay," she breathed.

    He laughed deeply as she worked against her words.

"Come on, I don't want you to miss it," he smiled.

Emmy pulled her head from the warmth of his body, pushing defiant strands of her golden brown mane from her face, eyes piercing blue through reluctant lashes. Cutter reached out to tuck a piece of hair behind her ear, eyes shining.

"You ready?" he asked.

"Okay." Her full lips curled.

He unzipped the tent, and offered his hand. The sun was young and did not yet sting Emmy's raw eyes. She inhaled deeply and absorbed her surroundings, trying to cleanse herself of last night. The faint crunch of loose stone shifted beneath their feet as they walked. The strong gust from last night's hike drew closer and as the fog worked out of her head, she could hear the birds sing behind her. The faint sound of lapping water grew louder. They rounded a hillside and the small lake came into view.

In the turmoil of reaching their destination, she must not have noticed it in the darkness, nor heard it over the gales of the hilltop. It licked sheepishly at them as they walked along the rim.

"I had no idea," Emmy breathed in delight.

"No one does but us, Emmy. No one thinks to ride up this way because you can't see it. From down there it only looks like another rolling hill."

They stood at the edge of the hilltop and Cutter watched Emmy soak it in. The wind pushed the hair from her collarbones as it snapped and swirled behind her. His hand wrapped more tightly around hers.

"Cutter, this is the landscape in the photograph!"

The color was sucked away into shades of blacks and whites, and each rolling hill was filled with the texture of a painter's brush. Emmy's eyes slowed as she savored each detail in front of her, allowing herself to be engulfed into the image that had once bewitched her.

"Only it's different," she said minutes later.

"Yes." Cutter smiled.

"We are on the far end of it, near the mountains aren't we?"

Standing at the crest of his sanctuary, she looked like a natural goddess, melting into the heaven of the land around them. She had been fearless in the face of her pain, and he had only buried his. He didn't feel worthy. He moved to stand behind her, wrapping his arms snuggly around her waist, pressing his lips gently to her ear.

"It was early on a Sunday morning," he spoke against the wind, "when I took that photograph. I had been upset about the chain of events that had lead me here. I was feeling particularly uncomfortable to live in Wyoming. So I decided to walk. No manipulated influences. Just the honesty of the land around me. I was thinking of home. Los Angeles. When I realized I wasn't sure where I was going to go, I stopped and looked at the incredible variations in the land ahead of me. It reminded me of the twists and turns in our own lives, so I snapped a photo of it. I wanted to walk through all of its textures, its rises and falls. I wanted to get to the end and turn around to see if it still looked the same as it did from the beginning."

"Was it?"

"It had grown familiar and less daunting. The jagged mountains stood at my back, and only the soft, rolling hills rolled in the breeze."

"What made you leave home?"

Cutter kissed the top of her head and squeezed her tightly, taking down the wall he had built so carefully.

"I was born and raised in Los Angeles. I lived with my mom. I grew up with nothing. She started drinking when I was a little kid. The stress of making ends meet was too much for her. By the time I was seventeen, I was the one taking care of her. Our relationship crumbled. She was angry and quit working. I'd wander around the city when I should've been with her. I used photography to distract myself, an excuse not to go home and listen to the screaming and crying. I didn't know how to handle it."

Emmy listened to the strain in his usual velvet toned voice as he spoke. She closed her eyes and felt the short rise and fall in Cutter's chest.

"I started seeing this girl. She made me forget what was waiting at home. We went out, drank too much. Soon, my life mirrored all I was trying to escape. The lines between what tortured me and kept me going blurred. My pictures were all fueled with the things I wanted to neglect. I grasped more heavily to my means of escaping and forgetting, drinking and partying harder, becoming my mother and not caring."

"I walked in on Rachael with some other guy. She was too drunk to even recognize who I was. That was when I realized I didn't even know who I was. I packed my stuff the next morning and left. It wasn't long after that I heard my mother had died from an overdose. I wandered for almost a year, waiting for the numbness to die down. Went east and started back, all of it mostly in a haze except for the photos documenting it. I stopped for gas here one day and stayed."

His arms gripped tighter and tighter around her as he spoke. Cutter had nearly forgotten what he had done and hoped she could see through it to the man he now was.

"I sound like a horrible person," he admitted.

"You don't, Cutter."

She turned around, burying her face against him. She knew perfectly well what judgement was coursing behind his thoughts. Emmy knew it was time to let the past stay where it belonged. The lake licked at the blue-gray stones behind them, and she finally felt free.

.......

Ms. Beckett's cheeks glistened in the sun like sallow gems. Every door in Henry's house had been broken open and she sat on the porch step with Emmy's letter dangling between her fingers. His body was lifeless behind her, just inside the living room. Life after life they had given into death, but it never got easier to find each other lying as an empty body. Henry hadn't gone peacefully as he had so many times before. She could feel the agitation of the change still lingering in the house, his uprooted energy was still dispersing.

She got up and walked to the kitchen to find a lighter. Behind the closed windows and concealed walls, she burned the only evidence of Emmy's location. Watching the ashes swirl in the air, she couldn't help but feel that this death was more final than before. Something had changed him, made him tired of going peacefully in hopes of protecting his granddaughter. Henry had spoken to her many times about his frustration in not being able to raise Emmy as he wanted. Just as he knew who she could grow to be, so did they. They made it impossible for her to live safely in her honest form. Instead, Henry had to be clever about teaching her, hoping that one day she would put together the puzzle and morph into the soul she had created at birth.

When Ms. Beckett's tears had dried, she walked back out the door through the upturned interior. Whatever they had wanted to find had already been shipped to her vacation home weeks ago. The pattern of their existence prepped her for what came next. Looking around, she thought it was unusual for Ethan to leave such a mess. The contorted truth of his lineage would be obvious to anyone who could see it, and she felt as though the old Roman in him was showing.

She could see the infamous face of a previous life form in her mind as the lunacy of last night lingered around her. This was unmistakably the work of Ethan's notorious past life. Emmy's wasn't the only one being brought to surface by the prophecy. She moved quickly and soundlessly away from the house, knowing his foot soldiers would come to clean up. She needed to pack and leave right away. The pattern was changing and she needed to be ready to adapt.

*Chapter Eighteen*

Lillian woke feeling more secure than she had in weeks. Scents of a tincture lingered as she woke, and she reached for her notepad to scribble it down. It felt satisfying to dream of herbalism again; it'd been far too long. Lillian smiled, letting the paper fall on her bed. Her weekend was nearly over and she looked forward to a long hike in the countryside out of town. She tugged on a green sweater and long skirt before heading to the car. It was unusual for her to feel spontaneous and Lillian was going to take full advantage of it. Getting away from the cottage would help keep her mind off anything that might creep into her sparse freedom.

Lillian had vowed to live outside of her thoughts and felt quite successful. Having caught up on all the responsibilities she had neglected with Dougal's arrival, she finally had some down time for herself. She felt a quiet power curl around her as she drove. The productivity felt satisfying even if she had exhausted herself and most of her supplies. She had gotten ahead of her business demands. Now, without the intensity of her practice, Lillian was determined to keep herself busy. It seemed to drown out what haunted her.

If anything odd started to form, she forced herself to forget it. She was tired of the whimsical distractions. She simplified, shut it out and moved forward. It was the only thing Lillian knew how to do besides healing. Answers about Aillig's death would never come from the imaginative fabrications she had created. All that had come was Dougal's temper and a renewed sense of hurt from digging up old memories. Lillian had worked too hard to let the serenity of her new life slip through her fingers.

The air outside her window chilled her cheeks. Her eyes were wide and ponderous as she glanced at the gentle slope of the mountain tops. Grass rolled in waves, and she forgot about everything outside the very moment she existed in. The pressures of entrepreneurship lifted and the claustrophobia of constantly being alone diminished. The sky seemed bluest this time of year. She wanted to feel free. She pulled into a car park and got out, inhaling her surroundings. She deserved to indulge in the world around her and Lillian's soul was awakened with sensory delight. Her medicine bag hung at her hip as she strode through new country and the outline of a stone wall pulled to her in the distance as she gathered new plant life to study.

The dew from the morning kissed her long skirts as she walked. Plants sang to her in a familiar song and the confines of reality fell away from her. Lillian hummed as she plucked rock rose and maiden pink flowers and set them in her bag. Her mind wandered through the list of uses she could create from them and smiled. The sun was warm she marveled in feeling the breath of what lived around her. The cloak of nature was the comfort she sought from a mother she never knew. It was on a day like this that she could feel the magnitude of the life givers she worked with. She felt expanded and alive in the familiarity of the earth around her.

Hadrian's Wall was deteriorated but no less foreboding as she drew closer. Like so many ancient relics in the country, it had been left for the slow death of time. The Romans had come to conquer a wild land and abandoned it when the native tribes proved to love it more. Lillian identified with the struggle for control. A mild anger stirred in her belly as she imagined the destruction their armies must have brought to the natural world. She looked longingly north of the line and sighed in sympathy for the old tribes that never seemed to recover the kinship they had before Roman invasion.

There was a buzz around her as she finally reached the old stones, and it grew more acute as she passed through an opening in the stone line. Her eyes tightened and the air seemed to constrict around her. The idle curiosity of history blurred. Lillian could feel pressure between her spine and her stomach twisted. She stumbled forward, surprised by the sudden sickness. She searched the details of her surroundings to see what had caused it. The northern countryside pulled at her equilibrium. She fumbled through her medicine bag, making sure she hadn't accidentally come into contact with anything poisonous. The ground rolled underneath her feet and she tried to gain some balance. Memories she didn't have formed behind her eyes and she shut them tight. Lillian fought against the words that tugged for her attention. She had escaped them for a few days, but she was well practiced in the warning signs of another attack, and Lillian knew what was coming.

She wrapped her arms tighter around her waist, hugging into her sweater as she backed to the wall for support. The wind sent her long, inky hair to curl around her back like serpents. The vibration in her ears grew louder. She lowered herself to the ground, trying to recenter. Her head teetered and the whispers returned as if they had never gone. She pressed her palms to her ears and tried not to succumb to the spinning ground. Sweat poured from her temples. She tried to relax.

"Shh, Lillian."

Voices filled her head but there were no faces to find. She glanced over her shoulder, looking south of the wall, and a white light seared her vision. Metal clashed in her ears and misshapen forms moved. She screamed as terror and rage tore through her body. She flung herself to the floor, hoping the cool grass could quench the fire burning her skin. Then silence. It dissipated as quickly as it had come.

Broken Latin lingered in her ear and the recognition of his voice calmed her. She groped for the wall.

"Don't leave me," she whispered as the last of her psychosis trickled away.

Her breath was ragged in the silence. She wiggled her toes to make sure she wasn't dreaming and dug her fingers into the earth. She tried to gain her equilibrium. How she had tricked herself into ignoring her visions and ghosts was beyond her. Lillian whimpered once in surrender. Whatever she had repressed since childhood had been set free after the moonflower incident and would no longer be contained. Lillian's head felt like it would explode from trying to control it. A few days of pretending it wasn't there had only made it worse.

She opened her eyes, looking at the uneven crevices of the ancient wall and rose methodically before heading back to where she parked, feeling sick and uneven. The ground vibrated underneath her feet and the wind blew in gentle waves around her. It was time to accept what was happening and work through it. Aillig would have encouraged her to do that a long time ago. Lillian let the sea of uprooting experiences form a line in her mind as she walked. She looked back on all the strange things that had brought her to this very point, picking through them neatly with resignation. She knew better than anyone that running from problems solved nothing. Without the pressure of stock maintenance and Dougal's demands, Lillian surrendered to what she had put on hold. Since his grumbling brother had come into her life, Lillian's entire perspective on Aillig's death had become possible. For as long as she had lived, she had marked her choices by the safety of common sense and science. Now it seemed to dwindle against the light of all the intuitive emotions she had hidden since Sister Roy. She had unlocked a part of her that she'd hidden since she was a girl, and ignoring it had been a mistake.

Ignoring him had been a mistake.

As much as she wanted to dismiss his existence with theories of logic, she didn't want to lose whatever strange bond she had formed with her ghost. She couldn't explain what had sent her into such a mad spell at the wall, but hearing his whisper was a comfort. Ignoring him had only made her feel isolated.

"If I'm destined to be insane, I suppose it's better than being alone," she sighed with surrendered humor.

Life was shifting again and she would readapt as she always had. She would find her balance in lists and tasks, starting with what she needed to address first. She had the drive home to plan a way into the PO Box. It was time to face her fear and find out what Aillig needed.

.........

His face brightened under the grime as the walls of another prison came back to view.

"We did it, old man."

He jumped up despite the pit of hunger in his stomach.

"For a moment, I thought we'd lost her in that strange vision she had. I thought only the Hooded Spirits were capable of conscious veil walking."

"Aye," Aillig smiled youthfully. "But you mustn't forget your woman once lived as one herself. In fact, she was among the very first of them."

"But if Lillian doesn't know that, how did she do it?"

"An old life of hers must have lived near the wall. Standing in a place of two lives caused her to momentarily live both at once. We have a hard time staying away from what we love most and tend to gravitate towards those places again and again, like her decision to move to her cottage. Whatever was north of that wall was very dear to her at one time."

The young man smiled in hope of his life after death. He worried less about finding her if his memory did not come with him. Lillian was the dearest thing to his heart and he would search for her even if he couldn't remember right away. He glanced to the folds of the druid's robes, afraid of what sacrifice came with maintaining his memory after death. The plan he and Aillig had created for his next life was not a promised outcome. He had learned quickly that nothing was.

"My black dove has shifted back to us," he reminded himself. She was starting to display the strength of her past lives. The corners of his mouth twitched in anticipation.

"Her road will get much darker before the prophecy sheds all its light," Aillig warned. "We must be vigilant. Lillian needs to learn that her dream wakes are not psychosis if she wants to find what has been left for her. I must teach you these ways also. My time is short, they will take me to my death parade soon. You have to be able to walk alone."

The man's strong jaw clenched and his shoulders grew tight. His little dove needed him most now and he would not leave her like he had before.

"Do not upset yourself with it," Aillig determined. "She was happy in those years and she was safe."

The young man had grown accustomed to being read by the druid. But speaking about what weakened his strength never got easier.

"I can't help but wonder if it's me who ruins her life. When I was absorbed with war, it seemed she was happiest. Perhaps I am the cause of all her struggle."

Aillig smiled. "The greatest change comes out of the greatest darkness. We cannot reach the light of morning without walking in the dark of night. When we grow complacent, we lose our sight and fall into line with the control trying to swallow you and I now. The agitation of change will force her to unwind what is tangled. You are the only thing that will wake her from her closed perceptions and link her to the reality of her dreams. She cannot feel complacent in your presence. Her love for you won't allow it."

.......

The sky edged into late afternoon as she pulled into the parking lot of the post office. Nerves fluttered across her chest as she opened the door. She had fabricated a detailed story about being a niece of the deceased. However, it all flew away at the counter. Maeve MacKay sat across from her, smiling in welcome. The woman came to her shop regularly for motherwort tea. The sweet, Scottish lady suffered from bouts of depression and the graying edges of her hair gave it away. Her honeyed eyes twinkled in surprise. There was no way she'd believe Lillian's story, the two had become fairly acquainted.

"Well hello, lass! What brings ye so far south?"

"I took a drive and ended up needing to run an errand. It's not too far from home, really."

Maeve laughed. "Love, when ye never leave your street it must be! What can I do for ye?"

Lillian blushed despite the woman's good hearted nature. She slipped the mailbox number across the smooth countertop and tried not to make eye contact.

"I've come for my PO Box. I set it up and never checked it," she lied, praying it'd work. "I'm afraid I've actually got mail and I've no idea where to pick it up."

Maeve smiled as she studied the address, her eyes widening in delight.

"So you're the one! I was wondering who that sweet man had left it for. Was he your father?"

Lillian hesitated. She adored Mrs. MacKay but didn't want to give anything away. Aillig had been concerned before his death and she couldn't be sure who to trust or what she would need to hide once she opened the mailbox. She smiled elusively and let Maeve interpret it.

"To the right. Third section on the left."

Maeve tried not to give herself away. She had waited years for Lillian to come, unsure when, or if, Aillig would ever tell her. She'd make the phone call after the girl left.

"Thank you," Lillian nodded and made her way.

Her nerves ticked more heavily as she approached. She had no idea what'd be in there. The fear of disappointment was looming over her. After all this time, Lillian might finally have an answer to all her questions. The key shook in her hand as she fumbled to put it in the lock. She cursed under her breath and rudely shoved it in before she had time to think. She opened the door and a puff of stale air sifted to her nose.

Two worn leather bound books sat collecting dust. Whispers circled faintly in her ears and she tried to grasp at them. She'd seen these books a thousand times but couldn't remember where. Perhaps she'd seen them in Aillig's study. Delicately, her ivory fingers grazed the yellowing edges of the closed books, gaining a memory of them. Her surroundings fell away and she could smell the turf from earlier that morning. She could feel the coolness of the damp woods just beyond her house. She could feel the lull of the moonflower. A song rose in her throat, the same song she had sung before the wall. Lillian focused on keeping the visions from spiraling out of control in front of Maeve. Hugging them tightly to her chest, she headed for home, distracted.

"So what did he leave ye? A bucket of gold?" Maeve laughed heartily as Lillian passed.

"No," she said distracted, "just old memories."

The road home did not favor Lillian. Every turn left her more dizzy. Her mind was disoriented and the pressure behind her eyes pierced her vision like shards of glass. She stumbled through her door, clinging tightly to the books. It was not too soon that she reached her bathroom and wretched. She crawled from the toilet and rested against her sink cabinets, wondering why everything seemed to upset her so intensely today. The floor was cold beneath her and she glanced carefully at the books. When stability curled around her, she picked them up and made her way down the hall. She winced under the pressure between her eyes and it took all her concentration to move her long legs to the bed. She set the books aside and took a moment to try and clear the fuzziness that edged around her. Lillian couldn't stand being sick, and the magnitude of the morning had taken its toll. She ran a hand over the cover of the brown leather book. Her green eyes glowed from under half opened lids and her limbs felt subdued. The heady scent of clary sage mixed with something unrecognizable in her nose. Lillian smiled. Aillig had clearly preserved the book in some sort of ritual oil to relax her. The wiry old man knew her too well. Aillig had always known her better than herself. All the nights he had spent waiting for her to startle awake had probably taught him a lot. She could only imagine what she had mumbled to him in her sleep. She ran her fingers fondly across the embossing on the cover. He was still taking care of her.

Though Lillian had never dabbled in anything beyond herbalism, Aillig had always believed in the mysticism of more detailed work. A list of herbs ran across her drifting mind as she tried listing what oil could have been rubbed into the old material. The cover design was worn beyond recognition and in a language she was not familiar with. She could almost see his white hair wagging in front of his face as he mercilessly studied theses pages for something new. She lifted the cover and let the weight hang between her fingers, wandering farther, remembering her own connection to healing wisdom. Her breath grew deeper as she toyed with the edge of the book. Her fingers flipped it open and she could hear the pages whispering, begging to be turned and read.

Her eyes felt heavy from Aillig's coating. A gentle psychosis washed her and Lillian's attention waned from the words on the book. Her palm explored the smooth surface of the first page and the woman appeared, smiling at Lillian. Her eyes were so piercing, so blue. Her hair was set in a challenge of mahogany and gold around her but she had the same sadness, the same loneliness that Lillian had. The sound of horse hooves beat in the distance. A tear rolled down the woman's cheek. The dream of the burning barn called to Lillian and connected with the stranger in her dreams. The face faded away. Lillian was alone.

She flipped the first page without thinking and could smell the aged ink rising to her nose. It reminded her of the spiced apples and roasted hazelnuts of late summer. The paper felt so unusual under her fingertips and just as she started to lift her lids to study what was written on it, she saw the shadow from the corner of her eye. The hair on her arms stood and her trance slowly fell away.

Lillian remained still in her fluent state, allowing her heart to override her fear. She tried to erase the haunting ideas of her caregivers. She wanted to accept the shadow man's comfort. Lillian forced a smile, pushing her self ridicule to the back of her mind. The edge of her bed bent. A deep whisper floated to her ears; the broken Latin. The harder she strained to hear, the fainter it became. She let her body go heavy against her sheets, feeling hopeless. She didn't understand how to communicate. Her hair moved off her cheek. She didn't move. A pair of lips delicately pressed into her forehead.

"*Invenies in statu... Ego te semper amavi*," he whispered.

She gasped lightly as the deep voice lingered in her ear. She felt her hand float to her pen and paper to write it down. Before she could let logic pass over her, she ached for the man that did, or didn't, exist. Her mind cleared and the weight in the air dissipated. She grabbed the translation book still on her nightstand to figure out what he had said. Her throat clamped shut.

"You will find me in stillness... I have always loved you," she whispered, tears collecting in her eyes.

........

He pulled away from her, unprepared for the moment he'd waited so long for. His eyes grew wet and he stared into the darkness of the prison. She'd finally allowed the stillness of acceptance to open the barriers between them.

"I've done it, Aillig," he whispered into the empty air.

His heart faltered and weakness overcame him. He wished that the druid could have seen it. They had already hanged him in the square of the village. The young man cried for his departed friend. The last of Aillig's people no longer existed here. He had to continue on the path Aillig had left in front of them. Aillig had veil walked to his future self before his capture and taught him the ancient, Egyptian oil on the books so that Lillian could be subdued for their next attempt of communication. They had been working together since Lillian had come to live with him.

The druid had instructed him to use the same oil to reach out to her once the books were in her possession, hoping to accelerate the possibility of her acceptance. Never did he think it'd actually work. She had finally seen him, and tried to know him for what he really was. His teachings in prison couldn't fail him now. The light that had been left by her old lives was finally reignited. Lillian would need help deciphering the truth. The books were the first step to Aillig's grand plan. The young man smiled. Tomorrow he would try to contact her without the druid's oil. The excursion of veil walking weakened him and he needed to rest. It was time to evolve the prophecy by letting love shed light into Lillian's lost memories.

........

Dawn had come quickly after a dreamless night and Lillian walked toward her bathroom already lifted from the scent of rock rose sliding beneath the bathroom door. She felt in tune with herself, even if a little shaky from yesterday. The man had confessed his undying love for her, and as strange as it all seemed, Lillian woke undeniably happy.

Her towel was wrapped lazily around her body. She opened the door and smiled. The water idled euphorically, interrupted only by waning bubbles. Her antique tub was oversized with brass knobs and the small window behind shed the gentle light of morning. Lillian turned to her counter to twist her hair atop her head before dipping in. The dry, delicate floral notes were warmed with a scent of amber as the bath oils filled the room. They proved to bring her to a still, meditative state. She was testing the flowers near the wall. The warming aroma could easily be pulled into a unisex perfume.

Lillian had one more day to herself before needing to worry about business, and she looked forward to scouring Aillig's old books. She hummed, quietly content with the possibility of still learning from sweet Aillig and for the potential to clear the mystery glowing around him.

She turned toward the bath. Her body stiffened. The shadow man stood behind the tub, his bare chest toned in the waning light. He smiled gently, hands resting in quiet strength against the rim of the tub as he waited for her to calm. A whisper reached her ear and she stared, hands grasped tightly against her towel. Lillian was certain she was awake and yet the man that came to her in dreams was standing right in front of her. She hadn't seen a ghost awake since she was seven in the church gardens. She was staring at a naked man. She should be afraid. But he was so beautiful. The shock of his presence vibrated in her chest.

"It's been me since we were children," he spoke in a rugged tongue, damning himself in his struggle to learn her language. He had been listening to it his whole life and felt inadequate now as he hoped to impress her. His heart beat wildly in his chest.

Lillian felt light headed from the vision. His gentle, silvery blue eyes lead her to a calmness, her breathing slowed and the longevity of knowing him was completely realized. He had been with her since they were children. He had always been there for her. She'd wanted him her whole life without giving a single thought to it. His broad shoulders relaxed slightly in understanding and he outstretched his palm in invitation.

She delicately made her way to the edge of the bath.

"Nolite timere," he choked, reaching out his hand, glad he had been forced to learn Latin.

*Don't be afraid.*

He stepped to the side and his full body was exposed. Her heart tumbled in butterflies as one muscular leg followed the other into the bath. Her face was hot with prudish embarrassment. He didn't fit with modern propriety. He didn't care that his entire body was exposed. She suddenly wondered where he came from, what life he once lived. Here was a man who loved her and she knew nothing about him. All the years she had spent griping about being alone were a falsity. He had been waiting for her to listen to him the whole time. She could recall so many dreams and whispers that she had ignored. Lillian's heart sank. He was the lonely one. She forced the voice demanding that he wasn't real from her temples. She couldn't allow herself to kill his presence with logic. Lillian just wanted to feel loved.

The soap covered his body irregularly and she felt her cheeks flush in modesty. She stepped forward and loosened the grip on her towel. Lillian could not deny the pulsing in her veins. She looked at him in sheer bravery. She had waited her whole life to feel connected to someone. Her towel grew looser around her body. He frowned.

"Paenitet me non possum."

*Sorry I can't.*

Sorrow swept across his face and he vanished.

She glared into the empty tub, letting one tear fall down her cheek before stepping in the scented water, his last words burning into her memory as she washed.

......

He let his projection fade with practiced celibacy. In his excitement of her breakthrough, the years of waiting for Lillian had blinded him and his subconscious had projected his astral form to paralleled the emotional nudity he gave to her. The forces of awareness it'd take to truly feel each other was nearly impossible. He could intercept her innocent heart breaking upon his denial. He was here to protect Lillian and that was not the right way. He swore one day they would be together, but only when the fabrication of time wasn't weaving between them.

*Chapter Nineteen*

After a busy morning shift, Emmy found herself lying heavily in her bed, the afternoon light rinsing the walls of her motel room. She closed her eyes and could feel the dust tickle her cheeks. Thought and dream mingled in her mind as slumber called to her.

*She ran after the horses who had broken through a fence at the rodeo grounds. Her limbs strained as she pushed herself to keep them in sight, extending further with every stride until her body fell forward and she dug her hands into the ground to keep moving. Emmy exhaled once and felt her body change into one of the herd. She could hear her nostrils flare and her hooves pound into the ground. Her heart sang as she caught them.*

*Indians rode alongside, whispering words she couldn't decipher. When she glanced over to the men, her delicate ears could hear the bones chiming in their hair. She saw the dark haired woman. Her arms were wrapped tightly around one of the men and she looked gently into Emmy's equestrian eyes. She parted her lips to whisper to Emmy, reaching a hand to touch her mane. A red Celtic cross was painted in her palm. Emmy shifted back to human form and reached out towards her. Knocking rang in her ears and the wind rushed in her head. She was pulled backwards into darkness.*

Emmy sat up in bed with a start as she unwrinkled her surroundings. The air no longer stirred, the walls felt stale. A knock came again and her heart stopped.

"Emmy."

She exhaled and stood to open the door. Cutter leaned against the door frame in greeting.

"I have a surprise for you."

She stepped sleepily into his lips, wrapping her arms around him.

"What is it?" she sighed breathlessly.

"Come with me."

It didn't take long for Emmy to figure out where they were going. The road had become familiar enough and she relaxed as it spun under them. She thought about the change between her and Cutter since they shared secrets on the hilltop. There was a sense of strength weaving them together. She had come a far way since the first time they met. Henry had been strict in making sure she understood mistakes were vital teachers. Without them, the truth was difficult to navigate, and they gave value to what made a heart sing. He never wanted her to live in shame of the decisions she made in life. Emmy glanced instinctively to her side, feeling grateful to have met Cutter because of her mistakes. She slid her hand against the console to weave her fingers with his. When they pulled up to the Big House, Emmy's stomach twisted in anticipation.

"Cutter, what's your surprise?"

The waning afternoon sighed at their backs. Though the sun had an hour or so to set, Emmy could feel its energy burning closer to her neck and the anxious feeling grew worse. She knew it wasn't from the excitement of not knowing what was coming. Something didn't feel right. He said nothing and lead her way around the main house, avoiding the guests readying for dinner.

"Cutter, can't you tell me? I can't stand this nervous feeling."

"We're almost there," he said smiling, squeezing her hand.

She sighed reluctantly and wished she could calm the small pit in her stomach. The faint aroma of alfalfa lingered on the wind. They turned a corner and Emmy's throat tightened. The wooden logs of the pen were thick and lonesome in the landscape, bleached from so many summers in the sun.

"Cutter," Emmy whimpered.

She caught the sight she nearly dreaded most. Two horses sat idly, tacked and waiting for them.

"Don't you have to work?" she begged pathetically.

"No, Sundays are typically rest days, and evening supper is tended by the land owners for Sunday prayer." He paused and looked at his hands. "And since I'm not exactly religious," he trailed off, grinning lopsidedly at her.

"Oh," she mumbled, shifting her weight.

"Look, last weekend on the hills, I could tell what the horses meant to you. Plus, we end up by the range herd every Saturday night at the rodeo. It's crazy the way they respond to you."

"But, Cutter," she interrupted skittishly, "I can't ride. I don't deserve that gift after what I've done. They'll know what's happened, they always can."

Cutter smiled, gently pulling her against his chest. He wanted to help heal her. He stood silent a few moments, preparing for her heart breaking refusal if her nerves weren't capable. He stroked her hair, thinking of a way to coax her. He smiled sheepishly. What he was about to say could be dangerous ground to tread.

"Emmy, just try," he cooed. "Try because Henry would be happy for it."

She shot her head back faster than he'd anticipated. Icy blue eyes nearly leveled him as they worked through the delicate bait he dangled. Just as quickly as it had come, the storm passed.

"You're right," she sighed with resignation. "He could stand what I've done, but not what I'm doing."

She tried calling for the comfort of her grandfather and couldn't feel it. It'd been gone for days now and she tried not to consider what it meant.

"Ready?"

She nodded, her heart pounding in her throat. She could feel her palms getting clammy but Cutter's confidence never waned. The two quarter horses stood unbothered by Emmy's shaking. Her legs ached to feel the back of a horse again, but her head wouldn't allow it. It had been so long since she was capable of opening her heart to riding. Ethan had kept her from it for so long, claiming that it made her devilish and hard to deal with. It was a cruel thing to have done. Tears collected in her throat and she ached to reconnect to what made her feel alive.

"You can ride Apollo," Cutter nearly whispered. "Goose is my work horse, he's the bay on the far side."

Emmy let out a nervous laugh as she lay a shaking hand on Apollo's thick neck. His attention shifted towards her. A horse's eye saw nothing but truth. She was staring into the face of her guilt. Emmy blew her fear into the air. His nostrils flared once in response but his body stood stoic. She reached to the horn of the saddle, lifting the bridle from where it hung. Emmy wasn't sure she could do it. Energy was building fast inside of her and rattled in between her ribs.

"Are you sure they're okay to use? I mean, haven't they been working hard all week?" she stalled, looking at Cutter.

"No, Apollo isn't ridden by our guests yet. He's newer to the herd and still getting acclimated to his new home," he smiled.

Emmy's eyes widened. This was her last chance to escape.

"Shouldn't he be ridden awhile first? What if he flips out away from the property?"

"I've been working with him all week," Cutter lied. "You'll be fine."

With no other option, she turned, quietly slipping off his halter. He curled his head around her to take the bit. She whispered Gaelic into his ear and it flicked once in response. In one silent motion, Emmy slipped her foot in the stirrup and swung up into the saddle. Cutter watched breathlessly. It was just as he dreamt it.

"You getting on?" she teased, distracting herself from the wave of emotion washing over her.

"Ready," he laughed, springing into the saddle with ease.

The sun hung lazily in the sky ahead of them. He didn't want to tell Emmy that Apollo had been hauled in only days ago, launching out of the trailer like the reincarnate of hell. He had seen her unbelievable communication with the most wild herds at the rodeo grounds. They were naturally drawn to her and Apollo thus far seemed to be under her spell too. His surprise was going according to plan this time.

"We'll be back before sunset, just a quick test drive," he muttered.

She only smiled. Emmy was rigid with guilt, though her spirit warmed to being on a horse's back again. An electricity coursed through her body and she looked to see if Cutter could sense the change she felt. Apollo's muscled back shifted underneath her; he recognized it.

Emmy admired his shining, pitch black coat as she reached a clammy palm to stroke his neck. Kentucky melted away as her fingertips slipped over his shoulder. She was intoxicated by him. Her bones felt alive. There was something empowering about containing a thousand pound animal between the strength of her thighs. A breeze rushed around her, lifting the bottom of her T-shirt to press dangerously against her knotted stomach. His feet danced nervously in response to her own excitement. Emmy's back was taut, but her shoulders were relaxed as she hushed the tightly coiled animal underneath her. A gale grew behind them and pushed at their back, spinning Emmy's hair all around her. Without warning, Apollo shot upward. Emmy's legs flexed and Henry's focus game started to take over. Her vision blurred. His hooves hit the ground. She pressed her heels into Apollo's side and they took off.

"Get it out of our system," she whispered.

Apollo's hooves ground deeper into the Wyoming dirt, her body reaching forward, melting into his. Each muscle coiled and exploded under the desperate speed for freedom. Her delicate fingers twined through his dark mane. His night coated ears lay flat against his skull and she found herself baring her teeth against the cracking of the wind. The summer grass turned fluidly gold at their sides. Her heart pounded as his did, her breath ragged as his was. The atmosphere fell away from them, and the only measure of time that existed was in the pounding of his feet. She could feel his dorsal muscles shifting beneath her body as he maneuvered effortlessly through the brush. Her own body felt as though it floated. The sky grew darker and Emmy felt the walls of her surroundings fade. She lost the feeling in her body. The light was weaving them together.

The gentle rise of the hills fast approached them and she spotted riders in the distance. Indians. She dropped herself lower, and Apollo thrust from his hindquarter to fly uphill. She could see their white hair and the bones that hung from it. Old, wrinkled faces beckoned to her. The ground leveled beneath them and she made herself sit upright, pulling away from him and the snapping of light around her. She blinked her eyes and tried to clear whatever she thought she'd seen from her mind. Apollo slowed to a stop. Emmy was dizzy and disoriented from forcing herself out of the connection. Her entire body throbbed and she fell forward onto Apollo's thick neck. No one was there to greet her.

The gusts on the hilltop tangled their hair together like midnight on fire and his amber eyes quietly steadied below them as she lay panting into his silky coat. Weightless and exhausted, Emmy closed her eyes halfway. An outrageous fire burned out of them both, like the late sun that seemed to return to their surroundings. She saw no one, heard no one. Whatever world she had glimpsed was not this one and she was angry that it wasn't real. Emmy was searching for something, but she had broken the connection Henry had taught her to use. She had never been able to hold onto it, and now she'd lost whatever reached for her because she'd abandoned Henry. She relented to her tears. She cried one last time for the horses she lost. She cried for the bond she could not understand and for being deprived of feeling it in Kentucky. Henry would have loved to see her practicing the game he had taught her so long ago. Apollo nickered nervously and Emmy sat up, wiping the wetness from under her eyes. Cutter was loping up to them from below.

His strong back flexed in confidence and long, lean thigh muscles moved with the horse's movement in quiet companionship. His hands were gentle and still, and relaxed on the horn as he stopped beside her. His grin was wide, cutting his face into beautiful angles. She smiled and forced herself back into the present moment, echoes of Henry's laughter dissipating with the wind that calmed around her.

"Seriously, Emmy, I knew it! I knew this would happen," Cutter stuttered through his exuberance. "I had a feeling you could ride, but man!"

"Knew what?" she muttered, distant and exhausted.

"And the way he just bolted! You made it look simple!"

"Cutter, know what?"

"I cannot wait to tell Roger about this!"

"Cutter!"

He whipped his head around, green eyes glowing brightly against his honeyed skin. She swallowed hard.

"Cutter what did you know?" she nearly whispered, knees weakening.

He smiled devilishly before he spoke. Apollo shifted his weight.

"I have never ridden Apollo," he said slowly shaking his head. "No one has."

"What do you mean?"

"He came in a few days ago. His owners thought putting him in big pastures would take some of the fire out of him. Roger didn't see his potential but when they were hopeless to control him, he felt bad and took him in. He came in the trailer quiet enough, but the second the boys opened the gate, he busted out and it took me hours just to get him saddled and tied. When I tried lifting a boot to his stirrup, he went straight up. But you!" he exclaimed, running his hands through his hair, "you got right on him! Do you know what that means?"

She shook her head, watching her fingers slide through Apollo's mane. "No. But whatever it means, Roger doesn't need to know. Or anyone else."

What she had was sacred between her and Henry. She wasn't supposed to show it to anyone. She learned the hard way by trying to show Ethan.

Cutter laughed. "But Emmy can't you see it? I've never seen anyone ride like that!"

"That's exaggerating. And no, Cutter. You're lucky you even managed to get me on this time. I don't have the nerve to do it. Once we stopped up here, all I could do was lean into him. It's too hard. Too many things come up and I can't maintain my control."

She was being vague. Being truthful would make her sound crazy. Then she'd get locked up, away from what she loved most.

"Emmy, Henry would be ashamed to hear you give up on your gift," he sighed.

She stared at him coldly and Apollo's back stiffened.

"Henry is surely ashamed of me for countless reasons. But you cannot imagine what the brutality of that gross human being has done to me," she paused, icy blue eyes cutting through him. "No, Cutter, I can't. I wish I could with every inch of my body. But I can't. Too many memories are linked to it."

She looked down in defeat, pressing her calves against Apollo's side to start a casual decent. The animals had been ripped away from her. They always were. She couldn't bare to have it happen again.

"I'm sorry, Emmy." Cutter spoke softly next to her, "I only thought that if I could get you on a horse, you'd remember how much you loved it. Maybe you'd want to enter the rodeo and make a name for yourself by taming one of the herd the right way. You could get out of the diner and the motel room."

He spoke thoughtlessly as he trampled through the reason for his surprise.

"You deserve so much more than all of that. You were born for more, I know it. It radiates from your body without effort. You can't see it? Emmy, just try. You are made for something special, I feel it in my bones every time I see you."

She rode quietly atop the hawk eyed horse. She wanted to yell at him. She had grown accustomed to the constant criticism of her own thoughts, but hearing them out loud from someone else made it worse. She wanted to tell him he was insensitive and assumed to know things he didn't. But he was right. She knew it and the flare of defense dulled. Emmy knew her ride today proved what Cutter believed in, but her fear strangled her. Her guilt shackled her to the past she refused to let go. All the effort she had made to overcome her past crumbled. There were too many layers to face and Emmy was feeling raw.

When they reached the big pen, Emmy slid off Apollo's back like water, tying him quietly before Cutter was able to lift his leg over his gelding's back. She said nothing as she loosened the cinch, and lifted the heavy saddle off his back with ease. Cutter tried not to watch, fearful that his frustration would explode and distance her more than it had already. He untacked Goose slowly, methodically, trying to gain a little more composure before speaking to her. Cutter clenched his jaw. It was as if she had no regard for the uncanny connection she had to horses. He just watched this little body framed in wild hair melt against the most unruly horse in a hundred mile radius and ride off like they had known each other all their lives. He watched the pain lift from her in the minutes it took them to reach the hilltop, and yet it was as if she hadn't recognized it at all. Cutter wondered if she'd always be plagued by the devastation, and if he'd ever be able to show her how much more the world was waiting to offer her.

"Thank you for the ride, Cutter," she spoke softly. "I really did enjoy being on a horse again."

Emmy leaned comfortably against the rail, blowing into Apollo's nostril, watching it flare with acceptance. His ears flicked as she let her secrets fall from her breath, and into his nose as confession. Sorrowful fingers fell down his wide forehead in unspoken friendship. They were both trying to subdue the fires within them. She sighed and stood straight, rubbing the tip of his ear before walking away.

"I'm sorry if I've upset you, Cutter. I just can't do it."

"But you just did, Emmy!" he exploded. "What can't you see about all of this? You are here for a reason, surrounded by horses and people who would appreciate this gift you have for a reason!"

He ran his hands over his hair and exhaled. His biceps flexed against his shirt. Butterflies danced in her stomach. Green eyes seared through her and she froze, barely shrugging in response. The ride back to the motel was a silent one.

When they pulled into the parking lot, she slid out, meekly trying to avoid the glare Cutter pushed between her shoulders. She unlocked her door, preparing to walk in without a word, but he caught her arm and she turned around, eyes threateningly wild. Cutter softened his grip and apologetically looked down at her.

"Look, I'm sorry. I didn't mean to be so aggressive about it. I just think a lot of you."

She said nothing, frozen by the feeling of being held against her will. He bent down and kissed her cheek, wanting to calm the nervous energy popping and crackling around her.

"Just think about it."

Cutter's heart fell into his stomach.

She nodded once and slid into her room, closing the door without a sound. Emmy fell heavily into her bed and cried without caring. The shock of Cutter's explosion had startled her. Her body was heavy as stone and she didn't dare to move. Every bone called back to Apollo. The child inside of her begged to go back, cried to talk to the horses like she used to. It was like she was trying to go back to a completely different life. So much had happened since she was an innocent little girl on her grandfather's farm. Exhausted, she fell asleep with the earthy scent of patchouli in her nostrils, and the gaunt cheekbones of the Indians gazing at her from the backs of her eyelids.

*Chapter Twenty*

Dougal sat among piles of paperwork at a complete loss. He had spent the past few weeks stripping the locations for anything Aillig could have left for her. Finding proof and gaining knowledge on the secret life of his brother would have given him the edge. Dougal's opportunity to move higher in authority was extinguished. His large frame slumped heavily in his desk chair, spent with the feeling of failure. There were no clues. He knew part of him should be relieved. This meant he would most likely close the case and never need to deal with the tragic woman up north again.

A knock came from the other side before his office door opened.

"Anything?" she asked.

He shook his head slowly.

"Our little birds tell us after you left she doubled her stock and seemed different. Whatever you did needs to be fixed. Now."

Dougal rubbed a gnarled hand over his eyes, trying to forget about the manic letter he had shown Lillian.

"The lass is the biggest mess I've known. She runs to her herbs for comfort ye ken. Nothing to trouble yourselves about."

"Nothing? The biggest problem is her herbs! She shouldn't have been allowed to practice after she left. Go out to her, Dougal, and *fix* the mess you made."

He glanced up at her insinuation.

"How do ye propose I do that?" he asked.

"However is necessary," she hissed before leaving.

......

*Lillian hugged the books to her chest as she walked on the trail behind her cottage. She stopped when she came to a headstone and knelt before a green cloak full of herbs. Lillian opened the brown book to record what she saw, but every page was filled with the same strange lines she had drawn around Aillig's hidden addresses. When she glanced up again, a woman stood in front of her. Her long, dark hair was similar to her own. Her eyes were a brighter version of her own. Her skin was made from moon glow and swirled like water. She met Lillian's gaze and knelt next to her before speaking.*

*"This is the Ogham. My sister, the poet, made it to hide our secrets from Father."*

*Lillian nodded, unable to speak to the strange mirror image in front of her.*

*The woman smiled before turning into a white and green light. It drifted off towards the sun. Lillian followed it until the light grew so bright she had to shield her eyes. A shadow formed in front her. Lillian reached out her hand and saw the woman from her dreams. She stood with a wolf on her left and a foal curled against her side.*

*"Find us," she whispered.*

Lillian shot straight up in bed, gasping. She flicked on a light and tossed her covers around before finding the books underneath her extra pillows. Not wanting to be induced by the oil, she pulled her sheet to her nose and opened one. As she suspected, a list of herbal remedies graced the pages she flipped through, all marked with an Ogham symbol on the opposite page. It was the Ogham year, the old tree lore of wise folk like herself. There was a chapter for all the symbols, all represented by a tree and its healing properties, both physical and psychological. The written language looked like a series of scratches to the unknowing eye.

"I can't believe I didn't see it before," she muttered to herself, half asleep.

She pulled the stack of papers from her drawer, glancing at the time with a sigh. Lillian knew better than to stay up all night deciphering mysteries. She still wasn't sure she wanted to find them. The answers may not be what she hoped for. She had never wanted to be right about his murder. Lillian glanced at the Ogham that often filled the spaces around her dream notes. She would need a key. It had been too long since Aillig had tried to make her memorize all the different meanings and symbols. It was so like him to teach her the riddles of the language before she could know the importance of it. Her finger ran down the vertical line found in the drawing of each letter, trying to remember what it represented.

"The separation between this world and the others," she whispered, straining to keep her eyes from burning as she concentrated.

The horizontal lines decorated either side in spaces around her writing. Lillian closed her eyes, hoping to recall what it meant, but only felt slumber beckon her. She placed it delicately back in her drawer. Her eyes were aching.

"I'll have to work on it tomorrow," she muttered before drifting off.

*Aillig sat in a circle of silhouettes, candles burning all around them. Lillian tried to focus on the shadowy figures as she neared, but they only grew darker. Aillig smiled upon her arrival, patting the ground beside him in invitation. The books he'd left for her centered the group,* and Lillian turned to ask Aillig to decipher what she couldn't. His large, knowing eyes crinkled in his translucent, aging skin as he shook his head to quiet the foreign language falling from her mouth.

"Relax child," he whispered. "Then he will always come to you. You must go to him, Lillian. I can no longer help you."

Her heart pounded against her chest. Lillian tried speaking again, but only produced gargles. Upset and frantic, her tears welled in the dim light, desperate to understand how he knew. She cried an assortment of herbs and flowers until she felt calmed. A paper folded into her hand and she knew she'd written them down.

"Oh, my sweet Lillian, one day you will learn."

She smiled weakly and rubbed her eyes, trying to clear the blur and focus on her beloved mentor. The candles grew brighter and when she turned to him, his face grew sallow and more wrinkled. His eyes lost their vibrancy. The long cardigan he loved best turned to rags, and shackles dangled from his bony wrists.

All the dark figures sat watching her, all with a face similar to Aillig's. A panic rose in her throat and she stood to flee from the disconcerting images. Lillian knocked over a candle in her haste and the flame ignited all around her. The books were burning. Lunging to save them, she fell into the flames. Lillian felt her arms wrap around them, but when she looked down, the blue eyed woman lay in her embrace. The woman smiled and held up nine fingers. The flames around them disappeared and spilled out of the woman's fingers, crawling around their wrists, trying to bind the girls together. Lillian watched and looked to the woman for answers, but she only shut her eyes. The light dulled and Lillian was pulled from the dream.

......

"Clary sage, cedarwood, spikenard, and everlasting," she repeated again in wonder.

Lillian locked her mixing room with a sense of success. Her eery dream had revealed the coating on the books. The list of herbs were simple, but inducing his hypnosis was not. It had taken her several tries before she tempted Aillig's message from her dream. When she allowed herself to relax, the oil drifted from her chest, deep into her lungs and activated. Within a few minutes, she accessed what she'd normally only see in slumber. Curious about his dissipated rejection, Lillian's mind had shifted instantly to a vision of her shadow man. The planes of her mixing room had foiled, and she had seen him sleeping in shackles, which gruesomely startled her out of the meditation.

She walked between the shelves of her apothecary still shaking off the lucid inebriation from her trial run. Lillian tried not to dwell on her shadow's decision to disappear without success. She had finally opened herself to the idea of accepting him as something real, and had brazenly considered the exchange of baring her body for the first time in her life. She could see the resignation on his face when he left, which didn't aid in an explanation.

"Am I really upset about a ghost rejecting me? Lillian, you've gone mad," she muttered to herself.

She toyed with the thick ends of her hair and very timidly, hoped he'd return soon. She couldn't help but wonder who he was. Lillian couldn't shake his unique demeanor and how misplaced he seemed in her cottage. She wanted to know how he could come and go as he pleased and if he'd resurface in her wake state again. She looked to the clock over her mixing room. She pushed some more stock onto shelves and turned to continue with work, settling to think about it in the privacy of her own home. If she could barely manage to accept the insanity of the concept she was creating, surely her customers would consider an exorcism or witch hunt if they knew. She unlocked the door feeling defensive and misunderstood amongst the clients walking in. Aillig would have known all about what she was going through.      His books were tucked away on her desk. She watched them vibrate with impatience for translation as she conversed with customers. She had woken up early to study their pages, and her discoveries thus far were not completely surprising. The first one she'd opened had been written about the Ogham and herbal remedies. It had taken her a few minutes to realize that Aillig had only used the Ogham symbols as a key to write in English. There had been nothing odd or secretive about the outdated remedies listed, but Aillig always had a purpose behind his quirks, and usually the stranger they were, the more hidden he wanted the information kept. Whatever clue he planted in healing sword wounds and rotted flesh eluded her. She would have to dig into the spiritual meaning of the trees next. She waved to another customer as she watched them go from her desk, resting her hand upon the second book like a doting mother.

The book bound in blue leather, however, was impossible. It did not transfer to any language she was familiar with. She guessed that it could have only been a precious item to him. It didn't seem right that Aillig would put such urgency into the possession of a favored book, and she wondered if the frenzied nature before his death had gotten in the way. Lillian glanced at the books a last time before returning her focus to work as the day dragged forward.

When she got home, she plopped her books on the bed before preparing meals for Hoot. He had greatly improved and was ready to be let go. She had noticed his withdrawn nature and though he watched her curiously in constant companionship, his vocalizing had all but dropped away. She decided to leave his cage door cracked open and give him the chance to decide what he wanted. It was hard for her to imagine the cottage without his company and tried not to feel abandoned by his inevitable departure. She wanted to sink into her usual sense of loneliness, but knew it was unnecessary. Lillian indulged instead in the image of her ghost as she started her own hearty dinner. He was a man she couldn't name, though something inside her called to him, knew him. She searched through her memory to the boy who haunted her as a child at the church. Her ideas of ghosts seemed to be evolving.

"But a ghost is a stagnant soul, stuck in death, aren't they? They can't grow up," she said out loud, crinkling her nose.

Lillian smiled in spite of her confusion when the once ominous density appeared behind her. He came back. She had become more finely tuned to his presence since he'd appeared and her acceptance at the tub felt like she had finally given him permission to stay. Her vegetables sizzled as they sautéed over the stovetop. *So this is what it could be like to have a man,* she dared to tell herself. Lillian laughed at her vivid imagination, not allowing or denying the strange relationship developing between her and the possibly real shadow man. She bit her lip and let the confession sink in with desire, trying to accept it as she had promised at the screaming wall. *Being insane is so much less lonely,* she jested. She was irritated that she was making fun of herself. The purist part of Lillian wanted to believe it was more than her own imagination.

His shadow grazed against her arm and she closed her eyes. She hadn't noticed how upset she was making herself as she toiled to make sense of him. Lillian exhaled deeply and she imagined his heavily muscled arms wrapping around her waist. The picture of him in her meditative mind was fuzzy. Lillian hadn't been able to see him vividly awake again and blamed it on her excessively scientific brain. She closed her eyes and marveled slightly at the memory of his rugged frame. Lillian couldn't think of a single man living that looked quite like him. A single breath sent goosebumps up her neck. He whispered gently to her, but the words flew out of her ears when she smelled something burning.

"Oh dear," she sighed, opening her eyes to the charcoaled vegetables in front of her.

Turning the flame off, she lifted the pan and dumped them into the trash, pouting as her stomach grumbled. She settled for some simple chicken noodle soup from her freezer instead, and tried to recall what he had whispered. When it didn't register, her shoulders slumped.

"For God's sake, Lillian," she scolded herself half heartedly. "You can't possibly be falling in love with a ghost."

The whole idea seemed outrageous, and yet she couldn't help but let honesty rule out her judgement. For one moment she admitted that was exactly the truth. She spooned her soup into her oversized mug and toted the steaming liquid to her bedside. She folded long, angelic legs underneath her and shed the sweater from the day's work. Her lace camisole allowed the cool breeze circulating in her cottage to grace her skin, tingling it to a delicate awareness of the things around her.

She opened the blue book, hoping to find anything interesting that Aillig would have wanted her to see. Grabbing her deciphering key, she went to work on the Ogham, transferring it from ancient symbols into English a last time. The words did not create anything comprehensive, and she'd already tried Latin with no success. She sipped her broth and furrowed her brow as she studied it, trying to sound out the phonetics. Lillian flipped through the pages, looking for an irregularity or something familiar that could set her in the right direction, scanning its entirety twice before shutting the back cover with a thump. She flipped it over in frustration. She slumped against her wrought iron headrest and glared at the antique in front of her with complete confusion.

There was nothing about it that caused her curiosity to pique. Nor did the other for that matter. She couldn't understand why Aillig had left these in such secrecy. Her suspicion of his high stress was creeping back into her mind as defeat seemed imminent. She felt like a failing student, and wished that she had been more adept when Aillig was alive. If she had been more secure, like she was now, maybe these things would have made sense. Maybe he placed too much faith in her.

A flash of anger spiked her body. She reached her foot to kick the books away, forcing them to slip off the bed. The blue bound mystery landed with a louder thunk than she expected. Lillian fell forward to grasp it in fear of damage, mortified over her childish behavior. When she brought it to her breast in apology, a key fell from inside the spine, rattling as it hit her wood floor. Slowly, she leaned to pick it up.

"You tricky old bugger," she laughed as she held it between her fingers. "Even your decoys fool me. Well done."

The brass shone under her lamp light and Lillian knew then it would all make sense. The key had to be for his vacation home, the other address she swore to memorize in secrecy. She giggled softly. Certainly he wouldn't have left a key laying in a place so easily accessible to prying eyes. Lillian should have realized that to start. She had to stop questioning what Aillig was leaving behind. It was time to look for answers, not excuses, she reminded herself.

She would have to close the shop to travel to the beach house and for how long she wasn't sure. In fact, Lillian couldn't remember a time she'd ever had a vacation. The thought thrilled her and she crawled under her covers, closing her eyes in the satisfaction of her evolving reality. Lillian welcomed slumber easily and moved languidly under the covers, reconnecting with a more fluid state of mind. She imagined the quiet lapping of lake waves as she shifted her hips back and forth. Quiet pops lengthened her spine as she started to relax. The smell of rose petals floated around the tips of her hair and she parted her lips when she heard his whisper against the pillow.

"Paenitet," he breathed against her neck.

*Sorry.*

"Don't be, just stay," she replied in her last breath before sleep.

Her hands curled instinctively in slumber.

*He lay beside her, arm draped over the dip beneath her ribs in protection against the looming danger just outside. She couldn't name what it was, but they both felt it lurking beyond the window. The dangers of Aillig's death moved all around them.*

.......

The bitter cold of his cell melted away as he allowed himself full access between time parallels once more. His blatant appearance in the soaking room had been an enthusiastic attempt at his new training. Once he had decided to return from her reality, he had become sick from the amount of energy spent to project himself so clearly between veils. He had needed time to restore himself and recenter for a more appropriate appearance. The druid told him he'd feel less dizzy as he acclimated to the untrained parts of his mind. Tonight, he ignored it for the simple pleasure of feeling near her. So many years he spent wishing for moments such as this. He smiled, peacefully inhaling the scent of roses as she slept.

.......

Lillian woke slowly, trying not to notice the emptiness of her bed. Romance lingered in the air as she got up and headed out the door for work. He had stayed with her through the night and Lillian couldn't remember a time she had slept so well. She shifted the weight of Aillig's books under her arm and sighed. As much as she wanted to bathe in the delight of her dream, she had to focus on what was real and tangible. It'd take a day to drive to the coastal home and with all the business recently, she could close for inventory maintenance without looking suspicious. In a moment of inspiration, she decided to take a week off.

It was too bad she had to lie, her customers would be so ecstatic to hear that she'd be relaxing by the crashing waves down south. Again, Aillig's insistence on secrecy nagged at her and she relented to devise yet another fib to keep his information safe. If Dougal was able to find her at the shop just by talking to her customers, then it'd be just as simple to find her there if they knew the truth. She cringed at his memory. It boggled her how he and Aillig could ever be related.

She unlocked the door and sat at her consulting table for a moment in silence. She curled a lock of hair around her finger, calculating the percentage of success this would have if she went for it. Lying was not her forte and it made her uncomfortable to think that she'd be doing it to people she cared for. She grew unsettled with dishonesty and even more so as she remembered the eery circumstances that led her into doing it. It was hard to believe that anyone would want to hurt Aillig. She wished with wild abandon to discover a truth that was more than the mistreatment she found in childhood, but the world has exposed its crueler side long ago. She knew better than to believe it was going to end happily.

She posted the flyer announcing her absence without anymore deliberation. Lillian had to know. She had to do something or she was no better than whoever had burned his shop. The door flew open with a swish and Lillian hauled herself back to the moment, it was time for work. As her first customers arrived and read the flyer, she watched their jovial expression change and realized it was going to be a very long day. The small town was run on an expected schedule, and questions went flying between the crammed aisles of her apothecary.

"I know Mrs. Lackey, but you've got enough turmeric milk to get you through the week," Lillian explained as she turned to another. "And Mr. Beauchamp, if you drink your tea every day you shouldn't need to come in so frequently for that cough."

Lillian was torn between the satisfaction and frustration of being needed. She glanced at the newer customers watching with half hearted attention and sighed over the possibility of losing them. The bell on the door rang and she looked tiredly to see who would be next. Mrs. MacKay's twinkling eyes caught hers and Lillian smiled. Despite her depression behind closed doors, Maeve was a genial woman who was always smiling in town. Lillian nodded her head in invitation and the strong woman walked to her. Lillian just hoped she wasn't coming to talk about the incident at the post office.

"So I hear you'll be closing for a week, lass," she smirked. "Well, good for you. I always wondered how ye managed all of this on your own. Vacation for ye, then?"

"Oh no," she lied. "I just need to catch up on inventory with all the new people passing through."

Lillian tried to sound enthusiastic to put weight to her words and was relieved when the woman played along, though her eyes said differently.

"Aye, I can see that," she said, looking at the shop crammed with the distraught and bemused. "Well then, lass, don't forget to rest now and then. I suppose since I'm here, I should grab a couple extra bottles of the stuff."

Lillian motioned her to follow. They weaved through the waiting people to the front desk where Lillian plopped down with more anxiety than she wanted to show. Mrs. MacKay watched carefully as she wrote up her ticket and placed her oils, teas, and creams in a bag.

"Ye know," she said casually, "I always wondered why ye gave me the cream. It does wonders for my skin, but I canna understand how it helps with the sadness."

Lillian smiled and placed a hand on her arm. "Sometimes the power of touch is more healing than we know. Especially when it's loneliness that's biting at you. The ingredients encourage self love, though it's really the touch, Mrs. MacKay."

The woman smiled back at her with a warmness in her heart. She patted Lillian's hand before turning to leave.

"Well, then I expect that ye should be taking some home on your time away, lass."

Lillian watched her go and shook her head. She could not figure out for the life of her why everyone over forty wanted her to fall in love so badly. Her heart fluttered thinking of him and suddenly she was ready to start home.

Mrs. MacKay picked her phone from her purse and dialed. When it connected, she spoke in a near whisper as she walked.

"Yes, she's closing, it's true. I think she's going to leave. No, I don't think Dougal's heard, but I will keep an eye on the girl."

........

"What'd you find out?" Dougal asked into his office phone, toying with the edge of a file.

"Not much, my grandson said she keeps a window in her bedroom open," Mrs. Duckett recited between a yawn.

"Is it anything unusual if we needed to get in there?"

"Not really. She lives alone and leaves it that way when she's gone to work. I think the dear probably forgot it was ever open."

Dougal sighed, feeling the pressure of his superiors dragging their nails in his back. "When will be a good time to get in then? When she's at work? Do we need to worry about neighbors?"

Silence hung in the air of the call and he could feel his impatience growing. He hated the relaxed pace of the country.

"Well," she spoke slowly, "word is she's closing the shop to catch up on inventory. She's taking the week."

Dougal's fist curled. "So what does that mean then?"

She sighed. "It means it will be difficult to get inside to look around if she's home all day."

He threw a pen across his office.

"Fine, have your son and his friends keep an eye on the house for anything that seems odd. After the week has passed, have them go in and search."

He hung up the phone feeling anxious. He knew what his boss had suggested but he wasn't ready to have the girl killed just yet. A small part of him was holding out, hoping to find some presentable information on his brother's social circle. If he could find a way to destroy the last of them, they would never have to worry about an upheaval again and he'd be put on a golden throne.

*Chapter Twenty-One*

*Apollo stood inside the rodeo arena, the bright lights gleaming off his coat. Emmy smiled and walked toward him. From the night above, an orange burst shifted away from the Wolf Star and hovered near his shoulder. Emmy reached out to touch it. The orb swirled and stretched before her and quickly took the form of a woman. Her eyes were made of blue flame, her skin glowed like hot embers. Her hair flew around her like the flames of a wildfire.*

*"You must become him. You must listen to what the Elder has taught you."*

*A tear streamed down Emmy's face. She missed Henry.*

*"Tell Apollo, the sun chaser, to take you out of the otherworld, child. Show him what you want and he will take you."*

*Before she could ask another question, the fire woman morphed and returned to the sky. Emmy watched the stars above her for a few minutes before quietly slipping onto Apollo's back.*

*"I want to see Henry," she whispered into his turned ear.*

*With a single leap, Apollo landed on the ridge from their ride. She could see Henry amongst the Indians.*

*Chanting filled the silence and flashes of faces twisted in front her. The beating of drums grew louder and louder. She strained to see the waving shadows of dancers through a fire. Beating hooves drowned out the shrill, ancient voices of their ceremony. Emmy reached her hand out to the heat of the flames. The blaze parted and on the other side stood the black haired woman, looking to her with inquisitive green eyes.*

*"Find us," she mouthed over the drums.*

Emmy flew out of bed in the early morning light with sweat beading against her hairline. Goosebumps rose on her shoulders and she reached to wrap the blanket tighter around her. The room was still, not a particle fell in the air, her breath suspended.

"Okay," she promised with fragile resignation.

Time moved again and she inhaled to catch her breath. The haunted tribesmen still lingered in her ears.

"I'll do it."

She rose from bed, reluctant to go to work for the first time. Her entire body longed to be back in a saddle. She could still hear the sound of Apollo's breath as they ran to the ridge. Emmy needed to get to Apollo one more time. She wanted to find the Indians. She ran Cutter's words through her head as she walked to work. He had evoked the thought of her future. She knew the diner offered little but hadn't cared. The gift he had given her yesterday woke her from a long sleep. Emmy had been wrong to shove off all that Henry had taught her, and she was wrong to have ignored Cutter's encouragement.

Cutter had known she was meant for more. It was time to trust in what he had seen. She hoped he would be in for lunch despite the way she had treated him last night. He deserved more than an apology. He deserved a promise. A small shiver ran up her arms. Emmy was afraid of opening herself up to what she had learned to keep hidden.

She had spent her childhood learning how to keep secrets. Henry had told her some things were meant to be kept to yourself. Ethan had proved him right. The only time she'd ever disobeyed Henry's advice had left her locked in a room crying. She hadn't been able to get in the saddle after that. Her work horses became fat pets. She stared out the diner window. Emmy couldn't let it happen this time. She had to recreate her future.

Her focus waned as the hours passed. The repetitive motion of wiping counters down started grating her nerves. She wanted to be in the mountains. The people of her dreams resurfaced in her imagination and Emmy couldn't help but wonder what she had really seen on her ride yesterday. Cutter's truck rumbled and died outside the window. Her heart fluttered in her chest. Cutter walked through the swinging door with his eyes on the floor, shoulders unusually slumped. Through half open lids he muttered a small hello and she took place settings to his table. Emmy wasn't sure what she wanted to say. She brought out his lunch a few minutes later and let him eat in silence. She twisted the ends of her hair and paced back and forth, aimlessly wiping crumbs from the bakery case. A speech was slowly forming in her mind while she waited for him to finish. Emmy caught him stalling at his table while he searched for some cash. She went to pick up his empty plate, and stopped.

"I'll do it. I'll enter the rodeo."

He smiled and it was hard not to kiss him.

"I'm sorry for yesterday. I wasn't ready to hear what you said. I shouldn't have treated you that way."

He said nothing, but stared as the static around her subsided. She turned to go and he grabbed her hand before standing and leaving himself.

"I'll see you tonight."

She shook her head slowly.

"No. Not until Saturday."

"I want to make it up to you. I was too rough on you. I'm sorry about yesterday, Emmy."

"I know," she whispered.

He gave her a swift kiss on the cheek and left. Emmy knew it would be hard for him to stay away, but Cutter was a man of his word. She wouldn't need to worry about being caught. She watched him drive out of the parking lot and clocked out. Emmy straightened her back. The plan she had formulated upon waking was going to be risky. She couldn't ignore what she thought she'd seen on the ridge. Something about Henry's stories rattled her and that she had been dreaming of them so consistently had to mean something. Emmy didn't care why she was compelled to find out, she didn't have space to question herself. She didn't have time for a regression in confidence. Slipping out of town reminded her of life before Wyoming. Emmy reminded herself that she would be back to her motel room tonight. She had to find the ridge and understand the importance of the Indians in Henry's stories. Too many times she'd dreamt of them, too many times Henry had repeated their story. Emmy didn't know why they showed themselves now and wanted to find out. She tidied up around her room and waited for night to fall. Nerves danced in her body. It was time.

Emmy knew the way and let her mind straighten out the stories that turned between her ears. Her grandfather had told her about how the cowboys needed to learn to understand the natives instead of conquer them. He said that what they could read in the stars would change the entire world. She ran her hand through her hair and tried harder to get past the general moral of equality she grew up with. There were details edging around her memory that she needed to recall, things that seemed harder to believe when she started getting older.

There had been a story he told her once about a tribe that lived high in the mountains. They were invisible to most people because they had been so good at hiding. They had become scared of a world they didn't understand. So they fled to the spirit world near the sky. He had called them preservers of life. They ate the mountain sheep and mastered the skill of sacred learning. They were a people not far descended from his fairytales of the Star People. She furrowed her brow. Henry had made it up. It was only a bedtime story. Indians hadn't lived freely on American soil for centuries. Yet she swore she had seen them just yesterday. Her soul bounced with the anticipation of adventure and her heart pounded in her chest as she looked for a place to hide her truck. She could see the lights of the Big House just up the road and didn't want to be seen.

She glanced to her left and saw a dilapidated building to pull behind, satisfied enough with the coverage. She hid her keys underneath the hood and worked her way to the ranch. She moved carefully around the property to the back pens. The house was quiet and it seemed that everyone had called it quits for early rising the next morning. Emmy prayed she had picked the right time to borrow from Cutter's boss. She couldn't believe she had justified this to herself earlier, but according to Cutter, Apollo didn't like anyone else, anyway. No one would miss him for a few hours.

He was easy to find standing alone in the closest pen they'd untacked from, which made Emmy smile. Apparently Cutter wasn't exaggerating when he said no one could handle him. Her heart sang as she neared and his head popped up through the darkness. She tip toed to him, barely able to make out his silhouette in the night sky as her eyes adjusted to the darkness.

"I'm here handsome," she whispered, "here, *fear dóighiúil.*"

He nickered and came to her in a couple imposing strides. She could see the fire in his eyes and nothing else.

Life tugged between them and she could feel Henry's game easily in the solitude. She smiled.

"We've got to go back to the running place," she whispered as she slipped a halter around his head.

"I think there are some people who want to meet us."

She pulled him closer to the gate, and looped the lead rope around his neck to make some reins. She felt a little guilty that she was stealing a horse on a whim with no backing, but her impulsive vortex always beat logical reason.

"I need to trust you to navigate the way. My eyes cannot see as well as yours."

He turned a gentle nose to nestle her side. Emmy reached for the latch on the pen but the old metal wouldn't budge. Impatient to get out, she slammed the latch back. The sound rung over the property and bounced off the buildings. She froze. Boots scuffed against the dirt in the distance. She ducked between Apollo's front legs. A few guests were walking back to their cabins. Emmy watched their door open and close, waiting a few minutes before moving just to be sure. Gripping a handful of mane, she swung herself up on his back and waited until his muscles relaxed beneath her. Emmy slipped her fingers down his shoulder, thinking of the dream she'd had.

"Thank you for guiding me," she whispered.

Emmy held the hilltop in her mind's eye. With the athleticism natural to a stallion, they took off soundlessly in the night. Emmy's thighs tightened securely against his sides and she settled into the rhythm on top of his flat back. The light of the stars above washed her skin and set it aglow. It didn't take long before he brought them to a clear path and Apollo pushed up the hill with ease. She sat up and slowed him to a walk at the ridge. She wasn't sure where to look. They walked further into the valley nestled between the high, distant mountains, feeling as though they were slowly getting swallowed. Emmy's hands whisked against his neck, soothing both of them as they moved through uncharted territory. The threat of wildlife rang true in her bones and she needed to tap into Apollo's instincts to keep them safe.

Emmy blinked slowly, and in the protection of darkness, allowed herself to reconnect with the teachings of her childhood. It had been too long since she was allowed to experience the magic Henry had showed her. Emmy closed her eyes and imagined the starlight descending from above, forming a pillar around both of them. She could feel a cord run through her spine, into Apollo's heart, and out through the ground. The light was not as harsh on her body when she wasn't fighting against it. She synchronized herself with Apollo and opened her eyes to observe the area for movement through his superior vision. Strange shadows shifted in the distant tree line. They watched her, trying to still the horses dancing beside them. Emmy urged Apollo forward to get closer.

"Can you see it?" a man asked in native tongue.

Another, older man nodded and saw the glow of energy congealing around the pair in orange and red pops.

"It's her, Sky Brother."

The group simultaneously emerged from the pine. Apollo's back stiffened and his nostril's flared. He pinned his ears and focused on the approaching mass before them. Emmy's heart started thumping in her chest. They were here. She hadn't prepared to be right. She hadn't prepared at all. She didn't know what to do next. Apollo broke the silence with a blood curdling whinny. She grabbed his mane before he reared and charged towards them, protecting his rider. Emmy sat back, disconnecting from her mount.

"Easy, easy," she whispered, tugging on her makeshift rein.

He heard nothing and continued straight toward the pine, ready to bulldoze the men. *You can't control him, Emmy.* She forced her muscles to relax against his back and loosened her grip. The white light sunk from the sky. She watched the figures grow bigger and she held her breath in anticipation of the collision. The cord tightened through her spine. She could see them now only a few feet away. She closed her eyes and guided the light to ground in the earth.

"Easy, boy."

Apollo relaxed his hips and slid to a stop, snorting inches away from the horses in front of him. His ears were pinned and he breathed deeply, assessing each one. Emmy watched them with the intensity of Apollo still running through her veins. Her eyes were wild and it took a moment for her to pull out of the union she had formed with her hawkish animal.

They were still real. The men were bare chested and clad in animal skin pants. Bones hung from their hair and all of her dreams pounded into the front of her mind. She said nothing. Their eyes were hollow and dark without the sun to warm them. Except the tall one. His shone in silvery hues. He spoke in whispers, his accent thick with mingled languages.

"You are her," he said, struggling with English.

"Who?" she asked, confused.

"The Moon Horse."

She stared at him. Emmy wasn't sure how they knew her, or why they would want to. She studied their faces, trying to remember if she'd ever seen them before. She could only think of her dreams. She looked to the one who spoke and clearly remembered his unusual height. It hit her at once.

"I had a dream about all of you. I *did* turn into a horse in it," she marveled. "I knew I saw you yesterday too. What tribe are you?"

They glanced at one another cautiously before the same man spoke.

"*Tukudika.*"

She nodded solemnly, not recalling it as one Henry told her about.

"We have been waiting for you to come."

Their wildness twisted in the air. Emmy was alone with strangers. Her back grew taut. Apollo dug his foot in the ground, waiting for the signal to lunge. Their horses backed without command and the men smiled with admiration. Emmy watched the hardness fade from their faces, and for the first time became aware of how noticeable her power was.

"Come back again, Moon Horse, when we are ready."

"I'm here now," she argued. She wasn't ready to leave. There were too many questions to ask, too many things to share. She wanted to know if Henry's stories held any truth.

"You have come to us in stealth and we were not prepared. Find us again in the place of the Sky People. We will know it is you and then will be your time."

They disappeared like ghosts back into the pines. She waited a moment and when they did not return, she considered trying to find them amongst the trees. She looked up to the sky and saw no moon. She had pushed her luck enough for one night. Reluctantly, she turned Apollo to head back to the ranch. Their presence was still around her. Emmy could barely believe what had happened. The whim that drove her to the dark mountains had proved to be right. She replayed the approval in the strangers' faces when Apollo seemed to read her thoughts. She had become so used to using her exterior world to distract her, she'd forgotten the power of her own intuition. It was time to regain confidence in what had been stripped in Kentucky.

She felt like she'd betrayed the happy life she had with her grandfather by forgetting all the time they'd spent riding. He had nurtured her ability to synchronize with her animals. Henry had guided her through extensive soul lessons to do what impressed the natives enough to invite her back. Her grandfather had accepted her talent so easily she never considered that she was different.

She brought Apollo back to his pen. The breeze had grown cool and she was tired from Henry's focus games. She dismounted and put Apollo away, rubbing his forehead lovingly before turning to go.

"Thank you for taking me, you have changed my life."

She walked to her truck and drove home under the stars, the engine rumbling rebelliously into the quiet terrain. It was time for her to draw inward for the first time in years and call attention to herself if she wanted to make a difference in the reality she had been living in. Something shifted and Emmy could feel herself seeing the world with different eyes.

*Chapter Twenty-Two*

Dougal sat at home, sipping his scotch. He had called in sick the entire week, feigning a terrible cough. He was relieved at first when no one seemed to care, but it didn't take long for the bitterness of being unimportant to creep in. Aillig had sent him on a wild goose hunt and he hated him for his lack of loyalty. Dougal was his own brother, and yet Aillig denied him information. Instead, he had betrayed him by passing all his knowledge to a silly, little girl. The same girl that would force him against the laws of his faith again.

Now that Lillian had gained attention, his superiors requested more darkness of him. He was only their brawn. They had dismissed whatever theories he had about Aillig's kind and their importance to the prophecy. Dougal felt completely alienated. He had dedicated a long life to faith and a community, only to be alone in his thoughts. The alcohol burned as he counted the failures of his quest. He couldn't spend any more time sitting in a recliner getting drunk. He refocused and thought that Aillig had to have sent him to the girl for a reason. The man never did anything on a whim, and the less it seemed to make sense, the more important it was. Dougal use to enjoy Aillig's games when they were children.

"You've made a hard riddle this time, brother," he muttered.

......

The car was quiet through winding roadways, and Lillian rolled down her window despite the chill. She breathed in the salty air of the ocean. Whispers rose around her and when none sounded familiar, she shoved them out of her attention. One ghost was enough. Lillian shifted her legs in the car and tried to focus on the softness of her lined leggings. As exhilarating as it was to venture out of town, Lillian wasn't certain about what she'd find at the beach house. Her last trip had left her spinning and she couldn't help but feel that going through Aillig's things would bring a similar experience. It would be no vacation as much as she wished it were.

She drove slowly down his street, keeping an eye for the right cottage number. The homesteads were scattered together, all plastered white with chocolate roofs. Lillian reminisced of a time when they had likely been thatched. Every lawn was manicured, but yellowing, much like the rougher grasses near the shore. She caught the address and pulled to the detached garage. Uncurling her legs from the car, she stretched and admired the view. The ocean lulled below, and white cliffs called off in the distance. An air of solitude wrapped around her shoulders and Lillian inhaled the thick, sea air. She walked around to the front door, running her fingers on the cobblestoned wall leading to the doorstep. It was obvious the place hadn't been lived in since his death, though it seemed someone had maintained the outside. The neighbors must have wanted the street looking well for renters. Her heart skipped a beat as she pushed the key in and twisted.

Lillian opened the door and walked into the familiar smell of Aillig. Everything had been left from his last visit; tidy and slightly overcrowded. Books were piled on top of the stuffed bookshelves, and pots held plants long dead. She smiled sadly as she moved around the small house, seeing so many relics of her beloved mentor. Despite her hesitation, Lillian couldn't help but relax amongst the perfectly intact atmosphere. He used to get so excited when he was preparing to come here. His eyes would twinkle whenever he shared stories about it. It already felt like home. She floated up the short flight of stairs to the bedroom and placed her bag on the floor. Everything was white but for the dark wood and furniture that accentuated the entire house. Part of it was Aillig's practicality; he was of simple design. Lillian noticed a pen and notebook placed carefully on the nightstand next to the bed. She didn't have to open it to know it'd never been used. It'd been left for her. He knew she'd come. A coldness ran down her arms, sharply reminding her of the reason she was there. The romanticism decayed inside the quaint room, so she took herself back downstairs to start the kettle to boil.

It bothered her that it seemed he had set a path for her to find whatever secrets he had been hiding. The more she let her mind wander through that which made up Aillig's reputation, it was strange to think he had any enemies. His heart was so kind, his eyes so knowing, that people were always drawn to him. Lillian really didn't see how Aillig could have put himself in danger. He may have been openly offbeat, but never threatening.

"Unless he was loved too much," she breathed intuitively.

Lillian was not so dull as to forget the vehemence of those with opposite beliefs of Aillig. He had very open opinions about his spiritual perspectives. She had to admit she'd taken a lot of Aillig's views lightly herself. It never crossed her mind to consider how anyone else viewed them.

"Until Dougal came, and I started believing in ghosts and dream messages."

She poured the boiling water from the kettle. A cup of tea to take the chill out sounded like a good idea. After, she'd go to the living room and start writing a plan to best use the short time she had at the cottage. The view from the kitchen was surreal. The water ebbed and flowed in shades of neon blue and the cliffs were as whitewashed as the cottage, beckoning to ancient times far more foreboding. They too seemed to be keeping secrets between their high ridges. A whisper passed faintly by her, though she could not catch it. She shook her head and waved it away. It wasn't her shadow man, he had not been present since she left. Whispers had been passing subtly since she got closer, but none of them were clear enough. Lillian drew away from the idea of more ghosts. It was hard enough trying not to think of herself as insane for being so attached to one, let alone more. She moved to see what was left of Aillig's stock. She flipped open the cupboards, and sifted through labels and jars, carefully creating options as she mixed and matched what herbs were there for a tea. She started through the cabinet next to the sink and froze. In a big jar was a tea blend labeled with her name. Tears welled behind giant green eyes and she lifted a shaking hand to pull it from the shelf.

"Always a step ahead."

She placed it on the counter and spun it, feeling a second label on the back. A note was taped against the glass. She unfolded it between sobs. She read each word carefully, savoring the sound of his voice in her mind.

*My sweet girl,*
*If you've found this, I would not be surprised that I am gone. There is too much information to fit on the back of a tea jar (I hope you like it, it's one of your dream recipes after all). You will find all you need to know. Will not say more, my dear, to be careful. Remember: subtlety always.*

*Have some more tea now and search. Don't forget to enjoy the journey, though I know it is difficult.*

*Aillig*

She hugged the paper to her, tears rolling down her cheeks. The confirmation of an intended murder washed over her in a strange satisfaction. Lillian lifted the jar and unsealed the top with a click of the lock. It popped and sighed. She breathed deeply into the contents. The earthy tones were undeniably her trademark, and she vaguely remembered smelling it before. The particulars were layered and deep, taking her back to the recesses of her mind. A foggy vision formed before fading as quickly as it had come. She cared little, too absorbed by his memory and the need to find more of his hidden treasures. She wondered what else Aillig had written down through all those nights. Lillian placed a small amount in a tea bag and let it steep as she watched the slowly fading light. She tried to soak in the last few hours of her life, and dried her tears. Times like these always made her feel lonely. There was no Hoot here, and the shadow man could not be felt. She touched Aillig's letter softly, longing to feel a connection to anyone at all. She was growing so tired of working through such huge events on her own. Lillian sipped her tea, letting the dark tones burn her throat and spread in her chest. She could almost hear the crashing water beyond the walls and they called to her lustfully. The ring around her iris grew darker and a buzz started between her shoulders. She should have guessed. She moved away from the window. This couldn't be another moonflower experience. She went to sit on the living room couch to stabilize, lifting a book as she passed it. She needed something to distract her from the affects of the tea.

Lillian thumbed through, casually looking for a hint or another note. It seemed to be a history book, a part of his infamous collection. Aillig had loved history for as long as she could remember. Her head grew heavy and fell back against the couch. She let the book fall by her side, surrendering to the fact that Aillig had coyly submerged her into another hallucination. She could feel her body reacting to whatever she had sipped on, and she was impatiently numb and drowsy. Her eyes drew closed as she thought more deeply, exhaustion taking her over. Lillian hadn't noticed how tired she had become. She was so involved with healing that she never stopped to take care of herself. All the hours dedicated to others were realized, and Lillian thought of the church, where the demands first started. She thought of all the times her knowledge was taken advantage of because she was a child. The cage of expectation had been what pushed her away. She rolled her shoulders to relax the stress out of her mind. She didn't care to think of the memories in the midst of remembering Aillig. He had saved her, now she needed to save his secrets. Her breath fell heavier and she drifted off despite her effort not to.

*She stood on the cliff looking out to the water, golden rivers of light wrapping up her ankles. The wind slid through her hair and around her body. The ocean called to every living nerve in her system and she cradled it deeply in her lungs. On the beach below, Lillian watched a dark body move towards her. The whispers from the day converged in her dream and grew clearer as she focused. Strange chants rang in her ears and she squinted to see what was approaching. In a blink a dark horse stood in front of her.*

*The animal was proud and intimidating as his nostrils flared inches from her chest. Lillian closed her eyes for a moment of composure and opened them to the girl from her dreams. Her mouth moved in conversation but Lillian couldn't hear through her excitement. She tried relaxing more, listening to the lull of the waves, heeding Aillig's advice to relax and listen. She closed her eyes again.*

*"Are you one of them?" the woman asked.*

*The whisper shocked her. When she opened her eyes to communicate, the woman was gone. In the distance, the demonic barn burner stood watching, his dark hair frantically disheveled. Lillian's heart pounded and she called out for her friend.*

......

Mrs. Duckett's grandson felt guilty sitting outside of Lillian's cottage. He had been in love with her for years and looking in on her personal life seemed too intrusive for his genteel upbringing. Regardless, the old woman had ordered him to do it and he'd been taught to obey his elders. He pushed his boyishly cut hair from his eyes as he sat in the hedges across the street, waiting to see a sign of movement. He imagined her working tirelessly into the night, concocting new and magical recipes to fix what was broken inside of people.

He knew nothing about her lifestyle and considered it somewhat as he would a fictional story about witches and spell books. The taboo image aroused a small excitement in him and sitting alone in the dark, allowed himself the indulgence of possibility. The mystery of the girl had always been whispered through town when gossip was dull. She kept to herself and neighbor's knew nothing about her. People often liked to create whimsical stories and he thought maybe that's what put her in the trouble she was in now. Everything was so repetitive and secure in this place that when a fresh breath of air waltzed into town, it all went off scale.

The lights of her cottage hadn't flipped off at the time she usually went to bed, and Nathan grew curious. He wondered if she'd gone out for a late night walk, though she never had before. The fantasy of magical powers drew him to look closer and he moved in stealth across the street to her open window. The air was still and eery. It was a night made for the witches and black lore his grandmother had told him about as a child. When he lifted his face to peek in through the window sill, a pair of unblinking eyes met his.

From the bed, the owl called lowly to his intrusive curiosity. Nathan fell backward into the surrounding gardens with a yell. He sat there for a moment, catching his breath. When he recovered, he attempted again to approach the window. The owl was perched on the window sill now, watching him. The boy stood staring, too scared to move in case the bird felt inspired to do the same. Wild animals terrified him and even though this was her pet, it didn't deter his rising fear. Before he could blink again, he turned and sprinted down the way. The mass of feathers lifted silently out of her house and straight towards him, screeching like a banshee. Nathan did not bother to look back when the fluttering faded as he dashed for home.

*Chapter Twenty-Three*

Emmy had needed the solitude to prepare for tonight. She had been swept into a storm of truths about Henry's fairytales and spent most of the week recalling how similar her dreams had been to his stories, and how similar his stories were to what was unfolding in real life. Emmy could feel the dark circles under her eyes. Looking into the stands it didn't take long for her to see Cutter and Travis in a corner of the bleachers. Folded bills cushioned their handshake before they sat. Cutter noticed her and waved from his seat. Emmy's heart tightened.

"There's no way she's going to do it," Travis scoffed.

Cutter grew hot. "I bet you, didn't I?"

The anticipation was weighing on Cutter's nerves. He had spent the past week trying to keep Emmy's debut a secret with little success. He had recounted her ride with Apollo to his bunk mates, but skepticism swept through them instead of astonishment. He could still feel his muscles vibrating with anger at their disbelief. The familiar buzz of rodeo lights amplified the crowd's energy. News had travelled quickly in the Wind River area about the transplant diner girl daring to enter the Cowboy Challenge.

Emmy stood with the four others, all men twice her size. The crowd whispered and she knew every eye was watching beyond the blinding white of the rodeo lights. Waiting in the ring for the stampede of flustered young horses made her palms sweaty. Her senses were heightened and Emmy tried connecting to the young animals. Their nervous breath became her own. She could hear the click of the gate to their pen, and the overhead announcer made her jump. The excitement of the rodeo grounds intruded her thoughts and she looked around to find a familiar face. Everything started to run together in a blur and her legs turned cold. She couldn't control it. There were too many animals and they dominated the connection. She could only react as they were. Everyone had moved away from the disoriented creatures but Emmy. All she could do was find a fuzzy outline of Cutter in the distance as they ran towards her.

He stood up, white with fear. A yell tore from his throat; ragged as it drifted to her from the stands. Her eyes were as wild as theirs as they rushed by her in a frenzy. She stood like stone. Time ticked on the clock as the others made desperate attempts to catch the fleeting animals. All Emmy could do was look into the crowd, bewildered and disoriented. She was screaming in between her bones. The buzz of the overhead flood lights turned into the crackling of fire. Every yell from the bleachers sounded like the shrieking of innocent flesh burning in her mind. Her own voice begged to tear her body apart from the mania.

One of Cutter's coworkers roped the neck of a colt. He was dragged in the dirt until he managed to stand and dig in a few feet away from her. Emmy watched, motionless, as she was sucked into the colt's hysteria. His arms flexed against his shirt to bring the coiling beast closer so that he might be able to jump on its back. He yelled at Emmy to move out of the way but she only turned her head and tried to shake the feeling of being choked. She didn't have time to react to the colt's twisting body. His head snapped around in refusal to his constraint and slammed into her ribcage. Her body bent against the dirt. The man loosened his grip in surprise and the colt bolted backward, stealing the rope from his hands and taking off to the other side of the arena. She disconnected from the animal as it ran further away. Two minutes had passed in a blink of an eye and when the buzzer sounded, little noise came from the arena.

The horses were pushed back down the chute they came from. Emmy's body tingled and slowly recovered. The suction against her forehead was released and she winced. Pins poked behind her eyes, her head was pounding. The silence dragged on as she readjusted to her own body. Emmy rose slowly, stupidly making her way out. Her legs shook. Emmy could hear the sneering and the passing of money between hands. It had been a bad decision to test out her strangeness like that. Her heart slammed in her chest and she tried to control the fear and anger that swirled inside of her.

Cutter leapt down the bleachers and pushed people out of the way to get to her. Emmy leaned against the pen of the wild herd, watching them as if she had never been trying to tame them minutes ago. He stood inches away from her, raking his eyes over her body, before approaching slowly. Cutter touched her shoulder and she jumped back as though she'd been burned.

"What the hell were you thinking?" he almost yelled.

She stood, staring contentedly at the horses and said nothing.

"Jesus Emmy, you scared the shit out of me! I thought you were going to be killed."

She was silent.

"Let's get you out of here. Let's go get John and get a drink. You're in shock."

Emmy allowed herself to be coaxed from her frightened companions as Cutter wound through the crowd next to her. His shoulders were shaking visibly. Emmy was acting like she had the first day he saw her. He cursed under his breath. They moved through the parking lot in minutes. It was all his fault. John unlocked the bar, and turned on the lights. The air was fuzzy and the room was cold from the changing of season. He poured each of them a shot and busied himself with prep work before the rest of the crowd stumbled in. He couldn't meet Cutter in the eye.

Emmy was going to break down. She knew it. She just hoped Cutter was prepared. She stared at the woodgrain of the bar top. Millions of nicks textured the otherwise glossy surface, and she ran her fingers across it. Her fingers didn't look like her own, didn't feel like her own fingers. The room seemed foreign and far away. The shock running through her body kept her with the herd of traumatized little horses. She had felt the sheer terror streaming through them. It had paralyzed her. She couldn't unwind the confusion of the night, let alone explain to Cutter. He couldn't begin to understand the momentous things she barely grasped about her own life. It seemed like all the words in the world couldn't amount to a proper explanation about what had happened. All of a sudden it seemed as if he were a complete stranger. He stared at her, bewildered.

"Are you okay?" She seemed completely at ease. The whiskey burned in his chest as he swallowed and anger rose back up his throat. She nodded once, letting her fingers drag against the countertop.

"Emmy, what happened? You could have done it so easily," he spoke more desperately.

She said nothing, but stared at her denim clad legs, grazing a finger across a new tear in the thigh. She studied herself as if she had never seen her own body before. As if being human was suddenly unnatural.

"Damn it, Emmy!" Cutter slammed his fist against the counter, making the shot in front of her vibrate inside the glass.

Her head snapped back, eyes wild. "It's your fault."

She couldn't stand herself for failing him and everyone else anymore. All her pent up confusion turned to anger. Her voice seemed hoarse, deeper. When she spoke her words cut through him.

"I told you I couldn't do it. I told you I was worthless now. But you pushed me into doing it. I should have known better than to listen. I should have kept it all a secret."

John cursed under his breath and slipped out the back to diffuse anyone thinking they'd come in before they were through.

"I didn't tell you to just stand there! What's your problem? You can ride the wildest god damn horse but you can't stand in front of a group of people you know and coax an innocent little colt to trust you for thirty-seconds?"

Cutter was shaking and losing control over the volume of his voice.

Emmy laughed bitterly, unrecognizably.

"Can you, Cutter? Why can't you just go in there and do it? Just go do it for yourself next weekend and then you can win all the money you want. I'm nobody's pawn anymore. I saw you betting right before I went in."

Cutter stood from his seat, pressing his hands into the counter, leaning towards her. The ugly comparison to the man that ruined her sent him past sympathy. His attempt to remember she was lashing out in fear was waning.

"Is that it?" he yelled. "You think I'm using you to gain financial wealth? You can't be serious! I just wanted..." he trailed off, too angry. Sweat started to moisten the neck of his T-shirt.

"Yeah, just like *him*. Of course, I should have known. Nothing ever changes," she muttered, staring at a shadow too familiar. Henry had told her not to show anyone what she could do.

Cutter stared at her through an invisible wall. His blankness thinly veiled the rage stirring underneath. He had reached his capacity.

"I'm leaving."

He rose from the barstool, fists clenched at his side and stiffly walked out the door. She watched him go, hotly fused to her chair in defiance.

"Fine," she muttered emptily, not willing to give into the waves of sadness pumping blood through her heart. She knew she was being cruel, and didn't care enough to stop. Emmy slowly raised a glass to her lips and slid the amber liquid onto her tongue, allowing it to singe her taste buds before swallowing. She looked from the corner of her eye to see John slide in the door Cutter just walked through. She tapped the bar with her finger. He sighed, holding his tongue. For once she was thankful for his aloof nature.

She let her finger curl around the cool glass before sliding it mercilessly between her lips. The shock was warmly settling into her bones, the bruising from the colt's head throbbed, and all her demons were crawling out. A bitterness curdled in her throat, and she felt less inclined to keep her pain buried. She didn't care who saw the sorrow in her face, or the failure of a life she walked out on. She had abandoned the only loved things she had ever known. Emmy sat on the barstool until she sweat from the liquor pushing out of her pores. She looked at John with hazy eyes and he shook his head. She half smiled, standing to wobble to the door in numbness. She had work early and the night was burning quickly.

The cool air made her face feel dewy and she closed her eyes. A hand slipped gently around her forearm and she bobbed her head in alarm.

"What?" she muttered angrily.

"I'm taking you home, so I know you're safe."

Cutter was looked barrenly at the damage of the night. Exhausted from sitting in the cold, he had little to say. As much as he wanted to get in his truck and leave the whole town behind, he couldn't leave her to make an unsafe journey back to her room.

"Don't touch me," she slurred.

He reluctantly let his hand fall to his side, his shoulder tense beneath his jacket.

"At least give me your keys so I can drive you home."

She stared at him, belligerent.

"I can do it myself, I'm fine."

"No, you're not, Emmy. I won't touch you or talk to you, just let me drive you home."

She thought a moment before shrugging and digging for her keys.

"Fine."

Her truck started with a rumble in the nearing morning hours. She felt her head spin and it fell sharply against the cold window of the passenger side.

*The dark haired woman moved in glitches as she stared back at Emmy. The mirror in her motel bathroom was broken and made her sick to look into. She searched for a reflection of herself and found none. Emmy bent over the sink and puked. Orange and red light fell from her mouth and spiraled down the drain like a portal into hell. She lifted her head from the sink and haunted tree lines danced against mountain peaks in the reflection of the mirror. She tried to focus through her dizziness and stared harder at the image. It distorted and spun before everything went black.*

The blood from Cutter's knuckles was crusted on the door handle inside her truck. Her eyes shifted behind acid lined lids. Slowly came the realization that she was curled into the passenger seat, saliva caked to her cheek, sweat crusting the hair above her ears. Cutter's presence was absent, it was cold and empty in the cab. Emmy gathered by the stinging in the corners of her eyes that the sun had risen. How long she had slept was uncertain. Loneliness cut into the crown of her head and abandonment pounded against her temples. She opened the door and her stomach heaved with force as she wretched into the dirt. She stumbled to her motel door, feeling sick and hot. Not daring to try water, she crawled under the covers, fingering blindly for the phone and dialing.

"Kelly, it's Emmy. I know I sound awful. I can't get to work. Can Sherry do it? I know she'll be mad. I know he will be mad too."

Emmy squeezed her eyes tight as Kelly rambled, outraged at the spectacle of last night and her disappearance later on. When she started in on the scruples of George Fassenbach and his opinion of missing work she cut her off.

"I don't care. Then tell him I quit," and hung up the phone.

......

George sat across from Kelly as she recounted Emmy's phone call. The massacred attempt at testing her ability had left him a little in shock. Ethan had done a beautiful number on her. She couldn't strengthen her dark connection to the animals. He had considered calling him from the bar last night to come pick her up, but didn't.

He had watched the drinkers talk in animation over the incredible event. They couldn't believe she mustered the idea to compete. They had gone on about her working at the diner and how much they enjoyed her company. He had noticed an increase in the slow hours since she'd been working them. Cash still flowed in because of her, even if she wasn't a radical, demonic horse whisperer like the superiors foretold. They were a lot of superstitious old men, living in ancient histories anyway. George couldn't see what terrible destruction could come from a silly girl. He shrugged and took any publicity as positive, and whether her reputation grew from good or bad behavior wasn't his problem. The girl definitely stirred up the town and there was always profit in that. Kelly's dramatic monologue buzzed all around him.

"Don't worry, Kelly. We will deal with your friend appropriately," he placated her.

He'd wait as long as he could before calling them.

........

When Emmy woke feeling more human, she sighed and got up. She packed her bags and headed for the only place she thought she'd be accepted after last night's failures. She didn't care if she'd find them or not. Emmy was happy to die in the quiet peaks of nature after wrecking her last chance at life. She was never going to heal from Kentucky's damage. Cutter would never forgive her either. She hopped in the truck feeling like the nasty demon Ethan had accused her of being. Her mind swayed behind the steering wheel as she worked through the toxins of alcohol, her scattered memory, and her dreams.

Emmy's last shred of hope dangled from her red rimmed eyes, refocusing through her hangover. They wanted her to find their sacred ground. The strange tribe was waiting for her to come and she had wasted time being drunk instead. Emmy wasn't sure she was worthy of their attention.

"How do they know me anyway," she muttered out loud.

She was a nobody. There wasn't a reason for her to be invited to a place where real Indians lived. A place she had no idea how to find. She sorted through images of her dream, hoping to find a sliver of inspiration. The trees had looked familiar, but the mountain ranges hadn't. There wasn't a time she could remember where her and Cutter climbed anything more than the hill to his hidden lake.

Her eyes widened and the back of her head tightened. She had heard the chants before at the art show, staring into his photograph. The photograph that held the hidden lake out of view, where the wind rushed all around. She had to get to the lake and walk farther into the pines. They would be waiting for her there.

She found the old building near the guest ranch and parked her truck. Emmy figured the chance of Cutter missing it so close to his work would be slim, but she couldn't care. She slung her backpack over her shoulder and started the trek to the lake, scolding herself for pouting. It was time to take responsibility for the outcome of her actions and leave. She walked cautiously as she neared the property of the guest ranch, praying no one would notice her. She caught Apollo grazing in the pen she'd left him in. It made her sad to think he'd just sit, locked up because no one took the time to understand his ferocity. His head snapped upright. He could see her even from the distance she kept and it made her nervous. She didn't want anyone looking where he was. She didn't want to be seen, only wanted to disappear. Emmy tried to ignore the tearing of her heart as she walked on towards the tree line, feeling like she was abandoning him.

The Big House sat behind her, watching in secrecy. The snaps and clinks of workers rung behind her. She managed to make it to the field of tall grass before stopping. She looked out to the distant, towering mountains. Last time, she'd walked in darkness and under Cutter's guide. Emmy curled herself up in doubt. There was no way to tell where the lake was without walking up the ridge. Feeling tired from the hangover, she sat down, completely concealed in the grass, to take a drink from her water bottle.

"I guess they would be impossible to find, they've been hiding for who knows how long," she muttered to herself as she toyed with the grass.

Yells came from the property and her neck prickled. Squatting so that her eyes barely cleared the top of the field, she glanced back to see what caused the commotion. She smiled mischievously, seeing Apollo throw a fit in his pen. She knew it wouldn't be long until he would start protesting his confinement. The man below was unrecognizable and she laughed a little as she watched.

The black, muscle bound body reared in sheer frustration. The man waved his hands and yelled for him to calm down, but Apollo shied away, frantic over the attempts to control him. Emmy wiped the dampness of the field from her hairline. Apollo spun and charged towards the man. Her eyes widened and she begged for the horse not to hurt his assailant, knowing his temper had already sky rocketed. She held her breath as she watched Apollo gain speed, approaching with single intention, and hoped he would stop at the fence. The man understood just in time and jumped out of the way as the stallion went flying over the rails. Emmy's heart jumped in her throat as he cleared it and kept running. The ranch hand watched from the dirt as Apollo disappeared. He wasn't going to try to catch him, he was useless to all of them. Emmy stood once the commotion had died and turned her attention back to her plan. She smiled despite herself for Apollo's victory, wishing he'd find some wild herd to take care of. She focused on the sound of his hooves pounding faintly into the ground. It didn't fade as she listened. She looked below to the property, searching in the direction he had taken off in, but couldn't find him. The ground vibrated and a little way in the distance she could see the dark inconsistency of his body traveling through the tall grass towards her. Her stomach dropped. Apollo was not going to let her travel alone. When he reached her, he nickered. Emmy opened her palm for his soft nose. She looked to make sure no one had followed his direction. She pushed his long forelock from his eyes.

"I don't know where I'm going, but we've got to find those Indians again. There's a hidden lake somewhere around here."

She didn't have a halter and lead rope to swing around his head and stopped to consider the predicament.

"Well, who said I have to force you. If you want to come, then you can follow," she decided.

She glanced halfway over her shoulder as she walked. His head bobbed closely behind her. As they moved closer to the hillsides, she tried to find a familiar one. The imposing mountain range in the distance made it difficult to gauge. She tried to remember anything unique about it, refocusing to the morning she looked out from the ridge. Her sense of direction was twisted, and she felt her confidence falter. She felt helplessly small in the big terrain and stopped in her tracks. Apollo stood behind her in the hints of evening, blowing warm air against her neck.

Emmy was chasing a pipe dream. She wanted them to sweep her away from all the mistakes she kept making. She walked with her head down, too lost in thought to care which was the right way. The sun was setting swiftly behind them and whatever chance she had at reconnecting with the strange men from the other night was going with it. Once again she was looking to complete strangers to solve the deadness inside of her. Emmy had done nothing different since arriving in Wyoming. It seemed she was constantly trusting people who she had never met with the fate of her own happiness. Ethan, Cutter, the Indians. She should have been searching for it on her own, finding it within the parts that were left of her inside.

Apollo moved in front of her. She watched him move over the ground now swallowed by stars. The hair on her arms stood on end. When he started to blur from her vision she walked after him in swift, innocent steps, determined not to get lost from her companion. She panicked. Her cheeks moistened as she followed, wishing she had brought rope to make a halter. She didn't want to be alone. Her legs burned as she climbed, keeping his powerful hind quarters just in view. Wind rushed all around her and pushed her body over the ridge. The familiarity was overwhelmingly beautiful. Grass gave way to the stoney edge of the water and Apollo bent to take a drink. He had lead her to the hidden lake. She lay her small hand against his neck, stroking his sleek fur. The air was cool and she felt at peace.

"Show him where you need to go," she whispered, remembering her dreams.

His head snapped from the water to glare into the darkness. Emmy followed, allowing her eyes to adjust and focus. On the other end of the lake, a wild dog watched them. Her heart skipped while she strained her ears to listen for more movement. When the threat of a pack didn't appear, she moved forward. Apollo trailed suspiciously behind her as she approached, her hand out towards it; another stray to add to her pack.

It watched her, neither challenging or fleeing. When Emmy came near enough, it backed slowly, further and further as she cooed to him. Quickly, the threesome were up against the forest. The trees were ominous and ghostly as she stood before them in the dark. The dog watched her, waiting for her to follow. She exhaled slowly and walked in through the first jagged line of tightly knit trunks. She looked over her shoulder to see Apollo watching her with interest. He didn't budge. When she disappeared into the shadows, she watched him lower his head to graze.

Her heart pounded in her ribs, facing forward again to find out where the dog had gone. The wind rushed through the branches and she could hear them clinking like bones above her head. All the same sensations the photograph had sucked out of her lived in the night. She looked upward and saw shadows sitting coyly in the trees, watching her in silence as she walked. Emmy's dreams rattled in her mind, too exact to the reality unfolding before her. She could see the taut faces of men in the sparse moonlight, their clothes dangling off their bodies. Emmy couldn't help but wonder what desolate people they must be. Animal bones hung in their hair, dancing in the breeze. She could feel them scattered like watch birds.

They spoke in whispers as she followed the trail they were creating. She clenched her fists at her side. She could feel a sweat break from the nerves she pushed against and in the night it made her cold and shaky. Branches cracked and popped beneath her feet as the forest cleared. The valley was washed in the light of the moon, untouched by modern civilization. She could not believe what was in front of her. Tribe huts were scattered in the open grass that now swished at her knees.

She walked towards them, watching handfuls of dogs wandering through the hide tipis. Tall branches stood as the spine of the dwellings like spindly fingers reaching to the sky. Emmy's heart was in her throat. She could hear the chants from the glowing fire hidden somewhere between the clustered homes. Despite her fear, she smiled at the edge of the camp, seeing a band of young horses grazing openly with sleepy eyes. She wanted to see Henry here like she had in her dream.

An old woman edged near her from the outskirts of the village and wrapped her bony, strong hand around

Emmy's wrist, leading her inward. Emmy could feel the panic collect at her temples when the woman squeezed harder at her resistance. The woman's white hair wagged in scraggly strands around her shoulders and Emmy pulled harder and harder to go the other way, to stay on the outskirts where she felt comfortable.

"It's okay," Emmy rambled nervously, "I don't want to bother you, I just wanted to see. He told me to find the Sky People."

The old woman turned around and smiled, not saying a word, not understanding a word. Emmy could feel herself growing more nervous as they wound through the tribe of people, all of whom stopped to whisper as she passed. She had grown up listening to stories of the near mythical race and to see them in person was overwhelming. They walked through variously decorated tipis, some painted with bright symbols and animals tails. Others seemed like those Henry had always told her about; taut hides braced by tree branch. She watched children laughing and playing cat's cradle. Women peeked from their homes. Some were taller than others, some with more angular faces. Men were scarce and varied in age and physique, some of which were dangerously strong in appearance.

She could see the fire glowing from between the living quarters and the faint sounds of chanting floated to her ears. The woman tugged her to the opposite outskirts where tipis had been scantily erected of only pine branches from the forest. One of the skeleton dwellings seemed to be the woman's and felt fitting to her dilapidated clothing and near starving body. Emmy was tugged inside. Only a few piled furs covered the ground and a small fire burned in the other corner. There was barely enough room for them.

The old woman pointed to the furs until Emmy sat down. She spoke softly in a language Emmy couldn't identify though she'd sworn it was one she'd heard before in her dreams. The smoke swallowed the flames. The hot air was earthy and thick in her eyes. She closed them once as tears started rushing down her face. Her head swam with the fumes and she could feel herself leaning against the tightly laid branches for support. The vapor smelled nothing like a usual campfire and Emmy inhaled involuntarily, trying to identify it. A certain confusion overtook her and right before she sank down to slumber, she was distantly alarmed, realizing she had been drugged.

*Chapter Twenty-Four*

He watched as she slept, promising himself to meet her only in dreams. His little dove needed to find the source of her truth and he had to trust the druid's plan without interfering. The role he played in her life was different and to give her all the answers would not birth the strength she was going to need. It would have been easy to tell her the blue book had been written in his language, by her own hand. Teaching her a complex and dead tongue for reasons beyond her understanding would only cripple her acceleration. Lillian had to find the prophecy on her own. The shadow man smiled at the way the starlight kissed her bare shoulder. The premonition he'd had before the war had revealed what would be happening if Lillian started to remember her past lives; what was recorded in the blue book.

*Lillian sat at the edge of the coast, tears streaming from her cheeks as herbs lay scattered around her. Whatever order she'd arranged them in had been ruined. She looked to her side and the woman was there, staring out at the sea, a foal in her arms. Lillian tried again to speak to her, call for her attention but only soft mumbles fell from her lips. She didn't want to be alone anymore, she wanted to know who this woman was. A hand fell on her shoulder and she smiled, turning to see her shadow man next to her. He whispered soothingly in his foreign tongue, hoping she'd learn, but it was lost to her. He pressed his lips against her forehead.*

Lillian startled awake to the darkness that consumed the room.

"What in Sweet Earth was in that tea?" she groaned to herself.

She stood and headed to the bedroom and crawled under the covers. Lillian couldn't keep her eyes open and drifted back to sleep.

*He waited for her on the white cliffs. She sat next to him, contented by the monotony of the crashing waves below. His silver eyes brightened in reflection of the sea and his whole body seemed to glow. He pulled her slowly against his side and she nestled her cheek against his chest for warmth. He pointed to the water and she watched as ancient ships appeared and made their way towards the shoreline. He tried to tell her about them, wanted her to take note of their importance. She glimpsed at the crude models as they bobbed fearlessly in the water, trying to find something notable to remember. She could feel her fingers moving restlessly against a notepad and she pushed herself closer to his body, clinging to the dream against the sensation of waking. A chuckle rumbled deep in his chest and he kissed the top of her dark hair.*

Lillian woke to the barren light of a coastal morning, her fingers still clasped around a pen. She peeked through the slits in her eyes to see scribbles of Ogham, Latin, and English on paper flung about the bed. She felt the lethargy in her muscles and the sleep sifting through her conscience. The force of exhaustion from driving the day before hit her body hard. Without the responsibilities of daily life to encourage her forward, Lillian lounged underneath the covers, casually organizing her plans.

The thought of scouring through all of Aillig's possessions flooded her and she looked to the window as a means of escape. If she couldn't walk through her woods to clear her mind, she would have to make do with what she had around her. Slowly, she stretched out of the covers and delicately gathered up pieces of paper, piling them neatly on the nightstand. She flexed her calves and arched her back, letting her dark hair fall like water behind her. Already feeling more clear headed, she pulled on a thin sweater before heading out.

The salt in the air was tangible as Lillian moved her way along the path outside the cottage. The sea grass swayed and the strong wind whipped her hair around her breasts. Her sweater bent against her body and the sound of distant waves pushed thought far from her. She steered away from the cottages and toward the high cliffs in the distance. Lillian felt the broken reeds of grass underneath her feet as she walked along the ridge of the cliffside, following the weathered fence, smiling at the small purple flowers that grew in the bed of green. Cottages came and fell behind her as she walked farther, her skin growing tight from the salt and wind. The open landscape felt unusual after being constantly surrounded by forest. She hadn't realized how comfortable she felt being crammed between nature until now. Even still, she had managed to find the only barrier around to cuddle against. She let her fingers brush against the old wood and wire and admired the endless sea. The chalk cliffs cut away into shallow coves in the distance and their presence in dreaming drew her towards them. Maybe she would find him there. She unfolded her sleep notes and read over them with studious curiosity. Though she couldn't understand his language in the dream, she had transcribed some of it into broken sentences of Ogham. Lillian hoped he was trying to tell her about his life.

Aillig would be proud of her comprehension of the language, he'd been trying to teach her for years without gaining her interest. In the time she'd spent with her shadow man, Lillian had renewed enthusiasm for studying

Latin and Ogham, and wrote it more frequently while she was sleeping. The romance of a gentleman was indulgent. She missed him now as she looked down to the clear water, wishing that she might have a hand to hold or someone to soak in the scenery with. Aillig had written that she'd find everything she needed at the beach house. She wondered bashfully if he had known about her ghost and had included him in his tea jar promise. Certainly all the nights he'd sat at her bedside while she mumbled through her dreams would have revealed him.

She moved down the hill leading to the beach. The moisture from the ocean made everything slick, and her hands slipped off the railing. Lillian whimpered as she lost balance and reached for anything to catch her. Her heart dropped into her belly and her feet flew from the ground. She tumbled down the short decline into the sand. A weight wrapped around her waist as she sat up. Lillian gasped, unprepared for the surprise of his presence. He was there. His whisper came softly and was lost to the rolling waves. She shook her head, a smile creeping into the corners of her mouth, and waited for it to come again.

"Read," she repeated when she heard his whisper a second time.

She refocused on the notes and found a more complete sentence in broken English.

*My dove, you must journey this on your own. But I am always here, to keep you safe. Believe in me. Believe in my love.*

A giggle escaped shyly from her belly and Lillian closed her eyes in hopes to feel him again. A breeze fell against her cheek as his presence trickled to the distance and though a pang of sadness remained, she was relieved to know he was there. She recalled the imagery of her dream and tried to reimagine what it'd be like to sit next to him now. Lillian focused on the serenity of the deserted coastline. She closed her eyes, envisioning the ships that once roamed the seas, docking in the remote cove in the distance. The ships faded from her mind when she tried focusing too much on them. Lillian let them disappear. The waves rolled soothingly as she worked to the clarity she would need for the day ahead. She released the last remnant of her dreams and called herself back to the reason she'd come. Lillian opened her eyes, and inhaled the damp air before heading back. She silently thanked the love of nature as she climbed back to the house.

Lillian had learned long ago that giving herself some time to unwind and indulge in the morning provided her more space for the tasks of her day. She didn't need any distractions from her ambitious list. She glanced to the detached garage as she unlocked the front door. Lillian made a note to peek into it as well. She opened windows inside the cottage to let the briny air blow the staleness out. The ends of her hair were damp and she felt like a child again, finally living out all of her missed field trips. She started in the living room, and shelf by shelf, flipped through every book, paying attention to any information that seemed pertinent. The scent of the aged pages pulled her into their lives and she skimmed through them with her voracious curiosity. She separated the books between herbalism, miscellaneous, and Aillig's handwritten ledgers that cataloged his successes and failures.

A pen bounced between her fingers and Lillian bit her lip. Hours passed as she read about his misfires and failed concoctions, working through all of his notes, just as he must have done in this very room. She reveled a moment before looking around her. Books laid sprawled here and there, some open and subconsciously organized. Paper from her notebook was shoved haphazardly in between the pages she had edited. She hadn't particularly recalled doing any of it, though the dulling sun confirmed the effort she'd put in. Lillian ran her fingers across her forehead as she absorbed, her emerald eyes twinkling with wonder.

"Perhaps a spot of tea before I reorganize," she said to herself, standing.

Her legs were stiff and her hips popped as they readjusted on their way to the kitchen. She felt sound minded when she worked, as though she was moving toward something bigger than herself, that her capabilities were being reinforced. The excitement of gaining more knowledge from Aillig rejuvenated her and she found herself moving back to the living room before tasting her tea. The amount of new tinctures, oils and remedies seemed endless. She itched to wipe out her entire apothecary and start fresh. Many of the plants were listed in local areas and she thought to collect some before she left. Her fingers buzzed as she turned pages, passing from one book to the next. A worn cover caught her eye and she pulled it from the stack next to her. Its leather was soft and her heart stirred when she touched it. It was bound by hand with a sinewy rope she couldn't quite recognize. The geometric art of the Celts that Aillig was so fond of had been hand carved into it and was worn almost smooth with age. The paper was thick like cloth between her fingers and filled with a haphazard mixture of Ogham and other languages.

"Another of your treasures," she whispered, setting it carefully aside.

She glanced over the sea of books littering the living room and noticed a handful more of similarly handmade books. She stood and weaved between piles, picking them out and hugging them to her, lovingly making a stack of their own. Her eyes softened. Aillig had loved collecting old things. When she was done sifting through the cottage, she thought it'd be fun to peek at them. She flicked on a light and yawned. The day had grown late and she felt accomplished for the day. Heading upstairs for bed, Lillian stopped at the first stair, loneliness edging into her ribs. She turned and glanced at the small pile of books once treasured by her dear advisor. She turned back and picked them up. She imagined Aillig obsessing over their antiquity and it made her feel close to him. She slipped into bed contented.

*Lillian ran hastily through the thick forest, lifting her heavy skirts higher. Her chest was tight from excursion and her heart pounded in her ears. Dougal stood over a young man with malice. She had reached them too late, the lifeless body lay still on the forest floor. Lillian fell to her knees, too breathless to cry. The boy was barely in his twenties. Though his eyes were closed they had a knowing that burned behind them. She had felt it before.*

*"Brother!" she screamed.*

*Walls of blackness flew up around her. The hall was long and Lillian looked back to catch a glimpse of someone chasing behind her. She couldn't place the familiar face. Fear rose in her throat. The old woman called too sweetly after her, begging that she was only trying to help. The shadow man felt her distress and whispered into her ears. She followed his instruction as she ran. Tree roots illuminated and coiled in bright colors against the dark as she ran. Ogham flashed and banged in the night sky over her head. A magnetism pulled her down the long hallway and she could faintly hear the old woman calling to them from behind.*

*Lillian's hands shook as she scrambled to get away. Her heart beat upon her lips. He whispered in chants, raising his voice as she flew faster and faster in the shifting lights. She was running to find him. Her shadow had figured out how to be together. Lillian followed the feeling of his presence. Her body felt like it was tearing apart. She could feel her bones vibrate and she gritted her teeth against the sensation. A strange ball of light appeared.*

*"Not yet, child, not without her," it whispered inside of her head.*

*Lillian looked upward and saw the blue eyed woman being pulled upward by the tree branch lights. She tried yelling but no words came. Tears streamed down her face and she could no longer hear her shadow. Light pooled on the floor as her tears fell and wound up her legs. Lillian looked to the sky as light wrapped around her and tried to tear her body from the ground. But she could not move. Her bones creaked and Lillian screamed in pain.*

*Everything went black.*

She felt the uneasy sea sickness before she woke. A corner of a book stuck into the side of her waist and Lillian was nearly fearful to open her eyes. She was certain that the night terror had infiltrated the surroundings of her reality, and she prayed she hadn't destroyed anything precious. She lay perfectly still, not daring to inspire deeper nausea as she tried to process the mixed images of her dream. The strength of her nightmare was uncontested. Nothing had ever felt as real or as painful.

Lillian circled her feet under the covers, feeling the structure of her own body, grounding herself back to reality. The effects of the dream waned and Lillian's sadness filled the space where fear had been. Her shadow man would not be laying next to her. The woman she'd befriended in dreams did not exist. The only thing as real in life as in her dreams was Dougal and his aggression. Everyone she loved was alive only in her imagination.

The thought of more notes and scribbles left her reluctant to look around, and her throat tightened with tears. They came quickly and fell down her cheeks. Lillian hadn't realized how much she had been regulating her emotions while she hunted for an answer to Aillig's death. She had tried to ignore the fact that Dougal could return to frighten her again. She had covered exhaustion with diligence to make Aillig proud. Lillian reminded herself now that he was dead.

Lillian had been so close to finding the shadow man, she knew it. Then like everything else he had been ripped away from her. She wanted to go where he was, where she wasn't alone, where she didn't feel crazy and tired. She tried not ridicule herself for being in love with someone who didn't exist. She longed for his companionship no matter how much lunacy was laced into it. She didn't want to be in this life anymore.

Lillian tried to fall back asleep, stubbornly clinging to the idea of being with him and the other people of her subconscious. Her body ached with questions of the wild haired woman always flowing through her dreams, not speaking nor leaving. It made her feel unmanageably alone this morning and thinking of trying to decipher any more half thought out ideas put her over the edge. This trip was supposed to be rejuvenating and revealing and beautiful. It seemed now to be more of the same exhausting pattern she'd always kept. The bed felt heavy on her left side and a small weight lifted from her chest. Suddenly embarrassed, she wiped the tears from her face, not yet bothering to open her eyes in fear of losing his presence. The long strands of her midnight hair slipped away from her neck and goosebumps rose to her cheeks. Her fingers ached against her side and she inhaled a little deeper. His energy felt weak and she knew he wouldn't stay long.

......

He had to pull away, exhausted from the effort of being present in her attempt to veil walk. Aillig had warned him how dangerous it'd be to try to pull her through the folds of time when she was dreaming, but he was growing anxious for her safety. He could feel the pin needles of prying eyes. They interfered in her dreams and watched her as she walked around the cottage. Lillian had no idea she was being watched and he wanted to take her away where he could protect her. It had been an impulsive action that could have cost her a life. The most important life.

He had spent so long waiting for her to accept him again. Now that they were enjoying each other, it was hard to refrain. He sighed as he rubbed his hands over his thinning face. Dirt stained his beard and clothes, and the smell of his own filth irritated his mind. They had wanted him to suffer before he died. They wanted to pick his pride away in pieces, until he begged for them to bring him death. The idea was not entirely a fearsome one. He could find her in the next life. It was the transition to it that escaped him. He had little understanding of how death transpired or where he went when his body took its last breath. It worried him to think he could lose his memory of her, and all his fighting in this life would be for not. He laid down to rest off the sorrow. His fingers curled around a vile hanging from his neck. He had to stop fearing the unknown. He had to trust Aillig.

......

It was hard not being able to communicate with him like a real person, but the sensation of his presence had wound through her body and leveled her emotional equilibrium. Her head felt tight but she was more or less prepared for whatever disaster lay on the bed next to her. She peeked through thick lashes as she shifted to lay on her side. Paper and books were sprawled all over the place. Ogham was scribbled on sheets of paper that had been torn and tossed from her notebook. Lillian glanced at the pages left open in the books she'd taken to bed. She closed her eyes and sighed before giving in and pulling the notes closer to her. She had been trying to solve Aillig's mystery in her sleep.

She grew colder and the blood ran from her flesh. She was not prepared for the worrisome riddles she had written last night. Her eyes grew wide as she read faster and grabbed at the books and notes more frantically. The fearful movements of the dream clearly transferred and she forced her eyes to move more slowly over her cryptic scribbling. The symbols of Ogham were singular and made no sense. Aillig had said the tree language had layers of meaning, most of which were symbolic. A single letter or symbol could represent an entire idea or philosophy. She pushed her fingers into the base of her neck and tried recalling what else he had told her.

"Each letter is of three. A tree, a time, and a way to be. Journey to your center mind, and all fifths of Bith you will find," she whispered the rhyme.

Lillian shook her head. Aillig had been training her for this moment for years. She felt the game begin. Aillig was calming her nerves by distracting her with puzzles. Lillian looked again at the Ogham she had written.

The mark for Holly appeared over a haphazardly written note. She squinted to make out the words while she struggled to remember what it represented.

*Tightened patterns teach you blindness/break the shackles binding answers.*
*Travel to the center conscience/Tinne tea and steadfast mindset.*

*Fearful thinking tosses balance/harness stories under slumber.*
*Understanding hidden secrets/welcome equal sides of reason.*
*Treasure strangeness, timing, season/deepest kenning written ogham.*

*Perfect balance turns the time wheel/backward to the age of iron.*
*Begin again cosmic teacher /honor duty retribution*

*Crooked creatures threaten justice/vengeance buried under holly*
*Knowledge fallen, reborn again/conflict tempers broken pattern*
*Two fews of three are in existence/triple goddess tips the balance*

*Severed guidance treasured vision/traverse between spirit science*
*Eighteen years of broken magic/focus on your gentle nature*

Lillian ran her fingers through her hair, looking for keywords that might lead her in a direction of purpose. She knew that the Celtic word for holly was *tinne* which gave the symbol its letter.

"Eighteen years of broken magic, focus on your gentle nature," she whispered.

Eighteen years she'd spent at St. John's, where her natural desire to heal had been taken advantage of. Holly in herbalism was used in teas as a tranquilizer. She smiled. The tea she'd found with Aillig's letter. Its deep, earthy undertone had come from carefully dried and roasted holly leaves. She was certain it was only a contributing factor to her stupor, but she'd found a clue. This was not another dream about her childhood fears. He had taken the tea from her dreams and now her dreams were taking her to him.

Aillig had always dabbled in things too mysterious and surreal for her. She had watched him extract repressed memories from his clients through hypnosis many times. She'd been skeptical of his practice, always settling on his expertise to observe as the true tool for his healing success.

Aillig loved to make the world whimsical for a broken young girl, and as she'd gotten older she believed less and less in his embellishment. Now, she couldn't help but wonder if he'd used those very techniques to hide a secret within her own subconscious. She looked down to her notes.

"Tinne tea to keep me calm. The state of hypnosis."

Lillian looked at the slashes between certain words.

"Tinne and conscience. Hand in hand for all of his experiments," she laughed.

She grabbed at the books scattered on the bed. If Aillig was involved, then so were his books. Easily she found an open page with the sketch of holly leaves in the corner. She pulled her notes closer and grabbed for a pen that had been shoved under her pillow. The book seemed to be an old script, filled with pages about the herbs of ogham; a perfect blend of Aillig's love for history, healing, and lore. A horizontal line with three vertical lines reaching upwards from it was painted in thick ink in the center of the page. She was sure there was significance to the placement of the holly symbol, but couldn't guess what it was. Below, five words were listed next to an infinity sign.

"These must be the fifths of Bith. Oh Aillig, I cannot remember all of this information. What was Bith?" she muttered to herself.

"Was that the word for an ogham symbol? No, that is called a few."

Lillian tapped her pen against her notebook and bit her lip. She whispered the fifths listed, hoping to jog her memory.

"Steadfastness, rejection, judgement, vengeance, and preparation. A tree, a time, and a way to be. Five parts of a way to be. Be where? In life? On Earth!" she exclaimed with excitement as she wrote it down.

She looked back to her dream notes. There were five sections drawn, one for each fifth. Lillian assigned a fifth to each of them and sat back.

"A tree, a time, and a way to be," she repeated to herself.

She needed to know the general theme of the Holly before she could dissect it further. Next to the list of fifths was the sign of infinity, an eight turned on its side. She traced it with her fingers.

"Even turned on its side it's still perfectly balanced," she whispered. She looked back to the paper, looking to see if there was a connection within the text.

"The only word used more than once is balance."

Her mind spun and focused. She still couldn't decipher the symbolism in what she'd written. She tried starting from somewhere else.

"Harness stories under slumber," she scribbled separately. "Definitely all of my dreams. Aillig has put something in them."

"Severed guidance, treasure visions."

She made note of his death next to it. There was no denying he was murdered, even Aillig had known it. He had known it so well that he had used her subconscious to hide some kind of message about it. He wanted her to take her dreams seriously. Goosebumps raised along her arms. Lillian couldn't help feeling invaded. She'd trusted Aillig to keep her safe and it seemed she was in more danger by knowing him and knowing his secrets than she'd realized.

"Why can't you ever just be straight forward with things? This is too important to make into a riddle," she yelled into the air.

Lillian gave up and moved to something else, hoping that she could find something more direct. She brought the next closest dream note to her and rolled her eyes as she traced over the symbol for the hazel.

"Another riddle," she sighed, reading onward underneath the horizontal line with four vertical lines stemming towards the top of the page.

*Empty nutshells lying beneath my headstone*
*my knowledge transformed as fire in the head*
*listen to the world not made of flesh and bone*

*Perception's ashes create new wings to spread*
*beautiful spirit of light will rise with Lugh*
*grounding  true essence in the goddess' bed*

*Craft of the crone sovereign and deep within you*
*empathetic healer of arbitration*
*passion softens the hearts that have gone askew*

"Headstone, empty, Aillig's death," she was picking up on the overlapping theme. "Transformed as fire in the head. Probably the embedding of whatever he kept secret in my subconscious."

Lillian started to wonder how many of her dreams had nothing to do with her past, but perhaps with his. Maybe she wasn't as tortured as she'd thought all this time. It was becoming clear that Aillig hadn't been all he seemed on the surface. She shook her head, there was no time to get side tracked. She was finally working towards what brought her to the beach house and she had to remember that despite the flaws of a man, Aillig had been very good to her. She could share her subconscious for his sake.

"Listen to the world not made of flesh and bone."

Someone else had recently suggested she listen to him. He was definitely not made of flesh or bone.

"Perception's ashes," she wrote out on a new piece of paper. "Burn perception to ash. Kill perception. Perception of what? The world not made of flesh and bone, then perception's ashes, next line. A continuance?"

Aillig would have likely meant her rejection of things she couldn't explain. He had always told her to chase what she couldn't understand with the curiosity that possessed her. But Lillian wasn't sure that she knew how it related to his death. She pushed the papers aside and looked again for another marked place in a book. The ogham symbol for the hazel was scratched on a bookmark hanging out of a closed book. The leather was embossed with some symbol of sacred geometry. She sketched it roughly into her notebook, thinking to research its significance at another time. If she was meant to find this collection, there would be nothing unimportant about them.

The page for the hazel was scattered with illuminated art. A painting of a sun hung over a man, his head caught on fire by its light. The gold leaf shimmered as she studied and read aloud.

"Lugh, the sun god, fire in the head, knowledge. The hazel, the tree of knowing. For once a less dismal message."

Lillian knew the hazel well, as any healer would. It was part of a symbolic ceremony between the apprentice and the mentor when the torch was being passed. Aillig had given her his very own hazel rod just before his death, when he had told her she was ready to further her studies into a higher realm. She could see it in her mind, engraved with ogham and made to look as though it had come from the head of a unicorn itself. He was from Scotland, and their national animal seemed appropriate. Now it collected dust in a box with a few other precious items she'd managed to take north with her.

"I should have been listening instead of worrying. This would have been so much easier to understand."

Lillian studied the art and found the fifths next to a golden harp. Instead of politely writing off Aillig's enthusiasm for mythology, she should have realized it was part of the riddle.

"Eloquence, beauty, teaching, arbitration, and the arts. I need to have knowledge of these all as the hazel suggests."

Lillian rubbed her eyes and looked out the window. The sea was calling to her. She wanted a distraction from failure. Lillian could find a pattern, or a clue of Aillig's any day, but to understand his more philosophical mind was out of reach. She hadn't been interested in anything that wasn't concrete. She had needed stability then. She piled her notes according to the letters and picked up her last page of nonsense.

*Asleep within I beg forget me not.*
*Harmonic body binds what has been lost,*
*a silver tongue will tie the endless knot.*
*Embody my rope and walk the realms that cross.*

*Hermetic healer twisted within thrice*
*and concealed by the lunatic's fort.*
*Embrace the coat of esoteric mice*
*to see my name in perfect golden light.*

*Am I conception of eternal youth?*
*Elixir to make the maiden flawless?*
*Corrupt is the man who thinks this as truth!*
*For I am the unsung voice of the goddess.*

*Above, below, and also within you*
*Attune to Coll's light, find the hidden few.*

Below the poem was a horizontal line with five short vertical lines growing upward. She looked for a book that corresponded but found nothing.

"Attune to Coll's light, find the hidden few."

*Coll* was the old word for the hazel. She picked up the book with illuminated art and flipped past the pages about wisdom. Lillian's eyes widened as paintings sprang from the following pages.

"Avalon/Afallon, *Emain Ablach,* Eden," she listed the names heading each page.

They were the lands of the eternal, and the fruit was it's apple. Aillig had talked about them often, and they were stories she had enjoyed. She loved the idea of other lands, other realms, where the ugliness of this one didn't exist. It had also been a huge source of debate between her beloved mentor and those of differing beliefs. He had suggested that these heavenly homelands did not literally exist in the sky but in the higher planes of the mind, that they were symbolic to a person's essence. She worried that his open ideals may have gotten him in trouble.

"Hermetic healer twisted within thrice, and concealed by the lunatic's fort. Maybe someone thought he was so crazy that he was dangerous," she mused, recalling his odd behavior in the weeks before the fire. But how that tied into eternity she wasn't certain.

"Am I conception of eternal youth? Elixir to make the maiden flawless? Corrupt is the man who thinks this as truth. It couldn't be," she trailed off as she separated the parts of the poem.

Aillig was alluding to the mysterious elixir of life. Though he'd always had a terrible fascination with alchemy and science, she'd never suspected he believed in it. Nor would she think that anyone else in this modern era would think much of it. Puzzle pieces shifted in her mind's eye as she worked toward a bigger picture. She stared harder at the poem and the symbolic paintings in the book. She wished it had been accompanied by information like the others.

"It's the hidden few. The hidden letter, the hidden ideal. These books aren't going to reveal all of their secrets."

Lillian spread everything out in front of her and tried to look at the bigger picture.

"A silver tongue will tie the endless knot. Endless knot. The eight on its side is infinite. Embody my rope? Embody the eight. Embody balance!"

Lillian scribbled it down, feeling like she was catching on.

"What's balanced between all of this?"

Her eyes scanned through her dream notes, trying to find something that linked them. Like the illuminated paintings in the old books, one single word lit up on the pages.

"Goddess."

She stretched her neck and exhaled. Aillig had always steered away from the spiritual aspect of healing. He had been careful not to remind her of the past she had escaped. Now, she cursed herself for being caught up in her petty heartaches. Lillian was seeing how she had handicapped her knowledge for the first time. She had been so caught up in her own life, that she hadn't stopped to see his.

"There is nothing balanced about me," she whined to herself as she sat back against the bed frame.

She could feel the tension building behind her forehead. Too many messages passed and faded as she analyzed. Lillian stared blankly at the bed littered with books and paper and ink stains. At the edge of the mattress, an untouched companion to the others slept. It didn't have an emblem carved into the front. Instead, the leather was fresh and shiny, unworn from the abuse of time. Lillian hadn't remembered taking this from the stacks last night. She picked it up and opened it.

Her breath caught in her throat. It was Aillig's personal journal. The date at the top blurred as tears formed behind her eyes. Her heart pounded in her chest. The muscles along her spine tensed. Seeing his handwriting always got the best of her. She closed the book and fought hard to keep her mind clear, forcing herself to stare at the plain white wall in front of her.

"He's dead, Lillian. Stop it. Stop letting this get to you," she yelled to herself, fighting back tears.

She wasn't going to panic in the middle of her hunt. Her eyes shifted slowly to the window, far away to the scenery beyond the window. She could almost hear the waves lolling forward onto the beach, mothering her. The wave within her started to settle and Lillian edged the journal towards the rest of her findings, unprepared to read it. Whatever answers she'd come looking for would be in the pages just inches from her. The riddles softened the darkness of his death and started to look better than they had a few minutes ago.

"Perhaps some of that holly tea will do me some good now."

She went to swing her legs off the bed and hit her knees. The drawer of the nightstand had been left open.

"That's where the journal must have come from," she muttered to herself.

Something felt wrong as she walked out of the bedroom. Lillian never walked away from an unsolved riddle. She turned to scan the pile and shrugged. Taking a moment away would help. Still, as she walked to the staircase the feeling persisted and when she walked down the short flight she stopped and realized why.

The books she had started organizing and sifting through yesterday were thrown and tossed all over the entire living room. She walked by cautiously, as if she were viewing a crime scene. Lillian moved to the kitchen. A couple more books had also been thrown on the counter there, next to tea jars she hadn't left out. She must have been sleep walking. A pit formed in her stomach. Her habits were gaining strength with every new clue she unfolded. Lillian had only just begun to accept all of her quirks and this dream had taken it too far. She waited for the water to boil and plopped a tea bag into a mug. She didn't try to pick apart what was happening. She just simply turned and walked out of the door.

"Well, Susan, she's finally made it," a woman called heartily from her window as Lillian passed by their cottage. "Let's stay scarce through the day and let her settle in a little more before we let her know we're here."

*Chapter Twenty-Five*

When Emmy woke, the tipi was as barren and dark as it had been before, though the light creeping through the crevices told her it was morning. She peeled back layers of furs, and pushing her matted mane from her eyes, crawled out of the opening. She squinted her eyes in the bright sun. The camp was quiet and vacated. She walked quietly in the flattened grass, avoiding the ash of small camp fires as she went. She couldn't help but look around, still in awe of what she was seeing.

"They would be disappointed if you'd left before they met you," a voice spoke curtly behind her.

Emmy whirled around and stared. The tall man from the other night approached her. She couldn't mistake him, his light skin tone had stood out from the others in the moonlight. He was dressed in full regalia with the pelt of a wolf over his body, its large head sitting atop his own. His face was a little gaunt but not unhealthy. It seemed to her there was a bit of aristocracy in his demeanor. It was hard to tell under the teeth of a dead wolf.

"Who?" she stuttered.

"Everyone."

He was blunt and impressive.

"I thought you couldn't speak English," she blurted.

His smile flashed underneath the beastly hood and the long angles of his face caught a glimmer of light.

"I speak it quite well. However, you appeared unexpectedly. I was out of practice. My apologies."

He bowed his head, bringing the stark eyes of the wolf to meet her own.

"So, who exactly do you mean by everyone," she asked, trying to control the impulse to run as fast as she could.

"The *Panátĭ*, the *Siksika*, the *Toyani*."

Emmy had no idea what he was talking about.

A gentle patience passed over him and he turned to face the majority of the village.

"The entire tribe, the *Tukudika*, are mountain dwelling people from centuries ago. In English, some have been called the Bannock, Blackfeet, and Sheep Eater tribes."

She could recall her grandfather vaguely mentioning a few of the tribe names in his stories, and she strained to remember anything at all about them.

"But all the Native Americans were forced onto reservations," she argued.

He only smiled wider, and she wondered where she'd seen him before.

"There have been times in history where your pale men have looked only with their eyes and missed many things. We have been living in the hidden heavens of this world for thousands of years."

This wolf-man had to be lying. She wanted to laugh in disbelief but wouldn't dare be rude to someone of such stature. The last time she'd done that she ended up battered and threatened with death.

He watched her from the corner of his eye, sensing the distress she worked through in silence. He had been told by the spirits she'd find his tribe. His people needed to help her recall the memory of her lives. She would need them to help keep her safe from her pursuers. He could carry on with the story she was supposed to hear, but decided not to say too much at once. Just like the young horses in their herd, she was fighting her flight or fight mechanism. She truly was Moon Horse. Pride filled his heart, and the world he once had been a part of was lighted with hope. Change might come indeed.

"What is your name?" she asked, still on edge.

"I am a Sky Brother."

"I'm Emmy. So your name is Sky Brother?"

"No, sweet girl. We do not often reveal our names. It is the belief of the Sky People, the *Toyani*, that our individual names are sacred and that to share them too openly would diminish the power of the spirit who'd given it to you."

Emmy's blue eyes widened and she bit her lip to keep from smiling. Part of her couldn't help but giggle as she had in Henry's lap, hearing stories identical to these. In a moment of confused hysteria she let it bubble from her throat and she turned away to try and cover it. When she looked back up at the imposing man, she swallowed.

"I'm sorry, Sky Brother," she choked down more laughter. "It's just that I grew up hearing stories like these and I'm having a hard time believing that all this is real. That it's not a dream I'll wake up from and find the walls of my motel around me. I don't really know why I even decided to come," she rambled, pushing her hair off her face.

She thought of Henry and the strange coincidence of her location. Emmy wondered now if her choice to stay in Wyoming hadn't been as flippant as she thought. Maybe Henry's stories had been planted so deeply in her subconscious that when she came to a place matching her imagination's memory, she didn't even notice. It was just odd that all of his fairytales held so much fact. Emmy couldn't shake the feeling that Henry knew the whole time.

"I can understand your current perspective. Will you stay? Whispers of your arrival moved quickly through our people last night and they've gone to prepare for your welcome ceremony."

Emmy sighed. "But why?"

He only smiled, the curve of his mouth dangerously identical to the teeth bared on his head.

"Come. Let us find you clothes more suitable for your next journey."

He took her to the tipis made of simple hide and showed her inside. A young woman sat waiting for her.

"She is Bannock," he explained. "They are a peaceful and independent people. She has offered to help you dress for the ceremony if you will stay."

The deep richness of the woman's face was serene and welcoming, her amber eyes warming in Emmy's presence.

"Okay," she smiled, unable to resist her childish curiosity. "But I still don't get why I'm so important to you."

"You will start tonight," he said before leaving.

The woman's hair shone like the polished obsidian arrows sitting in the corner of her home. It made Emmy think of the dark haired woman in her dreams and if she was real and living here too. The Bannock woman motioned her to sit on the furs while she prepared. Emmy couldn't believe she was agreeing to this. Impulses had lead her here, and they were obviously working for her to stay. She reminded herself that there was nothing left for her to go back to. Anger drifted through her veins and she decided that this was as good as any other place to try starting over. At least they wanted her here.

She turned her attention back to the moment and strained to remember some of the words the wolf-man had used earlier to describe everyone.

"Toyani?" she asked pointing at the woman.

She grinned and shook her head.

"Panátĭ," she said, putting her hand on her heart.

She waved her hand around to insinuate the entire people.

"Tukudika."

Emmy nodded and admired her animal hide dress which was covered in colored beadwork. The intricacies showed crude images of deer and geometric shapes, and her head band had a large feather standing in the back. The more she watched and looked at her, the less she looked like a different race of people. If she had light hair, the woman could easily walk through the streets of town and fit in. She wondered if the Native Americans hidden beyond the small lake all looked less like the images of fairytales.

The woman placed Emmy's garments in front of her to change. Beaded into the hide shirt and pants were running horses of red and white. She reached out to touch it with her fingers, shocked to feel the soft and pliable texture. Emmy didn't understand why she wasn't given the dress of a woman, but not wanting to be inconsiderate and ruin the enchantment of the past twenty-four hours, she nodded once and touched her heart, hoping the woman would understand her gratitude.

She stood, slipping out of her clothes and into the new ones. The woman folded her pedestrian outfit and placed it lovingly in the corner near the arrowheads before positioning Emmy in front of her so that she could start braiding. Her hair was a tangled mess in comparison to the tribe woman's and Emmy felt self conscious as she gently tugged through it. The woman worked patchouli oil into her matted locks as she worked. Emmy had never had a mother, but thought if she'd had one, she would have liked a woman like this. The braids were wrapped and laid neatly against the tops of Emmy's breasts. The woman smiled after looking her once over and placed her hands delicately on Emmy's shoulders.

Emmy couldn't help but smile as the product of the woman's craftsmanship. They walked together in the waning light towards a gathering of people. A fire had been started and tribesmen parted and stood aside as the pair walked through, faces varying wildly from one to the next. Emmy looked at each set of eyes as she passed, feeling the rising importance of her presence. She looked for the tall man in hopes that he might explain the meaning for her, but he was nowhere in sight. The fire roared as they stood in front of it and a quiet rumbling of drums vibrated the floor beneath her moccasin clad feet. Through the flames she could see the blurred shadow of a wolf's head and knew that he sat waiting. She was guided to sit next to him in a place of honor, and Emmy's excitement amplified.

"So, are you the chief?" she asked, trying to understand her surroundings.

He smiled and shook his head. "No. We do not have set leaders here. Our people believe in the system of freedom. We step forward when we have knowledge to offer, so we can enlighten our entire tribe. In regards to you, I happen to have a knowledge beyond the old tales. This has put me in a position of leadership."

She nodded, caught up in the fantasy around her.

"What do you know about me? Does the wolf represent whoever is in charge at the time?"

Again, he shook his head. "The wolf was a personal journey."

When he didn't elaborate, she pushed no further and lost herself in the movements of the people. They seemed to be assembling into groups, collectively preparing to approach her.

"Each tribe has decided to separate and bring you a gift so that you may understand your importance to them individually. The last time any of our people chose to separate, they ended up on reservations. Do not take this gesture lightly."

Emmy swallowed.

"I don't understand what is so important about me."

"You have the power of many souls in you. You have tried countless times to save the people from the dictation of fear and hate that rule them. You have not yet won. But this story, the one you are living in now has the power of nine, and you have help. We have been the preservers of your story for generations. Even after the rest of the world has forgotten, we have not. You bring hope of living freely, of showing the way out of hiding, of growing our tribe to all kinds."

He looked down at her through glowing eyes and she had a hard time differentiating between the man and his robe. The air grew heavy around her, and she wanted to leave as fast as she could. Logic begged her to go, told her that something dangerous was falling upon her, but she was cemented to the spot on the floor where she sat. A tall and foreboding man approached them holding a mass of folded blankets and other contraptions. His nose was prominent and his golden eyes shone. She could feel herself wanting to cower in front of his intensity. Emmy consciously straightened her back. He knelt nimbly despite his large and muscled frame, and bent his head.

"He is from what you call the Blackfoot. They are our wildest people, proven to be brave and sworn to the duty of protecting our secrecy. They were the bold people who navigated the hunts of the plains and have a strong dedication to your communication with horses. They too regard the animals with explicit honor and he has brought to you their finest made blankets and bridles."

Emmy smiled shyly as the man pressed the gifts into her. The wolf-man nodded and released the representative back into the group of proud faced men and women.

"Weren't they a war tribe?" Emmy asked innocently, remembering Henry's stories about the Blackfeet and cowboys.

The man shrugged. "Their tribe was marked with an attitude like lightening. When they were pushed around by strange settlers, it was harder for them to be peaceful. We all believed in the harmonious existence between living things on this earth, and when it was tried by outsiders, they were proud to defend it. Even still, the ones who have accepted the way of life you're familiar with contain the undeniable pride of their history. In fact, we've had to keep our communication with them nearly nonexistent for fear that they would boast about us and reveal our secret dwelling places," he laughed happily.

"The Blackfeet have much to teach you if you choose to let them. Their people can help you remember the more instinctual part of the lives you've forgotten. They will help you understand your impulses in this life, the things you do subconsciously as old lives cling to the inner recesses of your mind."

Emmy couldn't understand why he kept rambling about previous lives, but in fear of angering him with questions he'd find silly, she stayed silent.

A gentle faced man dressed in a mixture of modern and traditional clothing approached. The serenity of his face calmed her nerves and his kind, sweeping smile was contagious. She leaned to her translator as he approached.

"Why does he wear a button up shirt under the hide vest?"

"He is a Bannock man, the same tribe as the woman who prepared you, as I think you guessed by their demeanor. They are an expressive and varied people who often times are capable of communicating with our family living in modernization. When the tribes had been asked to move to reservations, the Bannocks had gone rather peacefully. We think their natural curiosity pulled them in.

But when they were abandoned to starve, most left the reservation and wandered the area. Some came here and started their new history and others joined bigger tribes. Some found their way back to other reservations where they've blended in with surrounding tribes. They are the diversity of our people, those who inspire our expansion of intellect and trade. Their jovial exterior must not fool you for they are also a very independent group and they roam to be our ears and eyes. We know little else of what they do while they are gone. Their vast difference in perspective had once caused a rift between them and the Blackfeet, however, considering the evolution of our lives, even their old grudges have been put to rest."

The man knelt and presented her with a small satchel. The skin melted like butter in her palms, the objects inside rolling like rocks between her fingers as she felt it. She looked up into his serene eyes and understood how his people could blend into modern cities. He smiled, motioning with his own hands to open and look inside. Her icy blue eyes widened as she gazed at the myriad of glowing gems sitting between her hands. Her head snapped up in protest of such an expensive gift, but the sharp eyes of the wolf-man stifled her.

"It would be an embarrassment for you to refuse his gift. These gems are not of great monetary value to them, though it is not lost on them that you might need these in your journey to trade for money. His people have used them in modern towns for just that. But they hold highly spiritual power, and he hopes they aid you in accessing the language of your spirit. The Bannock keep expansive philosophies. Think carefully whenever you reach for this gift."

Emmy could feel a fluidity in her bones as she called attention to the precious stones. She nodded to the Bannock people in gratitude and an eager smile split across their leader's cheeks before he turned and slid silently back with his group. She placed the bag gently between her crossed legs and pulled on her braids as she worked through what was happening to her. She was responding to their beliefs with an acceptance she couldn't explain. She'd heard this all before though, and maybe it was the reason. She smiled at the subtle intelligence her grandfather had hidden between the lines of his bedtime stories. She never knew Henry to be frivolous and she could feel herself questioning the motives of his fictions for the first time. She missed him terribly tonight.

The hunched and silver haired woman from the night before came forward now, and Emmy grew nervous. She drugged her last time.

"It's okay to feel nervous in her presence," the man explained as he picked up on her tensing body. "Your soul is responding to the presence of a practiced spiritual woman. She has come forth to represent the *Toyani*, or the ones the pale faces confuse as Sheep Eaters. These are our Sky People, the souls who can communicate between lives and gain knowledge of how we exist."

She stood before Emmy, pulling a jar and a small satchel from the folds of her dress. Inside the pot contained a blue paint and Emmy looked to the man to explain.

"Tomorrow we will take you to the Sky People's dwelling place and you will need this then. She has heard the lives of past and probable future, and learned to give this to you from one of your past souls. We will learn more of it tomorrow. The satchel we will take with us then too, but it's important that you don't open it now," he said and he motioned the woman's dismissal.

Once she moved back amongst the darkness of night, all who gathered dispersed. The drums rumbled and people began to dance. Emmy watched as they moved methodically about the fire, chanting and calling to invoke the spirits that guided them. A wild eyed Blackfoot motioned for her to come closer. She looked to the wolf-man for approval and he nodded.

She stood and walked carefully to the group of athletically built men. When she stopped, they parted to show a young horse dancing nervously behind them. Instantly, she was concerned for the animal's distress and moved closer. She looked around at the expectant faces and they all motioned for her to get on. Having picked up on the idea that it'd be disgraceful to deny them, she placed a hand against the horse's neck to soothe it. Its amber eyes caught sight of the fire and the young animal reared up in fear. When Emmy looked back to see what had scared it, she was sent into a tunnel of confusion. Her eyes glazed over and she stumbled forward for the horse's rope. Her mind brought forth the visions of her old barn burning at the back of the property and sent her heart in her throat. She looked wildly around at the faces near her, half expecting to see Ethan laughing amongst them. She fell to her knees and heard the chanting drown out the screams of the horses in her vision of home. Emmy dropped the bag of gems she hadn't realized she was clutching and touched the delicate legs of the horse in front of her, managing through her haze to stand back up. A hand cupped her shoulder and she spun around, wildly trying to fight whoever it was.

"You're okay," the deep voice sang. "Do you know what happened?"

It took Emmy a moment to refocus on the glowing eyes of the wolf pelt before she shook her head. He picked up her satchel and handed it to her, motioning to tie it around the waist of her pants.

"You connect into the horse through the projected pictures in your head. That is how the black stallion knew to bring you here. I'm sure you can think of times that's happened to you before."

He paused and waited for her to process. Then pointed to her satchel.

"One of the healing rocks from your bag, the one you call labradorite, opens your passage to past lives where you were known for your communication with horses," he explained.

"These horses are not broken souls, trained into the robotics of obedience like the ones you are used to. Their ability to connect with you is much stronger, and your past soul will pick up on it with more intensity. This mare conveyed to you her fear of fire and your mind related it to a picture that was comparable in your scale of emotions. Now take a deep breath, there is no one here to hurt you. Approach her again and remember what I've told you."

Emmy's chest heaved as she tried to catch her breath. She turned to the sweet angel, more concerned about easing her fears than conquering her own. As she stepped in slowly, she could hear the dim crackle of her Kentucky barn. Emmy closed her eyes and focused on staying relaxed, wanting to encourage the same from the youngster. She thought of the long grass in the valleys and the gentle lap of the water at the hidden lake. She tuned her ears to the panting of the horse and when it seemed more subdued she silently reached out to stroke her neck.

Emmy opened her eyes and whispered Gaelic singsong into the filly's flickering ears.

"Now try to mount her. The Blackfoot people are believers in what they can see and have waited generations to witness this. Let them see who you are," the wolf-man encouraged in a low tone of excitement.

"Little Angel," she muttered to the young dappled gray.

Emmy twisted her hand into smoky mane and with an effortless tug pulled herself onto the horse's back. The filly's muscles flexed and she leapt forward a few feet before settling under Emmy's weight. The light Henry had taught her to beckon manifested in her mind's eye, moving gently to link her to the mare. She did not notice the awestruck faces watching her. The light fused to the ground and their serenity synchronized for only a moment. When she looked up, she blushed and slid off her back, suddenly self conscious about the talent that had been called into open air. There was no ignoring it now, and no demoralizing it by calling it luck. It was obvious in every face watching that she was inexplicably different. The men lead the gentle filly away and it suddenly became clear to her why she was given the ceremonial outfit of a man.

"They wanted me to show them," she said, looking at the wolf-man.

"Yes," he smiled. "And on a horse no one has been able to tame. It took all the men surrounding her to lead her to you. Part of the bridle they handcrafted for you is of hazel wood. Our people believe that it protects Spirit's wisdom. Now that you have proven your ability to shape shift and spirit talk, you can use the bridle to protect you and the mare from unwanted attention. I will explain more on your spirit walk."

She'd have felt more shocked if the same trick hadn't already been played on her by Cutter. Suddenly she was feeling homesick for him. He had seen it all along. Emmy's heart sunk to her stomach. It was all her fault. The night seemed late and she yawned before she could catch it. The tall man came just inches from her face, looking even more frightening against the light of the moon.

"Your day is very important tomorrow, go and get some rest."

He looked to a lingering woman and nodded for her to take Emmy to a tipi. She was lead to an empty Blackfoot dwelling, marked with the flamboyant images of running horses. The woman left her at the door and Emmy genuinely relaxed for the first time that day. She undressed without question, crawling under the furs and fell asleep with ease.

*Cutter appeared before her, worried. He roamed around the pens at the Big House muttering to himself. She tried helplessly to yell for his attention, but no voice came. Resigned to silence, she felt her transformation and knew she had taken on Apollo's form, running to the hidden lake in despair. The black haired woman stood waiting for her, plants cradled in her open palms. Emmy's own hair whipped in the wind when she changed back to herself. The woman spoke in languages she didn't know and she looked frantically for the wolf man to translate.*

.......

Cutter tried to stay angry as he thought of his empty bank account. Just like every woman he let into his life, she had wasted herself and his money away. His mother had fallen to alcohol, and his ex girlfriend had partied while he clung to the coat tails of good faith. His desire to see the best in people always left him burned. Emmy had not only stripped him of every cent, but forced him to go back home. He had no choice.

Cutter threw his camera against the wall, and cursed. He was too old to run from his responsibilities, and knew the disaster lay roughly in his hands. It wasn't her fault. He never should've pushed her. He'd apologize. He was too wildly in love to give up on her so easily. She was nothing like those that tortured his past. He hoped she'd forgive him.

*Chapter Twenty-Six*

Despite the chill in the air, Lillian pulled off her shoes to feel the beach. Her union with the natural world was the only thing strong enough to ground her. She waited a moment and when she did not feel him come, she was oddly comforted in knowing that she must be okay.

Her toes were numb and she dug her feet under the sand in concentration. She wrapped her arms across her chest and watched the rhythm of the water. Lillian found the steady pattern of the wave break, and moved into a meditation of thought. The vibration from the crashing water boomed to her feet and in her mind's eye, she laid out the pieces she found this morning and considered them as a whole.

She knew that while she dreamt, she had also been searching through Aillig's cottage. Lillian had never recalled herself being so active during slumber. Aillig must be using her subconscious as a guide to her reality.

"What tricks have you put into my mind, Aillig?" she whispered to the waves.

She couldn't ignore the sharp edge of invasion that crept inside her good faith. She had never agreed to his hypnotics.

"I would have if he could've asked," she sighed. She was tired of feeling defensive. Under her breath, Lillian recalled the first riddle.

"Fearful thinking tosses balance."

Lillian relented and reorganized, calling to the version of herself that simply enjoyed solving a good riddle. She couldn't allow old habits to deconstruct her intelligent mind. Aillig had made that much clear, and she smiled despite herself. He knew her so well.

She thought about his hypnosis. If it had inspired her enthusiastic stroll through the cottage while she slept, then there had to be a link between her dream and reality. Lillian searched for commonalities between her nightmare and the symbols she'd found sleep walking. Each clue had been connected to a letter in Ogham and she was starting to think the language had more importance than writing efficiency. They had also appeared in her dream like bright lights. Aillig was famous for creating layered answers into a single clue and the language itself carried many meanings.

It was clear that he wanted to relay the importance of her dreams as a symbol of all things hidden. Only Lillian had access to the world of her dreams. There couldn't be a better place to hide his secrets. Her long hair was damp from the air and she toyed with it between her fingers. She could only imagine what he had stored away in there that someone else would be desperate to get. The Ogham few marked by its hidden nature came to mind.

"Am I conception of eternal youth? Elixir to make the maiden flawless? Corrupt is the man who thinks this as truth," she repeated.

Lillian wasn't as loyal to the ideas of magic and alchemy as Aillig had been. He was the man who could see an entire life inside a leaf. She could only see its purpose. She closed her eyes and tried not to feel the pressure against her temples. It didn't matter what she thought about it. Lillian needed to think like Aillig if she wanted to understand his clues, even if it meant believing in his whimsy with the same devotion he had.

"You've really pushed my limits, my friend," she laughed softly.

Lillian sucked in the breeze, feeling goosebumps under her clothes.

"Understanding hidden secrets, welcome equal sides of reason."

"Here I am ridiculing Aillig for believing in magic while I'm in love with a ghost. Strip the emotional value of magic away and it's only herbalism and chemistry, really. Strip it off my love affair and what do I have? Lunacy."

She thought of his riddle.

"Hermetic healer twisted within thrice, and concealed by the lunatic's fort."

Lillian could understand the reference to secretive healing. Aillig had kept his most valued knowledge to himself and only a few others, none of which she'd ever met. Perhaps they would play a factor in unveiling his death in the future. Lillian blew into her hands for warmth; she could be hopeful she wasn't alone. There had been mention of three in his riddle.

"Crooked creatures threaten justice, vengeance buried under holly."

Her back tightened. He had known who was coming for him, and perhaps he knew where evidence to prove it was kept. Lillian made a mental note to memorize the line. She was suddenly annoyed that she hadn't opened his journal. There was no telling what knowledge could have been sitting in plain sight.

"Empty nutshells lying beneath my headstone, my knowledge transformed as fire in the head," she reprimanded herself. She should have known better. The entire riddle represented sacred wisdom, of which he had plenty, and had likely left in between the pages she refused to read.

"Asleep within, I beg forget me not."

She was reminding herself that his death was the reason she'd come. His cottage was not a vacation, but a duty she'd promised herself to. Even her shadow man had stuck to his promise better than she. A group of birds broke the serenity of the morning horizon and she watched them fondly as they twisted and swirled in unison. The giant flock of starlings stretched and collided. Their formations painted symmetrical waves of images and Lillian got lost trying to draw pictures in it. She missed the companionship of her ghost. She felt like she was drowning in the sea of Aillig's riddles, and longed to feel comforted by him. She had been so close to finding him in her dream. The power that had tried tearing her from her body had left her empty upon waking. She wanted to believe that it was possible he existed beyond her mind's eye.

"Severed guidance, treasure vision, traverse between the spirit science."

The papery sound of wings filled her ears and she watched the flock until they dwindled in the distance. A wind delicately toyed with the ends of her hair, and a chill came over her. She stood, rubbing circulation into her feet one at a time.

"Harmonic body binds what has been lost," she whispered.

Lillian walked back to the cottage more calmly than when she'd left, prepared now for the task at hand. Her intentions were rejuvenated, and the newness of her discoveries had worn off. Lillian had already come to terms with the fact that he had been murdered, but she hadn't accepted her responsibility to find out who was guilty.

"Definitely no vacation," she breathed out loud.

Lillian had never imagined that her life would end up where it was. She was trying to solve a murder. She was being asked to believe in things that had no factual foundation. She was falling in love with a figment of her own imagination. Yet, she'd never felt more alive.

"Strange to see ye here!" a voice called as she passed the neighboring cottage.

Lillian jumped. She looked around before catching sight of the woman calling from her window. Her thick build and broad shoulders seemed familiar. Lillian squinted, trying to make clear the face shaded from the kitchen. The woman poked her head out further, waving jovially as she came closer. Lillian's chest collapsed against her heart.

"Oh, hello Mrs. MacKay." Her lie crumbled to her feet and she grabbed for any excuse but the truth. Heat reddened her cheeks and words evaded her.

"Don't worry, dear," she laughed from her kitchen, "your secret's safe with me! We all need a little time away, don't we?"

"I suppose so," Lillian smiled, defaulting to her professional attitude.

"Have a nice walk, lass? Perhaps if ye aren't too busy this evening ye can come for a meal. Would be the least I could do after all the help you've given me."

Lillian only nodded, waving as she continued on towards the protection behind Aillig's door.

Mrs. MacKay watched her as she passed. Though it was tempting to see what the girl had been up to in the cottage, she refrained from risking what little trust she felt she had with Lillian. Mrs. Bixby came in from the garden, holding a basket full of fresh produce.

"Did you see her?"

"Aye, I did, said my greetings. I'm sure she's started through his things. Won't be long now until we can start poking around too."

"Do you think she could be the one, Maeve?" Mrs. Bixby asked with childish excitement.

Maeve MacKay nodded slowly.

"Aye, she fits the story well enough. Can't be certain until we look for ourselves. Only after we are sure should we tell the rest of the sisters, Susan."

Susan admired her fresh pickings, hoping dearly that the girl would come to dinner. She had always been drawn to Lillian's peaceful nature and had a soft affection for her. She looked at her slightly offbeat friend and hoped that Lillian wouldn't be afraid of Maeve's inconsistent personality.

"I can feel ye fretting, Sue. Ye canna worry about it. She will come or she won't. If she doesn't, ye may just have to encourage her dreams a second time with your veil walking. She will come, I can feel it."

Susan Bixby smiled. Maeve was rarely wrong.

"Poor lass feels exhausted is all," Mrs. MacKay whispered. "Best leave her until this evening. She'll be too tired to refuse our company then."

Mrs. Bixby shook her head as she looked. "It's her dreaming. She has no idea what it all means. She keeps fighting it with the ideas she was raised with. Do you think we could help her, or will it only frighten her if she knows we've been watching?"

Susan poked her head out the window before Lillian disappeared into the cottage. Out of the corner of her eye, Susan saw a little bird curiously bobbing through the air.

"Maeve," she almost yelled, grabbing her friend's arm. "Look at that, a starling has taken to her! That's the bird of the Holly is it not? Oh dear, this does seem promising. The sisters will be pleased. Aillig would have been too, the smart old hare. The starling is a sign of balance, she must be accepting some of what must seem so strange to her."

They both smiled in the silence. Whispers about the changes shifting all over the world had been growing since Lillian grew more attentive to the circumstances surrounding her life. They'd need to prepare for the chance to explain what Aillig had left behind for her.

*Chapter Twenty-Seven*

Rocky cliffs threatened Emmy's bravery. Slate gray stones stood like monstrous crystals overhead, and dared her to approach the sacred ground she was being lead to. It made her dizzy to look upward. A slight hum rang in her ears. Emmy couldn't figure out how they would scale the beasts. The wolf-man had forgone his dramatic apparel for a fur hat that stopped below his ears and clothing more common to trappers. His pale skin and angular, long nose gleamed in the morning light. Emmy couldn't help but wonder where he'd come from. She felt connected to him; both transplants in a world they were not born into. Respecting his privacy was hard when she felt so impressed with his ability to adapt, but Emmy was learning that the native people told you what they wanted and nothing more. She tried to practice the discretion she so often sought.

He moved in front of her and swiftly located their way up.

"The Bannock had looted paleface sites after being left to starve," he explained, pointing to the worn ladder in front of them. "The Blackfeet made these ladders to hide our best possessions in high caves long ago. They may seem wild, and they certainly are, but the Blackfeet were the starters of our community. Their restlessness inspires change, and also keeps us alive and hidden."

Emmy stared at the ladders, skeptical of their strength. They looked as ancient as he suggested.

"We must climb to go to the place of the Sky People. Our elders, mostly the *Toyani*, have travelled here since the beginning of time to communicate with the spirits. This is where we learn about the things we cannot always see. I must take you there now so that you may speak with the spirits and try to remember why you are here."

She hesitated. Too many questions filled her throat. He watched her patiently, but offered no comfort. Emmy had seen quickly in the events of last night that the natives didn't coddle the fear of what was unknown. They celebrated the courage of facing it instead. The Blackfeet had shown their respect when she had calmed the mare. Emmy took one last look into the silent eyes of her guide and reached for the ladder. He waited for her to climb a ways before following. He would give her no bail now that she started. She dared not look down as she went, placing one foot carefully after the other, feeling more secure as she found a rhythm. Her eyes locked onto the end high above her and her mind wandered from the danger she was facing.

Emmy couldn't understand why she had such an easy time trusting strangers when she barely trusted anyone at home. She knew she meant Henry. Her heart was heavy looking back at how easy it would have been to apologize and mend their rift. She saw so much of him in the Natives. For a man from Ireland, he had been so involved in telling her stories of people that were not his own. Knowing her grandfather, it was probably to bridge the gap between his land and hers. He was so good at making the world seem smaller to a little child. As she climbed, she tried to remember the stories of his people, but Emmy kept finding herself mixing them with the Natives.

When her wobbling knees had just about given beneath her, she managed to scramble to the top. She located a cave concealed from the view below, but dared not go in. She waited for her guide. He met her with ease and Emmy smirked.

"We have only begun, save your competitive nature for something more useful. You'll need all the strength within you to reach the top."

The two walked a few feet to the next ladder and climbed. They zig zagged endless levels of ladders before they reached their stopping point. Emmy's legs shook from exhaustion and she sat against a cliff wall to catch her breath. The altitude made her slightly dizzy and she forced herself to keep from looking down. She wasn't particularly afraid of heights but she was feeling disoriented enough to fear stumbling off the ledge if she stood. The man closed his eyes to the wind and inhaled the purity of the ancient grounds as he sat next to her. When he felt she had adjusted sufficiently, he lead her down a narrow pathway to round the peak.

Petroglyphs littered the walls of the mountain and the hum grew more intensely in her head. She pressed a palm against her temple and tried focusing through the altitude sickness.

"It's not the height that causes it," he spoke calmly. "It's our paintings."

The air was silent and not a sound escaped the atmosphere beyond her own breathing. A slight pressure built between her eyes and she tried believing him.

"They speak to you because they are you. This is your story, it has been written in pieces for hundreds of years by generations of our Sky People who have communicated with their spirit guides. Your spirit is strong, Emmy, and needed to be kept for you to remember."

She looked at the archaic designs, trying to decipher them. She wished Henry were there to ease the feeling of such importance. He would have known how to explain this; would have made it smaller. Her heart dropped. *He would have known how to explain this because he did know.* Empty holes in her upbringing were being filled.

The man smiled sympathetically. It was hard in his excitement not to tell her everything. He knew too well how overwhelming the burden could be without the natural pace of self discovery. He had carried a similar weight since childhood and couldn't be responsible to place the same onto her. His life depended on what she would do at the cliffs and nurturing her would do no good. He had to be certain she had the strength in her own heart.

"This is you sitting amongst the horses of a different land," he pointed. "The Sky People didn't know your name then, but I know it now. They called her Epona."

Emmy swallowed, knowing the name. Henry had told the story of Epona a million times as she had begged for it most often. The Gaulish horse goddess was her hero. The name the natives had called her at camp became clearer. Henry had told her Epona rode in Emmy's dreams to keep monsters away. Monsters like Ethan. Her head swirled as unconnected memories threaded together.

"You know her story then?"

All Emmy could do was nod.

"Of course you do, she is you. She is part of your *navushieip*, the soul that travels through dreams and other lives. She is in you now."

Emmy kept nodding. The hum was growing in her head. Henry had been working some sort of plan her entire life and she had been too stubborn to see it.

"This is you now," he pointed, continuing to a rider with arrows in one hand and an odd sack in the other.

"He is the black horse who brought you here, he represents a journey and is the one you ride to see what you have forgotten. The arrows," he said, pointing, "can relay many messages. These two face each other. You will or have warded off evil spirits. These arrows above you point right, which mean you will be protected."

He paused, furrowing his brow as he ran a finger to her other hand.

"But no one can understand what else you carry, the symbol is foreign to us."

Emmy stared at it and her throat grew dry. She could see the worn lines he had missed.

"It's not a sack," she choked through the sandpaper making up the back of her mouth, "see those lines? That's an Irish harp."

*Oh, Henry.*

The wolf-man looked at her with interest.

"They're symbolic to my ancient people," she managed to elaborate, her mind distant from the present. "My grandpa had one at home. He never used it and I always thought it was odd to keep such a large piece of nothing. He told me it was a memory of ancestors and their knowledge was important to preserve. I used to beg him to pluck the strings and he never would. He said when the time was right, someone would come to play it."

"Henry is a wise man."

"More than I ever realized," she whispered. "What is that behind me?" Emmy pointed to a large, cartoonish figure fitted with an angry face.

"That is the bad spirit who follows you in every life, in different forms. Since the early histories, he has destroyed you. You are made from the house of fire. This element has been in your soul always. It generates immense attention towards you. Your history has been passionately maintained which is why they have kept a tight noose around your neck. You are the light that travels in the darkness, the shock that wakes the sleeping mind. He is the only force that can contain you. He is fear."

Her hands started shaking as faint screams began growing in her ears. Voices filled her head with increasing volume. Though she was as silent as the air around her, she knew the screams were her own.

"You are remembering now," he assured her. "You know all the lives before this one and you're denying your subconscious its truth. You're fighting the constrictions of a singular time frame, a singular life. This is why you are bothered by the feeling of instant recognition. Let go of the preconceptions of your society."

The wolf-man turned to her then and waited for her mind to stop spinning in circles. When she made clear eye contact, he spoke quietly.

"He does not remember anymore either," he said, pointing to another figure holding a spiraled shield, "and you will keep breaking your hearts until you let them open. It has been countless lives since you and he were together. He amplifies you, is the guidance for your uncontrollable element, a gentle grounding force in this reality. You are impulsive, explosive and bright, Emmy, and he understands. My people knew yours and his story once, but it is very old. It's hard to say why you haven't reunited, it was not written and got lost when our oral historians were killed."

She thought of Cutter. An explanation to their strange connection was offered. Emmy's heart pinched. She stared again at the petroglyph, feeling as though she were falling into Cutter's shield. The spiral turned as she instinctively leaned closer. Wind rose in her ears.

"We do not know why, but he carries it in all the stories."

"It's painted on a wall in Henry's house. It's Irish. Henry said that the true Irish used it to help travel to magic places, to the gods that had created them. He said it was like time travel. I used to stare at it for hours when I was a child, trying to escape to the past to see my parents," she whispered, unblinking into the shield.

"Your *puhanavuzieip* has started," he whispered, "come with me."

She walked reluctantly away from Cutter's shield to follow. They moved along a thin ridge and rounded another corner.

"That spiral is called a memory tile," he explained as they slid along. "It's what triggers your past memories to come forth so you can travel to them. Your vision quest is calling. It's time for you to see the truth of who you are, Emmy."

Emmy focused on shaking the dizziness from her eyes. The world around her was blurry and the wolf-man's body was hard to make out as they curled around a giant boulder. Henry's game finally made sense. The memory tile had triggered the same feeling. She strained to look ahead of her and pull out of the spiral's effect. It was worse than anything the light had done. The steam of a hot spring crept into the corner of her eyes and soothed the sickness in her head.

"Undress and cleanse in the water smoke until I come and get you. I will turn away while you do so."

She slipped quickly into the water and felt her bones defrost. The air was cooler than she had noticed and the heat from the natural spring felt luxurious. Her hair had come partially out of the braids that soaked in the water. She watched the strands that had wriggled free, shifting in the warm spring. Her mind relaxed and healed the numbness in her body.

Every time she wanted to reject the stories being told to her, the man would eliminate her doubt. He explained everything with such a natural acceptance that it was hard not to believe him. Her skin grew swollen in the hot water. She glanced out to the clear sky around her. A breeze of whispers curled around her neck and she moved with lethargy to see that a pile of pelts had been left behind her. The silence of such a large man was impressive and without further instruction she managed to wrap herself as she stood from the water, walking back to the petroglyphs. She felt like she was in the right place for the first time. Even at home with Henry hadn't been right. Her life had been shrouded in secrets and controlled by everyone but herself.

"But you knew, Henry, and said nothing," she whispered.

The heavy fur kept the warmth of the sacred pool on her skin, making her lick her lips. She sat in front of the painted wall feeling dehydrated and disoriented again. The wolf-man reappeared then and crouched next to her, his palm outstretched. In it sat the most colorful flower Emmy had ever seen. Its star shaped, bright blue petals faded to the shining likeness of the yellow-white sun. He lifted it to her lips and encouraged her to eat a portion. She did so, mostly out of confusion, chewing the seeds as he watched. He left the pot of blue paint next to her.

"This is the *toyatawura*. It was in the satchel from last night. It will help you on your vision quest now. It is time to use the ability you have to shape shift into the horse for yourself. It is time to shape shift into your past lives and learn. The spirits will talk to you if you let them. You must eat one petal for five days, a day for each sacred world within this one, before you return to us. I will leave you until it is through. I have hidden small portions of nourishment near the pool if you need it. If you come back to us after your quest is finished, we will know the Fifth World, the world of change, has begun."

*Chapter Twenty-Eight*

Lillian grabbed her notes and walked through the house collecting all the books she had scattered in the night. The living room had turned into a complete mess. So had her plan of secrecy. She glanced at the titles of the books as she picked them up and cradled them in her arms, calculating the odds of seeing a client all the way down south. She only hoped that she'd not be seeing them again. Lillian looked to the couch littered with her sleep walking disaster. It'd be hard to make excuses for why she was there now. She pushed aside a few more books and made a hole to sit in. Lillian sighed and stood again. The kitchen table would have to be her work station instead. Its knot work had been preserved and Lillian smiled as she set her things on top of it, letting her fingers linger in admiration. She pulled a chair out and sat, pushing her hair back in a neat bun. The quaint court yard sat outside the big windows and she glanced affectionately to the garden that had been somewhat maintained. She made note to make time to replenish it tomorrow morning and take stock of what had been left by Aillig. Settling in, she eyed the stack of books and delicately pulled out the one she had not looked in.

Lillian tugged her notebook closer. It was time to face Aillig's truths in the most direct manner. She lifted the cover, her heart pounding in her chest, a sense of violation and secrecy mixing strongly within her bones. The world around her drowned as she read.

> *I recovered a young woman from the streets just a week ago, and a feeling has arisen in me that she may be what this world has been waiting for. The beings with whom I met in youth have foretold of this. My heart sings with the delicacy and natural competence she has for the healing arts. I do not want to make judgement in haste, so many meditations will pass before I am certain enough to spread news. For my own measure, I must record what happens next...*

Her whole body shook as she read onward. Aillig had taken account of everything in the years she had spent with him. He had been observing her since the day they'd collided in the market place. Her eyes scanned through early entries. She swallowed information about the dreams he'd sat through with her. Tears welled in her eyes as she relived her experience through the clarity of an observer. The diary was fantasy laden and full of detail from a man hungry to unlock secrets. Her secrets.

> *Lillian has been in my care for some time now and has excelled as a focus of hers is awakened. I've made books filled with the scribbles and mutterings of herbalism that she whispers in the moments before waking. My intuition tells me the before mentioned focus of hers is trying to communicate to her, but because she does not know or accept the idea of multiple lives, she is only able to communicate in the waking of the subconscious during sleep. The poor thing has been through such devastating loss and trauma that to speak openly of what she is now would do no good. Lillian sleeps restlessly, calling out names of people whom I don't recognize. Emmy, Cutter, Ethan, Henry. She speaks in the old tongue when she*

*dreams of a man familiar to her. They speak about memories of her past, but I am afraid my translations are inaccurate. I think Lillian likes to keep him to herself.*

*My own swirling equilibrium tells me I must have known this man in another life as well. I'm afraid whatever recollection of the past she dreams about has been lost to me. I plan to research the factual parts of her dreams in hopes of locating who her focus could be.*

Her mind teetered and her heart softened. She hadn't ignored Aillig, he had tried nurturing her recovery by withholding information. He had known about her dreams and said nothing. He had known about her insanity, and her bond with a ghost and said nothing. He hadn't rejected her like her parents for being strange. He had loved her more, taught her more. Lillian didn't want to cry anymore and fiercely held onto her composure.

"Aillig, why couldn't we have talked about it?" she choked.

It was nothing new to miss him as she read. Lillian closed her eyes and waited to feel her shadow man. When he didn't come, she took a deep breath and moved forward. Pieces of her life were trying to connect in her mind's eye. She shook her head, not wanting to see the bigger picture before she was done reading.

*Lillian spoke the name of a focus tonight! She was Airmid, the healer. How I didn't see it before is outstanding. She calls through every vibrant thread of Lillian's soul. Her unsurpassed talent in herbalism makes perfect sense. In this particular dream, Airmid called out a list of herbs followed by a riddle of directions. I have spent the entire night trying to decipher what she meant to reveal.*

*Lillian kept calling, "maiden, mother, crone." I feel she is part of a triple goddess, a triple alliance, or a triple aspect within, like the prophecy calls for. Whatever it is, I am certain that Lillian will need it in future. I hope that she has only murmured these words in the safety of my home. Revealing too much in slumber could have been dangerous for her in childhood. So much power should not be laid in hungry hands.*

Lillian sat back and stared out the windows. What had possessed and tortured her at the church was a blessing to Aillig. They weren't dreams at all. She didn't know what they were, or where she was going when she slept. He seemed to think it was linked to some sort of prophecy, but Aillig had a tendency to take fantasy to heart. She stood to put the kettle on the stove before returning to the table.

*My dear Lillian has made it clear to me that she is, in fact, what my brothers and sisters have been waiting for. Last night she rose from bed to sleepwalk around the room. This she has never done before. She muttered in an odd accent, not her own. Then she moved to write on a piece of paper. What was legible sent a chill through my bones. A focus of mine had woven into her subconscious to identify himself. He left a date and location of his existence, alongside a myriad of places about Lillian's past experiences. He also confirmed what I had hoped for. The prophecy will soon make itself known to her.*

*My focus had been alive in the time of Julius Caesar as one of the last druids of Gaul. He had to have been a veil walker to communicate through Lillian. A dear friend of mine has the same talent.*

*Once she had fallen back to sleep in her bed, I wasted no time. I managed to gain access to the records kept by the church and tried finding anything about why her parents could have left her there. Then I drove to the library at first opening to search for what lead this druid had given me. I found a necklace in the spine of a book. It had been left for Lillian.*

Lillian could see the golden chain hanging out from the edges of the journal but could not tear herself away from reading. He had tried searching for her parents.

*The woman behind the desk had grown suspicious of my snooping. I am not surprised that she watched over books of such antiquity, too much has been hidden in those texts. They always things secrets too closely. With the right mind, their secrets could be unveiled and alter their position of power. My kind makes them nervous.  They know we can be crafty since we have such expansive knowledge over them. Sensing my time was running out, I made signs and clues for Lillian to find in books that hold no obvious relevance.*

*I'm afraid I won't have time to make sense of this for Lillian. I can only set up a few clues to help her along, I'll need to let the Sisters know for Preparation in case. I fear I have glanced too close for Danger's comfort. My safety has been jeopardized and I must embed the knowledge I've gained through hypnosis for Lillian. Her heart is too true to maintain mandatory secrecy. I fear she will be none too happy when she discovers my intrusion.*

Aillig's death felt more like an unveiling of her own life than a mystery of his, and she felt responsible for his murder. He had been searching about her life this entire time. With a shaking hand, Lillian turned the last page over and picked up the delicate necklace in her palm. Her head felt heavy and she fought with difficulty to keep the dizziness away. The metal was old and stronger than any gold she'd seen. She handled the coin that hung from the chain between her fingers and thumb, flipping it over when she felt ridges against the pad of her finger.

Though the image had been worn, the crude profile of the face was unmistakable. She nimbly clasped the chain around her neck and let the coin with her shadow's face fall between her breasts. It hung heavily and the weight sitting against her skin was strangely comforting. She hugged her palm around the pendant, overwhelmed with the realization that everything happening was much larger and more to do with her than she could ever imagine. The kettle was screaming as the water boiled on the stove, but she did not move to turn it off. She called for him. She knew why the necklace had been left and it had taken so many years before his gift was finally in her possession. She wanted to know more, needed to understand what he also knew about her. If Aillig's journal was right, her shadowman existed. Somewhere. The coin proved it, and he must have been important.

The knocking on the door was near banging before Lillian heard it. She rose instinctively to turn off the kettle, too engrossed in the shock of what she'd learned. She called for her shadow again as the knocking became more persistent. He wasn't going to show himself with visitors around. Lillian sighed. Facing anyone familiar under these circumstances felt impossible. Yet her service to humanity compelled her to shove her overrun mind and malnourished emotions away. Lillian wondered if she'd truly find peace and quiet in her life. Her hair fell in soft waves as she untwisted her bun and walked towards the front door.

"Just a moment," she called from the other side. Lillian pulled at her sweater, trying to look more level than she felt. She dropped the necklace beneath her clothes to conceal it before opening the door. Aillig had been right to assume she liked to keep him to herself. She prepared to feign illness in hopes to discourage an evening of company.

"Hello, dear," Mrs. MacKay bellowed cheerfully as the door swung open. "We've brought ye some supper. When I hadn't noticed ye leave in hours, I figured you'd probably absorbed yourself in your mixing."

"Hello, Lillian," Susan chirped as she slid from behind Maeve's larger frame.

"Mrs. Bixby!" Lillian exclaimed, forgetting her act in surprise. "I thought you'd gone to see your sister? I must suppose everything is okay?"

The frail woman nodded sheepishly, biting her tongue. She couldn't reveal the truth all on the doorstep.

Feeling strangely happy to see them, Lillian stepped aside, motioning them in. The fumes from the ladies' pot made her stomach growl.

"It was awfully kind of you to think of me. I hadn't noticed how hungry I was."

A short supper wouldn't be terrible. She moved swiftly ahead of them to organize what she could, clearing the table before they could read her papers and books. Lillian cursed herself as she pushed her work to her chest, ruining her organization in haste. The women eyed each other as they carefully managed to fake a glance away.

"Go ahead and sit, I'll be a moment. Tea?"

They nodded graciously as Maeve set down the pot of stew. Susan let the bread basket linger on her arm as she looked around.

"It's not at all how I imagined his house to be. I was certain it'd have more color," she thought quietly.

Maeve smiled. Aillig had been such a lover of ancient art, she was surprised herself over the white washed walls.

"I've made some cardamom apple tea, I hope it pairs with the food."

Susan stared at Maeve in astonishment. Lillian's incredible intuition was not used only in her healing. Maeve shook her head imperceptibly. Susan's nerves tended to blow in these situations and it was imperative not to frighten the girl with all they'd been waiting to tell her.

"So what brings you down south? What are the chances of us running into each other?"

Lillian sat next to them, trying not to seem distracted. Her mind begged to go over the material she had just discovered. She grinned, her cheeks taut from restrained politeness. If she was going to have their supper, she at least owed them her attention. Lillian did her best to pull herself away from the presence of the journals.

"Well," Susan started shyly, "I did come to see my sister. We aren't actually related though."

"That's right," Lillian nodded, "and how is she? It seemed you were worried."

"I'm doing much better, thank you. So is she."

Lillian's eyes widened, glancing at the robust woman across the table. Susan had come to see Mrs. MacKay.

"But Mrs. Bixby left before you," she accused, looking at Maeve.

Lillian could feel the bristle of defense rise in her neck.

"Aye, lass," Maeve recovered. "But I had asked that she come to meet me here."

Mrs. MacKay opened the top of her pot to ladle some soup into bowls. Lillian's stomach rumbled when the steam succulently slipped to her nostrils.

"I made some lamb stew, I hope it suits ye. Susan's a magician at baking and brought some bread for dipping."

Maeve nodded towards Mrs. Bixby, her wide face lit up with mischief. This was their chance to make or break a bond.

"Ye see, Susan and I are old friends. We belong to the same," she paused, considering, "humanitarian club. Every year we meet down here. So when we saw ye, we were quite surprised."

"I'm sorry I lied," Lillian blurted between a sip of soup.

"Not necessary to apologize," Maeve dismissed as she continued. "We figured ye might be a part of the club too, being here in these cottages."

Engrossed in the flavors of the stew, Lillian was slightly lost and let her guard down.

"Well, I'm definitely not a part of any organization. Sounds lovely though."

Susan spoke without thinking.

"Trouble is, these cottages are only owned by our organization."

Lillian could feel a static barrier surround her. Her face went carefully blank and she set her spoon down before speaking clearly.

"If you already know why I am here, then why should you play any longer."

Mrs. MacKay took a sharp breath of patience for the misgivings of her dear friend. Lillian was too smart to be played with. The older women said nothing as they tried to adjust to the shift of energy in the room. Susan hoped they'd be able to explain a little more first, wishing she hadn't said a word. They had anticipated a certain chilliness from her when truths were revealed, but they had not been prepared for it just yet.

"I do not own this cottage, and I can assume you know who does. I am not presently willing to divulge much more, and since you've been so intrusive to come snooping around under the guise of friendship, I would much rather you carry this conversation."

Lillian's could feel her heart thumping with nerves, her mind racing to figure out how they knew Aillig. She'd been so engrossed in looking for the clues Aillig left her, she had nearly forgotten that there could be others doing the same. Others who may not have the same intentions she did, and considering what she'd just found out, may not have happy intentions for her as well. She was suddenly very aware of what was happening around her.

"You've nothing to worry over," Maeve spoke more fretfully than she'd sounded before. "We aren't here to hurt ye, or find anything of Aillig's. He was a dear friend to us. He was a part of our community. We met here every year to keep our beliefs and stories alive. Though I'm certain ye know him more intimately, we don't doubt his good heart and incredible intelligence. In fact, because of those traits, we've been watching over ye in his absence, as he requested."

She had heard these sweet words dripping from the mouths of nuns when they had wanted something from her. She couldn't know who had harmed Aillig, and it very easily could have been someone close to him. Her hands quivered in her lap under the table, but her eyes remained clear and vibrant, calculating their movements. The barricade she had built around her personal life felt violated and the idea of being watched without knowing shocked her.

"Why?" she whispered.

Susan looked at Maeve before rising to sit closer to Lillian. They had formed a special bond up north and Susan intended to call on it now, placing a frail hand on Lillian's, drawing them off her lap. She could feel the physical contact soothe the girl and when Mrs. Bixby was certain Lillian had calmed, she began to explain.

"Aillig possessed a kenning that has been unrivaled. He knew when he took you in that you were a very special person in this world. But it took him a long time to share this belief to a few of his closest friends," she said, motioning her open palm around the room.

"There's a story that's been passed down from the generations of our kind, giving us hope for a global change in the world. It's been kept a guarded secret, held only in the heads of few, though all of us know a general version. Aillig's mother had passed it onto him. Before he died, he had mentioned a little to us. He thinks you could have a part in what's been prophesied for this change."

Lillian stared at the grain of the table, watching it turn to flowing rivers in her imagination. If it hadn't been for Aillig's journal, her anxiety would have overturned her coping skills and the women would have been hysterically begged to leave. Instead, she let her mind flow through her life in a different perspective, and she could feel herself balancing her reactions. The wood became idle again and she thought of the holly ogham. The riddles were coming together in the way Aillig intended. She needed to adopt the likeness of the holly; rough and strongly defensive to the outside dangers and open in the spaces within. Balanced. Lillian nodded to encourage Susan to continue.

"We have little knowledge of what he meant about the prophecy itself, but he urged its importance just before his death. Since then, we have kept a distant eye for any sign to aid you in your journey. We know him little outside of these beach cottages as we tend not to make it too obvious of our friendships. We learned generations ago that we can attract unwanted attention when we are too open about who we are, and we fear that could have been Aillig's downfall."

Susan looked at Lillian's blank face and knew the girl was inside the deep workings of her own mind, absorbing what was being said. Susan often functioned the same way.

Maeve closed her eyes a moment and focused on Lillian, feeling the swirl of nausea the girl was ignoring. If anything, she was resilient to shock which both saddened and encouraged her opinion of Aillig's intuitions.

"Who do you mean when you say we?" Lillian asked.

Maeve and Susan sat thoughtfully, considering the best answer to explain.

"Uneducated people would call us a covenant," Maeve finally spoke, "because the media and those in control want to emphasize the fantasy and folklore they've created around the term. But we are only normal people who have been taught, and born with, the ability of higher awareness. We are capable of seeing, both literally and metaphorically, more than the majority of humanity. We have been raised and taught differently. Aillig was a healer and a mathematician. Susan works in the transition of dreams and subconscious known as veil walking, and I am a feeler, or empath. I'm not sure if any of that makes sense to ye, but now is as good a time as any to get ye caught up."

All of Lillian's strange habits and happenings started lining up behind her eyes, flashing in moments of clarity. Aillig had written about her uncanny talent for healing. She had even outsmarted Aillig's failures the other night. She saw the communication she used in dreams, and her strange interaction with a nonexistent man. She remembered Aillig mentioning a veil walker in his journal and wondered if it was Susan. The cracks in the beliefs that had structured her life were shining with light.

"I understand."

Maeve nodded, moving slowly in her own mind as she felt Lillian's distress levels rise and wane. She could hardly believe the level of tolerance Lillian was maintaining. She felt it would be an unsuccessful venture to press too much on her at once and moved back to more generic speech.

"Aillig could see the way ye could heal others and wanted to see that ye harvest your ability to its utmost potential. Unfortunately, it seems someone disagreed, and having ye under his roof rubbed them the wrong way. We don't think Aillig died by accident and we were hoping to work together in finding the truth."

Lillian looked at them as though she'd never met them in her life. She stirred the last bit of her soup aimlessly, watching the broth trail behind the path of her spoon. It all made sense and didn't. It was too convenient for them to show up, but it wasn't. Aillig was a planner. She wasn't sure what to do or say to them.

"It's getting late, dear, ye need some rest. I'm sure you've already pulled this house apart. I do not want to pressure ye further. Susan and I are here if ye need, and will leave ye otherwise to your findings."

Maeve could sense her exhaustion and decided to back off. They rose and she idly followed to see them out, watching the pair walk halfway down the path.

"Would you like to come over tomorrow morning for some breakfast and a chat?" she pushed somewhat forcibly past her lips.

Susan turned first, grinning from ear to ear and nodded.

*Chapter Twenty-Nine*

She sat in front of Cutter's shield, feeling sick. The rock paintings shifted and Emmy lost control of her reality. She watched them move with life. Cutter's spiral unwound and turned into three snakes. They moved together, then wound back into one. The giant snake sprout nine heads. Emmy's closed her eyes, wishing she'd not eaten the flower again. The separation from mind and body was taking its toll. She could feel her hands moving. The vibration against the rock numbed her fingers as she watched herself carve her vision like many had done before her. The wall was surrounded by the scratched petroglyphs she had created. The old Irish knot work from Henry's home filled the spaces around her strange snakes. Whispers drifted through her ears and Emmy looked around at the commotion growing louder on the surface of the cliffs.

Horses ran in between the moon in the sky and the pounding of hooves shook in her chest. Owls flew overhead, screeching like banshees and everything turned blue. Her fingers went to the paint, working nimbly against her skin. The clash of metal and distant war cries filled her ears amd rabbits sprung like flowers from the cracks of rock she carved into. The dark haired woman appeared before her. Pairs of eyes flashed in blurs and her mind worked furiously to recognize all of them. Emmy could feel her equilibrium twist mercilessly out of her control. She lay her head down, wrapping her furs into a makeshift bed and blacked out.

*Her face fell onto different bodies as her old lives moved in front of her like a flowing river. Though the color of her hair and eyes changed, basic features remained. Each one grew more ancient in dress and demeanor as they passed more quickly until the sky turned black and swallowed her vision. Cutter stood before her, bare chested and covered in blue paint. He held his hand out to her, but no matter how hard she tried, she couldn't reach him. The dark haired woman appeared next to her, the world around them darkened until she could see nothing. Strange symbols burst over her head like fireworks. She grew angry that she couldn't find Cutter. She could feel him, could feel that he was near. Trees came to life, illuminated in gold and silver. She grabbed their roots and tugged, unravelling their structure like a ball of yarn. She wasn't going to lose him. She wrapped the light around her, let it reach upward towards the sky bursting with symbols. She could feel her feet lifting from the ground and looked down in wonder. The dark haired woman stood watching her. A string of light curled up from the woman's feet and wound around her own legs, binding them together. Stuck in between the floor and the air above, Emmy felt herself being pulled forward. Two balls of light appeared not far in front of them. The woman below her screamed out in pain.*

Emmy woke drowsily to the distant screech of eagles. She looked at the sky through squinted eyes. Her wits were dull as she woke, trying to remember where she was. Her naked body felt cozy in the furs and she stretched her aching muscles. As the fog of another hallucination cleared, Emmy flung herself around to stare at her own petroglyphs.

They made little sense to her now. She had given up trying to decipher them after her first return from the vision quest. She shifted her weight and looked to count her tally. Emmy marked her fifth day. She needed to find Sky Brother to understand. Her mind was disconnected from her reality and she would need help finding her way back to a singular life. Emmy stood slowly and stretched her aching muslces. The cramped area was starting to wear on her. She found her clothes and reached for them to get dressed. It was going to be a long climb back to camp. Emmy lifted her leg into the hide pants, and froze, looking down at her skin. Her bare body was covered in blue paint. She had recreated her petroglyphs. Whispers lingered in her ears and she was too exhausted to listen.

She no longer wanted to remain in the haunted peaks alone, and dressed quickly. She located the first ladder and made her way down. Time had been tricky on the cliffs. It had felt like only last night Sky Brother was handing her the beautifully dangerous flower, and yet it seemed she'd been gone for years. The world was different now, smaller and larger at once. Her mind had been expanded into those she'd once held in the past. She could recall some of them now as vague dreams, and wanted to learn more. All of Henry's stories had been about her. All the times she had begged to hear the story of the horse goddess, she had actually been begging to remember who she was.

It was quiet and vacant when she reached the camp, and Emmy allowed herself to catch her breath. She looked anxiously for the other paleface. When she couldn't find him, she waited outside the tipi she had slept in before. Questions for Sky Brother started to bubble in her throat. Emmy wanted to understand her spirit walk and the marveling idea she could be Epona. To think, Cutter had recognized it without even knowing. It made her wonder about their past life together and why no one could recall it. She had to get back and find him. She had to apologize. She had to tell him about what she'd seen.

A shadow moved from somewhere beyond and Emmy caught sight of Sky Brother slipping between tipis.

"I need to go back," she called to him.

He smiled widely and made his way toward her.

"But first, I need to tell you about my time on the mountains. I don't understand any of it. Well, except Epona's story. Henry told me all about her. She was a woman among horses," she repeated in Henry's tone, "who traveled under the moonlight to deliver stories to all the sleeping people. She was so popular that her reputation had reached Ireland from Gaul, and she was worshipped under their own name for her. Even the men trying to conquer the Old Word worshipped her in secret. One night, a man captured her and kept her in confines like her beloved creatures. She was tortured. She decided to escape. So when the moon was full and the roses bloomed, she ran away on the black horse of the sun until she was swallowed by the light and never found again. But what does that mean for me now? And what about all the other drawings. Like the owl. I've dreamt I was an owl before, but what does it mean? There were snakes and rabbits and fighting too."

Emmy paused in her recounting and looked at the man in front her, his wolf cape still as intimidating as before. His silence didn't feel promising.

"I guess you can't understand what I've seen up there. I left my own paintings on the rocks for the Sky People to decipher. Hopefully better than I could."

Emmy hesitated. She wasn't sure if she wanted to offer what else she'd painted, but her eagerness to understand got the better of her.

"The last quest I took though was different. I painted almost all the pictures on my body with the blue paint. Did that old woman know I'd do that? Does everyone do that? Am I supposed to show you? Maybe if you can see the paintings, you can help me understand the secrets."

His silvery eyes faltered and all the hardness of his exterior melted for an instant before he recovered. He wasn't sure if he should see anything more. Some things were meant to stay sacredly mysterious, and so little mystified him anymore. He looked at her small body knotted with the fire that marked her. She wanted him to look, dared him to see the images and offer what he knew. It was hard not to succumb to Epona's persuasive spirit. It wouldn't be the first time he had. He nodded once.

Emmy's heart skipped. She hadn't thought about what she was doing until now. No one had seen her body since Ethan had stolen it from her. She lowered her eyes and tried not to tremble. Her hands lifted the hem of her shirt and she bared her tight stomach to show him some of what she'd done. His heart pounded seeing the first image that caught his attention; three snakes wound together. Before she could lift her shirt off her body, his hand shot out and grabbed her wrists. His grip was hard and Emmy's throat tightened.

"That's enough," he said hoarsely.

"Your journey must continue. But I ask that you wash your vision paint from your body. It will be hard enough to hide from the eyes that are searching for you. You are going to vibrate intensely now that you've awakened and they will respond. You have ignited the powers they have suppressed in you. It will be harder to exist under their radar. Their own deep subconscious will grow agitated with your presence as their ideas of right and wrong conflict against what you are. What we all really are. Take note from the mouse spirit. Let yourself blend in and you may be able to escape somewhere that is better protected by our people. The tribe has already made preparations to move and cover our tracks. Travel carefully now, sweet girl."

"Who is watching me?" she asked desperately.

"I cannot say beyond the bad man on the walls. I have not ventured to these towns for a very long time. But just as you and I have lived many times, so have they. Do not be blind to the idea that they are trying to extinguish you. If you need anything, do not hesitate to find us again."

She swallowed hard and nodded before turning inside to wipe most of the paint from her body and dress in her civilian clothes. Emmy tried not to feel disappointed by his cold rejection of her journey. She wanted to share it with someone who understood. Cutter flashed in her mind and she bit her lip. If anyone would listen it would be him. She needed to believe in something. When she emerged, she stuck out her hand to her new companion. He shook it firmly, working hard to keep the solemn expression on his face.

He did not want her to see his worry. He couldn't shatter the delicate awareness she had just built. Allowing her dominant weakness to weave into it would be unwise. Fear had been crippling for her, just like the animal spirit of her sacred guide. Emmy had a dangerous road ahead of her and she'd need all the strength she could find to survive what was to come. He watched her go, pleading that the rest of the prophecy he had kept to himself all these years could be realized with her natural intensity. His life depended on it.

........

George Fassenbach threw his phone across the living room. The girl had disappeared after the disaster at the rodeo grounds and no one could find her. He had misjudged Ethan's toy and hadn't given him enough credit for the damage he'd done. She'd broken again and ran away. George paced to the cell phone and picked it up.

He considered dialing Ethan, having lost his investment, but paused. If Ethan realized she had been here all this time, George would surely suffer. He knew Ethan's methods were extreme and he could only imagine how he'd get repaid for his disloyalty. George had heard vaguely about the gruesome murder of the girl's grandfather, and the drinking binge Ethan had gone on when Emmy still hadn't shown up. The superiors had let him sit in the local jail for public disturbance until they could figure out how to handle him. If Ethsn found that Emmy had been here all along, everything that mattered to George would be destroyed.

Kelly passed before his eyes and he set the cell on his couch, plopping down next to it. He rubbed the deep crease in his forehead. He had played too closely with fire and now he was getting burned. It was only a matter of time before they found out what he had done. The truth screamed so loudly in the silence he couldn't hear anything else. Certainly he would be condemned for disobeying his superiors. They'd done it to him before and he couldn't stand to see Kelly pay for his mistakes again. Losing her mother because of it was enough. He had to figure out where Emmy had gone.

Breaking into her room hadn't given them any leads. After two days with no trace, he had hired one of the boys around town to pick the lock. All they had found was Cutter's photograph. The woman lived like a recluse. Cutter had been the one to find her truck hidden in a shack on the side of the road, but when the ranch hands were asked about her, no one had a clue about where she'd gone after the rodeo. Even Cutter couldn't offer a suggestion, they'd had a fight that night and he hadn't heard from her since. George could feel the sweat of desperation roll down the side of his face as he stared out the windows in his living room.

"This is what I get as punishment in this forsaken land. A bunch of incapable idiots to do my work. I don't care if I have to dispatch a search and rescue unit to find her. I will get her back."

*Chapter Thirty*

Tea and coffee steamed endlessly over piles of scones and biscuits. The early light of morning crept into the kitchen and for the first time in her life Lillian had someone to talk with. She and Susan exchanged stories about dreams and Maeve pointed out Lillian's subconscious knack for channeling her clients' ailments. Maeve was an empath herself and told Lillian she could help strengthen her ability.

"Now ye know why my emotional meter bobs this way and that," Maeve laughed. "Again, I am so grateful for your ability to heal. When I get around too many people who ignore their feelings, I go toes up. Your gift always brings me back."

Lillian blushed. "If I'm correct, you should be thanking Airmid, not me."

"Your focus, the part of you from another life, does not give her knowledge to anyone, child," Susan whispered. "And what she gives to you is outstanding. In all my years I don't think I've met someone who was a focus of Airmid. Even Aillig could not extract what you do. When he tested you under the guise of a teacher, he was handing you things he could only write down but not create. You did it with ease. Airmid was legend for herbalism and communication with all living nature. Her story is a sad one though. Her healer brother was ripped from her by death at the hand of their jealous father. Herbalism was the only link she had left to their high born talents after his passing. A lot of their sacred knowledge died too."

Lillian thought privately about the dreams that were starting to make sense. She had mixed a past life with her present one, and she couldn't help but wonder why. Perhaps Dougal could be from a past life as well. She wondered if lives had patterns, or repeated. Lillian let her imagination idle and hauled herself back to the conversation.

"Herbalism has always been there, as if I've been doing it for years longer than my own. Now I kind of see why, except for the focus part. Long ago, I was Airmid herself?"

Susan smiled, her gentle patience best suited for teaching Lillian their perspective.

"When someone dies it is largely accepted to believe your soul leaves your body. We believe the particles of energy that make up your soul disperse after death and move through the parallels of time to create new forms with other parts of released souls. So when you are born, you are a culmination of particles from past lives. A focus is what we call one part of what makes you. Does that make sense?"

Lillian tilted her head. "So that is why I was so drawn to herbalism? Because part of me had already done it? Does it also explain certain emotional triggers that I can't properly analyze when they come on? Perhaps it's because I've been through it before in a previous life and not this one?"

Susan nodded with pride. "Yes, my dear, that is the most basic idea. You may feel dizzy in a place you've never visited. In another life you probably held vivid memories of it. The convergence of time veils confuses your reality, or the singular and linear reality that you believe in."

Lillian curled a finger through her long hair and thought deeply about what she was considering. She wanted to ask about her shadow man, but a part of her didn't want to risk disappointment if they explained him away.

Maeve glanced at Susan, feeling Lillian's static defense rise. It blocked her from reading how she felt.

"Well, lass, there's much more to tell ye on another day. Right now we must get to finding Aillig's clues. Ye said he seemed odd before his death. He must have seen it coming. If so, the old man had to have left something behind to protect ye."

The stout woman could tell Lillian's brain was foiling under the weight of information and redirected her to something tangible to work through. Lillian nodded and pulled the stack of notes she'd made. She had edited the information to make sense without the involvement of her shadow man or secret riddles. There was something too personal about them. The riddles she'd written made her self conscious and she wasn't ready to expose her psychosis to the women. Lillian didn't want to be ridiculed for having a love affair with a ghost. He was sacred to her. The thought made her heart beat wantonly for him and both women picked up on the change in her energy.

"It's okay," Maeve cooed, misunderstanding. "You've every reason to mistrust the whole world, but we will not betray ye."

"Maeve, how can you tell what I'm feeling?" she asked coyly, wishing they wouldn't be able to read her thoughts about him.

She smiled. "Ye feel what the other person feels. It's tricky to learn, but I can help ye. It's more about relaxing than concentrating on them. Ye probably do it all the time when you're not paying attention. Just now my own heart fluttered nervously, but my conscience understands that I am not nervous, so it must be that I'm picking up on someone else's emotions. Ye see?"

Lillian smiled weakly and nodded. She toyed with the ends of her inky hair. She wasn't an excellent liar, and to agree that she was nervous about showing them what she'd found in the cottage would be one. Truthfully, she was relieved to finally share the weight on her shoulders with someone else like her. For the first time since Aillig's death she didn't feel like the only person in the world. She didn't feel insane. Susan picked up the scrambled dream notes and looked bashfully to Lillian.

"This happened the other night, didn't it?"

Glancing over, Lillian nodded.

"Part of dreaming like you and I do is learning how to navigate the realm of the subconscious. They call those practiced in it veil walkers. I am one and I fear I may have been the woman you ran from."

"But why would I be afraid of you?"

"The danger in veil walking is that you can only control your own subjective reality. I have no control over your dreams, I can only make myself present in them. There are ancient stories of those who had greater talent, but I'm afraid as our kind have diminished so has our ability. Your subconscious will always feel a veil walker in one form of agitation or another. I was worried about your safety, and hoped to encourage a thought to visit us. But I was unaware of what fear lies within you and my presence morphed into your own association of strangers. I'm so sorry to have scared you, Lillian."

Lillian patted the old woman's hand to soothe her. She could not deny the relief she felt in finding the answer to the woman's identity.

"It's okay now, Mrs. Bixby, don't mind about it any longer. Now, let's get to work, shall we?"

Smiling to herself, she turned to open a book. Lillian thought about the other presence in her dreams, fantasizing about the possibility that he too was a veil walker. The coin was dense and smooth against her skin and her eyes were bright green.

The three worked tirelessly, writing down various bits of information through the day, speaking sparsely as they absorbed the volumes. Lillian rose to stretch, massaging the crease forming between her brow. She could feel the pressure at her temples and moved through the house, hoping to smooth out the confusion of so many words. She plucked at books, trying to unwind. It seemed too easy to believe what they were saying and she wanted to fight it for the very reason. Life wasn't as easy and mystical as the women were presenting it. *Yet, every time you decide to just go with it, everything falls into place, Lillian.* She saw a leather cover peeking through a pile and knew what it was before she even touched it. She slid the diary from between books. The worn casing was as soft as his other journal and when she opened it to the first page, the paper stirred restlessly in her palms.

She started to read and as she turned the pages, all she ever wanted fell in heavy cursive between the lines. There in blotched ink and extravagant swirls was what he could find on her parents. The writing was hurried, and her heart pounded.

*It was nearly impossible, but I was capable of sneaking into the church for a look about her parents. Records were carefully hidden and not complete. I'm sure it was a safety measure. Her parents knew who she was and had to flee as a decoy to save her life. She'd have been killed at birth otherwise, I'm sure of it. Hoped that by leaving her the one place they'd least expect, she'd be safe. Poor dear couldn't have understood the magnitude of her daughter's importance. It was only a matter of time before the church found out who was in their care. Don't know if her parents are living or dead. Trying to find out, but eyes are on me in every direction. Afraid they've caught on.*

The book was sprawled open in her arms when she walked back into the kitchen. Maeve and Susan raised their heads, eyes widening as they saw what she was holding.

"My parents," she whispered.

They said nothing.

"Did you know?"

Susan shook her head. "No, darling, tell us?"

"They left to keep me safe. Aillig suspects that the church I grew up in had something to do with it, but he wasn't sure. He couldn't find much beyond the location of where he'd found my records. He said he was being watched too closely and he didn't want to be obvious about it."

Maeve tried to assess Lillian's emotional level and felt nothing. She guessed that the girl was a little in shock and stayed still until she was certain what to say. No one had known anything about Lillian beyond the prophecy. The woman living in their present reality was a mystery and suddenly, she felt bad for not taking the time to ask. She was still a young woman living a singular life. Maeve scolded herself for forgetting the girl didn't see herself like they did. All of this was unusual and probably frightening to her. Susan filled in the space with the same emotions, but her nervous character had a harder time refraining.

"I didn't know, dear," she whispered sorrowfully. "I'm so sorry I never asked. I should have taken the time to get to know you, as you are presently. I'm afraid I got caught up in all that you will someday be."

Lillian shook her head. "It's not something I think to tell. I'm sure it's obvious that I keep to myself, there's no need to apologize for not having an impulse to ask about my life."

She pressed her palms on the knotted wooden table.

"I think I need a bit of fresh air to clear my mind."

Lillian moved silently out the back door towards the garden. The women made no protest as they watched her go, understanding that trying to work through it for her would only be a crutch for what was coming. Susan looked at Maeve, wanting to be consoled over the girl's fragile state.

"She'll be fine, Sue. If she was able to survive and get out of the church as a child, there's no telling what she can do now as a woman. Just give her time to breathe."

Lillian shifted around the plants that had been largely unattended since Aillig's death, grazing each one with a loving pad of her fingertips. She had never been worthless like she had felt as an orphan. She had been so important that everyone she loved most had been put in danger being near her. The weight of truth was heavy on her chest and she breathed in the night to clear her lungs. A whisper came across her ears and she smiled.

"You're breaking your rule," she whispered back.

"Ego te deseram."

*I will never leave you.*

She smiled and knew it was true. The door creaked behind her and he disappeared as quickly as they came.

"I'm sorry," Susan squeaked when Lillian spun around. "I felt another presence out here and got worried. We never know who could be following you."

Lillian's cheeks flamed and she tried to scramble for another lie to throw them off, but had none. Thankfully, they did not press and assumed on their own.

"It must have been the plants," Maeve chimed in as she stepped out herself. "They call to her."

Susan's small, boney shoulders shrugged quickly and the tension dissipated. Lillian looked around for anything to change subjects to and remembered the detached garage.

"You know, I haven't looked in Aillig's garage yet. Maybe we could find something important in there."

She was too eager, and Maeve picked up on it, smiling. Everyone was allowed to keep secrets, and she was certain Lillian had plenty of her own. They followed Lillian's graceful strides.

"His mixing room!" Susan whispered excitedly.

Lillian looked fondly at the scattered array of herbs he'd left, no doubt in a rush. He had always been a bit messy when he mixed, a trait that Lillian had not absorbed. Silently, she moved through his stock, reorganizing with the loving affection that made her memory of him. Maeve, always observing, took a chance.

"Would you like to show us how you mix, dear? We could show you how to intentionally use the dreams and visions you're subject to."

Lillian was surprisingly willing to try. All these years she'd wished for a moment like this. Finally she was able to share the things that didn't make sense, and with someone who understood it.

"What should I make," she asked shyly.

"Something simple for ye, tis only an exercise."

She nodded and delicately went about, collecting herbs for her favorite infusion. Susan watched with intensity, knowing quickly what she was about to make.

"Lillian, you know what that is?" she asked excitedly.

"It's my favorite scent infusion. I use it for everything at home," she mentioned casually.

Maeve looked to Susan, but she said nothing.

"So what happens when you mix, dear?" Susan coaxed.

"Normally, when I mortar and pestle, I get little visions of things in my head. They always connect to the purpose of my healing. It's kind of like an imagery association to confirm that I'm on the right path, I suppose."

"Very smart, you are right. But might I ask what vision you get from this infusion in particular?"

Lillian stopped to consider. Nothing popped into her head.

"I suppose I don't know, Mrs. Bixby. I can't recall anything."

The older woman giggled childishly, approaching Lillian. She wrapped an arthritic hand around hers and spoke in a whisper.

"Roses induce veil walking. You've been mixing to veil walk without realizing. Well, at least your present self didn't. It explains the erratic nature of your visions. Watch now. Keep mixing with this in mind."

Lillian exhaled nervously before trying. She could feel the dried petals crush beneath Aillig's pestle and she inhaled the aroma floating to her nostrils. Her chest expanded with fresh air and she could feel herself lift away from the confines of the room. Nothing came at first, and Lillian reminded herself of what Susan had encouraged.

Her eyes closed and soon the velvet texture of her visions appeared. She saw the scattered herbs along a green cloak, and Hadrian's Wall. Facing to the far north, with the wall behind her, Hoot and the woman appeared in a blue light and she opened her eyes with a start.

"I went with you," Susan said, releasing her grip. "Those were objects from your past lives. They finally came clearly to you now that you've let them. You won't need to wait for sleep to understand messages anymore. Airmid has given you the gift of vision through her herbs. That was her cloak you saw."

Lillian stared at her, shaking her head.

"Not all of it was from a past life, I mean, from my focus. Hoot lives with me now."

"Tis not the first time he's found you then. But there's time to understand all of that. How'd it feel?"

"Lovely not to spin out of control." She laughed despite herself.

"Is this similar to the coating on Aillig's books that I told you about?"

"No. That was a potent mix to...well...force you into a meditation of sorts," Mrs. Bixby laughed. "If Aillig used anything natural it was because he got it from you. As you might know, his specialty was with the sciences and mathematics of chemistry."

Lillian thought of his double burners and smiled. She hadn't really noticed how little he practiced herbalism until now.

"Mrs. Bixby, who was that woman I saw? I see her all the time in my dreams, though never in...this...life?"

Susan crinkled her forehead. "I didn't see any woman, Lillian. She could be anyone, maybe yourself in a different time frame? Since it wasn't my walk, I'm subject to obscured vision. At least until you and I form a closer bond."

Even amongst all the chaotic possibilities of who she really was, she could feel a rooting deep down inside of her. So many years of confusion had passed and all because she couldn't accept what was outside the box of a reality she didn't even like. She thought of the church and how much she had clung to her upbringing without knowing. So many people had bravely blazed a path for her, and now that she'd found it, she couldn't let all her loved ones perish without reason.

"I've got to go back home tomorrow. I've got to go find the rest of the clues left for me."

"I thought he mentioned them being in the city, near the church, not Northumberland?" Maeve asked.

"I need to go home first and get a few things I've left, and check on the shop. Then I will return to Norwich."

..........

Dougal prepared to make his way back to the northern country. The encounter of the owl irked him, and having forced Nathan back the next night, it was revealed that she'd left town. The boy would not return after the second attack. Dougal cursed himself for thinking he could leave the uneducated sheep to do his dirty work with such a clever woman.

He had been so desperate to find anything about the interworking of his brother's organization that he hadn't kept a close eye on what she was doing. He swore to himself that he would strangle her with his bare hands if she jeopardized his position. The woman he worked for was not beyond punishing him again. He tried squeezing his fists together and winced. Anger rose in his throat and he locked the door to his office, blaming the stupid girl. He could have let all of this go if she hadn't gone off and disappeared. Now the superiors were pulling their hair out trying to find her, and it all fell on him to fix. They had given him permission for murder if he felt it was his last option. Dougal wished to make it his first.

*Chapter Thirty-One*

"Where's Cutter?" John asked, sliding a shot of whiskey across the bar, eyeing the layer of grunge on Emmy's clothes.

"Hell if I know," she breathed, toying the spicy smelling amber between her fingers with repulsion.

"Bullshit, Emmy, you know where he is."

She smiled and shoved the shot back at John, untouched. When she had returned a few hours before, there wasn't a trace of the man she felt ripped apart from. Desperate to know what had happened, she had wound up in front of the New Yorker. Now, she was starting to feel hopeless. All of her excitement and clairvoyance from what she'd seen in the mountains was dissipating.

John raised his brow. Cutter was a good friend of his, but it was hard to defend him when Emmy sat alone because of it. He swallowed hard, forcing the soft affection for her from his voice.

"Emmy, he would never tell you, and I shouldn't now, but that's all he had. He has to drive back to Los Angeles."

"What do you mean?"

"You didn't know? Last Saturday he bet every dollar he had on you. Everything. Without hesitation. I saw him do it," he shook his head. "Had to wait until payday so he had some cash to get there."

"Shit," she drawled under breath.

John held a weary eye, gears were turning and he knew well enough now that some crazy, rickshaw idea was being created. There wasn't a doubt that whatever she was planning next would be the craziest. Dirt coated her hair, making her more wild than a human should look. He wondered suddenly where she'd been this whole week.

Emmy grinned, slowly raising her head.

"You know, I've always liked you," she said, trouble curling her lips.

"No," he cut her off. "Whatever it is, no."

She laughed then, shaking the tips of her wavy hair.

"But John Boy, you already did."

With that, she left.

"Thank God," John mumbled, relieved he wasn't involved. He pulled the tap, watching the velvety liquid fall and slosh into a mug. He laughed. The ceiling fan wobbled over his head, and an old man sat at the end of the bar like always; just a particle of dust settling atop the shelves. A truck stuttered and spit somewhere outside. She had no regard for what was realistic and reasonable. John couldn't help but fantasize about Emmy's plans. She and Kelly were always at it. Sweat beaded at his hairline and the truck rumbled just beyond the open door of the bar. Somewhere in the depth of his conscious an alarm went off. Suddenly realizing, John jumped right over the bar and sprinted out the door way.

"Emmy! That's my truck!"

Her toothy grin sparkled in the daylight. She didn't bother slowing down as she hung her head out the window.

"Don't worry, John, it'll be back in your hands tonight!"

"How am I supposed to get to the rodeo?!"

"Walk!"

She turned the corner, gone. John stood, arms limp at his side, lower lip drooped open.

"I just got that car," he whined.

Despite the irritation that glowed dull on the top of his skin, a slow grin came over him. He knew Emmy would be back without a scratch on it.

"If she isn't, she's dead," he scoffed.

.....

Cutter sat on the edge of his bunk, flipping a business card in between his fingers, waiting for the other line to pick up. The empty pit in his stomach sat heavy since Emmy had taken off. When she hadn't turned up for work on Sunday, he had walked to her room with flowers to apologize for his temper. The stress of losing his savings was taken out on her because he needed an excuse outside of himself. He hadn't slept in days and stubble grew roughly on his face. He rubbed his hands over his eyes as he heard the voice on the other end.

"Yes, my name is Cutter Maben. This summer, one of your agents gave me his card. I was hoping to speak with him now about taking a job he offered."

A few minutes later he hung up the phone and looked at the softening sky out his window. He sighed and lay back against his bed. He couldn't bear to go back to the rodeo grounds tomorrow. The memory of last Saturday still burned in his flesh like a branding iron. He had chased Emmy off with the same harshness that she had been trying to escape. He knew he had completely screwed up whatever beauty they held between them, but he just couldn't believe it was in her nature to leave her friends without a word. He'd heard her struggles and the pain she carried between her shoulders at the hidden lake. Replaying the night after the rodeo made him wince. In a clear state of mind, it all seemed like such an awful reenactment of the horror she fled from. Perhaps in the state of shock she was in, she had done what came robotically to her and fled. Cutter dissected all the things he did wrong as he sat, hating himself on his cot under the stars. It felt like he had spent lifetimes he didn't live trying to find a woman like her, and in a moment she was gone forever.

·········

Emmy only had a few hours to get herself to George Fassenbach's home and persuade him to let her enter the Cowboy Challenge. After her disappearance, she knew it would not be for the weak stomached to sit eye to eye with the man and boldly ask a favor. But she was determined to right the wrong she did Cutter, even if it was too late. She swallowed hard. Even if it was too late.

She pulled up to the Fassenbach ranch under the setting sun. The house sat on the rugged ground, boldly facing the distant mountain range she had just wandered out of. She shrugged her shoulders, wondering how far the man could really see. The windows reached from floor to roof, and she swore he'd have a telescope to keep watch on the secrets of his town.

Her sneakers seemed to slap too loudly as she made her way up the steps to the door. She rang the bell and winced. There was a heavy creak on the other side of the modern cabin mansion. The giant door flew open with ease and she found herself staring into the eyes of the slightly unpredictable mayor.

"Well I thought you'd up and gone," he mused tentatively, trying to keep the shock from his face. "Kelly will be happy to see you hadn't left without a good bye. It isn't kind to disappear on a girl like her, perhaps an apology is due. She's not here, but I think you knew that. Come in."

She felt like a trap was being set, and she walked right into it. The house looked like a hunting lodge, scattered with stuffed game that she didn't doubt was killed by the man she was now following. Her throat went dry. They reached the giant, oversized leather couches, and she sunk into it at his gesture.

"So, what brings you here? I won't hear any apologies or begging for your job back. You quit."

Emmy stared at his heavy frame. Though full boned, he was not the man you'd take for slow or incapable. His jaw was set hard, and she took a breath before facing his scrutiny.

"I don't want my job back, and I won't apologize by your request. I came here to ask for permission to enter past cutoff into tomorrow's Cowboy Challenge."

George's eyes widened in consideration. A deep wrinkle set between his brows as he recalled the disaster that unfolded just a week ago. He worked through his logical mind. He figured the ordeal inspired her disappearance and his sweet Kelly's days of crying. He looked at the compact woman in front of him. There was a taught, wiry tension to her body that had been only barely visible before. George found himself more than curious about the outsider living inside his town in such privacy. It made him agitated thinking she could outwit his eyes around the city. Part of him thought it'd be smart to call Ethan before she could slip through his grip again. He'd not be this lucky a second time, that he was certain of.

Money jingled in his ears as he stared at the transformed girl. There was something fearsome in her eyes that made him uneasy. He smiled dangerously. He was willing to gamble on anyone that could look him in the eye and make him a profit.

"Why again?"

She knew it was a loaded question. She had to be careful not to give him any leverage.

"I have to prove to myself that I can do it."

His smile didn't waiver.

"Not for Cutter?"

Her heart twisted at the mention and she tried not to let it show in her face. George would undoubtedly use anything against her in his negotiations. She shook her head. He slammed a fist on the table between them with a loud crack. Emmy blinked once, slowly, before staring through him in defiance. Her fire was definitely impressive.

"Fine then," he laughed heartily. "Get yourself killed, or save your man. Though I think the first is most likely."

"Thank you," she replied coldly and rose to go.

He showed her out, watching her down the drive. When he closed the door, George turned to look out the expansive wall of windows at the jagged mountain range. He was going to need to tighten up his team if he was going to keep a close watch on her. If she succeeded tonight, he'd need to collect his profit quickly, quietly and off the books. He picked up the telephone and dialed.

"Hello?"

"I think it's her. I'll know more tonight."

"Talk to you then."

George hung up the phone and resisted the urge to look for a glass of water. Talking to Ethan Scipio always left his throat dry, no matter how short the conversation. George was dedicated, but Ethan was ruthless and took this loss of control personally. If George decided to tell his sect boss that the girl was indeed his estranged wife, he would have a hard time making a cover story about her permanent disappearance to his innocent, frivolous Kelly. For a short moment, he wished he'd never called.

.........

The dirt rattled beneath her toes. She could feel the vibrancy of the young herd being driven into the holding pen. Her hair stood on end, and she could hear the grunts as bets were placed against her. She smiled devilishly and looked to her left. Emmy wasn't surprised at all to see the looks of disapproval from the other competitors.

"You're dumber than I thought," a voice grated into her ears. "This time I ain't gonna let go if you get in the way."

"Okay," she muttered.

Suspense made the air around them tight and Emmy focused on the still in her heart. She heard the click of the gate just beyond them and moments later the thunderous hooves. She stayed frozen in place as the herd came rushing at her. Her heart fluttered and she pushed it out of her body towards the insecure babies. Blue eyes hawked through the tangled mass of legs and Emmy caught the flash of color. She recognized the filly instantly.

"*Anamchara*," she breathed.

Emmy calmed herself, understanding who she now was. *Epona,* she whispered into the recesses of her mind.

*Epona...*

Emmy's body felt expanded and the stars grew brighter. She shifted her sneakers in the dirt and saw the aura of innocence around the filly. Tuned into her racing heart and nothing else, Emmy whispered in a thick accent she'd never heard.

"I am your mother, dear creature, do not be afraid."

The crowd sat completely silent, the announcer muted in disbelief as Emmy set herself up to be trampled by the filly flying straight towards her. The confusion of sound fell away from her ears and all she could hear was the ragged breath from the filly's nostrils. She opened her palm and as the filly came running inches in front of her, Emmy stepped aside to grab a fistful of mane.

Life slowed as Emmy flexed her biceps and pushed the last grounded foot from the dirt. The crowd blinked and Emmy's small frame sat taut on the filly's back. Her ears flickered wildly as she leveled her neck, outstretched her head and ran full force to the other end of the large rodeo arena. Emmy sat fluidly on top of her, whispering Henry's sweet nothings in Gaelic, watching the quickly approaching pipe fence.

"Calm now, angel. Do not be scared. We are the same," she cooed, gently fusing their energies.

The filly's back muscle relaxed under Emmy's thighs and for a split second Emmy felt their two souls converge. She closed her eyes and exhaled once, thinking of her night amongst Blackfoot men. The filly darted to the left and stopped parallel to the fence.

There was no roar of the crowd. Silence penetrated their existence and Emmy opened her eyes, watching her hair still floating around her breasts. The expansion faded, her body responding again to the dense gravity of her reality. Epona was gone. Clouds of dust billowed as she slid off, running a hand over the painted filly's forehead. Her legs were numb and tingling as she regained control of her body.

"Thank you, little girl, for your bravery."

Big blue eyes blinked once through long white lashes before Emmy turned and walked to relieve the connection. She strode the length of the arena to quiet murmurs outside the white pipe fence. Halfway down, she felt a push in between her shoulders. She turned slowly around to see the paint standing loyally behind her. Emmy smiled and blew into her nostrils.

"*Anamchara*, my soul friend, let's get out of here."

The two walked freely, untied and unafraid, out of the arena and to the holding pen just a few feet away. The crowd watched in shock, and the announcing booth buzzed overhead in silence.

It wasn't until the horse was safely locked into the holding pen that the crowd burst into a voracious roar, and Emmy couldn't help but let a grin flutter across her face. She walked to the payout booth to cash in. The man, still dumbfounded, grabbed the bag of earnings and handed it to her. She turned and left before the cash amount could stumble across his lips. Emmy had placed a few of her precious stones on herself beforehand, praying she'd not lose the expensive gifts from the Bannock.

Emmy stood protectively near the holding pen as passersby gawked and nodded with praise at the newest champion. Her nerves bit at her as she tried to figure out how to get to the mountains without causing too much attention. She needed to make sure this little filly was in good hands after the courage she displayed. She deserved more than ever to be with the Tukudika, in the land that could not be discovered by anyone. She decided she'd wait until after the bar closed to return to her.

"Come on," John yelled from the crowd surrounding her, "you'll be drinking free all night!"

Rounds flowed freely in celebration at Ale Haus, and Emmy's eyes twinkled in John's direction.

"What are you drinkin' sweetheart?" a voice called out.

"Vodka," she requested, staring dead into John's eyes as she responded.

He barely smiled, and slyly poured water into a shot glass. The night seemed to drag on as voices blurred together in congratulations. She watched the clock and grew more anxious every time someone pleaded for her to tell them how she did it.

"I can't tell you how I did it. Luck, I guess," she explained absently.

Cutter hadn't been there to see her, and he was nowhere to be found now. She worried that he'd already left town. She sighed heavily and turned back to the handful of people left waiting to talk to her. When two o'clock finally came around and John hollered for everyone's exit, Emmy waited impatiently behind to head to the rodeo grounds unnoticed. She had already disobeyed Sky Brother's advice to stay under the radar by entering the contest. Now, she could see why the wolf-man had encouraged her to stay out of the spotlight. When the last lingerer stumbled out of the bar she got up to leave.

"Emmy," John stopped her.

She whirled around smiling.

"Thank you for everything, John."

"Whatever, it's fine," he brushed aside, knowing that his truck was parked safely outside. "But I have to know. No one has been able to crawl on that herd in over twenty years it's been said."

Emmy only shrugged.

"To be honest, I couldn't tell you completely, and what I could tell you, you'd never believe."

..........

George sat back in his recliner, incapable of wiping the small grin on his face. His knack for following gold proved strong as he had made money on Emmy's foretold talents. He thought it strange to be alive and see the living version of a story he'd grown up hearing. In the excitement of her display, he found himself conflicted on what to do next. Ethan was half the country away. Had he been living in the same state, his decision would have been easy.

She had gone from a worthless, mousey thing to a money earning equestrian sorceress. It was amazing what a little distance from that violent man did for her. No wonder they liked to keep her near him. His fear of Ethan was probably minuscule in comparison to Emmy's. He couldn't help but consider the idea of Kelly being put into a marriage with the man. Fatherly instinct washed over him for a moment, and he couldn't help but side with Emmy.

"Ethan can wait a few weeks," George sneered to himself, pushing off the uncomfortable emotion. "This girl is going to make me a huge profit and just in time for the off season. I will put him off the scent."

*Chapter Thirty-Two*

His limbs were heavy and covered in dirt as he sat in his solitary confinement. He could feel his ribs poking his side as he tried to rest and focus on the light his little dove brought him. He had long passed the time he thought he'd be kept alive, and the minimal nourishment he received was starting to rattle his well being. No longer did he look like the mighty leader he had once been. His shoulders slumped and the idea of death seemed nearly satisfying. The only strength he had was gained from seeing Lillian.

He had to believe that they would be together in one life or the next. He inhaled deeply and refocused on his mission. He could not fail her and would survive long enough to make sure she was safe. He recalled the first night he had dreamt of Lillian's prophecy and smiled. He missed the warmth of his home and the smiling faces of his family. His bony fingers wrapped around the vile hanging from his neck. The druid had given it to him to take just before his death. Grimy hair fell in ragged lines against his sharp cheekbone as he concentrated on staying present in Lillian's life. Danger crept around her and she'd need him to be strong.

.....

Lillian could see his shadow far before she could recognize his face, but the stature was unmistakable. Dougal was waiting for her outside the shop. The vague presence of her shadow man made her cautious as she approached. The mist seemed thicker her first morning back from the coast and her breath caught in her throat as she neared. Her neck hair prickled. Lillian could feel her feet slow as she came closer. Dougal's back was facing her. He was preoccupied with her door. She stood and watched, speaking upon him too quickly.

"Good morning," she nearly yelled.

Dougal spun around, startled.

"Oh, hello."

She said nothing.

"How odd," he chuckled. "I had come to see ye and was just reading your letter."

Lillian smiled to conceal her suspicion.

"How's inventory coming along, lass?"

Dougal could feel his anger rise and tried to manipulate it. He had wanted to break in to find answers and instead received the presence of the girl, which complicated things.

"Grand. I wasn't expecting to see you. Is there something you need?"

Aillig's journals made her wary of Dougal's motivation. Anyone involved with the church could be a threat, and Dougal had already displayed dangerous behavior.

"Well, yes," he said too sweetly. "I said I'd be back if I found anything and I have."

A lump caught in her throat. Whatever he'd found could lead to what she'd learned. Lillian couldn't be sure what side he was on, but being raised Catholic made it less likely he believed in the borderline mythical circumstance of her life. She shifted her weight.

"That's lovely," she said too eagerly. "Shall we have a look at it inside?"

He grinned and Lillian felt a pressure against her arm. Despite the warning from her shadow, she unlocked the door anyway. They walked in and headed for the consultation desk. Dougal walked behind her.

"Looks like you haven't been here in days. Your mixing room must be a mess, however."

He knew it wasn't.

"I haven't been here in days," she reminded him, "and I do inventories in the comfort of my own home."

Though too personal, she wanted to secure her false story in case he'd been by before today. Dougal nodded.

"I'm sure you're tidy as it is. Just like my brother."

Her leg twitched. Dougal had swung and missed. Aillig was notorious for his messes. They sat, and when she made no inclination toward making tea, he spoke.

"I found Aillig's birth records. It was shocking to find out we were only half brothers. It sent me on a long and meaningless paper trail."

Lillian nodded, processing what was important. Aillig had left Dougal to find her for a reason, she reminded herself. He had sent him the note that had initiated the entire search. There had to be something she needed from his brother. She wanted to ask about what purpose his findings served, but Dougal raised his hand.

"It doesna matter. Nothing seemed suspicious. His father is unknown and I knew our mother's side. She was the only one left by the time she passed. I also found my brother's interest in old literature. I'm not surprised, considering his line of work. He was always chasing fairy tales."

The statement hung in the air as he raised his wrinkled brow. Though acting the casual man, he never looked more threatening. *Think like Aillig.* Lillian moved a piece in his game of chess. She chose to stay silent to draw out more information.

Dougal shrugged, somewhat more irritably than he liked.

"I thought to come and tell ye that the search was over unless ye had some knowledge about his curiosities, in case it could give us an idea where to continue. I'm afraid I've reached a dead end."

She knew there'd be clues hidden in the pages of the books he'd looked at, and maybe more to find than Dougal realized. He obviously wouldn't connect the clues to a discovery of her past selves and the prophecy. He couldn't. He didn't think any of it was real. He couldn't have thought to look too carefully or he wouldn't be sitting so amiably in front of her. Lillian tried to apply what Maeve had taught her about being an empath.

Lillian relaxed her body and visualized an open door where her abdomen was no longer tense. She could feel the mild irritation he was staving off to save face, and she picked up more acutely on his game playing. Her mind raced as she considered her next words carefully.

"We've all grown up reading stories, Mr. MacIntyre. Aillig enjoyed literature. I may not be much help, but I might try. If you want to leave your findings with me, I can go through them this week."

Dougal's mouth twisted into a dark smile, his excitement getting the better of him.

"Problem, dear, is that I don't have them. All the records are in the antiquity room down in the city."

Lillian's palms felt clammy. It wasn't the blatant slip of Dougal's scheming that frightened her, but more the thought of having to return anywhere near the dungeon she grew up in.

"There's no reason to be afraid lass. There's no reason to fear the church."

"That's not what I fear," she whispered, trying to forget Sister Roy's face.

Dougal knew without asking what was linked to her terror, and it was justified. She sat staring for minutes as he waited, growing more impatient as the clock ticked behind him.

"I'll go then," she finally whispered.

He nodded, following her to the door as she rose. She locked up silently behind them.

"When shall I expect ye?"

"One week. I'll need to make arrangements and ready my clientele for another absence."

With a grunt, Dougal parted from the girl feeling triumphant. When enough distance had been put between them he picked up his phone.

"Yes, I got the wee lass to come back," he reported with confidence. "Whatever he hid, we'll find now."

"Do not be too sure, Dougal, she is a flighty thing and will run at the scent of danger."

The other end went dead and he shoved his phone back in his pocket. He knew little about why they watched her so closely, beyond the fact that she was a part of Aillig's organization that wanted the church destroyed. Dougal's hate towards her was automatic. If they had sent a man to do the job when she was born, nothing would have gone wrong. His half brother may have almost blown the lid off their cover, but Dougal had taken care of that. This girl should be simple. He could smell a promotion on his fingertips. That woman had no clue how in control he was of Lillian.

Lillian got through her front door with shaking hands, and picked up her telephone to call the women.

"Hi, Maeve. No, I'm okay, really. But Dougal was at the shop when I went to check on it and said he had information on Aillig. No, I didn't have a chance to grab the moonflower, though I may have some here at the cottage. Would you and Susan be able to come by?"

"We'll be there within the hour."

Lillian plopped onto her bed and closed her eyes, pressing her fingers into the sockets. Susan had volunteered as a more practiced veil walker to attempt contact with any of Aillig's past lives. She'd need a heavy sedative, and Lillian's expertise, to go so far in a realm without the restriction of time. Lillian needed the moonflower oil, but she had never replenished it after her episode. Now it'd have to wait. She couldn't help but wonder if it was not the time to try, as if fate was correcting their haste. She sorted through her mind, wishing it didn't have to be the unpredictable moonflower that took them to such a deep recess. She longed for time to walk through the woods for more inspiration. Lillian could feel the woodsy air tugging for her attention.

"The tea!" she exclaimed to herself, remembering the imagery she'd created when drinking it.

The tea Aillig had left her at his beach house induced her into a strange trance of its own. She leapt up to open her cupboards where she had placed it upon her return home. No wonder Aillig had taken an unusual interest in hallucinogens before he died. He knew Lillian needed to access her deeper self with help before she could do it on her own. Whatever needed to be found had to be by herself, not Susan. She had a feeling Aillig wouldn't have shown himself even if they had tried. He was leaving clues for her to understand, not for him to provide answers. She put the jar in one of her suitcases as she started to pack.

The knock on the door was swift and delicate. Lillian opened it with relief.

"I apologize," she mumbled, as she welcomed them in. "I do not have a kitchen table, nor do I have a couch. Never really planned for visitors."

They walked passed the entry way, seeing her bedroom to the left where couches and a television should be. They said nothing, but smiled with gracious manners. Her cheeks flushed.

"I hate closed spaces," she muttered hopelessly.

"It's lovely," Susan said, grabbing her hand.

Lillian smiled. "I have a seating area in the atrium. It's in the back. I'll give you the whole two minute tour on the way. Kitchen's on our right."

They moved down the hallway, walls barren but for the dried herbs hanging in half decoration.

"Toilets here," she said pointing to the door. "Mixing room on the left."

Both women looked to the door on the left with curiosity. Lillian didn't offer to open it and though disappointed, they were not surprised. Healers seldom shared their sacred ground. A small, slate colored door stood in front of them. Lillian looked over her shoulder grinning.

"And this is the atrium."

Maeve and Susan's eyes shone as they walked into the quaint area. All the walls were made of windows, surrounding them with the world beyond. The Cheviot Mountains idled far in the distance like sleeping giants and the stretch of turf reached with desire to the forest line in the near background. An iron table was cozied between pale wooden chairs and a pot of tea sat steaming for them. The women admired the serenity of colors in the potted plants and the rich selection in the garden just outside. Maeve couldn't subdue her effervescence for Lillian's world.

"It's like ye live outside our existence," she murmured in a heavier brogue than usual.

"It certainly feels that way," Lillian smiled as she gazed to her walking path.

Susan stayed quiet as she bounced around in the bright vibrations of the worlds around them. Lillian's sovereignty was strong here and it was easy for her to move into all the realms Lillian lived between.

"The plants sing to you," she said softly.

Lillian nodded. "Yes, I suppose they do in a way."

All three sat down and poured a cup before she started in.

"So as I said, Dougal was at the shop when I got there. I can't decide if it was a bad coincidence or bad intentions interfered. Either way it was unsettling."

"He said he had information on Aillig?" Maeve asked as she drummed her fingers against her thigh.

"Yes, though he was very vague. Found out Aillig was only his half brother. But I don't think he would have found that at any of the addresses I had given to him unless he was snooping for something."

Lillian searched their faces but they were as shocked as she. No one had known about Aillig's mysterious parentage.

"Dougal said it was all unimportant to his death. Father's an unknown and his mother was the last of her line. No one was alive to be motivated for murder. The rest of what he found is kept in the city. Books Aillig had checked out and such. He found it useless, but we know better."

"Well, Aillig kept him involved for a reason," Susan cooed. "He'll get us what we need one way or the next."

Lillian nodded. "Indeed, because I'm going back to get it with him."

Both women shot a piercing look of opposition as she spoke her intention, but Lillian quietly arranged her gaze on the comfort of her surroundings outside the windows.

"But it's too dangerous for you to go back near that church," Susan protested.

"Especially if they think you're important or on to something. Just like we've got stories of ye, they have their own," Maeve argued.

Lillian held her gaze steadily on the trees in the distance.

"Aillig was always two steps ahead. It has to be this way. It would have been better to go unannounced and without escort, but I have no choice. Like you said, he involved Dougal for a reason."

She remembered her dream from the beach house. She had been running to her shadow man because he was calling her to safety. He had called her away from the dream when it grew too intense. She knew there was a purpose to his presence in the beach house nightmare and had to believe that if she found herself in too much danger, he would find her a way out even if it meant sacrificing herself.

"Susan, do premonitions exist?"

Susan hesitated as she thought carefully.

"Well, literally, no. Nothing in this world is ever concrete. We are constantly changing, learning, evolving. Movement dictates our survival on many levels. However, there can be belief in probabilities. We can hold faith in most likely guesses based on patterns or previous information."

"So a premonition is more like a possibility of events based on the knowledge we are given to date?"

Susan smiled. "Yes, that's a good way to put it. There's never an absolute of the future. Not even your prophecy."

It made her wonder why it was this life that was so important and why she hadn't brought the prophecy to fruition in a past life, when she was clearly more capable of understanding it. *Aillig would have been able to figure it out.* She missed him dearly.

"Have ye had one, lass?" Maeve asked edging toward her.

Lillian only smiled. "No, but I've had a probability."

*Chapter Thirty-Three*

The truck door slammed with a metal ring. Emmy had found it parked safely on George's back property. Dust finally caught up with the giant beast, and danced anxiously around jean clad legs. The tear mid-thigh stretched and laughed with every scuff of her sun bleached sneakers. The engine was still hot and ticking by the time her hand reached the door of the diner. The cow bell rang once and fell still. She stood a moment before running her fingers through her hair, flipping it behind her shoulder in a mess.

Heavy bellies twisted in their Sunday suspenders as they watched her walk past, jaws dropping, food hanging on their tongue. The piously infested place stopped operating for the hard curves swaying down the isle. She had started making an impression last night and clung to it with confidence. Cutter's back was facing the entrance. He picked at the fries on his plate, scooting them through ketchup as he pretended to listen to Sherry Jean's chatter until she was choked silent. She glanced over his shoulder with a tightened face. Curious, he looked over his dirt coated shirt. He saw the pair of blue eyes a few feet away, glaring at Sherry Jean, who huffed and walked away with a straight back. Emmy walked to the edge of his table, but didn't sit down. She was silent, staring into him, void of anything but proud anger. She dug into her sweatshirt pocket, and pulled out a giant wad of cash, throwing it and a copy of the day's newspaper over his hands.

"Here's your cash back."

She cursed at herself for losing control of her anger. Emmy turned and walked out of the diner before she could say anything worse. She was too desperate to see him, to feel him, and too angry to admit that she'd been hurt.

Cutter sat for a few minutes, staring at the photo on the front page of a ragged haired girl swinging up onto the back of a wild horse.

"She did it," he whispered.

He separated a few of the crumpled bills from the wad and tossed them on the table next to his empty plate. He jogged outside and stopped. Cutter's chest caved inward as he looked around. Her truck was sitting in between semis and he ran to look inside. The cab was empty, but the keys were left hanging in the ignition. She had left it for him, and he knew then that John must have told her he got rid of everything just to make it back home. He was the only one Cutter had told the truth to. Hopping in, he set it to roar and flew onto the road. She was walking with her head defying the skyline, staring longly toward the motel. He slowed alongside her, stretching to roll down the window.

"Get in, Emmy."

"No, Cutter."

She wouldn't look at him. He followed her and pulled into the motel parking lot.

"Emmy, just stop would you?" he called, getting out of the truck.

She whirled around. Her heart fluttered seeing the dark circles under his eyes and the gauntness she didn't remember seeing under his cheekbones. She fought hard to keep from running into his arms.

"What, Cutter," she breathed.

"Emmy I'm sorry," he started, not moving. "I should have never yelled at you or pushed you into doing something you weren't ready for. I never wanted to hurt you. When I found out that you'd disappeared, I was sure you'd never be coming back. I didn't know you were here or I'd have come for you. I hadn't seen anyone but Sherry Jean today. I had no idea..." he trailed off.

Her shoulders slumped in defeat. The terror that looked so familiar on his face only mirrored her own desperation for him. Cutter wasn't anything like Ethan, the anger that had sent him raging against her was out of fear for her well being, not because he had lost money on her. The hardness in her heart disappeared. She held out a hand and smiled weakly as the hurt worked its way off her breast. If the Sky Brother was right about them, Emmy wouldn't get anything from fighting. She needed to trust him. She needed to learn from the mistakes she made with Henry. She needed to remember who Cutter was to her.

"Come inside, I have something to tell you."

Cutter's stomach twisted in fear of whatever he'd let his little horse fall into. She seemed different, though no less beautiful, and her skin glowed against the disarray of her clothes. The room seemed dusty and stale, as if no one had been sleeping there for some time. Cutter studied her and the strange demeanor she had adopted. He wasn't sure he could sit through another story of her pain, especially if it had happened because of him. He sat stiffly on the edge of the bed, feeling improper and foreign in her room. When he had adjusted to a certain level of comfort, she spoke slowly.

"Cutter, remember the day I rode Apollo?"

He nodded slowly.

"Before you caught up to us, I thought I had seen someone else on that ridge, but by the time I got up there, they had disappeared. It bothered me enough that I snuck

Apollo out another night to go searching, and I was right. There are people up there. A whole tribe of Natives."

"You stole Apollo?"

She shrugged in momentary bashfulness, but the excitement of what had happened pushed forward. She pulled up her shirt to show the paint that she hadn't scrubbed off. His eyes ran up her abdomen, studying the half visible, crusted paint. Cutter's body tensed, recognizing the blue symbols from dreams he'd been having.

"Cutter, they showed me how to use my talent intentionally. I can communicate with horses like people communicate with each other. Sort of. You saw all along. I'm so sorry I didn't trust you."

He wrapped his hand around hers, but said nothing.

"Cutter do you believe in multiple lives?" she rambled, not giving him time to respond. "The Sky Brother told me it's real, and that you and I have met before a long time ago. I don't know about you but I've been spending most of our time wondering why I felt like I knew you." She looked at their hands, feeling a gentle tug inside her mind. Now that she wasn't fighting against it, Henry's game did not control her. "Do you feel that weird tug every time we touch, too?"

His throat tightened. He wasn't really listening. He was trying not to choke her with the desire running towards his lips. He wanted to kiss her. To quiet her. To tell her what words couldn't.

"It happens because we *did* know each other before and you're supposed to be in my life and no one knows why we got separated. It's been so long that Sky Brother said even his people forgot. I'm part of some important prophecy and you're important for me. Something about fire and being able to understand me. There's a lot I still don't understand, but I believe it. I believe what they told me, Henry had been telling me in bedtime stories all along.

I have the book with me. He knew too. It's got to be right, Cutter."

"Sky Brother took me to their spiritual grounds and I saw the paintings of our story. They've been there forever, before I was born. And you have a memory tile that helps me remember. It's a spiral. I sat up there for days going back into lives from before, remembering."

Emmy bit her lip and waited for him to say anything.

"You don't believe me, do you?" she sighed.

Cutter wanted to savor the fullness of her lips when she was excited. He leaned forward, cupping her strong jaw in his hand and kissed her cheek with gentle restraint. He sat a moment in silence, quelling the fire, toying with the ends of her hair.

"Emmy, since I met you I've been dreaming about memories we've never had together. I dreamt about you on the side of a river, and riding under moonlight. I dreamt of you doing things I've never seen you do."

Her eyes lit up.

"I have spent every day trying to remember those dreams as they faded with your disappearance."

He let the agony of losing her show in his trembling hand. He let her see the worry that dulled his face. Slowly, achingly taking his time, he lowered his mouth onto hers with the uncertain gentleness of a man who thought he'd lost everything. Cutter wrapped his arms around her entire body, pulling her as closely as he could. They were being ripped apart again.

"Emmy, I leave tomorrow."

His departure hung in the air. He regretted the contracts he had already bound himself to.

"I know," she smiled sadly, placing her hand on his thigh.

"I'm sorry," he whispered into her hair.

"So am I."

They sat, feeling the strange familiarity return between them. He didn't want to think about what she'd just told him or what it could possibly mean. He couldn't indulge in her fantasies right now. Cutter only wanted this moment. They were together.

.......

Ethan's pride was burned by her successful disappearance, and the harder he tried to recover what he had lost, the more he spun mercilessly out of control. He looked around at the house laying in interior shambles, wracking his brain. He had upturned every floor and smashed every wall, looking for leads to her location. He threw another piece of furniture across the room with a dull yell.

He stumbled to find his brandy, drinking the honeyed liquid like water. He should have let her keep more possessions in the house. She would have been too stupid to hide them, unlike her grandfather. Now he relied solely on the asinine idiots below him to find her. A handful of times someone had called claiming sight of her. He had only arrived to a false identity each time. Ethan was growing impatient with useless trips and his position was unraveling fast. His superiors' contact with him had been minimal in the last few weeks and he guessed they had taken matters into their own hands.

"Can't ruin their reputation," he sneered.

"They should have just killed her to start!" he boomed, throwing his last glass against the wall. His disheveled hair fell in his eyes.

"She's the last of their damned blood line. It could have been done already. They wait too long for everything."

He blamed his superiors for her escape. They let him rot in jail too long and she slipped away. Stumbling to the front door, he decided he was done waiting for the approval above him. He wasn't going to be excluded from their plans anymore. Ethan would call first thing in the morning with opinions of his own.

The screen door cracked open and he guzzled the last of his brandy decanter. He was going to conquer and kill until he found her himself.

"I am going to get her," he hissed between his teeth, heading toward his car.

Ethan caught an uprooted floor board with his boot and fell forward. His ribs slammed hard against the stairs of the porch and he passed out before his cheek tore against the gravel of the drive.

*Chapter Thirty-Four*

It was strange that the hysteric rush for product didn't manifest as Lillian announced her second leave. In fact, it was oddly quiet at the apothecary. All the frenzy had come at home while the three women spent the week gathering items for removal.

"If Aillig had decided to keep all of his findings in places of secrecy, then we must do the same. Nobody knew about his beach house."

Lillian looked to Susan and Maeve as she put her bags into her car.

"If you have always traveled there, it won't seem odd if you go now. Just be careful if we are assuming you've been seen here. We would be done for if they follow you and find that house."

"I have a few days to find what he left in the city. I'll ring once I'm back."

......

He protested Lillian's return to the city in every dream she had. He knew too well what happened when anyone came too close to their secrets. His entire army had been mutilated because he had attracted too much attention about their falsity. Their ability to harm her would be tenfold near the church and she was going without backup of her own.

It took all of his energy to stay constantly near, even as she drove. He worked hard to move past the aching around his bony wrists as the shackles grew heavier. He knew what an approaching war felt like, and he hoped that her naïveté might serve her now. If she could see the trials he had lived through in rebellion against them, she'd not dare attempt her return.

"She is stronger than even she is aware," he reminded himself, "and you are to love her."

His dwindled body distracted his mind once singularly focused on his purpose. With struggle, he ignored the starvation snaking through his ribs. The longer veil walks were taking a toll and he grit his teeth.

.....

Driving into Norwich felt like a vice grip around her skull. The tight roads glowered under steep buildings stacked into the misting clouds. She glanced at street signs as if someone might recognize her and turn her in. The shopping mall buzzed with every day commotion, and the imposing St. John's thinned the air. She had rung Dougal the day before to announce her arrival.

Lillian turned slightly to Gaol Hill and neared her accommodations. She couldn't help but sigh over the typical modern elegance seeping through to the money funding the crowded city. Only hours from home and she already longed for the open peace of Northumberland. She took a few minutes to unpack her bag, wanting to waste as little time as possible before heading to the church. Lillian tried to focus on the business end of her journey in hope of leaving her nerves numbed.

She shuffled past groups of people in a brisk pace, feeling the tension rise in her shoulders. She slid through the market place she'd first met Aillig and smiled fondly before the humor was lost. In front of her stood the hell that raised her. The sharp peaks of the building stared over her in judgement. Its pallid exterior threatened to swallow her whole as she approached.

"So ye actually came," his voice sang behind her.

Lillian whirled around to see Dougal in the most jovial state he'd ever been in. He was dangerous indeed.

"Well, let's head inside shall we? Been a few changes since you've last been here."

Her heart slammed against her chest as they walked through. Everything felt as it had when she left. High ceilings bent forward to strangle her and every carving seemed to be telling a different warning. The stained glass shone as bright as a beautiful distraction and the chill grew more stifling. Their footsteps echoed against the tall walls and she pressed her pen and paper to her chest, forcing her eyes to look ahead. She didn't want to engage any lingering emotions about this place. Dougal lead her through corridors she could remember like yesterday. But as they approached the gardens, it started to change.

"Och," Dougal grinned. "I see ye noticed your beloved garden has been replaced."

The map in her head erased. A quick escape would be more difficult now that she felt a little turned around. Lillian's nerves started to penetrate her mission.

"This is the library and records hall now. When I searched the database, his name appeared here, but nothing else. However, he had written it in his coded letter to you all the same. Perhaps you will have better luck than I."

Dougal unlocked the heavy door and swung it open. Whatever shred of nostalgia had been kept for her in the gardens faded. They entered into the warm tones of oak ceilings and shelves brimmed with religious works. Lillian couldn't help but wonder what Dougal had found of Aillig's here. Entrapment loomed in the walls of the library and she scolded herself for not considering that he might already know about her supposed prophecy. If she could tell a lie, so could he.

"Closed to the public today," Dougal mentioned as he acknowledged the empty facility. "Makes it rather easy to look around."

"So what is it that you found linked to Aillig's death here?"

"Despite his choice of daily living, it seems Aillig had a thirst to learn about my religion. I cannot see what he ever gained by having a membership here for all the strangeness that made him."

Lillian listened intently to the open judgement of his half brother. She found it surprising to hear in contradiction to his early concern about Aillig's potential murder. They had their opposing beliefs, but it hadn't deterred his attitude about Aillig before. Dougal seemed strange, and Lillian didn't like it.

"Was there anything promising to lead us in a different direction for his cause of death?" she probed.

Dougal watched from the corner of his eye, irritated by the soft whiplash of her reminder. He did not like pretending to care for Aillig or the little darling in front of him. There was always an air of arrogance around their type as if they knew something he did not. He would enjoy stripping that from her.

"Just find it odd that he was ever here. However, ye grew up with the education of this very church, and also the education of my half brother. I was hoping ye might find a connection."

"You mentioned a membership. Aren't libraries accessible to the public?"

Dougal turned impatiently towards her. He wondered if she ever chose to listen to the important parts of a conversation.

"The library is maintained by the donations of our church members who are rewarded by having access to the library for deeper devotion, lass."

Lillian looked around at the history in front of her and thought. Aillig had to have been a member of the church to get in here. She glanced quietly to Dougal as he headed for a table to see if he'd put it together. Aillig had used it as a cover to find information on Lillian.

"So when did Aillig become a member of the church?"

She swore the stubble on Dougal's chin stood on end when she asked. His eyes narrowed. She could feel her throat tighten and managed to shrug.

"I never knew him to be a religious man myself. I'd be curious to know when he made the switch," she paused, searching for a motivation he'd agree with. "Maybe his conversion had been a quiet one. If someone had found out, they could have been upset about the façade. It's not a secret between us that Aillig openly disagreed with most of this," she admitted, waving her hand around the room.

The burly man watched her a moment. Dougal hated how she jumped between competency and listlessness. There was little he could do to guess what she might know. One minute she was afraid, the next too sly for his comfort. Despite his better judgement, he led her to the information desk and sat down.

The ring of keys jingled like bells as they were tugged from his jacket pocket. Each chime brought light into her brain as she realized Dougal's role. Aillig was using him as easy access to the information he couldn't bring to her. Her fingers twitched against her leg as a piece of the puzzle clicked into place. Maybe he'd found information on her parents here. She moved behind him as the thrill of the hunt began. She watched the neatly written index cards flip through his gnarled fingers. In moments, he located Aillig's reference card and pulled it out.

"Looks as though he joined a few years ago," Dougal pointed to the date.

Lillian speculated. "That was a few days after my nineteenth birthday."

Dougal didn't react to the bit of a clue she offered and Lillian swallowed hard in contemplation. She had to risk revealing what she was looking for if she wanted to be sure what Dougal knew. *Think like Aillig, always one step ahead.* If he didn't know the importance of this discovery, then he likely didn't know much about her. Aillig had joined as soon as he thought he needed to uncover what they'd hidden here.

"Maybe he was looking to find something about my upbringing so that he could return me to my proper home?"

Dougal knew Aillig to be the harmonious type. It wouldn't have been strange for his brother to consider returning her. But he had decided to nurture her, which seemed too coincidental. His role in their heathen community had only amplified the possibility of her self discovery and that was frowned upon. He watched Lillian's innocent eyes glazing over the shelves. Aillig couldn't have told her about her own prophecy, or she'd not have dared to come so close to the church. He shrugged and considered the possibility that all the worry was still for not.

"Seems quite right," he finally decided.

He lifted the card to replace it. Lillian noticed a small, familiar scratch on the card behind it. To anyone else it would have seemed to be an imperfection from the hand who wrote it. But Lillian had seen the same symbol millions of times in her sleep notes.

*Ogham for Holly,* she thought, seeing the mark. *The riddles. Crooked creatures threaten justice, vengeance buried under holly.* Lillian scanned the name below the symbol, surprised. Naturally in alphabetical order, Dougal's own membership fell behind his half brother. He joined the day before Aillig's death. Of all the churches Dougal had to be associated with, it had to be this one. The room shrank, and Lillian forced her growing nausea away.

"Don't you think he would have used the references here to find the names of who may have raised me?" she thought quickly, wanting more time to process.

Dougal prickled at the thought of his brother prowling. Certainly she thought his intentions were pure, but he'd known Aillig to be very keen in his younger years. Despite his better judgement, he played along to concrete his feeling of her ignorance. He had to admit his curiosity was piqued with the different route the search was taking. Eventually, her point of view could better lead to something about the damned souls his brother had consorted with. Perhaps Dougal could outsmart his brother for once. Aillig was not the better son, he was.

"Why would that be important to finding a clue about his death," he asked.

Lillian winced and instinctively took a step backward.

"I was only thinking he may have spoken to them in private about me, or maybe he had gone to confessional about something obscure in the days before his death. He could have told someone then about a potential lead. He had been so odd before his shop burned, and he had asked me quite often about returning to the church," she lied.

Dougal rolled his eyes. He wanted to strangle her, but he had already been warned to keep his temper in check. He couldn't understand how anyone could be so daft to their own importance. *Unless she's not the one they speak of at all.* Nonetheless, the College of Cardinals would be furious if he blew it and sent her running when they were so close to finding out what she did or didn't know.

"Good point lass," he agreed gruffly. "Let's flip through and look for names that seem familiar to ye. Surely he talked to all of them. Twas such a chatty man."

He pulled the drawer open and Lillian stopped him.

"Don't you think there are files out here?" she asked, pointing to all the shelves. "He wouldn't have been able to look through these cards, right?"

Dougal slowly shook his head. Of course there were plenty of files out there, and no doubt Aillig went through them. But he was not about to let her see all the information holding thinly veiled secrets. They hid things in close quarters and behind restricted areas for a reason.

"No, lass," he lied. "I'm afraid personal information isn't kept here besides these membership cards. I suppose we can rattle them off to help ye remember any name that might sound familiar."

"How could Aillig find out who to ask about my caretakers if all of this is just generic information and that drawer is locked?"

His lie faltered.

"Just because it's locked, doesna mean one canna ask for someone to look for ye."

She nodded impartially to conceal her own bumpy lie, glancing at the cards over his shoulder. She watched sharply as he flipped and sang off names. She hardly listened, already knowing every name of the nuns who raised her. Instead, she focused on looking for Aillig's imperceptible signs in case he left any more. Nothing caught her eyes as they flipped.

"Helena Roy," stung every bone in her body as he said it. If she had been anymore distracted, she'd have missed Aillig's mark on the card.

Dougal didn't need to look at the girl to know the weight that name carried.

"She's still here," he coaxed with oozing hospitality, "if ye care to say hello."

Lillian said nothing, feeling her hands grow clammy in memory of the pain the woman had inflicted. Her back twitched responsively and Lillian fought the desire for fresh air. The moments passed somberly, Dougal also reflecting on the actions of his bosses. He too did not escape the brutal lesson of respect in his years. He rubbed his gnarled hands as a memory. Out of nowhere, a dull bitterness inspired him to practice compassion.

"What'd they do to ye?" he asked, spinning in his chair, raising his hands.

Her dark green eyes widened at the revelation.

"You mean it wasn't arthritis?"

"No, but that's what I tell everyone."

She searched his face with pain staking sorrow, but could feel little response from him. She couldn't access feelings if Dougal didn't even allow himself to.

"I told ye I was hard headed," he stated more gravely than his first admittance.

For a moment, they shared the same pain and she decided to reveal her secret, despite the mistrust between them. She turned slowly, lifting her heavy sweater over her shoulders. Her skin rose with goosebumps in the crisp air. Delicately, she pushed her silk camisole up her back. Dougal inhaled through his teeth at the sight. Sinewy scars lay in thin white lines across her back, cross hatching the devotional word into her flesh. Lillian closed her eyes to shut out the tears welling up.

"Helena?" Dougal asked.

Lillian nodded as she pulled her sweater back on and turned around.

"I had a hard time sleeping when I was young. She swore I was possessed and tried beating it out of me."

Dougal shook his head. Helena was his boss, but he knew little about the woman outside her involvement with the girl. Helena's little birds had been sent to keep an eye on Lillian over the years since the Vatican decided it'd be too much for Helena to visit. A public outbreak from Helena was an ugly tabloid they weren't willing to chance.

She knew Lillian had arrived and it was only a matter of time before she'd seek her out. He almost worried for the girl. Dougal despised the whole lot of his half brother's type for their flippant disregard for order, but his moral code drew limits around the abuse of children. He was certain the hierarchy wouldn't have knowingly encouraged Helena's methods.

"They have their ways, lass," he said distantly.

She nodded, staring off into old memories. Dougal knew he'd lost her again. They'd been holding her prisoner her whole life without knowing it. The whole task of his assignment suddenly seemed redundant. This girl would never get past her childhood, never wonder what could've been beyond Northumberland. He'd babysit her through the trip and report there wasn't a thing to worry about. It was rash to have considered her murder, she was just a waif of the person they thought she was.

Lillian looked around the room, holding very little information on Aillig though she was surrounded with knowledge. She'd only gained what she had in secret which made her wonder why Dougal thought to bring her here at all. He had no lead.

"Why'd you bring me here? We found nothing."

Dougal couldn't tell her the truth. It was a fear tactic to keep her in check, to remind her of the power she disobeyed. He had to think quickly.

"I was hopeful for you to find something. I suppose his reasoning for St. John's address eludes us. Shall we go to City Hall? Ye seem to be better at creating possibilities. I can ask around here later to see if anyone knew him."

Dougal didn't want her to snoop anymore. He needed to keep her away from the files before he could move them out of the building. He had come close to revealing the truth about her once, and he wasn't going to risk it a second time.

"Yes, let's move on," she whispered.

Lillian couldn't bear to stay in that building any longer. It was hard for her to concentrate among all her old memories. Her mind spun around Aillig's two clues, hoping whatever else he left behind would link them to something more substantial.

*Chapter Thirty-Five*

Cutter woke naturally to the young sun. He looked at the pale purple sky outside her window, his muscles heavy and reluctant. He needed to get up and prepare for his drive back to Los Angeles. He had pushed all his responsibility aside to spend an innocent night in her motel room. Cutter smiled and watched Emmy sleep peacefully in the crook of his arm. He dangled his free hand off the bed to grab his Polaroid and burned the memory into something he could hold. The buzz of the ejected photo woke her and she opened an eye, smiling.

"I'll be back in a little bit," he cooed, running his hand over her hair.

She nodded and drifted off again.

Cutter slipped out from the sheets and grabbed her keys off the table. He drove to the Big House to gather his things. The sun shone in his eyes as he thought of Emmy lying in bed where he left her. Her hair was a mess around her shoulders and her sharp jawline jutted outward in defiance even in slumber. Cutter spent his entire life wanting to believe in fairy tales. It was what saved him in times of darkness and Emmy's wild experience seemed to revive him. He could see where a fire element stirred in her.

"I can't believe I'm going for this," he breathed inside the cab of the truck.

Even as Cutter tried to protest, the young and tireless soul inside of him knew it was right. He just couldn't explain the unexplainable. He imagined their previous lives and how it must have been, how it could be now. He'd lost sleep between soaking her into his memory and trying to figure out how to stay. Emmy didn't speak frivolously and he wanted to hear more of her story, to help her work towards a logical meaning.

Cutter knew he had to go home. He needed to tie loose ends so they could start a life without anything to inhibit their happiness. The money he made there would allow him to provide a promising start for their future. He packed what little he had, wasting no time so he could return to Emmy. He looked once at the giant pens and found Goose grazing lazily. He smiled crookedly in goodbye and turned to go.

"No goodbye for me?" a voice boomed behind him.

Cutter turned to his boss.

"I'm sorry, Roger. Emmy came back and I want to spend all the time I have left with her."

Roger smiled.

"She sure did. I saw her on Saturday and am still in disbelief."

Cutter thought quickly.

"I bet you could see it again if you wanted. I hear one of your men is leaving and the position needs to be filled."

"You're right. The sucker's leaving us for the big city, and in a hurry. Will need to have those young legs worked in the winter and I've lost my best hand," he winked, extending his hand to Cutter.

"Give her a call, Roger."

Cutter hopped in the truck, indulging one last time in the Wyoming outside his window. Wild vibrancy sang on the tops of the terrain, and drifted in the mountain air. An aquamarine sky filled his lungs and the peaks shook in haunting departure. He could see the deep enchantment of his hidden lake in memory and ached to be there with her.

Cutter could no longer remember the love of this frontier without the sound of Emmy's laughter. The intensity in her eyes rivaled the cloudless sky and her hair flowed as wildly as the horse herds. He grinned in satisfaction. His heart was wise in choosing her.

She sat waiting in the doorway for him. He drifted into her room and sat on the edge of the bed. She let herself stretch out on top of it. Cutter allowed himself a longer look at the curves of her body as his T-shirt hugged them, trying to maintain a gentleman's fondness to their innocent night.

"Emmy I got you something," he said, handing her a small box. "It's nothing special, but important for you to have."

She sat up and opened it to find a cell phone inside.

"I don't want to lose touch with you ever again, Emmy. I wanted to make sure that you could call me if you needed," he stumbled, trying to find words in light of the last week. "I'll be working long hours, but you can always call. I'm contracted to work there for a few months. I'd like to come back to see you afterward."

He swallowed hard and looked out the window. The thought of living without her seemed impossible now. The idea of their past lives apart stretched too long and too real between them.

"I don't want to leave. I don't want to think what it'd be like without me here."

He looked at her with dewy green eyes, wishing he'd never called the agency.

"But it will be good, Cutter. We have got to know who we are as individuals before we're any good for each other. There's a lot to learn before then, now that we know what we are, I guess."

She wrung her hands, wanting to believe it more firmly, like she had yesterday.

He nodded and rose.

She walked him to the door. They spoke not a word and she leaned in slowly for a last kiss. She let her hands run up his chest and intertwine behind his neck, leaving a trail of goosebumps on his skin. She stepped closer, pressing her body against his, and in a moment of bravery, pushed her hips into him. She could feel his abdomen tighten in response and she drug her eyes to meet his. She could feel her body reacting to their old memories, coaxing him to stay just a little longer. Emmy didn't bother fighting against it.

"I feel like we are always getting pulled apart. Don't forget me, Cutter."

He lifted her against his chest. She wrapped iron thighs around his body and arched her back as his hands ran up the back of her thighs. He tilted his head backward, relinquishing control. She kissed his neck and flames rocked his body. Her mouth lingered like butterflies. Sweat was forming on the back of their necks from the heat passing between them. Slowly, he let her body slide against his as he lowered her to the ground. They tried not to regret the chastity of their relationship.

"John's going to bring the truck back from the airport. I'll come back as soon as I can. I promise."

She nodded, and watched him get in her truck to drive away. Her heart was heavy as she sauntered back into her room. Being aware of their story made it more painful to hear him leave. Emmy wasn't sure what was supposed to happen now. She was sure that rekindling their past memories would offer guidance. She fell on top of the mattress with a sigh. That wasn't going to happen now and she wasn't sure she knew how to do it anyway. Henry would have known what to do next. She glanced at the old story book she had carried with her since she left Kentucky. Maybe if she read it again, there'd be clues. If nothing else it would be a good distraction from the sadness depleting her body. Emmy drug herself up and walked to the desk to open it. The motel phone starting ringing. Taken aback by such an unusual sound in her room, she let it ring a couple of times before answering.

"It's George. I have a business proposition I'd like to discuss with you. Can you come to the house today at noon?"

"I guess. Will Kelly be there? I'd like to apologize to her," she drawled.

"Yes, I suppose I can arrange that. See you at noon," he said, hanging up.

Emmy ran her fingers through her hair, catching every tangle with popping agony. Dealing with George Fassenbach was the last thing she felt like doing. She glanced at the clock and decided she'd take a shower before going over. She barely had the water running before the phone was ringing again.

"Hello?"

"Hi, Emmy. I'm not sure we've officially met, but my name is Roger. I run the guest ranch Cutter was working for. I was hoping to speak to you about working with some of the horses here. It's my understanding that you were able to ride Apollo. I admit I didn't believe it when Cutter told me, but I did after Saturday. Anyway, now that Cutter's gone, I don't have a capable hand to work the horses. I know it's sudden, but I'd really like to meet with you today if you have time."

She smiled. Her eyes twitched at the clock to calculate the most efficient schedule. She could stop at Roger's on the way to the Fassenbach property, and give herself a backup plan in case. It'd be a better distraction than missing Henry to forget missing Cutter.

"I can come by in an hour," she answered happily.

"Great, see you then."

Emmy jumped in the shower. Cutter would have been so proud to see her get back to what she loved. She felt she had finally found the road she'd been looking for in Wyoming. She silently thanked the tribes for bringing her back from the dead. She had risen from the ashes of her life in Kentucky to fly under the light of the moon with her horses in the bed of Wyoming. She dried herself off and dressed quickly before hopping in the truck. She was eager to prove her new foundations were solid.

Since she'd come back from the Sky People, she'd only managed to prove herself once. Now she'd be able to practice every day with horses and learn more about the mystery of her life through it. Tapping into Epona might allow her to look back in to others that could surface an old memory about the prophecy. Emmy smiled as she pulled into the Big House.

Roger was waiting for her. He was a tall and wiry man, bristled with gray hair.

"Pleasure to meet you. Cutter has told me a lot about what to expect, I hope you can live up to the standard he's made for you," he laughed.

Emmy shook his hand, beaming.

Roger had a gentle way about him that immediately made her feel comfortable. He lead her to the pastures and leaned against the rails where Apollo stood.

"He showed up a few nights ago. We found him grazing around the area."

She watched Apollo move in full awareness of their surroundings, looking occasionally out of the corner of his eye to keep track of her. She knew beyond doubt that he had run from the Tukudika after realizing she was gone. She could feel his contented demeanor in her presence. Her own heart quieted, knowing that the only other living thing witness to her secrets had given up paradise to be near her.

"So what do you think about working here, Emmy?"

"I love it here. But I'm not sure how comfortable I feel being a guide. I know it may seem strange after Saturday, but I'm a little shy around people. I prefer the horses," she laughed a little hesitantly.

Roger nodded.

She and Roger had spent an hour discussing the possibilities of her employment. She had explained that she was coming off of a dry spell and still needed to shake off the dust before she felt comfortable working with other people. He was agreeable about her perspective.

"With winter coming, our younger horses aren't as capable of waiting out the weather for exercise. You should be busy enough keeping them sound of mind in our covered arena," he chuckled. "Would you ever be interested in teaching our hands, or offering lessons to our guests?"

Emmy bit her lip. She was supposed to be careful about showing off what she could do. It could be very dangerous if the wrong person saw, but she really didn't want to miss this chance.

"It's been a very long time since I've ridden on a consistent basis. In fact, Cutter had just convinced me to get back in the saddle after years of avoiding it. Is that a question I can answer closer to spring?"

Emmy hoped she had handled it the right way.

"That's fair enough. So when can you start?"

"Well, Mr. Fassenbach called too and I'm supposing he will have a pitch of his own. It would be disrespectful of me not to hear him out. I can let you know this evening."

Roger frowned, hesitating to speak, but the affection Cutter had showed for her won out his better judgement.

"He is a powerful man, but be careful," he warned.

She nodded once before shaking his hand and leaving. As she walked to her truck, a gust of wind pushed against her shoulder. She turned around instinctively searching for Apollo. He stood with his head and ears alert, watching her leave. She smiled in acknowledgement and he lowered his head to graze once he was certain he didn't need to go after her.

Emmy prepared herself. She had asked that Kelly come to the meeting because she missed her. Truthfully, she wanted a buffer in case things got violent. Anyone thirsty for profit reminded her of Ethan, and she was not going to put herself in that position again. The man may think his daughter was only a ball of fluff, but it didn't diminish the love he had for his only child. He would never show his true colors in front of her. She sucked the air in between her teeth, anticipating the reaction of seeing Kelly again. She felt bad for the way she last talked to her and intended to reconcile her wrongdoing immediately. She hoped Kelly would understand. The house loomed in front of her when she pulled in the drive, and the feeling of danger rose in her throat.

She knocked on the door and was relieved to see Kelly on the other side of it.

"I can't believe you," she scolded. "How could you just leave me hanging like that? We are best friends."

Emmy wrangled her patience and humility.

"I know it was wrong, Kelly, and I'm sorry. I wasn't in my right mind and I apologize."

Kelly rolled through her usual dramatic episode, staring with exaggeration. After a moment, she gave up and smiled, wrapping her arms around Emmy's body.

"Whatever, girl. I'm just glad you're back. You're lucky I like you or my dad wouldn't even consider what he's about to propose."

Kelly lead her into the living room. The familiar air of being lured into something lethal whipped around her again. She couldn't shake Ethan from her mind. George sat looking out at the mountain range from his couch, a glass of brandy half empty in his hand. Emmy swallowed. It was never easy to guess what Mr. Fassenbach had working behind his eyes.

"Emmy, I want to hire you to feature your horsemanship. I'd like to give you your own time slot during the Saturday night rodeos to show people what you can do. I will give you a cut of the profit from ticket sales," he boasted generously, "so that you can make a start for yourself."

She eyed him from across the table. The couches and sitting room seemed just as ominous as they had a few days ago. The wildness she respected in his eyes was carefully veiled behind business matters and it made her shift her weight. The idea of such public display made her uneasy, and she knew that she'd never be able to properly explain the way she understood horses. Not to this town. She could feel the buzz of the P.A. system and how it distracted the horses from her. It'd be a circus to try to wrangle things she'd only just learned.

George was growing restless as she considered, and there was something familiar about the anger. There was a sense of control that he must be used to as mayor, she guessed, and maybe the fact that she had options made him uneasy. She had to admit that refusing George was frightening, but not as much as melting down in front of a huge crowd. No, she needed a little solitude to strengthen herself first. She had to take the advice of the wolf-man and try to blend in.

"I'm sorry, Mr. Fassenbach, but I just don't think I'm ready for what you're offering, as generous as it is."

He nodded slowly, carefully displacing whatever he felt about her decision.

"Very well, my loss then. Perhaps we can approach the offer again at a later date."

"I would like that," she lied.

She stood to leave, outreaching her hand to him. He shook it briefly, drawing back too quickly. She caught the release of fire from beneath his carefully controlled demeanor before he recovered.

"I'm sure I'll see you in town," he said casually, watching her leave.

Emmy only nodded, her throat too dry to speak. The drive home seemed long and she had forgotten her cell phone at the motel. Emmy wanted more than ever to call Cutter for comfort. She clenched her jaw and took it as a sign. If whatever she was meant to do split them apart, she had to respect it. He couldn't always be there to save her. She just hoped it wouldn't take a hundred lives to find each other again. Emmy wanted him back in this life.

She called Roger from her room when she got back.

"That's great news, Emmy." Roger beamed on the other line. "Would you be willing to bunk here? It's included in the pay I offered you."

"Yes, I would," she agreed, excitement seeping nervously through her voice. "When should I start?"

"Tomorrow?"

"Okay, see you tomorrow," she nearly giggled and hung up the phone.

Roger ran a weathered hand over his face. George was undoubtedly a business player, and was used to having his fingers in everything profitable. It wouldn't be long until he found a way into Roger's. He knew he'd have to pay for beating him out on the girl, he just wasn't sure how or when.

.......

Ethan lay drunk in bed, his house phone smashed to pieces with almost everything else. Finalized divorce papers had been fabricated and sent to him shortly after his flowery call to the Vatican's Secretary of State. They wasted no time in making sure he understood their disapproval, and dismissed him from his duties without a twitch of guilt. He was no longer responsible for finding his wife, and had been excommunicated by the organization. Everything that gave him control and power had been stripped. It wouldn't be long before his monetary luxuries would be taken as well. His slow road to Rome was over. They had called him Peter the Roman. They had said he would be responsible for their demise if they couldn't find Emmy. He turned slowly under the sheets, not upsetting his equilibrium, and grunted when he opened his eyes.

The woman lay limply next to him with a black eye and drool on the pillow. She reeked of booze herself and Ethan couldn't remember bringing her back to the house. The lazy end trails of sex made his limbs heavy and he couldn't negotiate what had happened between them. He was a free man, he reminded himself, and shoved the woman's arm. She stirred in mumbles which made him more angry.

"Get out," he warned, wanting to get rid of his sin.

The woman protested in a gurgle. He rose from bed in one swift motion, picking her lethargic body up in his arms and threw her on the floor. Her head slammed hard before she sat up to cradle her hangover.

"I said get out!" he screamed, his voice cracking.

He stared at the disaster he had created in his home and blamed Emmy. If she had never walked onto his farm he could have been happy. He could have lead a normal, prosperous life, and his superiors wouldn't have dumped him. She disobeyed the laws of creation and she needed to pay, not him. It mattered not in the eyes of God if he fulfilled his holy loyalty under the guidance of the Vatican or on his own. He pictured the last time he had seen her, bent on her knees in the face of death. The sweetness of bringing the wretched to the edge of hell excited him. He pictured again the chance to complete the promise he had given her. *How her flowers will rot with her black soul beneath them.*

There had to be something he was missing. Someone had to have seen her leave the house that day, the town was too small. It was time to start upturning stones at the neighboring houses. Ethan huffed and wheezed in excitement as he pulled on his wrinkled clothes, kicking the woman on his way out. She crawled daftly down the hallway trying to find her way through a swollen eye.

"You could at least give me a ride back," she grumbled.

Ethan swirled around, stomping heinously back to her with all the rage he couldn't satisfy on Emmy.

"You aren't going back to town, whore."

*Chapter Thirty-Six*

The drive was silent as they rode down city streets. She tried to hush the healer in her listening to Dougal's quiet wheeze. The damp air was getting to him, and a list of purity herbs filed in her head. *Licorice root, ginkgo biloba, chamomile tea.* It'd be useless to tell him anyway.

"This is where I found what little there was. All of it dead ends, unless ye might find something. I'm starting to feel like he had left a burner on after all," Dougal encouraged, ready for the endeavor to be over.

Lillian said nothing as they went in, wondering why he even wanted her to come on such little paper trail. She had found it strange they'd been the only people at the church. It had always been filled with passersby or at least the sauntering friar. All of this was stored neatly in her brain as they approached the front desk.

A small framed woman sat behind it and looked over the brim of her glasses.

"Hello again, Mr. MacIntyre," she chirped quietly.

"My guest and I will be reviewing the records I had on hold."

"Certainly, Mr. MacIntyre."

The woman unlocked a deep file drawer, pulling out a stuffed manila folder labelled with his name. She peered at Lillian as she slid the folder across the monstrous desk. Dougal smiled briskly and moved by to find a research table. The girl never stopped staring at Lillian, and clutched her rosary as she went by. Lillian's mouth went dry.

Lillian looked at the incredible amount of information around her and couldn't help but want to sit and sift through it all. The concentrated folder Dougal offered seemed small in comparison to the generations of books towering above her. She suddenly felt so unimportant. She'd been on such an intense journey where everyone around her thought she could be larger than life, but these shelves held endless histories of endless people. Generations of brilliance surrounded her. Her history started and ended with herself, the orphan who killed her parents.

"Are ye gonna look or not?" Dougal interrupted in his usual prickly manner.

"Sorry."

Lillian opened the folder and pulled out the stack of papers, immediately seeing ogham nicks of importance. She studied Aillig's records slowly, trying to memorize all of it without being obvious.

Aillig's father was not identified on his birth certificate, but his mother, Fiona Blackwood, had a long history streaming behind her on the family tree. Lillian recalled she had also been a healer. She read onward, learning that the family had descended from overseas, made claim in Scotland, and even dated back far enough to have mention of piracy in their blood. She noticed the subtle ogham left for her by Aillig and committed the history to memory. Dougal's careful attention made her nervous to stare too long. Quietly, she pulled out a piece of paper and tapped her pen against it.

"Ye find something then?" he probed.

"Oh no," she said, mocking distraction. "Just a habit to have it out, I suppose."

Dougal grunted and rubbed the stubble on his face. Lillian scanned, pretending to doodle as she went, writing down the information in Ogham, out of order in case Dougal noticed the similar scratch marks on the papers. She wished she had been less selfish in her time spent with Aillig. His lineage fascinated her and she wished fervently that she could have asked him about it.

"They're all dead, lass." Dougal eyed her.

"Just curious," she smiled. "It's my nature. Plus, Aillig spoke little of his family."

He hated her blank stare. It made it impossible to know what she was thinking, if anything at all.

"Dougal, you seem to be right, however," she sighed in mock disappointment as she turned the last page.

"There's nothing here. None of these people could be motivated to hurt him, their potential enemies are surely dead with them. You mentioned record of what he last checked out?"

Dougal thought before speaking. He wasn't sure it would be good to share. Her interest made him uncomfortable. She had been more willing to stay closed off until now. He couldn't make another mistake after showing her the letter, but he couldn't think of a way to decline her request.

"Yes, but I didn't request they hold it with everything else. All the literature I mentioned was in the antiquity room. I can request access, I suppose."

She nodded, watching him move towards the front desk. The woman there was staring. That must've been the one Aillig referred to when he said he was being watched. Lillian tried to smile and looked back down at her paper without interest. There was no way she'd be able to pick apart her puzzle here. She resolved to piece it together in the safety of her hotel room. Lillian tapped her fingers against the desk. She had to look around before the opportunity slipped by her.

Lillian dressed herself in a dreamy nature and slid out from the table, nonchalantly browsing exactly where she wanted. The personal records section. Aillig's mark on Helena's name card in the church library made her curious. She slipped down the appropriate aisle, scanning quickly for the her last name. She pulled the drawer open and flipped the papers through her delicate fingers. The name felt like knives across her eyes. Lillian read over the little bits of information in haste.

"Look, she's disappeared," the woman hissed when she looked up from her computer. "She's tricked you to go snoop where she doesn't belong. I knew it was a bad decision to bring her here. I don't trust her."

"Quiet," Dougal commanded. "That is blasphemy against your elders."

The woman clamped her mouth shut as the gruff old man went searching. The feeling that Lillian was on a lead made him dark. He didn't like being tricked by a little girl.

Lillian's palms sweat as she shoved the papers back in the folder, silently closing the drawer and slipping down the next aisle.

"What are ye doing?" Dougal demanded from behind her.

Lillian jumped, whirling around to face him.

"Oh, dear!" she gasped, putting her palm to her chest to conceal the pen scribbled on it. "You almost gave me a heart attack."

"Ye find something to look into after all?" he probed with black anger.

She smiled sadly.

"Oh no, unfortunately not. It's just that all these shelves of records seem so curious to me. I do love a good history lesson, especially when it involves someone's personal history."

Her heart slammed in her chest.

Dougal narrowed his eyes at her drawn and dreaming expression.

"It must be my profession," she whispered.

The hint of mockery was not lost on him and his opinion of her shifted. Dougal was starting to feel like he was dealing with a schizophrenic.

"Anything in the computer?" she asked sweetly.

"What? Yes, but our request can take a while to get approved. The record hall closes soon," he fibbed. "We may as well resume tomorrow in the antique books. I'll meet ye at ten in the morning."

She nodded and started out. Dougal stopped to return the research.

"You're right, she doesn't belong so close to all of us," he whispered. He was going to need time to rework his strategy.

They walked out in silence and more tensely suspicious of one another. She hailed a cab back to her room, waving him good bye. Once she turned the corner, Dougal picked up his cell and dialed.

"Helena, this girl is insane, but ye were right about her subtle observation. Something in those pages had to have irked her. She didn't bother looking around at our library, yet here she went wandering."

"Don't let that paranoid twit at the desk get in your brain. The girl ran away from us, why would she suddenly have interest in religion now? Of course she didn't look in the church library. Did you see what she looked at in City Hall?"

"No. She was strolling through the census sections."

"Tisk, tisk, Dougal. One slip and this whole thing can come crashing down on you. Information has a way of finding her. We must be vigilant so that she finds only what we want. Or the danger of her prophecy could materialize."

"How could a person as lost as she fulfill the downfall of our structure?"

"Now, Dougal, are you questioning the higher power?"

"No," he mumbled and she hung up the phone.

Instinctively, he asked for repentance and refocused his faith. Maybe he underestimated the power of the girl. She had him questioning his faith without realizing it.

*Chapter Thirty-Seven*

Emmy inhaled the sweet smell of alfalfa and bedding as Roger lead her through the pristine breezeway. Small nickers sung in the air as they passed.

"Your bunk is attached to the barn on the far end of the breezeway, I hope you don't mind," Roger explained.

The seclusion from the bunkhouse and guests was appealing. The quiet that enveloped the back property was needed to tune into what she'd learned with Sky Brother.

"There is a small kitchen and the laundry room is across from your room," Roger carried on as they opened the door.

They walked through her small apartment quickly and moved on, her head whirling with her new surroundings. He showed her the large covered arena and the rest of the small things he thought she'd find useful as she worked. When the tour was complete, he stopped full circle in front of the door to her room. He dropped the keys into her hand and smiled.

"I picked a variety of personalities for you to work with so we can find out which horses will benefit under your training. There aren't any set work outs for you to follow, so just do your thing. I trust you know what they'll need to stay sound. We have big dinners Sunday nights at the house, and though you aren't required to come, you are always more than welcome. Supper is held at five-thirty every evening, same offer is extended. I'll make my rounds in the afternoons during the off season which starts in two weeks, but will be mostly absent leading up to that as we close out guest season."

He sucked in a happy breath of air.

"And welcome to the ranch."

"Thanks, Roger," she said shyly.

He smiled at the small woman in front of him, and left her to gain more familiarity with the facility on her own. Emmy put her bags down to unpack later. She wanted to wander through the barn and see what horses had been brought in for her to work. The high ceiling of the barn made the eight horses seem small and childish. They peeked happily at her over their sliding doors and she let her fingers linger on each velvety nose, allowing her scent to become familiar. Emmy found herself disheartened to see that Apollo was not behind any of the stall doors.

She moved into the tack room and ran her hands along the countless saddles she had to choose from. Each horse's bridle had been hung neatly under their name tags. The excitement of returning to the saddle was growing rapidly within her. Emmy knew her new life had genuinely begun.

......

Cutter unlocked the door to his mother's apartment with reluctance. He had sublet it to a friend and was not prepared for the disappointment that hung stale in the air. The furniture was faded and rotting just as he had left it. Polluted daylight seeped through the windows and the density of her death clung to him like the pill bottles he'd found in her hands. Cutter touched nothing, feeling no nostalgia for the memories of his childhood. The city air stifled him with smog and oppression and he longed to be back in Wyoming. With her.

He left the master bedroom locked, not wanting to see any of his mother's likeness and made a point not to look near the far end of the living room either, though it was hard not to see it from the corner of his eye. He turned to his old room and dumped his stuff on the bed.

It was as barren as his mood. He could barely imagine the boy who had once slept here. Cutter looked at the boxes of photographs that he had sent back from his travels. Beyond a reminder of his tortured journey, they meant nothing and sat on the floor unopened. Cutter felt like he was haunting himself. He pulled his cell out of his pocket to call Emmy. It went straight to voicemail and his heart fluttered a moment in disappointment.

"Hey it's Cutter. I got here safe. I miss you. Give me a call when you get this."

His mind turned back to the living room and he knew it was inevitable, he had to look at it at least once. The piano was dusty. Cutter flexed his shoulders under his worn black shirt as he walked towards it, unsure of the heartache he was approaching. He sat on the bench and ran his finger along the keys; cold and smooth. He could almost see his mother laying on the couch, half dazed in the confusion of alcohol and pills as she listened numbly to his music. A weathered, grown up hand struck a key and it sucked the wind from his lungs. He had loved playing once. With a deep breath, his hands danced over the length of keyboard, his sorrow striking out a composition he thought he'd forgotten. His fingers kept pace as though he'd never stopped playing, and Cutter's mind floated back to the dreams of Emmy.

*He could see her again at the river, where he loved her most. He wasted no time to hold her close to him, wading into the water with his lips locked hard on her mouth. She whimpered only in pleasure and they lowered their bodies into the shallow water. Her clothes became translucent to his imagination and he savored the detail of each hard curve. She closed her eyes and he slipped the blouse off her shoulders.*

The walls of the apartment came flying up around him. The music fell to silence and he didn't realize that he'd been crying. Cutter hated this apartment and stood from the piano. The further he walked from it, the more he ached to play again.

"No," he reminded himself. "Nothing good ever came from music."

Cutter shook the feelings from his head and decided to stop by the new office to introduce himself. He would submerge himself in the work he had to do to get back to Emmy and that was it. He grabbed his backpack and left.

The streets were as angst ridden and hurried as he had left them. Cutter didn't fit in with the stream of city people anymore. Instead he only saw his lost anger on the faces hurrying to their jobs, phones glued to their eyes and ears. He laughed thinking of how he used to want to be like them, with fancy cars and big lofts high in the skyline. Cars rattled by and for the first time he felt disoriented. Everything was wrong here, and the agitation settled in his sore ankles. He hadn't noticed the strain stirrups had put on them until he was back on concrete. It was going to be a long job to get through. Cutter took a deep breath when he reached the office. He tried to remember what it was that seemed so appealing about apprenticing a photographer and Emmy's black dress flashed behind his eyes. He smiled despite himself and pulled open the big glass doors.

"Welcome back, Mr. Maben."

Cutter stopped. Fate was punishing him for coming back.

"What are *you* doing here?"

Rachael sat behind the front desk with all the mocked up professionalism of the conniving fox she was. Cutter turned black inside.

"Don't look so happy to see me," she whined, walking from behind the front desk.

He backed away as she approached. She stopped.

"Are you serious?" she asked in disbelief. She had made sure to look unrealistically beautiful for his first day back home.

Cutter only stared at her with dull eyes, trying to understand the ill coincidence that brought them to the same place. Los Angeles was scoured with people, the last thing he had ever imagined was the possibility of seeing her again. He expected her to be crammed up in some artsy complex in Silverlake with the guy she had cheated on him with, playing guitar and singing folk music. Yet, here she was, torturing him again.

He knew her too well to think she didn't figure out he was coming back. His buddy must have mentioned it to her. *When? Probably in bed,* he sneered as he reluctantly caught glance of her curve hugging skirt.

"Well, if you've got nothing to say after all this time, I will show you to your boss' office then."

He nodded once and followed far behind the swinging of her hips, feeling suffocated. The modern interior of the modeling agency was something out of a movie. People passed him in zipped up deadlines, hectic with their own self importance. He was surrounded by the rat race he thought he'd thrive in, and seeing it with fresh eyes skewed his old opinions. It should have impressed him, but Cutter was busy questioning the goals he had set before finding Wyoming.

"Thank you, Rachael," Mr. Taylor said as his eyes slid over her body.

She smiled coyly and left as quickly as she had come.

"Great piece of ass," the older man chuckled.

Cutter grew hot under his skin and worked hard to smile over his rage. Frank Taylor had no idea what went on beyond his own self involvement. He stood in an expensive suit to shake Cutter's hand.

"Welcome to the team. I was really impressed by the work you'd shown at old George's place. I'm certain your talent will be a great addition to the department of photographers here. You can start tomorrow, call time is 7 am."

Cutter nodded and held his breath. His shoulders were taut and he wrestled with the desire to abandon the city. The front desk was empty.

"I can make three times the pay here," he reminded himself out loud.

He took the long way home. Cutter had no one to talk to, and nowhere to go. He knew he wanted to spend as little time in the haunted apartment as possible. He checked the time on his cell phone and caught the blinking light.

"Damn it," he grunted, realizing he had missed a call from Emmy.

"Hey, it's Emmy," she breathed dreamily through the voicemail. "Sorry I wasn't by this thing. I'm glad you got there safe. Everything is fine here, Roger's a great guy. I can't believe the kind of facility he was hiding back on the property and I can't wait to start the horses. How's everything at the new job? Hope to hear from you soon," she ended cheerily.

He was disappointed that she'd made no mention of missing him. Without being there, it was inevitable for the other men to try for her, especially since they'd never officially labeled their relationship. It made him feel dark to think that anyone else could pass hands over what was his. He rubbed his hands over his face and shook his head.

"When did I become so possessive and insecure?" he muttered to himself.

He had walked to his old stomping grounds in habit. The bar was dotted with the few early drinkers already lost in their dead end day. He shrugged and went in, hoping to find a bit of comfort in the surroundings he had left behind.

*Chapter Thirty-Eight*

Lillian walked straight to her desk. She turned off the television and flipped on a lamp. The dark accents of the room distracted her and she longed for the cool, light tones of her own home. Staring at the Ogham, she began untangling it from her own mess. Aillig had left singular letters in random places for her to pick up, next to information he thought might help her. He had undoubtedly spelled out a word, but because she had jumbled them for safety, she couldn't guess. The clock ticked as she rearranged again and again.

"Haul Gal, no. Auld Hag, no. Dughaill, no."

"Guildhall," she muttered. "Sounds familiar."

She pulled the directory from the desk and looked it up. The old records hall.

"But they stopped using it for that decades ago."

A small squeeze on her shoulder made her smile. Of course he'd not leave her alone in this place. Instinctively, she found herself tugging on the chain of her necklace. The page of notes fluttered and she nodded.

"Aillig wrote it, so I must not argue. The next puzzle piece has to be there," she smiled, reminding herself that Aillig always stayed ahead of the game. *His game.*

Lillian closed her eyes and sifted through what she already knew. Somehow, her involvement in Aillig's life had twisted into the reason for his death. Dougal's foreboding employment with the church had been a point of interest left by Aillig. It was becoming more obvious that Dougal's interest lay not in avenging his brother. The old man hadn't been subtle about his opinions of Aillig or the interest he had in what he'd left behind. If Dougal was searching for information about Lillian then he was no better than the woman who had kept her from the truth, and Helena was no saintly creature. Her file proved as much.

After being released from a correctional facility, Helena had been converted and hired by the church around the same time Lillian arrived as an orphaned infant. Lillian hadn't even come close to understanding how dangerous the woman truly was. Aillig's mark on her membership card had been a warning, though it was unlikely that Lillian would ever forget. Poor Aillig couldn't have known, he'd never seen the scars. She sighed, and readied for bed as the hours grew later.

A hand grazed her back and she tensed, realizing her shadow must have seen them. The wounds had long healed and the emotional value had numbed. In his softening presence, she couldn't hide the toll it had taken so long ago. She felt ashamed in his acknowledgement. It had been easy for her to forget the reason Helena Roy had marked her back with disapproval, but now with the very reason floating all around her, Lillian finally understood why she'd forgotten about her shadow man. Her heart skipped as she dozed off, feeling inadequate and mutilated under the flutters hushing over her back.

.....

He was not a stranger to battle wounds and easily imagined what the lashings had felt like. She must have been so alone, bleeding and nursing the abuse without him there to comfort her. Sorrow and fear twisted rapidly behind his eyes as he redrew the lines that marked her back. He had not been able to protect her in the past and this was the sacrifice they both bared.

She dimmed from his view and he stood in his cell, yelling at the top of his rickety lungs. Whatever fatigue had cursed him faded in rage and he swore they'd get what they deserved for hurting his little dove. He didn't care how many lives he had to live to see it happen, they would feel his wrath.

....

*The room was dim and dripping with condensation as he searched her face. His own was gaunt and tired, startlingly emaciated since she'd seen him by her bath. Her shadow man was absorbed in the gore of her past and she clasped his hand to assure him. His large frame tensed in frustration of the constraint that time had created. Despite the fatigue stealing color from his beautiful face, his eyes were ominous with a fire burning dark against their silvery overtones.*

*"Find her," he whispered.*

The alarm chirped like pins in her ears, and she groped for the digital by her bed, sitting up in the dreary city morning. Her dark hair stood in contrast to the gray skies as she dressed and readied for Aillig's mission. Lillian smiled despite the pockets forming under her eyes. The truths she'd wanted to find her entire life coiled before her. She walked to the desk where a sleep letter rested. The odd tilt to her writing was the signature of her shadow man. Running late on time, she decided to save it for when her attention could savor his expected romanticism. She folded it into her palms and headed out.

She was happy to walk to the Guildhall nearby. Her wool cardigan wrapped snuggly around her as she tucked her hands into the folds of her crossed arms in the chilly morning air. Lillian felt so astray from her surroundings as her walking boots banged against the inflexible cement. She wondered what Airmid would have thought of modern society. In all the turmoil of the past few days, she hadn't any time to learn more about her or the triple alliance Aillig swore she was part of.

"I've really got to expand my studies beyond the safety of herbalism," she whispered to the trees dotting the sidewalk.

The pale light reaching between rolling mists made the Guildhall feel more medieval than she had remembered. As she approached, Lillian recalled the times she'd passed it, bustling through the market that crowded around the building on weekends. She couldn't ignore the coldness in every menacing brick as they stood alone together.

"Okay, Aillig," she whispered. "Where'd you have me look if I were inside?"

She only had a short time before she needed to leave and meet Dougal. Lillian walked up the front steps and tugged on the door a few times before noticing the posted hours of operation. It wouldn't be open for another hour. Finding free pamphlets in a holder, she picked one up and looked through the divided sections of the building map.

"You cunning fox, this game of layers continues," she said as she came across the East End, smiling.

She thanked the harrowing blood of Aillig's pirate family. Underneath the Guildhall was a predated undercroft said to once have housed criminals. She looked around the empty facility, gaining the whereabouts of its location. She walked swiftly to the East before stopping in her tracks.

"And what do you expect to do, Lillian?" she scolded herself. "Break in?"

She looked at the low windows for a minute before disregarding the idea. Aillig had probably planned for her easy access with a tour for whatever clue he'd left. She sat against the wall and thought. Whatever was in there needed to be seen without Dougal and it'd likely be pertinent to whatever was hidden in the rest of the clues that were in her possession. Lillian considered in the worst situation she could always come back after going to the antiquity room. But Dougal might track her if he felt suspicious. She patted her feet against the cement and kept eye for passersby. She heard a scratching overhead, and looked up. She hadn't considered being followed now.

A peregrine falcon watched her intently from its perch. Aillig and his older clients had talked of them with high regard and fascination. No one had seen them for nearly a century. She thought of what Susan had said about her affinity with birds in past lives and smiled. Old wive's tales had circulated in her childhood, foretelling their return when the faith of God was restored to the city. The drawings in Aillig's books matched this one with detail, she thought, as she admired the bird's intense beauty. A pang of sorrow stung her. Aillig would have loved to see the creature himself. With a quiet flap of the wings it flew in the air, circling the area for rodents.

Lillian felt distracted by its hunt, having given up hope on the entrance to the prison. She allowed herself to spend time submerged in what little nature she could find. The slate shades of its feathers sang to her and she closed her eyes to follow it with her ears. The silence of the sleeping city lent to the intensity of the sounds and Lillian reveled in the bravery of a born hunter.

She opened her eyes, watching him dive in for a kill before disappearing from sight. It reminded her of Hoot, and she felt happy. She rose to her feet, resolving to figure a way back for a tour without Dougal, and turned into a jet of wind. Lillian ducked and covered her ears to the screeching above. The falcon made another pass before slipping through a crack in the window next to her.

"You little devil," she whispered as she peeked through the window, seeing him settle in the corner next to his mate.

"Protective of your family, I see."

Haphazard shelves held heavy stacks of papers long since viewed by the public. Lillian was certain it was the old prison. With a little force she managed to push the window open. The street was silent around her, and Lillian breathed through her rising pulse.

"I cannot believe I'm about to do this," she whispered.

Lillian leaned in to look for a landing spot, her arms shaking against the window frame. She crawled in slowly and lowered her body to the top of a shelf, testing its strength before letting go. Noiselessly, she found her way to the ground and waited for her eyes to adjust to the darkness. Dust covered the open stacks of paper and she gently picked one off the top. St. John's emblem was on the letterhead.

"Of course," she whispered to herself.

Quickly, in fear of being caught, she started thumbing through the stacks. Her precarious bond with Dougal was losing its stitching and she had no time to waste. Lillian racked her brain to decode Aillig's clues. The story of his mother had brought her here. The Ogham had told her where to go.

"Helena and Dougal," she breathed in process of elimination.

She looked on the ends of the shelves, finding worn alphabetical labels. Paper was strewn and scattered across the shelf in barely organized piles as she searched for Helena's last name.

"Here," she said, grabbing a marked folder.

"Helena Roy," she whispered to herself. "Converted after release from women's correction center. Acquired female infant, delivered to St. John's. But why would

Helena have brought me to the church? Aillig thought my parents had."

She stared at the woman's records, trying to decide if she wanted to know the reason for her arrest. She could only imagine what Helena was capable of. Lillian shook her head and steadied her focus. Guildhall wouldn't be closed much longer and she needed to be out of there with plenty of time. Nimbly, she went in search for Dougal's file so that she could read simultaneously. Within minutes she had shoved through folders to find his.

"Dougal MacIntyre. Roman Catholic secondary school in Glasgow, hired for apprenticeship at Norwich Cathedral, transferred to St. John's...a few days before Aillig's death."

A blurry picture started to form as she hunched in a corner to read between files.

"Helena was sentenced to jail for manslaughter and robbery," she breathed, running a finger over the reports. "And Dougal was a complete delinquent through his young adult life. Then nothing after their conversion."

Her assumptions came quickly as she read about the pair's unsavory past. The idea that the church intentionally utilized their violent personalities would be total hypocrisy. Lillian knew she could believe what was unfolding, but didn't want to. She wouldn't believe that their holy leaders might have accepted, and even encouraged, the abuse she'd suffered under Helena's watch. Lillian read on, praying to find one of Aillig's leads.

Flipping another dusty page, she stared down at Helena's file, reading over the letter until it was unmistakably real. Lillian's hand flew to her mouth. Penned in Helena's hand, and addressed to the holy leader in Rome, was the start to Lillian's murky past.

*Holy Father,*

*I have obtained the child and dispatched my men to complete her parents' disappearance. I can ensure my loyalty to your graciousness and will make certain she is raised to forget her potential but for the use of our holy divinity.*

*Your devoted servant*

Twisting through the true story about her parents was the confession of their acknowledgement to her strange prophecy. Suspicions turned to stone in her swirling stomach. Lillian could feel the panic prickling the outline of her composure. *Get the rest of the information and think later, Lillian, you cannot get caught in here. It will be death for certain.* Lillian shifted her eyes to Dougal's folder, refusing to absorb what was splayed in front of her. She did not receive relief, and her hands began to shake. The official report detailing Aillig's death lay in the bloodthirsty files of his brother.

They had murdered him in fear that his position with an organization called the Hooded Spirits, the Genius Cucullatus, might expose her prophecy. The reality of her importance had grown beyond the comfort and whim of Aillig's group. The belief of her capability to destroy their religion had climbed all the way to the Vatican.

It felt like an awful fairytale. A story told to give hope to the hopeless or fear to the fearful, twisting to each storyteller's liking. She was a savior and a demon. Lillian could feel the shock numbing her. Aillig had come too close to finding out whatever they were trying to hide. He had figured something out, but they made no mention of it. They murdered him to keep him from talking. The darkness of death loomed over her. Her back tightened instinctively. The helpless and fragile soul of her childhood awakened. *I'm not fearsome,* she protested to herself, giving into the terror she knew too well. *How could I be so threatening that I'm considered an antichrist? How am I so powerful that I'm part of some prophecy? I'm just Lillian!*

She was surrounded by killers and their power. Her fear of the city was rapidly growing out of control and the time had dwindled dangerously. She moved drunkenly to return the files and leave. If she was a minute behind, Dougal would question her. Lillian's mind spun and her balance weakened. Whatever strength she had built with Maeve and Susan was buried between the sheets of paper in this room.

Something stirred outside the door and voices faintly murmured a short distance away. Lillian scrambled to shut off the lights, terror streaking across her body. She'd only read two out of hundreds of files that were kept away. She could only imagine what else laying rotting in between the stacks of their dirty laundry. Anyone with permission to this room had to be just as awful. She cursed herself for breaking in. Lillian flew to the back of the room, crawling numbly up the half empty shelf she had used before. The lock turned and she crouched, frozen in the darkness, clinging to the flimsy metal. They'd catch her the second a light flipped on. The door creaked open and she closed her eyes. Somehow she knew it would all end in death. *It did before.*

A sharp wind darted over her and the falcon screeched in a fuss over more intruders. The door closed with a start and before Lillian could think, her body lifted through the window, stumbling to rest against the ground outside. She could hear the disgruntled men yelling outside the door. Lillian tried to get up and couldn't, her legs were rubber, her breath short.

"I'd like to strangle the thing and stuff it for decoration."

Lillian covered her mouth in forced silence. She couldn't move, wouldn't dare move. The voice below left her in shock.

"No, Jim, I've got to babysit in an hour. Helena doesn't want to take any chances, so just destroy the files. The girl is too unpredictable, or rather my brother's involvement with her was. We can't tell what he's communicated to her in this ridiculous goose hunt, if anything at all. He sometimes was too clever for his own good."

"Yes, Mr. MacIntyre."

"Good boy. I'll see ye at devotion this evening."

She waited to be sure they'd left the room before standing on her weak legs to run the short distance back to the hotel in fear of being caught. Lillian surged up Gaol Hill, locking her sight to the entrance as she neared. She managed a brisk, controlled walk through the lobby and into the security of her room. The deadbolt locked into place. Lillian couldn't regulate her breath. She looked at the clock and calculated a few minutes to compose herself before heading to meet Dougal, the murderer. She could feel the shadow hovering in her frantic state. Lillian wished now more than ever that he would materialize into a body that could protect her at the hands of a killer. The trap that she had stupidly paraded into was closing around her.

*Chapter Thirty-Nine*

Cutter sat dully behind the camera, prepping for the next set. Everyone had left for lunch while he stayed behind, wishing he hadn't quit smoking. The high strung tension that built the industry was biting at his self preservation and he could feel himself falling into the negative mindset of his peers.

"You don't want a drag, Cutter?"

His entire body twitched and he said nothing. He felt cold in her presence and had largely avoided talking to her.

"Look can't we just talk? You left so quickly I never got to apologize," Rachael sang.

She had a way about her that sounded so sincere when she chose. Too much time had passed for him to remember what they ever had. His shoulders slumped before he straightened from packing set bags and turned to her.

"I have nothing to say to you. I didn't then either."

She stared at him, misty eyed, and he felt bad for being so harsh. Cutter's strict chivalry got the better of him.

"I'm on my ten now. You have that long to say what you need."

She smiled faintly, following him outside, her giant heels clicking against the tiled floors. He turned abruptly when they reached the sidewalk, giving no more kindness. Rachael leaned a slim hip against the building wall, crossing her arms over the dangerous curves he at one time enjoyed. She flipped her blonde hair around her shoulders and set blue eyes innocently on his. The façade made him think of the lightness in Emmy and he grew uncomfortable in Rachael's presence.

"I'm sorry for the way I treated you, Cutter. I've missed you every day since you left. When word got around that you'd be coming back, I had to nab any chance to see you."

"So you got hired here? I'm sure I can guess how your interview went," he replied bitterly.

Her tricks were as devious and adulterous as they had been. All his repressed darknesses resurfaced and exploded in his face. Emmy was right, he needed to come and bury some stuff before they'd be any good together. He shifted away from the woman in front of him. He needed to tell Emmy about Rachael. He should have mentioned it immediately. He cursed himself for giving into the sympathy games, Rachael didn't deserve to toy with him like that anymore.

"I came looking for you once, you know."

Cutter looked at her sharply.

"Yeah, I managed to find out that you had settled in Wyoming. I had come dolled up in a black dress, the way you liked. It was a little over a year ago. But there you were among a handful of other cowboys and I lost my nerve. You weren't the boy I fell in love with anymore. So I came back home," she breathed, taking a long drag of her cigarette.

He didn't think of her. He thought of Emmy, walking in all her beauty at the art show. He looked at the broken girl in front of him, seeing the dark circles she tried covering with makeup and the dark roots of the hair she wasn't maintaining. She was as broken as the city she lived in, and as much as his habit wanted to fix the wings she was nursing, he knew his pattern had to change. Emmy was the only heart he needed to mend. The wind of Wyoming circled in his ears and he recalled the week she disappeared. Its importance had dulled since he'd been back. His ability to believe in love stories had taken a beating.

"Won't you have a drink with me after work?" she begged. "For old time's sake?"

"No, it wouldn't be a good idea. I'm in a relationship."

Her eyes widened and she smashed the cigarette under her heel. Cutter never remembered her to be envious of his attention. In fact, she'd cared little about it. He was agitated with the woman and went back in without a word. He absorbed himself in his work as he assisted the head photographer. He would utilize anything as a distraction from the ugliness inside his chest. The afternoon session clicked by in millions of strobe and soft box flashes before wrap. Rachael left a bad taste in his mouth and he only wanted to hear the voice that would soothe it. He wasted no time getting home to call Emmy. He threw his stuff unceremoniously on the counter as he walked into the empty apartment, sitting roughly on the couch. He was tired from the hectic schedule he was maintaining at the agency.

"Hello?" she answered from the other end of the line.

"Hey," he breathed, feeling her smile.

"How was work?"

"Good," he said, considering how he was going to present what he'd been excluding in their conversations. "You?"

"Great! Apollo finally reached my rotation and he almost jumped out of his skin with the excitement of being near me. Cutter, you would have died laughing. He's a completely different horse now and I've got him turning on a dime with no more signal than my thoughts. It's hard not having someone who knows to see it all. Some days I still can't believe it. It's like magic."

"I bet," he mumbled, preoccupied.

"You okay?"

"Emmy, I need to tell you something. I should have earlier, but I didn't think it'd be a big deal."

"Okay," she said hesitantly, waiting for him to continue.

"Rachael works at the agency. Front desk. I don't know how in the hell I could have such bad luck."

"Oh."

"I made it clear today that I wasn't interested."

"So she tried hitting on you?"

He could hear the short tone she was trying to hide.

"No, not really. But she wanted to reminisce about old times when I went on break today. I swear there's nothing to worry about. I shut it down."

The silence dragged between them. Cutter was nervous.

"I wish you would have told me to start. Is there anything else you forgot to tell me?" she clipped hotly. The distance between them became very real.

"No, Emmy, nothing. I promise," he rushed, staring at the piano.

"Okay. Well, I'm really tired. I should get to bed."

Cutter rose to pace the room, distressed over the change in her voice. He didn't want to hang up without closure on the matter.

"Are you okay, Emmy?"

"It's just that everyone that's ever been close to me has kept secrets, Cutter. Now you're no exception and I'm trying not to be mad. I mean, you're a grown man and you're free to do as you please. We never titled what we were anyway. But if you want to go around chit chatting with your ex-girlfriend, you could at least hold me important enough to mention it. I don't want to be under another illusion, I've been subjected to enough lies," she rambled, building a wall of security to block her hurt. "I don't know why I'm getting so mad. I'm not mad. Just forget it. Thanks for letting me know."

"I didn't lie to you, Emmy!" Cutter urged through his cell. "I just didn't want the whole thing to be important because it's not to me. She crossed a line today, so I wanted to tell you."

"So what happens now? What if she keeps bothering you?" Emmy couldn't understand why she was getting so angry. *We've done this before.*

"She won't."

Emmy smirked through the phone.

"Okay, Cutter, I believe you. Do whatever you want, I'm going to bed."

The line went dead. He redialed and got voicemail. He dialed again. A dull anger rose in place of her assumptions and he tossed the phone on the table. He cursed himself for his stupidity and got up, needing fresh air.

"Fresh air and a drink," he muttered.

He walked to The Foxhole and sat down.

"Whacha drinkin', buddy?"

"Whiskey and water," the feminine voice rang from the other end of the bar top.

Cutter moaned and looked up to see her sitting with a martini in her hand. He couldn't get rid of this broad. She was ruining everything.

"Get away from me," he grumbled as she sat closer to him.

She smiled delicately, too interested in him for his liking.

"I won't say a word, Cutter. But it's a free country and I can have a drink where I'd like."

He ran his hand through his hair.

"Remember our times here?" she cooed.

"I thought you weren't going to say a word."

"It's still in the back room, Cutter. We should play again, for old time's sake."

He glared at her. *Nothing good ever came from music.* He could feel the presence of the piano between the walls of the bar. They'd spent many nights drunk in the back room. He shunned the memory.

"Get away from me."

"I don't want to," she whispered, leaning too closely. They had something once, and she needed it back. Her career spiraled the second he left town, and she wasn't going to let it happen again. She knew Cutter too well to fail at winning him over.

He slid the last of his whiskey down his throat and stood, leaving without a shred of interest in the girl behind him. Cutter curled his hands into a fist and made his way back to the apartment, slamming the door shut when he got in. He was more angry than when he had left. This place was turning him back into the old version of himself. He looked to the table, remembering his cell phone, and his heart skipped seeing the blinking light. He jumped over the couch and dialed his voicemail.

"I'm sorry, Cutter," Emmy relayed. "My temper's awful and I think the distance between us is taking its toll. I'm glad you told me about her at all. Just be careful and please tell me what goes on. I can't be there to show her how I feel about you. I miss you, Cutter. We'll talk tomorrow."

He smiled with relief. Emmy's strength was admirable. Cutter had to make it up to her. His shoulders relaxed and in an effort to remind her of how important she was, he swore to find a library to learn about the story she'd shared of their past lives.

"It's obviously what's keeping us together," he muttered, "while the city is ripping me apart."

*Chapter Forty*

He waited outside the antiquity room for her. Lillian's pulse raced as she tried to control her anxiety. Dougal noticed her shift in attitude.

"How'd ye sleep, lass?"

"Nightmares," she lied.

Dougal suppressed a grin. The visit to the church must have done its work.

"Well, Aillig leads us to the land of fairytales. It should soothe the darkness of the night," he said in sarcasm. He was tired of this game and this child.

She smiled weakly and followed him past security. At least the gentle young man behind the desk did not grab for his rosary to ward her off. Dougal handed her a short list.

"These are the last books he checked to study before his death. I find nothing out of the ordinary for my brother."

He could hardly be bothered with the superstition of the fable that outlined her life. Dougal had decided yesterday that she was a nobody. He had never once seen proof of a prophecy like her in the written word, anyway. If it was true, it would've been in the Bible. He leaned against his chair in boredom. Not being allowed to scare her took the fun out of babysitting.

"Thank you," she whispered, praying her shaking voice didn't betray her.

Lillian thought Dougal seemed distracted, presumably reflecting on the resurfacing events he had been a part of. Whatever the case, she took the opportunity to search through the Dewey Decimal system and locate the books. She looked once to find Dougal sitting at a table, uninterested in the search. Lillian located the first book and pulled out a volume of Voltaire's philosophy. The pages were thin and yellowing. She flipped more slowly through them and noted the quote marked with the Ogham symbol for the holly.

*It is dangerous to be right in matters on which the established authorities are wrong,* she read to herself. She slid it back in between volumes. There was no need to make note of the message Aillig was leaving. It became clear that he had not been sure where she'd start her search. This had been a precursor to what she'd found in the Guildhall. She committed it to memory and planned to compare it with the rest of what she'd found. Lillian moved down aisles, looking for the next book, wanting to seem as though nothing had struck her interest. With shaking hands she located the title and opened its pages.

*The Divine Comedy* had been such a favorite of Aillig's. She remembered seeing him read it over and over with a humor in his eyes, never understanding what he found so amusing about the ideas of hell and the cycles of the afterlife. Now, she was beginning to see the joke. *If the church could believe I am from hell, then the whole place must be filled with bunny rabbits and roses,* she tried humoring herself.

She glanced over her shoulder. Dougal was dozing off in his chair, arms crossed over his heavy midsection. She flipped through the book, looking for any sort of Ogham, knowing he'd been rushed. She smiled, despite her weakening confidence, over how hard it must have been for

Aillig to deface such an old copy. There were so many of his nicks for the Hazel Ogham, her memory was easily lost. Lillian took a deep breath. The chance that she could steal it was slim, but if she could get a few hours to compare it to a translated copy she'd be better off.

"*e 'l sol montava 'n sù con quelle stelle, ch'eran con lui quando l'amor divino,*" she tried whispering, noting a prominent mark of the hazel next to it.

She peeked through the shelves to check on the murderer. Dougal was where she'd left him, still dozing in his chair. Before her moral code could deter her, Lillian dropped the book into her bag without a word.

"I'm sorry Aillig, but I can't leave it here. I don't have time to memorize it."

She moved to the next work listed, pulling *A Midsummer's Night Dream* from the shelves. She knew the play well, as Aillig had often read her the enchanted tale. She scribbled down the title for memory and scanned again for his marks. She found an underlined section. Ogham for the eternity symbol was drawn lightly in the corner. *The hidden symbol and all that is beautiful,* she recited to herself.

"Through the forest have I gone, but Athenian found I none. On whose eyes I might approve this flower's force in stirring love. Night and silence-Who is there? Weeds of Athens he doth wear: this is he, my master said, despised the Athenian maid, and here the maiden, sleeping sound, on the dank and dirty ground. Pretty soul! She durst not lie, Near this lack-love, this kill-courtesy. Churl, upon thy eyes I throw, all the powers this charm doth owe. When thou wakest, let love forbid, Sleep his seat on thy eyelid, so awake when I am gone, for I must now to Oberon," she whispered.

She sighed, "Aillig it's too long."

She ripped the page quietly from the book and shoved it in her shoe. Being in any proximity to the man who murdered his own brother was growing unbearable for her nerves, sleeping or not. She checked on Dougal, but he was no longer sitting. She turned the corner, moving away from any evidence that she'd caught on to the truth. Lillian was terrified that it had all been an act and she had been caught. She wondered if she'd been seen fleeing the Guildhall this morning. He might only be playing along. Lillian's throat grew dry as she crept down another meaningless aisle. She saw something move from the corner of her eye. She picked up a book and pretended to read it.

"No leisurely study today?" Dougal asked from the other side of the book.

She snapped it closed, jumping.

"No. I'm afraid I feel defeated, Mr. MacIntyre. I'm starting to think my beloved friend had been careless. Nothing here s-s-seems abnormal," she closed her eyes and exhaled.

He watched her. Her dismissal of the hunt sounded too close to the one he'd received the first time he tried returning her to the city.

"These books are all favorites of his," she lied. "It wouldn't be strange for him to come admire more ancient copies than his own."

Her heart pounded at the nearness of such a dangerous man. It suddenly made her own life seem so breakable. The edge of the stolen book poked her from inside her canvas satchel and she prayed he hadn't seen her.

Eventually, he nodded.

"It's a hard truth to come by, but I think the same thing. Shall we depart?"

Dougal felt confident as they left. He had derailed her from their secrets. Her fable was hidden and her dawning age of prophecy concealed. He could taste a raise on the tip of his tongue. The murder of Aillig had dissolved the last link of knowledge she could have acquired. He couldn't understand why they hadn't just killed her to start, seeing how helpful it had been with his brother. No one would have to worry about her if she were dead. Maybe they doubted the prophecy themselves, as wise men would. An unnecessary murder wouldn't be good to have on any record. He thought of Aillig. *No, there was no hiding his heresy.* He looked at the nervous thing in front of him in ridicule.

"Thank ye lass for your time. I suppose ye will head home now, to your pleasure."

She smiled and turned to go. Her paranoia was getting the best of her. She absorbed her surroundings as she traveled back towards the hotel, looking over her shoulder to be sure she wasn't being followed. She needed to find a bookstore quickly. Dante's story needed to get back into its holding place before anyone noticed. Lillian walked swiftly into the first bookstore she found and wasted no time locating Dante's translated masterpiece to take back to the hotel.

In the room, she regrouped herself before going over the information. She didn't have time for a breakdown if Dougal expected her to leave so quickly. She pulled out her stolen objects a little bashfully and leaned over them. She browsed through some of the places Aillig had nicked in *The Inferno*, decoding the translation with her new copy.

"The devil is not as black as it is painted," she muttered. *They really must think I'm the devil. Look at the severity of your circumstance, Lillian.*

"Consider your origin. You were not formed to live like brutes but to follow virtue and knowledge," she read, thinking of Helena and Dougal.

"The day that man allows true love to appear," she paused calling for the presence of her shadow. "Those things which are well made will fall into confusion and will overturn everything we believe to be right and true."

*Well, he has certainly made me reconsider the truth about ghosts. That would knock the church's foundation right off its blocks,* she thought. She was starting to see why Aillig ruffled their feathers.

"As one who sees in dreams and wakes to find the emotional impression of his vision still powerful while its parts fade from his mind- just such am I, having lost nearly all the vision itself, while in my heart I feel the sweetness of it yet distill and fall," she sang.

Lillian thought of her herbalism and how it felt familiar to her even in youth when the rest of the world was still new. Her dreams had brought her knowledge from past lives, though she hadn't known upon waking. The realm of her subconscious had its own marker of truth and its importance settled into her bones. *What seemed right in dreaming must now be right awake,* she noted.

Lillian scrolled to the last quote he had marked with Ogham and read. "That with him were, what time the Love Divine."

"Why does that sound so familiar? Love Divine," she muttered.

Nothing came to mind and she was too frantic to spare time on it. Lillian efficiently moved to the ripped page of Shakespeare and reread it:

*Through the forest have I gone, but Athenian found I none. On whose eyes I might approve this flower's force in stirring love. Night and silence-Who is there? Weeds of Athens he doth wear: this is he, my master said, despised the Athenian maid, and here the maiden, sleeping sound, on the dank and dirty ground. Pretty soul! she durst not lie, Near this lack-love, this kill-courtesy. Churl, upon thy eyes I throw, all the powers this charm doth owe. When thou wakest, let love forbid, Sleep his seat on thy eyelid, so awake when I am gone, for I must now to Oberon.*

"Pretty soul," she smiled in memory of Aillig's nickname for her. "She durst not lie. When thou wakest let love forbid sleep, his seat on thy eyelid."

*He knew about my shadow.* Her eyes welled. Aillig knew and validated the idea of love she had skirted around since her ghost's appearance in the cottage.

"So awake when I am gone," she whispered, letting a small sob dance away with all the illusions the church had chained her to.

"I promise, Aillig, I will."

"The maid sleeping on dank and dirty ground. My master despised the Athenian maid," she mumbled, tapping her pen, reworking the pauses in the structure of the text.

She thought of Helena. It brought memories of her makeshift room, away from the church where her sickly body wouldn't infect anyone. Reading the truth on the floor of the Guildhall gave her perspective of sickness new light.

"I was never physically sick, they didn't want the demon to infect the pious."

Shaking her head, she read on.

"Flower's force in stirring love, she durst not lie."

Lillian wrinkled her brow, rattling off an impressive list of flowers, trying to find one of importance.

"My roses for dreaming! It focuses my visions and the abilities of Airmid."

"It also brought my shadow man," she added, thinking of the rose petals in her bath so long ago.

She smiled in memory of their lifelong relationship. He had always protected her, even in youth. He had never left the night Sister Roy had drug her back and beat her for sneaking out. Lillian's eyes widened and she fell back hard against her chair. Lillian had prayed to Lady Julian for help, the patron of the chamber she lived in. She'd seen the statue so many times, she was surprised she'd forgotten.

"Divine Love had been engraved on the statue outside the building."

Her heart stopped. Aillig's last clue was in the dungeon of her upbringing. He had only gained membership to walk the grounds and search her old home for himself. His marks on their cards were only part of his game.

"You couldn't let me solve your mystery," she lamented to the emptiness of the city, "without solving my own."

His game wasn't over until the reason he sacrificed his life was brought to light. Grimly, Lillian searched through her notes, looking for more clues within the clues. Feeling responsible for his death wouldn't avenge him.

"I don't know where they could've hidden anything in that barren cage."

Tired eyes scraped over everything she'd collected. Lillian's head pounded under the dim desk lamp, and her shoulders burned from hunching over her notes. Exhaustion was toying with her and she closed her eyes to ease the aching. Words floated from the page in her mind's eye, searching for patterns.

"Three locations, three books, three passages, three dream notes, three goddesses. What was there three of? And where? Where would they have hidden something I wouldn't have seen?"

Lillian tried building an interior of the room she had wanted to forget. Her eyes flew open.

"The windows."

There had only been three windows in the chamber where she slept. She vaguely recalled reading that they provided a source of communication with different parts of the church for Lady Julian. She never had to leave her room.

"Sounds like jail. Certainly was for me."

Lillian wasn't sure what to do next. She needed to get into her old chamber, but her checkout was tomorrow and to stay longer would bring the wrath of their attention. She'd have to go tonight. Flying under their radar would be impossible. Lillian put her head on the table, feeling hopeless. Praying had never helped her, but she was desperate for any guidance.

"Devotional!" she whispered, remembering Dougal's comment at the Guildhall, pressing her palms into the desk to raise her head.

"The entire facility will be in the main church."

She packed her bag without another thought, fearful of changing her mind, and left for Lady Julian's chamber. Aillig died to get her to this point, she couldn't turn back now.

*Chapter Forty-One*

George hung back in the shadows, increasingly agitated by the attention Roger's ranch was receiving. He had asked Roger to pay added fees for the liability of the people wandering his property. His profit was smaller than he was expecting and Emmy's reluctance to take his offer had only grown stronger in the time she'd spent here. He didn't like seeing someone else prosper from the kindness of keeping her secrets. If he couldn't profit from the prophecy she wasn't supposed to realize, no one else should either. The town thrived because of his efforts and now he got nothing in return.

He watched her work, as entranced as everyone else. The enchantment of her talent persuaded the whole town of her greatness. He was disappointed for doubting his superiors, seeing now how dangerous she was to their control. Everyone catered to her every need so they might be able to watch her work. She had them eating out of the palm of her hand. It was Eve who tempted Adam to eat the forbidden fruit, and she had come to life again to coax the holy to sin. George needed to take control of his city.

He looked at Emmy with a crowd around her, even though she was silent, and felt the jealousy rattle in his chest. Without him, none of this would be prospering, especially her, yet no one crowded him in thanks. He walked away with the graceful movement of her body impressed beautifully into his brain. George wanted her gone, and thought little about what would happen if they found out he'd housed her for so long. He went home in an ugly mood.

The relocation to Wyoming was supposed to help regenerate his good standing as a priest and mayor after his gambling scandal. Instead, it had only given him a divorce and a baby girl to raise on his own. He sat down and poured a glass of wine. All the promises they'd made about his temporary situation had been broken. He thought of what they might do for him now that he had a hold on their beloved prophecy. He'd look like a hero. He'd be able to return to a position of stature, where his business skill could be catapulted. George picked up the phone.

"Ethan. It's her. She's gained quite a bit of attention here, however, and her removal has to be carefully done so that no one protests and causes a scene. I will keep a close eye on her until we can formulate something that will leave my town unsuspicious."

.....

Ms. Beckett could hear him approach. She moved inside of her home, leaning against the wall just to the side of her screen door.

"I don't care if she's made friends there or not!" Ethan yelled into his cell phone as he paced the sidewalk just in front of her house. Ms. Beckett's heart pounded in her chest as she intercepted the energy exploding from the pores of the unpredictable man. He had been utterly reckless since Emmy left, and she had been careful never to come in contact with him. She feared that she'd suffer violent interrogation should his suspicion of her knowledge rise.

"Fine," he sighed irritably. "I'll give you five days to get it done and get her back to my property, or I'll be coming there myself to do it. And don't think it was anything other than dumb luck that she showed up in that miserable town of yours."

He hung up the phone. She had no doubt that he was headed to drink himself into oblivion in celebration, she could feel his body crave an addiction. Ms. Beckett waited minutes before moving to her desk. She drew out a single sheet of paper and scribbled hastily. She folded it inside of an envelope and looked closely to make sure Ethan had gone before locking her door and heading to the post office. Emmy had to know that he was coming for her, and a safe house needed to be ready to receive her as the prophecy grew in intensity. Ms. Beckett would leave immediately.

"Larry, I need this overnighted to the marked address. It's urgent and under discretion," she whispered to her old friend. It was the only way she could get around Ethan. He couldn't hack into a handwritten letter.

.....

Ethan wasn't going to wait more than a day to recover the demon. He was chomping at the bit to replace his position and secure the comfort of his wealth and business again. The house was too quiet without the work of his superiors coming down on him.

He paced the living room fantasizing about what he'd do to her once she was back. He envisioned her angelic body lying as it had on the bed beneath him, quieted for the pleasure of a husband. She'd look much healthier than when he last saw her and he felt a pulse surge through his body in excitement. He threw clothes into a suitcase. He needed to look pristine. After her death, he would certainly be recognized for saving their religion from the Devil herself. Ethan sat on the edge of the bed and poured a drink.

He couldn't wait to boast in their face. His family had been saving the Vatican since its creation and he would maintain the legacy. The long lineage of royal blood coursing through his veins was made for moments such as this. He thought of his father and the foundation he'd built for the succession of his son. Ethan refused to look at the damage he had caused in his frustration to find Emmy.

"She's going to pay for all that has been wrecked because of her defiance," he muttered, getting drunker as he thought.

It pleased him to imagine strangling her like the old man. He would like to compare the similarities in their face as she sucked on her last few breaths of air.

"Shame the carcasses rotted before I could hang them for her to see," he thought in memory of the burned barn. A smile lit the darkness in his eyes and he slammed his glass on the nightstand. Ethan slipped off the edge of the bed and lowered his head.

"Lord, you have sent me to protect the Holy word and I shall just as my family has done for centuries. I thank you for the graciousness you have provided in return. Amen."

His head hit the floor hard, swimming with another bottle of booze.

*Chapter Forty-Two*

Lillian parked a few blocks away and walked to the building with little trouble. The area was deserted for the gathering in the main church. The suffocation of her confinement returned and she focused on breathing deeply. Her shadow man was heavy on her back and the dream she had considered a premonition with Susan and Maeve crossed her mind. She was prepared to find him if someone came chasing after her, even if it meant surviving the pain she'd felt in the dream. Even if it meant death.

She could see the statue marking her entry as she approached. Lillian had known little about the Lady beyond the fact that her room had once been a confessional when Julian was alive. She had asked Sister Roy about her often, only to be answered with a swat or worse.

"Orphans are too sinful to learn the word of Julian," she used to sneer.

Lillian held her breath and pushed against the unlocked door, the statue watching in stoney silence, and she slipped in. The room was as bare as she remembered. Looking at the bench that used to be her makeshift bed, it was hard not to feel afraid. Her memories tugged at her, redrawing how it had looked so long ago. Her lavender blanket once draped over the wooden bench. Her dried flowers had littered every surface top to create a fullness toys would never bring. It was impossible to think anything could be hidden in the small, empty space. His whisper lifted to her ear and she smiled, remembering how they used to play on the floor. *Before she beat him out of me.* His presence grew heavier in the air, pressing against her feet. The damp smell of Sister Roy's frock returned to her nostrils and she fought with strength to push off the spiral of a panicked vision. She could feel her shadow densely against her and tried to focus on his presence as she waned into her fears.

"What, my love," she whispered, confused.

"Subter," he hushed.

*Beneath.*

She tried to clear the spinning in her head. *Beneath*, she repeated to herself. *Vengeance buried under holly. My dream notes. Three of them.*

"Windows. Three windows. Beneath the windows."

Lillian flew to the ground and pushed the panels below the nearest window. She leaned all her weight and felt nothing budge. A cry of frantic desperation escaped from her blushed lips and she started knocking, hoping to hear a hollow spot. Nothing. Her heart was in her throat now.

Quickly she shifted to the second window. She pushed the board below it. It creaked but did not move. Lillian couldn't hold onto her reality. Her panic was rising and the vision was making the edges of the room blurry. Tears rolled down her cheeks as she pushed harder and harder against the floor. She tried lifting herself and stumbled, grabbing the side of the bench for support. Her knees were weakening, she could feel the anxiety attack her body.

Lillian slid to the floor and leaned against the bench, hearing Sister Roy's voice echo between her ears. She forced herself to look to the third window. Hanging below it was Jesus, crucified on the wall cross, forsaken for what people didn't understand, just like her. She could feel the blood trickling from his forehead and down her own throat.

"Vengeance buried under holly," she gasped in between short breaths. His crown of thorns was the clue. She pulled her numb body towards the third window. Lillian had no idea how much time had passed. Shaking hands reached the wooden plank under the Savior and with little force pushed the board away. In the darkness below, and covered in the filth of secrecy, were a stack of disheveled papers. Lillian's body shook as she gathered them, trying to read through her tears.

*My dreams had not failed me and I gave birth to our sweet Lillian as the prophecy foretold. Afraid that others have suspected, we have formed a plan to separate from her to send them after us instead.*

Lillian crumbled against the floor, sobbing over her mother's account. All the years she spent suffering through the questions of abandonment made her weak. The truth had been inches from her little hands the entire time. She placed the papers in front of her, pressing her palms against the cool wood, hoping to calm herself. There wasn't time to have feeling now. She sat up and read on.

*We dropped her off at Fiona Blackwood's home, hoping she'd be safe. Word was sent that her husband had figured out who our dear baby was and put her in care of the church, where he thought she would be best handled. I have not slept since I've been told.*

"Blackwood, Fiona Blackwood, my mother had known Aillig's mother!"

Her mind whirled around the lineage of their families. Aillig's placement in her life was more planned than either of them had understood. They'd been wrong to guess that her parents had dumped her at the church. Tears streamed down her face and all the courage she had bustled in with dissipated, fading her shadow man's existence in the rising storm of her dismay.

One by one they'd eliminated all the love that surrounded her. Even in all his knowledge, Aillig had not escaped and Lillian could feel the walls closing on her own chances.

"I wish I could have used the dead brother. He was far more clever than the one I had to use against you."

Helena Roy looked down on her with joy. All the blood in Lillian's body drew towards her heart. Her hands lost feeling.

"My poor man, Dougal, was too tired and old to think much of you. I was hoping his temper might scare you off because I knew you were too smart not to put Aillig's subtle hints together. I raised you after all," she smiled wryly.

Helena bent inches from her face, her breath hot against Lillian's cheek. Lillian swallowed as she clutched the papers against her. The woman had aged with dangerous severity, and her eyes hardened in cruel motivation. Each graying strand that replaced her once blonde hair reeked with the humor she found in Lillian's frailty.

"Scared as you ever were, aren't you? You should be. I'd have killed you after I killed Fiona, but the Vatican frowns upon the murder of children. You are no child now and I cannot risk you passing this and whatever else you know around."

Lillian screamed and leapt for the door in hope to escape, but Helena intercepted her, grabbing a fist of her hair, and yanked her backwards. Lillian fell against the bench with a crack, feeling cold hands coil around her throat.

"I'll rather enjoy strangling you for all the sleepless nights I suffered from your visions," she sneered. "So amusing I thought it was for you to live here, just like the last visionary we plucked from your community. No surprise your parents named you after her. Bit of bad luck for you, I suppose, gave it away. You'll die here just like she did."

Lillian could feel her grip loosening on the papers and the edges of her peripheral vision grew fuzzy with light. Her eyes were wide as she listened between her own gasps of air.

"You never put it together, deary? Didn't you ever wonder about our sweet Lady Julian? She had visions about the falsities of our religion just like you. She converted to stay alive. The poor thing hoped that the common people could sift through her riddles and find the truth. Sad, really, that she gave them so much credit. They don't ask questions. Just like you. Didn't you ever think that Lillian sounded so closely to Julian? You saw her every day as you walked to bed. You had the answers in the palm of your hand since the day you were born. You have failed again to suppress the power that is the Vatican."

She could feel the dry heaving replace her thoughts as Helena squeezed pleasurably harder. The prospect of impending death calmed Lillian's nervous system as it prepared to succumb, and she could feel the presence of her past lives cradle around her. Lillian knew this would not be the end. It would only start again as it had a hundred times before. She thought of Aillig and her parents. Again they had wasted themselves for her failure. Her body relaxed involuntarily against the grip of the older woman, and she could feel her eyes dulling. *What if I forget who I am again and more people die for my sake?*

"You've always required such little effort to control," Helena whispered somewhere far away from her in satisfaction.

Lillian's glazing eyes looked longly towards the door in defeat. Her shadow man appeared. His body vibrated brightly in anger, and she smiled at seeing him. The memory of his stark body aside her bath tub seemed like such an old memory. He looked thinner than she had remembered, and his face was washed in panic. She watched softly, wanting to be near him. If death brought her their union, she was willing to let go of her body. He shook his head and pointed to the table she was pinned next to.

"What are you smiling at?" Helena screamed, shaking her.

Lillian looked back into Sister Roy's hellish eyes, and could smell roses drift from Helena's face. *Her* roses.

"The elixir for beauty," Helena mimicked. "If we couldn't have your gift, then we couldn't risk it going into the wrong hands. Not everyone deserves to live forever, but I'm stocked to the brim with your beauty creams." The life was leaving the wretched girl, and Helena wanted her to die in misery. She nodded to the perfume bottles from Lillian's shop, boasting about her knowledge of the prophecy. Lillian reached her free hand to the table, groping for her perfume, and Helena smiled.

"That's all that's left of your precious plants. Your dreamy little cottage and magic shop have been erased and burned, just like Aillig's," she lied. "We found your little pet and killed him. Dougal fancies stuffed birds and spoke admirably about placing yours on his shelf. And now you will die too, without the chance to use your witchcraft to destroy us."

A rage built in Lillian as the image unfolded before her. A shrill and unusual scream penetrated the lock around her throat and in one last attempt, she managed to rip the lid off the delicate glass bottle and throw the liquid into the woman's eyes.

Helena stumbled in shock and released her grip, rubbing the burn away between shrieks of anger. Lillian staggered backward, gasping for air. She looked through her light headedness to find him. *I can't forget my dream.*

The woman lunged blindly at her and Lillian tripped out of her way, feeling the blood rush back to her head. His whisper pushed against her ear and she focused to find him. *I can't forget my dream.* Lillian strained to follow the pull of his presence. Helena's tears fell from her reddened eyes as she came running more accurately towards her. Lillian dashed to the side and the woman's shins hit the hard wood of the bench.

The shadow man pulled the last of his frail energy to materialize again and pointed to the heavy candlestick holder in the windowsill. Faithfully, Lillian dove to it and without thinking, laid a blow backed by all the years of pain into Helena's head, knocking her out. Lillian scrambled to grab what scattered pieces of paper she could.

"Come," he whispered.

She ran to him as he dissipated, blind with shock.

"Come back my love," she sobbed. "I'm terrified. I can't do this alone."

A gentle push came from behind and she ran into the open fields of the night. Not a soul saw her as she fled, the soft voices of their hymns beating into the back of her neck. Lillian could not feel the tears that soaked the raw skin Helena had strangled. She ran numbly by the guidance of her shadow, unsure of how long the woman would stay down. Her hands shook as she tried frantically to unlock her car door. The key scratched all around the lock and cries escaped desperately from her swollen lips. Her shadow weighed against her hand until she felt the ridges of the key slide forward. In a heaving gasp, she managed to get in and start the engine. Lillian drove without thought, desperate to leave the city behind. She would not go back to the hotel to grab whatever remained of her clues. They were no longer necessary. It wouldn't be long until Dougal, or one of their henchman would be there to ransack the place anyway. She had no home to drive to, and she prayed Helena Roy couldn't guess where she was headed.

*Chapter Forty-Three*

Emmy sat down in her small kitchen for a lunch break. She nearly jumped out of her chair when the phone rang.

"Hello?" she answered, slightly bewildered. The landline hadn't rung since she'd gotten there.

"It's Anne from the motel. There's a letter that arrived for you here, would you like to come pick it up or should I have it sent over?"

"Oh. I'm on my lunch break now. I can come and get it."

"Great, will see you soon. Be nice to catch up with you."

Emmy hung up the phone and went to grab her keys. The phone rang again.

"Hello?"

No one answered.

"Anne?" she called to the silence.

Emmy shrugged and hung up. She checked the clock, knowing she could just make it back if she hurried.

Driving back into town gave her some time to wander away from the submersion of her work. The horses were such a happy experience that she thought of little else while she was near them. Cutter had been gone long enough that the initial edge of his absence had worn away.

Even the story Sky Brother had recounted of their love had less shine than when she'd seen it on the cliffs for herself.

She was content where she was, having the small dreams of her childhood in her hand. Trying to live up to the prophecy she had been told about seemed uninteresting, and the responsibility of being such an important person daunted her. Here, she could melt in with the background of Wyoming and never be bothered again. She pulled into the motel parking lot and wasted no time grabbing her mail and heading back. She'd have to look at it later after her last round of colts. The week had been filled with the rowdy youth of masculine equines. Roger said the real test would start with them, and he wanted to see if she could live up to the legend of her first ride with Apollo.

Emmy laughed recounting the first day, trying to wrangle the energy of her little boys. The mindset of men was one she had a hard time understanding, but eventually she found that using the strength of her physique rallied their attention. They were boys, they wanted to play games to outdo each other.

"A little rough housing from Mom never hurt anyone," she laughed, remembering how tired they looked at the end of this morning's workout. She stretched her sore legs before hopping out of the truck.

"I've been waiting for you."

Emmy stopped dead in her tracks, startled to see him there. Fassenbach looked wilder than he ever did, and the horses hooves danced nervously in the stalls behind her.

"I'm sorry?" Emmy stuttered.

Something didn't feel right.

He approached her with arrogance and placed a hand too heavily on her shoulder. She tightened instinctively.

"I have a new opportunity for you," he proposed with cloaked impatience. "I will be building a training facility just for you, so that you may acquire and sell horses as you wish. No more dead end work with Roger."

Emmy stepped back until his thick arm fell to his side. Her heart slammed in her chest. She may have been long gone from Kentucky, but the look of a cheat was burned into her brain.

"I'm sorry, Mr. Fassenbach, but I'm really happy here."

"Could you at least stop by? Kelly was so excited at the prospect of living on the same property as you. It'd break her heart to feel you've ditched her again," he sighed in mock exasperation.

Emmy watched him carefully, feeling nervous about the promise she was about to make. But George never involved his daughter in anything crooked.

"I need to get back to work, George. But sure, I will come by. For Kelly."

He smiled roughly and nodded.

"Come tonight."

He left without a word and she watched him until his truck disappeared. She hadn't realized the horses' frantic uprise until the settling silence burned in her ears.

"That was weird," she breathed, walking into her room.

She would never quite understand George Fassenbach. She never wanted to, either. She sat down at the table in her apartment and ripped the envelope open with her nail despite her tardiness. A moment more to quiet her mind before work would be smart. When she unfolded the letter, the familiar cursive sent chills down her arms.

*Emmy,*

*I am unsure of what is happening, but Ethan knows where you are. He plans to come. Horrible things have happened in your absence and I'm afraid for your safety. I've called my Sister who lives in Oregon. Emmy I*

*urge you to meet me there immediately. Call the number
on the other side once you are safe. More information then.*

*Ms. Beckett*

Bile rose in her throat and her knees felt weak. Her vision was edged in blackness and it was hard to concentrate on staying coherent. She rose from her chair and ran to the bathroom to wretch. She wondered how long it'd been since the letter had been sent. She had no idea how quickly he would find her.

"What the hell am I going to do?" she cried.

Emmy sat heavily in her kitchen chair, trying to gain composure. She could almost feel the gun pressed into her forehead and suppressed the urge to scream. Losing her mind wouldn't do her any good. She had to think quickly. There were too many people working around the facility to leave now. She'd have too much explaining to do and that'd put them all in danger. She'd have to leave tonight.

.....

Cutter sat in the library, absorbed with his findings. He bounced back and forth between the histories of the Native Americans and the multiple origins of the spiral Emmy had mentioned. His imagination and good heart had recovered in between the lines of his research. There was so much more to what they'd taught her and he couldn't wait to tell her about it when he got home. He doodled her memory tile on his notepad, daydreaming of his nearing departure.

Soon they could be back in Wyoming together, starting fresh. Maybe she'd even be able to take him to the hidden tribe so he could ask questions of his own. He fantasized about what he would find on the cliffs they'd shown her. Cutter looked at the clock and stood to gather his things. He walked back to his apartment in the early night, feeling enlightened, focusing not on the crowd of the city but on the gentle breeze that floated between buildings. He felt like himself again and couldn't help but wonder if it was because he was on the right path of discovery. He was learning about his past in a depth he'd not known about and it felt empowering. His life was endless. It made the hardships he'd endured seem so unimportant. Cutter felt like he had been reborn, reawakened.

He walked into his apartment unable to ignore the piano. It hummed loudly in his ears and there was little he could do to resist his desire to play. He sat on the bench, running his fingers over the keys without making a sound. He stopped and set his fingers in the correct position, spiraling an index finger over the ivory bones in front of him. Cutter became transfixed by the motion and fell far away from the surroundings of the city. He could vaguely hear the music and his fingers stretched and arched over the length of the piano. Visions of open country rolled in endlessly green grasses and shadows of men. The gentle cry of his instrument transformed into plucky vibrations against his fingers. He stared down at his open palms, trying to figure out where he had gone.

.......

She stumbled in the night, packing her bags. When darkness blanketed the Wyoming range, Emmy stepped out of her room and locked the door behind her. She slipped into her truck and prayed the ignition couldn't be heard from the Big House in the distance. She pulled the Thomas Guide from her glovebox, and Henry's storybook tumbled out with it. She threw them on the bench seat and pulled out of her parking spot with sweating palms. As she rolled towards the exit of the property, she heard one long, shrill whinny in the distance and slammed on her breaks.

"I can't let it happen again," she said to herself.

Apollo called out to her from his pasture. She couldn't risk losing him like she had her others. That was one thing Ethan would never take from her again. She backed down the drive and found the nearest trailer to hitch up, leaving her truck running. She prayed the clanking of metal wouldn't call attention to anyone in the bunkhouse. Emmy unlocked the door and pulled down the loading gate. Strong legs swiftly carried her to the pasture where Apollo waited.

"Okay boy," she whispered to the eyes burning in the dark sky. "We've got to go now."

She opened the pasture gate, sliding a rope halter over his head. Again, she was stealing Roger's horse and hoped he'd understand why she left. She had grown very fond of Roger in the time she'd spent there. Emmy knew whatever disappointment he might have over her disappearance would dissipate once Ethan showed up.

She closed the trailer and turned.

"You said you were coming to meet me," George threatened as he stood behind her. "I should have known better than to think you'd come."

Apollo kicked inside the trailer with fury.

"You see, we have a little problem. *I know who you are*," he sneered as he walked closer to her, "and you can't leave my sight. I'm sure you can guess why. You have some big secrets stored in that little body of yours."

George's beady eyes raced over her body. The lust oozing from him was too familiar to Emmy, and she turned blind with fire. Already on the brink in anticipation of Ethan, Emmy's instincts were purely primal. She didn't make a sound as she leapt at the hefty man, her body strong and taut as she pushed him down. He hit the ground, startled by her power. Dust billowed around his soft body.

"He's coming for you, and there's nothing you can do about it now," he sputtered.

Emmy turned and sprinted for the idling truck. She no longer suffered from the weakness of Ethan's control. She could feel Apollo's electricity and her focus was singular. George managed to his feet and grabbed her arm as she curled her fingers around the handle of the car door. His grip was like iron and she could feel her skin bruising. Emmy searched for something close enough to strike him with. There wasn't a thing he couldn't get to first. Apollo was shaking the entire trailer and it wouldn't be long before someone heard the commotion. She thought of Cutter and wished he wasn't so far away. Emmy's eyes widened and she plucked the phone from her pocket with her free hand, curling her fist around it, and snapped her shoulder back. Her fist hit his jaw with explosive force. George's eyes widened and glazed over as he stumbled backward from the whimpers of her busted hand. Emmy jumped in the truck and tore down the road before the fat man could recover.

George couldn't help his shaking hands as he scrambled to find his phone. He stumbled to his own car while it rang and headed for home before anyone could see him on Roger's property.

"Helphho?"

"Ethan? Ethan, are you awake?"

"What do you want?" he growled.

"Ethan," he gulped, "she's gone."

"What?!" he screamed, his voice cracking in George's ear. "How'd this happen? You've already let her get away from you? She's a worthless little girl, George!"

Ethan threw the empty bottle across the room and watched it shatter. His face was hot and veins popped from his neck. He spoke slowly through his teeth before he hung up.

"I am coming to you, and I'm going to ruin the entire state of Wyoming on my way. You will perish, George Fassenbach, you and your pretty, little daughter. Be certain of it."

*Chapter Forty-Four*

Helena woke from the blow, mania rising like venom in her head, realizing the girl was nowhere near. She stumbled across the yards to the main church where devotional had just been released. She spotted Dougal and in a few steps she reached him, teeth bared inches from his face.

"You are a worthless, fat man. She knows everything!"

Dougal stared at her in nonchalance.

"So what, Helena. The girl is a nobody, what's she going to do? Run home and cry in her wee cottage?"

"No. Because you are going to burn it before she can. Burn everything that is hers."

The aged man looked at her tiredly, waging the outcome if he refused. He was getting tired of the game she had dragged him into.

"If you don't, there will be no better life for you," she sneered. "You can be sure that I will find a nice headstone for you to place next to your brother's."

He nodded once, absorbing the severity of the situation, feeling whatever promotion he had been searching for slipping away.

"What about the girl?" he asked dutifully.

"I will handle her now. She went hiding where no one would find her. Except me."

Helena Roy always made good on her threats.

.....

Maeve burst through Aillig's beach house to the garden where Susan sat watching the moon.

"Sue! They've just burned her apothecary. They've burned her cottage. I've just been rung about the fire trucks gobbling up the streets to put it out."

The women could feel the heightened lunacy of what the legend had predicted. Lillian had broken a barrier that the church had been able to keep for centuries.

"The prophecy foretold the power of nine would be the beginning of the change, Maeve. We've got to find them all," Susan chimed, still staring into the moon, lost in her visions. She closed her eyes and couldn't feel Lillian anywhere in the dreamworld. It both worried and comforted her.

The burly woman nodded and truly believed for the first time. Never did she think she'd be alive to witness the downfall of their reign of terror. She tried to think of what to do next.

"We have no way to contact her," Susan fretted, after her failed attempts to find Lillian's energy. "How do we know she's okay?"

"We must have faith that she will come to us. In the meantime, we're going to need to prepare to keep everything safe."

Susan's eyes welled, knowing too easily how many times the prophecy had failed. Maeve set her jaw in a hard line and encouraged her friend to do the same.

"We got involved, so let's do our part. Maybe there will be a reward in the next life."

Made in the USA
Charleston, SC
30 July 2016